D1419047

5 4073 02140486

RECKLESS
GIRL

BOOKS BY EMMA TALLON

Runaway Girl
Dangerous Girl
Boss Girl
Fierce Girl

RECKLESS GIRL

EMMA TALLON

Bookouture

Published by Bookouture in 2019

An imprint of Storyfire Ltd.
Carmelite House
50 Victoria Embankment
London EC4Y 0DZ

www.bookouture.com

ISBN: 978-1-78681-806-5
eBook ISBN: 978-1-78681-805-8

This book is a work of fiction. Names, characters, businesses,
organizations, places and events other than those clearly in the
public domain, are either the product of the author's imagination
or are used fictitiously. Any resemblance to actual persons, living or
dead, events or locales is entirely coincidental.

For my whole world – Christian XX

PROLOGUE

She stared down into the murky waters beneath and squinted. It was dark, but street lights flooded the bank of the river. Shadows fell across the sharp rocks below. As her eye caught something red bobbing up and down near the small rowing boat her breath caught. It was the hood of Ethan's coat.

'Ethan!' she screamed. Seeing a break in the low wall a few metres down, she ran towards it and catapulted herself through. Scrambling down the rocks, she hurried towards him.

'Have you found him?' came a voice from behind her.

'There,' she sobbed. 'In the water. Ethan, get *up*,' she cried. He was face down and not moving.

She launched herself further and cried out as she went over on her ankle. Someone swept past, quicker than she was at scaling the treacherous rocks.

'Get to him – quickly.' She watched as the other woman threw herself in the water and reached for his hat. As she pulled it towards her and out of the water, her eyes closed and she began to weep.

'No,' she whispered. 'No, no, Ethan!'

Her scream echoed off into the darkness.

CHAPTER ONE

Freddie pulled the thin white sheet back slowly over Anna's taut stomach, exposing her bare flesh to the light breeze that was coming from the open balcony doors.

'Stop it,' she said with a laugh, her eyes crinkling prettily at the sides.

Freddie looked up at her, a glint in his eye. 'And why would I do that?' He grabbed her thighs and in one deft movement flipped her over onto her front. She laughed harder as he crawled up to kiss the back of her neck.

'Because,' she said, wriggling out and pushing him away, 'we need to surface for food and water for a while. We're going to starve to death if we stay in bed for the *entire* trip.'

They were in a hotel halfway up a mountain on the Amalfi Coast. Outside the open doors and beyond the wrought-iron rungs, sapphire-blue waters gave way to an almost identical sky, the sun glinting off the waves in the distance. The warm air smelled of salt and fresh bread and the small town of Vietri sul Mare below buzzed with activity. Fishing boats and pleasure boats bobbed up and down. It was a perfect corner of the world where stress and worry didn't exist.

After everything they'd been through and as things were relatively quiet, he'd suggested they get away from it all for a while. There was still work to be done, problems to sort out, but nothing that couldn't wait for a few short days.

They had barely had time to come to terms with the loss of their baby and the death of Freddie's brother before an old threat had reared its ugly head. The mafia had rolled into town, looking for one of its chiefs, Frank Gambino; someone Freddie had been forced to dispose of after a business deal went south. It had been a tense time, finding the right way to cover it all up, a time made even more stressful by the sudden appearance of Tanya's estranged mother, Rosie.

Not easily fooled by the Mother Teresa act Rosie was pulling, Anna had known something was wrong and had gone out of her way to uncover her more sinister motives. Rosie had been lying, using Tanya's weaknesses to grow close to her, all the while planning to kill her off and steal her business.

Life never seemed to stop, and every time they thought they were coming through the clouds, another problem came storming round the corner.

Freddie shuffled up the bed and lay facing her. 'OK. You win. Dinner and wine and a walk around the town – that sound good?'

'It does.' Anna leaned in and gave him a lingering kiss.

Freddie trailed his fingers down her side and rested his hand on her stomach. 'What do you think about trying again?' he asked cautiously.

Anna tensed. 'What do you mean?'

'You know what I mean, Anna.' Freddie half sat up, resting on his elbow. 'What if now that things are settled, we properly try for a baby?'

'Freddie, you know what the doctors said.' Anna sat up and swung her legs over the side of the bed, running her fingers through her hair to tame it. 'I can get pregnant but the chances of me carrying to full term are slim,' she said, her voice flat.

'Slim isn't impossible,' Freddie pushed, 'and we can make sure that we—'

Emma Tallon

'Make sure that what, Freddie?' Anna rounded on him, agitated. 'Make sure that I lie perfectly still for nine months in the hope my body won't reject it? Because that won't make a blind bit of difference. Whether I'm cocooned in bubble wrap or dancing on tables, I can still lose the baby. They told us that.'

Freddie moved to sit next to her. 'Don't you want to at least try?'

Tears filled Anna's eyes and threatened to spill over as the all too familiar wave of grief returned. She was still trying to heal from the nightmare she went through at the farmhouse only a few months before. Tanya getting shot, the knife against her neck as Freddie's younger brother Michael dragged her down the stairs, the cold, hard gun in her hand, ending his life and finally, the feeling of her baby slipping away from her body as she bled out on the floor.

'I want to be able to give you a family more than anything in the world. I know you want kids; I've always wanted them too. But after losing our baby at that farm' – her voice wobbled with emotion – 'my arms have ached every day to hold him close to me. I already feel like something is missing.' She swallowed and blinked away the tears. 'I can't lose another one. I can't get my hopes up only to watch them bleed away from me again.'

Freddie nodded, his expression sombre as he took her hand in his. 'It's OK. We don't need anyone else to make us a family. You *are* my family. Nothing else matters, OK?'

She heard his sadness as he saw his visions of a large brood melting away and smiled sadly. 'It does matter, though. You want children and you have every right to have them.' She bit her lip, trying to control her emotions. 'And I want you to know that I understand if you need to be with someone who can give you that.'

It was the hardest thing Anna had ever had to say. It was something she had known she needed to say for months, but she hadn't had the courage. But now Freddie had finally brought the subject up, she knew it was time. He had to know that she loved him enough to set him free if that was what he needed.

Freddie pulled away from her, shock and anger replacing the sombre concern on his face. 'What are you saying?' he asked, aghast. 'Don't ever say that to me again, Anna. *Ever*,' he repeated strongly. 'I love you more than anything. It's you and me against the world, alright? Kids or not.'

Visibly stressed now, Freddie stood up and lit a cigarette, walking over to lean on the balcony.

Taking a deep breath, Anna composed herself. She had said the words; she'd done what the deep feeling of guilt had forced her to do. And she was relieved that Freddie had not taken the way out she'd offered. It would have killed her to see him go. Though she would have let him. Because that's what you do when you truly love someone.

Walking up behind him Anna wrapped her arms around his bare torso and rested her forehead between his shoulder blades. After a few moments the tension left the muscles under her cheek and Freddie turned to embrace her.

'I love you,' she whispered.

'I love you too,' Freddie replied. 'We have a great life together. Let's just focus on that. Because when we get back' – Freddie gently pulled her chin up and a grin crept up his face – 'you have a whorehouse to sort out, *madame*.'

CHAPTER TWO

Sarah Riley straightened her fitted suit jacket and pushed her dark, bobbed hair back behind her ears as she strode towards the door to the office that housed her new team. It was her first official day back as a DCI on the force and in her new role managing the Organised Crime Task Force for Ben Hargreaves. Ben was the Secretary of State for Justice and had been her boss many moons before. She'd been working for him when she'd first met Freddie, on a case involving the abduction of Ben's daughter.

It had been Freddie who'd put an end to her career in the force, threatening to out her dark past if she didn't leave. But in a twist of fate he had later hired her into his underground firm, needing someone with her particular skills. It had been a rollercoaster of a ride from her last day in this building until now. This time she was not a straight-laced DCI here to protect and serve. This time she was here as Freddie's mole, a double agent.

Pushing through the doors, she could see the team were already gathered together facing away from her, their attention on Ben.

'And here she is, your new leader DCI Sarah Riley. Give her a warm welcome.' Ben smiled tightly as she walked over to his side. The group of people, ten in total she knew, cheered and greeted her warmly. All except for one.

'Thank you, I'm glad to be here.' Sarah rested her hard gaze on the petite blonde woman sitting at the back with her jaw dropped open. Detective Holly Miechowski quickly shut her mouth, but a look of shock flashed across her face. Sarah smiled at her coldly.

'DCI Riley has run many very successful task forces in her career,' Ben continued. 'I have every faith in her abilities to get things done and I advise that you learn as much as you can from her in your time on this team. You will answer to her from this point on. And now I will hand the floor over.' He stepped aside and Sarah walked forward.

'Thank you for your kind words, Ben; I'm looking forward to this team achieving great things.' A few people nodded in agreement. 'Our main target right now are the Tylers. I have personal experience of this family, having worked on a case involving them before. I know you've done your research and even tried to take them down, though I understand this came to nothing.'

'Worse than nothing,' Ben piped up in an irate tone. 'I had legal representatives making claims of harassment. So now we have to tread very carefully.'

'I see.' Sarah fixed her stare on Holly. She thought back to the night Freddie had spoken to her in his office.

Sarah had discovered the bugs Holly had placed whilst she'd been undercover and had caught her red-handed on a secret camera. Freddie had sent her packing with a warning – he knew where she lived. He told her clearly that if he ever caught her sniffing around the club again, or if she breathed one word about meeting Sarah, he'd slit her throat in the night. Of course, Holly had no idea at that point that Sarah would end up coming back to the force as her boss.

'This isn't something to be overly concerned about, I don't think,' Sarah said, her gaze sweeping the team as she paced slowly in front of them. 'If anything we're lucky that these threats were through legal channels. They're above board and as such the consequences are above board.' She paused. 'It's when the Tylers start threatening you personally, behind closed doors, with promises of violence' – she stared into Holly's eyes – 'those are the ones you want to be worried about. If there's one thing I know above anything else, it's that the Tylers don't make idle threats. These are dangerous people, possibly the most dangerous in the country.'

Holly visibly paled under Sarah's piercing gaze, fully understanding the clear message. No one could know what she knew about Sarah, or she would suffer the consequences. She looked down to her notebook and Sarah moved on.

'So watch your backs.' There were murmurs of agreement. 'It won't be easy – they're intelligent, well established and don't play to the rules we are bound by. But we can do it, if we're smart about it and take our time. Please remember that this is a marathon, not a sprint. It's more important to have an airtight case than to rush in and lose them later.' She eyed them all accusingly, reminding them that this was the mistake they'd made before. 'I've been briefed on each of you and I'm looking forward to getting to work with such a skilled team. Any questions?'

'Yes, ma'am,' one of the men at the front spoke up. He was stocky, tattooed, with bright blue eyes and a man bun. Adam Chambers. She knew from his file he'd pulled off several good undercover operations in various gangs. 'How'd you take your tea?' He grinned. Everyone laughed.

'You're the team suck-up then,' Sarah replied in good humour.

'Just getting my extra brownie points in early, ma'am.' He gave her a cheeky wink.

'Noted. White, no sugar. Now' – she clapped her hands together – 'let's get to it. I'd like a summary of your work and findings so far from each of you on my desk by the end of the day. I'll review tonight and form a plan of action for tomorrow. Off you go.'

The team disbanded.

Sarah breathed in deeply, taking in the buzz of activity in the room. Her eyes briefly met Holly's before the other woman turned away.

Sarah was going to have to manage this situation very carefully if she was going to come out of this smelling like roses on both sides. Holly knew exactly what Sarah was doing here and that was going to be a problem. Because if Holly was worth her salt as a policewoman, not even Freddie's threats were going to hold her back from meddling for long.

CHAPTER THREE

Paul took one last drag on his cigarette and flicked it away, grinning broadly as Freddie and Anna reached his car. He grabbed Freddie in a big bear hug, patting him on the back.

'Ah, brother, it's good to see you back,' he said with feeling.

'Good to see you too, mate. Everything alright?' Freddie replied as Paul gave Anna a squeeze too.

'Yeah, yeah, everything's pukka,' he said in his deep, gravelly voice. ''Ere, let me take your bags.' In one swift motion Paul swung both suitcases up into the boot of his brand-new Range Rover. 'What do you think?' he asked, gesturing towards it.

Freddie looked it over appreciatively. 'Nice motor. Does James like it?'

'Oh yeah, he loves it,' Paul replied with a short laugh. 'Told me this morning we should move to the country. Says we'd fit right in now.' He rolled his eyes and Freddie grinned.

'What did you say to that?' he asked.

'I told him to fuck right off. I'm not poncing around in a bunch of bloody fields, thank you very much.'

Anna and Freddie laughed.

'Yes, I can't see you loving country life, Paul,' Anna said.

'James wouldn't love it either, if he actually thought about it,' Paul replied, getting into the driver's seat. 'He'd soon go running back when he realised there ain't a Starbucks round every corner.' Starting the engine, Paul pulled out of the car park.

'So, what's been going on back here then?' Freddie asked.

'Not much.' His easy smile dropped.

Freddie noticed and frowned. 'What's up?' he asked.

Paul sighed. 'One of the Manchester crews. They've been supplying product here, infiltrated our chain.'

'Coke?'

'Yeah.'

'Fuck.' Freddie balled his hand into a fist and stared out the window with a frustrated expression.

Ever since their old supplier Marco's operation had been raided and shut down, they hadn't been able to source enough decent product to meet the demand. They'd acquired small stashes here and there, but it was never enough.

The problem was that this left them vulnerable. They weren't meeting their area's needs and therefore their dealers' incomes were drying up. Loyalty or not, there was a point at which any dealer would turn elsewhere to make sure he could earn enough to feed his family. And this meant that other firms could see an opportunity. One that some were brave enough to go for.

'Who are they, Paul? Are they to be worried about?' Anna spoke up from the back of the car.

'They might be,' he admitted. 'Usually this sort of thing is all talk, but this firm is pretty big and they hold the monopoly in Manchester. If the rumours *are* true, they know what they're doing.'

'Are you talking about Drew Johnson's crew?' Freddie asked, turning to face Paul.

'Yep,' Paul confirmed with a nod.

Freddie stared at his brother in silence for a moment, his expression serious. They didn't know Drew or his crew personally, but Freddie had always made it his business to know who the big fish were in any major city that may, at some point, wish to do business through London. Drew's crew were not as well established as the Tylers, but they practically ran Manchester.

'I want you to call a meeting, get everyone together tonight. We need to cut this off before it becomes a problem.'

'How do you propose we do that, Fred? If this is for real, we've got no weight behind us. One traitorous dealer we can make an example of, but if they infiltrate the chain and our rivers run dry…'

'Just call the meeting.' Freddie's jaw formed a hard line. 'We'll cross that bridge if and when we come to it.'

*

Paul pulled up outside Club Anya as Anna had requested and she jumped out. 'See you later on at home,' she said to Freddie. 'And thanks again, Paul.' She waved them off and turned towards the club with an eager smile. As much as she had enjoyed their time away, she was looking forward to getting back to work and to Tanya.

Feeling a strange warning prickle on the back of her neck, she glanced over the street towards the alley. As she did, a blonde head jerked back and the front of a khaki coat swiftly melted out of sight. She paused and waited. *Was someone watching her?*

Two men talking avidly walked down the alley past the point she had been watching and the strange feeling evaporated. Loads of people walked down that alley. Whoever it was probably just changed their mind about where they were going. She was getting paranoid. For once there was nothing sinister going on in the background. She needed to chill out and stop her instincts from assuming the worst all the time.

Walking through the doors, Anna made her way towards the bar. As it came into sight there was a loud screech and a mass of red hair came hurtling towards her. Tanya wrapped her arms around Anna, enveloping her in a hug and nearly knocking her off her feet.

'Oh wow.' Anna laughed, regaining her balance. 'I've missed you too.'

'It's so good to have you back. You know' – Tanya winked – 'just because I hate doing the paperwork and all that.'

'Sure, OK,' Anna said fondly, linking arms with her and walking over to find a seat at the long bar.

'Just kidding. Though I am excited to crack on with our new project,' she added enthusiastically. 'I still can't believe it's actually happening. Never thought you'd go for something like this in a million years.'

Anna gave her a wry smile. 'Me neither.'

After finding one of their showgirls offering extra services in the back alley, Anna had gone ballistic and fired her. She'd been clear from the start that she would not allow the club's reputation to be tainted by dirty deeds. She wasn't from the underworld of London and as such had always wanted to keep their business above board. When Tanya had suggested they open up a whorehouse, she had only been joking, really. But lately Anna had changed. Recent events had done something to her, darkened her soul in a way that she knew she would never be able to change back. Suddenly, in comparison to the horrors she had faced and overcome, something as simple as a whorehouse didn't seem like such a big bad deal anymore. It was just business. It was illegal, but these days there seemed to be very little that scared her anymore. So she'd decided she might as well embrace it.

'Good to see you back,' Carl greeted her warmly and pulled out a bottle of white wine and two glasses. He presented it with a flourish and raised one eyebrow in question.

'Go on then,' Anna said with a happy smile.

'So, how was Italy?' Tanya asked excitedly, crossing her long, slim legs and leaning one arm on the bar.

'It was just… perfect,' Anna replied. 'The hotel was beautiful – we looked out across the sea from our room. The weather was great; the food was amazing. I think I must have put on about half a stone with all the pizza and pasta we ate.'

'Oh, jealous,' Tanya interjected with a laugh.

'And it was just really relaxing. I needed that. Well, I think we both did actually.'

'Yeah, you did. I could do with a relaxing break too,' Tanya said in a wistful tone. 'Maybe I should book something. We could go together, have a girly one.' She sat up. 'Let's do it! Let's hop on a plane and go somewhere exotic, you and me!'

'You haven't got a passport,' Carl and Anna said in unison. They looked at each other and laughed. It was a running joke between them. Every now and then Tanya would decide to book a spontaneous holiday, an adventure somewhere in the world. And every time they would remind her that she still needed to get a passport. Tanya would put it on her to-do list and swear that it would be the very next thing she'd get to, but she never did.

'Oh, for fuck's sake.' Tanya rolled her eyes and picked up her wine. 'Fine. I'll get one. First thing tomorrow I'm going to apply and then when it comes through, we're going on a girls' trip. Deal?'

'Mhm, sure,' Anna replied, hiding her amusement.

'The day you walk in here holding an actual passport, I'll shave my head,' Carl said, laughing.

Tanya narrowed her eyes at him. 'Yeah?'

'Yeah.'

'OK. I'm going to hold you to that,' she replied. 'I'll even bring the razor.'

'You do that,' the bar's manager said with a laugh. He winked at her and walked away to serve a customer.

'He's getting cheekier by the day, that one,' Tanya said, turning back to Anna.

Anna laughed. 'And, like me, you love him even more for it.'

'True,' Tanya replied grudgingly. 'Anyway. You were telling me about Italy. Have any adventures? What were the blokes like? Bet you came across more than one Italian stallion on your travels, eh?' She wiggled her eyebrows up and down saucily.

'Christ, Tan.' Anna snorted and nearly choked on her wine. 'I was there with Freddie, I was hardly going to be scouting the area for random men.'

'Oh, come off it,' Tanya tutted. 'You might be all loved up, but you're only human. You must have had a good look.'

'I really didn't,' Anna replied. 'Sorry to disappoint you.'

Tanya pulled a face and shook her head in disappointment. 'Anna Davis, that is truly shocking. You're a disgrace to hot-blooded women everywhere. But' – she jumped down from the bar stool with a grin – 'I shall forgive you.'

'What a relief,' Anna replied with deep sarcasm.

'Yeah, well, only because I really need you to come and fix a little problem in the office.' Tanya began walking away and Anna quickly followed, her forehead creasing in concern.

'What sort of problem?' she asked worriedly.

'The sort of problem that occurs when you and the accountant both fuck off for a week at the same time and I'm left alone to sort out the VAT,' Tanya called over her shoulder.

'Oh shit,' Anna cursed. She hurried after her. 'What have you done…'

Carl chuckled to himself as he poured the French martini he'd been mixing into a glass. He was glad Anna was home. Those two were like two halves of a whole. Much better together.

CHAPTER FOUR

Freddie rolled his glass in his hand, watching the deep amber liquid within swirl around. He was in his office at Club CoCo, listening to a rundown of all his men had heard so far about the firm from Manchester. If the rumours were true, it wasn't looking good. He knocked back the whisky and savoured its fire.

Bill Hanlon coughed as Sammy finished speaking. 'I've also heard that and a bit more to boot.'

'And?' Freddie focused his gaze onto his old friend.

'I was in The Black Bear last night and overheard a couple of our dealers discussing pick-up. They've already been supplying on the quiet.' He shifted his weight and sighed heavily. Bill hated to be the bearer of bad news, especially news like this. 'So today Dean and I did some digging around, tapped up a couple of rats with ears to the ground. They'll tell you anything for a price. It appears Drew Johnson has already infiltrated nearly half our chain. He's been sending dribs and drabs but now he has enough orders to start sending bulk loads.'

Freddie nodded. ''Course he has.' He pinched his nose. 'Half our chain is a fucking hefty catch.'

'They're going where the money is, Fred,' Dean said quietly from the corner of the room. 'They've been asking us for weeks – we've had nothing to give 'em. Their loyalty is only ours as long as we provide them with a living.'

Freddie lit a cigarette and puffed on it. 'How are they getting the bulk load in, Bill? They'll need someone here to distribute. Who've they got?'

'They've loaded the dealers with enough to keep them going for now. In a week's time they're sending one of their men down with the first big bulk load in a caravan. He's going to distribute from there until they have more permanent premises down here.'

'Do you know who they're sending?'

'Some guy called Jacko. I don't know much about him yet.'

'OK.' Freddie sat back in his chair and took another deep drag on his cigarette. 'This stuff they're selling, is it any good?'

'Yeah,' said Dean, his voice glum. 'It's fucking excellent. Bastards. Took some off one of the dealers I spoke to earlier. Here.' He took a small pouch out of his pocket and threw it onto the table.

Freddie opened it up and dipped a finger in before rubbing it around his gums. The tingling numbness was instant. He pulled an expression of grudging approval and gave the rest of the pouch to Paul. 'Test this.' His gaze moved around the room and rested on Bill thoughtfully. 'Where on earth are they going to park a caravan up in London where it won't stand out and won't be under threat by Old Bill?'

'Apparently Drew's been in talks with the gypsy site underneath the Westway near Shepherd's Bush. They've agreed to let him keep the caravan there and protect it for a price,' Bill said grimly.

'Gypsies? Fuck,' Freddie said, wiping his hand down his face. Firms in their own game were one thing, but gypsies were a whole other ball game. They were the most dangerous people around if you were on the wrong side of them. Cunning, clannish, completely unpredictable and violent without care for consequence, they were loyal only to themselves and their own way of life. This was the reason Freddie had never worked with them before. Whilst he had no doubt that they could have been lucrative business partners on many occasions, he had no family link and therefore could not guarantee their loyalty. If Drew had gypsy protection, this would make things a lot harder.

Suddenly a chuckle broke the silence in the tense room and all eyes swivelled towards Seamus who had been sitting quietly to the side, listening.

'What's so funny?' Freddie asked.

'What's the one thing that's more important to a gypsy than money?' he asked, his grin broadening with every word.

Freddie shrugged. 'Family.'

'Exactly. That Westway site has been there for decades. The same families have lived there for generations. And one of them just happens to be headed by me da's brother. I have an uncle and two cousins over there and they just so happen to be the head family,' Seamus finished with a twinkle in his eye.

Freddie processed this for a moment and felt a spark of excitement run through his veins. Seamus's blood link to the Westway gypsies changed everything.

'Now that is a very interesting piece of information indeed,' he said. 'That might just help us trip these Northern fuckers up for good. If we use it wisely,' he added. 'Go get yourselves a drink, boys. We've got a firm to take down.'

CHAPTER FIVE

Tanya cast her eye over the VIP tables and gave a satisfactory nod. Leaning back against the end of the bar, out of the way of all the customers waiting to be served, she rubbed her cherry-red lips together and ran her hands down her tight body-con dress. She looked good tonight and she knew it. There had been several appreciative glances thrown her way already by some of the customers – and a few dirty ones from the women with them. But this mattered little – the effort in her appearance was not for them. Tonight she had a date.

'Jesus Christ, if it ain't Tanya bloody Smith herself!' a voice shrieked from a little way down the bar. Tanya turned, looking for the source. As her gaze landed on the short blonde woman facing her with a look of excitement, her own face opened up in surprise.

'Oh my God, Jules! What the hell!' Tanya ran over and grasped the smaller woman in a great big hug before pulling back, holding her by her shoulders and appraising her properly. 'I can't believe it's you,' she said, shaking her head in wonder. 'It's been so long. I tried calling you when you left, but I couldn't get through. You just disappeared…'

'I know.' Jules squeezed Tanya's arm. 'Listen, what you doing 'ere anyway? You working?' She nodded towards the stage where one of the burlesque acts was stripping behind her feather fan.

'Oh, no.' Tanya shook her head. 'No, this is my club.'

'Your club?' Jules took a step back and frowned in surprise.

'Yeah,' Tanya confirmed, smiling happily. 'Well, half mine. I own this one and another with my business partner, Anna.'

'Oh, I see. Wow. Good on you,' Jules said enthusiastically. 'That's amazing. From the bottom to the top. Just shows what you can do when you set your mind to it, eh?'

'I guess,' Tanya said. She subtly took in Jules's appearance. Having put a little extra weight on over the years, she wasn't exactly fat, but she was no longer the cute little blonde that had pulled the punters into the club every night. That had been how they'd met. Jules had been one of the stars of the show when Tanya was first introduced to the scene. Petite with a generous bosom, big blue eyes and pale golden locks that fell to her tiny waist, men had loved her. To them she was the girl next door, the fruity farm girl or the naughty babysitter.

Now Tanya could see that her waistline was gone, her breasts sagged low and her face looked grey and pinched underneath the thick make-up she wore. Her big blue eyes were ringed with dark hollows and her hair was cropped short, neglected and dull. Her outfit was OK, but it had seen better days and Tanya noted the absence of the jewellery and designer wear she had so coveted all those years before. Life had not been kind to her. She wondered what had happened to her friend to change her so much. No one even knew where or why she had gone. She had just disappeared one day.

'I was just about to get a drink,' Jules said, facing back towards the bar.

'It's on the house.' Tanya caught one of the barmen's eye. 'Anything my friend here wants, put it on my tab.'

'Ah, you sure? Thanks, Tan,' Jules said with a grin. 'I was only stopping for a quick one anyway. Was en route to meet an old friend, but I'm a bit early so stopped off to see what all the hype was about. I've heard good things about this place.' She looked around with interest.

'Listen, I've got some time to kill myself.' Tanya glanced over towards the hostesses once more. They seemed to be handling the rush just fine. 'So why don't I grab us a bottle of wine and we can catch up properly?'

'That sounds like a plan,' Jules said with a grin.

One hour and two bottles later, Tanya leaned her head back over the booth they had managed to nab from a leaving party and laughed. 'Oh God, yeah, that was so funny. I haven't thought about that night in years.'

'I'll never forget it. Kevin, the bouncer, got the sack for that, do you remember? While he was off getting his knob noshed on round the corner by that new girl, no one else was watching the door and that punter's wife walked straight in. You was in the next room, do you remember?'

'I do.' Tanya laughed, tears of mirth rolling down her face. 'I came running in when he started screaming, thinking something had happened.'

'Something *had* happened! His bloody wife walked in whilst he was pumping away on top of me, telling me to call him Sergeant Major. He was getting there too, just about to blow his load and then there she was. *Phillip!*' Jules mimicked the outraged wife's voice.

Tanya shrieked with tipsy laughter. 'Oh God,' she cried.

'Best part was, after she battered him out the door she turned around and asked me how much he owed. Paid me an' all – said no one should have to endure him for nothing.'

They both collapsed into hysterics as they recalled that hilarious night. It had been one of many. Tanya's professional roots were something she rarely talked about these days. Now that she had changed her life for the better, it was something she didn't like to dwell on, an embarrassing history. But tonight Jules had reminded her of some of the funnier moments in her sordid past and it was nice to have a good laugh about them.

Tanya was wiping away the tears of laughter when she noticed Anna approaching them with an amused smile.

'Hello, and how are you this evening?' she asked, chuckling at the sight of her drunk best friend.

'Anna! I'm so glad you're here,' Tanya said, standing up and balancing herself. 'God, I have had quite a bit more than I'd planned to.' She checked her watch and snorted. 'I'm supposed to be on a date in an hour. Ah fuck it. I'm cancelling it – this is way more fun anyway. Come, join us.'

'Sure.' Anna smiled at the blonde woman opposite her as she slipped into the booth. 'Hi, I'm Anna.'

'Jules,' the woman replied, holding out her hand.

Anna shook it but noted that the woman had quietened upon her arrival and was now sizing her up critically. Anna hid a frown. 'So…' She turned to Tanya. 'What are we celebrating?'

'The return of an old friend,' Tanya replied. 'Let's get you a glass – oh, hey,' Tanya called over Anna's head to a passing hostess. 'Becky, grab Anna a glass, will ya, babe? Thanks.'

'Actually, Tan, I gotta bounce, mate,' Jules said with an apologetic grimace. 'I've got to be somewhere.' She stood up and collected her belongings. 'I'll catch you again, though.'

'Oh, wait, let me get your number and that,' Tanya said.

'Don't worry, mate, I'm not going to disappear again any time soon,' Jules said smiling at her. Her gaze moved over to Anna where it lingered, the smile dropping slightly. 'I'll come back another time. See ya.' With that, Jules left them.

Tanya laughed quietly and shook her head. 'She used to be a right livewire, that one. The stories I could tell you…'

Becky came over with Anna's glass and Tanya took it, pouring in a generous amount of Pinot before handing it to her friend.

Anna narrowed her eyes thoughtfully as she watched Jules's retreating back. 'Who is she again?'

'I used to work with her – met her when I first came to London and started in the clubs. She was a right laugh. We went out together a lot – her, me and Denise, my old flatmate. But then one day she just upped and disappeared, not a word to anyone. We were all really worried – I even called the hospitals.' Tanya's tone sobered up as she remembered how worried she had been. 'But then we got this postcard one day saying she had moved and was fine and good luck with everything.' She shrugged. 'Was a bit pissed off, but what can you do?'

'So where did she go?' Anna asked.

'I don't really know, to be honest,' Tanya answered. 'She said she lived here and there, moved about a bit. We've just been reminiscing more than anything really.' She shrugged. 'Girls like her, they don't like to lay their cards out on the table, even to friends. I used to be cagey too.' Tanya glanced at Anna. 'Why the interest?'

Anna picked up her wine and shook her head. 'No reason really. She just seemed a bit odd.' After the recent history with Tanya's mother, Anna felt even more protective of Tanya than ever. Everyone had thought she was mad when she'd said something was off with Rosie. She'd even questioned her own sanity a few times along the way. But she'd been right. Perhaps, though, this was making her too paranoid. Jules was just an old friend.

'Well…' Tanya took a deep sip of wine and settled back into the comfort of the booth. 'Most toms are a bit odd.'

'So, she's still on the game?' Anna asked.

Tanya shrugged. 'Who knows. I didn't ask, she didn't say. But she was, back in the day. Just like me.' There was a silence as they both looked around the room at the heaving club.

'Busy tonight,' Anna remarked, changing the subject.

'It is indeed. Which is all the better for us. So' – Tanya brandished the bottle with a grin – 'let's continue with this fine bottle of Pinot and make that the cause for the rest of tonight's celebrations.'

Anna laughed and held her glass out for a top-up. 'You had me at Pinot.'

CHAPTER SIX

Sarah paid the barman and walked back over to the back booth in The Black Bear pub, where Freddie sat waiting. Sitting down across from him, she handed him a beer and took a deep drink of her gin and tonic.

'Ahh,' she said. 'I bloody needed this.'

'Yeah?' Freddie replied. 'Everything still going OK?' He glanced up at her.

Freddie and Sarah had a rocky history, initially fuelled by a mutual hatred throughout their battle to be the first to bring the other down. Over time, their mutual dislike had dissipated into a mutual respect and these days they could almost forget how they'd come to their strange professional arrangement.

'Yeah, it's all running smoothly, but I don't know how much longer Holly is going to sit by and watch quietly. She knows that I'm there to undermine everything the team does and I can see her bubbling away. She's finding it hard not to blow.' Sarah's expression was grim. Already she was learning that her role had basically been reduced to putting out the fires her team were setting around Freddie and alerting him to all their traps. Hiding this from her staff and looking as though she was proactively helping to guide them towards success was exhausting.

'If she knows what's good for her, she'll stay out of it,' Freddie replied. 'And if she knows as much about me as she thinks she does, she'll know my threats are never idle.'

Sarah nodded. 'She knows that. It's what's stopped her so far.'

'Can you get her transferred?' Freddie drank from his glass.

'I've thought about it,' Sarah replied with a heavy sigh. 'Technically yes, if I had a good reason or if she asks to move. But I don't and she hasn't. Holly has an exemplary record. She's worked hard to get onto a team like this, put in the extra hours, gone the extra mile over the years. There's no reason that wouldn't be suspicious as to why I wouldn't want to keep someone like her. I've been making things as boring and awkward as possible for her in the hopes she'll ask for a transfer, but no luck yet.' Sarah stared gloomily into the depths of her glass. 'Going to have to change tack, though. That file Bill put together for me, have you seen it?'

'Yeah, I glanced at it.'

'The boyfriend.'

Zack, a kid Freddie had taken on a few months ago who was a whizz at hacking pretty much anything, had hacked Holly's phone and was monitoring her activity, a summary of which was in the file. Sarah was glad Freddie had such a handy tech guy.

Holly didn't seem to be into much other than her work, nor did she have much of an online presence, but this didn't hugely surprise Sarah. With the sort of people they dealt with and the nasty situations they could find themselves in, it wasn't wise to leave personal details exposed.

She frequented a couple of cocktail bars with a group of girl-friends. This same group had a WhatsApp chat which Zack had summarised as a *bland boring chick chat* and marked as irrelevant. There was one person of interest in Holly's WhatsApp, though. A long-term boyfriend, called Roddy. It appeared that he was into motorbikes and bike shows, though Holly didn't go to these and they led quite independent social lives.

'You think he'll be an issue?' Freddie asked.

Sarah pulled a face. 'Not really. But I need to suss it out. Going to have to try playing nice for a bit, see if I can get her to open up about him.'

Freddie didn't reply straight away, the chatter of the people in the pub around them the only sound as they drank. Eventually he shrugged. 'You're just going to have to keep an eye on her, try to stay on top of the situation. Because it's your arse that's on the line,' he reminded her.

'Yeah, thanks, I'm aware of that,' Sarah replied caustically with a roll of her eyes.

Working for Freddie was very lucrative financially, but it came with its own unique set of dangers. If Sarah was caught and accused of working for him, she would have to deny it to the end. Even if that meant being struck off the force and sent down for sabotaging an investigation. It wasn't a prospect she liked to dwell on.

'Here.' She tossed a file across the table. 'That's the latest intel they've gathered and plans for the next stage. There's nothing you can't work around fairly easily.'

'You can't bring kids in 'ere, love,' they heard the barman call out towards the other end of the bar.

'Well, I need to find his father and from what I hear, he's in here,' came the sharp reply.

Sarah pulled a face over the table at Freddie and he frowned. Leaning his head to the side, he looked down the bar towards the commotion.

'That might be the case, but you still can't bring kids in here,' the barman replied more loudly.

Freddie watched him cross his arms stubbornly. He glanced over towards the woman standing with a little boy, a tight grip on his upper arm. He couldn't really see the kid's face; it was bowed as if embarrassed at the spectacle his mother was making. Freddie shook his head. *Poor little mite,* he thought. The mother turned her head defiantly, staring out some of the men around her who were sniggering at the situation.

'I'm not leaving until I've seen if his father's in here, OK? I won't be a bleedin' minute, you sour old bastard,' she said defiantly.

'Oh, for Christ's sake…' The barman looked up to the heavens. 'Go on then, who ya looking for?'

The woman stepped forward into the centre of the pub and looked around, her eyes quickly searching each table and up the row of booths. As her gaze reached the last booth and rested on Freddie's face, she stopped and lifted her chin.

'I'm looking for him,' she said. 'My son's father. Freddie Tyler.'

CHAPTER SEVEN

'You fucking what?' Freddie exclaimed as he registered the woman's words, his voice rising in horror. 'I don't think so, love.' He looked at the sea of shocked faces around him and his heart sank like a stone. There was no way there was any substance to this claim that the woman's young boy could be his son, but that didn't matter. Half of London's underworld was in this pub; it was a hotspot, a safe haven for organised criminals. News of this would spread within minutes. Freddie didn't care much for idle gossip, but he did care about Anna and that was all he could think of in this moment. Hearing a rumour like this, with everything she was going through, it would hit her like a brick.

'You might not want to believe it, Freddie, but it's true.' The woman held her head up defiantly and Freddie felt anger begin to creep up his neck.

He stood up with a murderous expression and stepped out of the booth towards her. He saw panic flit across her face momentarily, but the hard confidence soon reasserted itself. Something in her expression made him pause and he began to study her properly. His anger was ready to unleash itself on this scumbag who had decided to try and palm off her kid's parentage on him. It served to remind him that he was a target for tricksters and con artists – powerful men always were. But a voice niggled inside that told him he had seen her before. Despite her run-down, weathered appearance, her bright blue eyes were familiar.

'It's damn well *not* true,' he said strongly, looking around and making sure people heard his response. 'I think I'd know if I had a kid, especially one that big. How old is he anyway?'

'He's just turned seven,' she replied. 'And you don't know because I never told you. But I'm telling ya now.'

'You're mad,' Freddie replied, shaking his head in disbelief.

'Am I, Freddie? Don't you remember me? We had a lot of fun together back in the day.' The woman jutted her chin out and pushed her dirty blonde hair behind her ears, as if suddenly aware of her scruffy appearance.

Freddie frowned and thought back to seven years before. It had been a crazy time. He'd been rising high in the ranks of the underworld under his mentor Vince and the world had been his oyster. He'd bought the clubs and had started taking the lead on some of the firm's ventures. The money had been rolling in, more than he had ever thought to be earning. His days had been filled with hard graft and his nights had been spent drinking away the stress and living it up. Many girls had come and gone. Mostly he had hooked up with strippers. They knew the score with men like him and were thick-skinned enough to not get too emotionally attached, or if they did, they were too hard and proud to show it. Most of them anyway.

The memory of how he met Tanya flickered to life, as it always did when he cast his mind back to those days. After meeting her in one of the strip clubs he frequented, he'd dated Tanya for several months before casting her aside when she appeared to be growing too attached. Moving on, he hadn't given her a second thought until years later when they met again through Anna and became good friends. He didn't like to think back to their past these days; he wasn't exactly proud of how he'd acted.

As his mind raced through the faces of all the women he could remember, one suddenly stuck out with great clarity and he felt his stomach turn to ice. Blinking, he stared at the woman in front of him again through fresh eyes and mentally groaned. Of all the women who could have turned up with a child in tow now, none of them could have bitten him in the arse more than this was about to if what she claimed was true.

'Jules,' he stated flatly.

'In the flesh,' she replied with a cold smile.

Freddie looked around. Everyone was still staring, the room completely silent except for their exchange. She had picked her platform well, knowing full well that he'd have to hear her out and wouldn't be able to cover this up. Hot anger boiled in his veins at the thought of the corner she'd trapped him in. Surely her claim couldn't have any truth in it? He had always been careful. This was a set-up.

'We might have had some fun back in the day,' he said through gritted teeth, 'but that don't mean your kid's mine. Do you really think I'd fall for that?' He stepped forward menacingly and she took a half step back before stopping herself. 'You really think you can walk in here after all these years and palm him off as mine to get a bit of cash?' Freddie snarled. 'With all due respect, you were a stripper who liked a good time. I was hardly the only bloke around at that time.'

'No, you weren't,' she admitted with a shrug. 'But you're still his dad. You were the only one it could have been, for a few reasons. And if you don't believe me, perhaps you'll believe your own eyes.' She shook the small child, who was still cowering with his head down, under her tight grip. 'Look up, Ethan. Let your dad see ya.'

Freddie looked down and almost stopped breathing as he stared into the terrified hazel-green eyes of his younger double.

CHAPTER EIGHT

Loud beeps echoed around the old warehouse as the small truck backed up towards the open lock-up. The driver watched his boss in the side mirror, waving him back gradually until eventually he held his hand up in a signal to halt. He pulled the handbrake up and jumped down from the cab.

'Shall I start unloading, boss?' the driver asked in a broad Northern accent.

'Yeah, go on then.' Drew Johnson fiddled with the toothpick that could be constantly found sticking out of the side of his mouth and waited for Richie to pull up the roller door at the back of the truck.

Rumour had it that Drew kept a toothpick on the go because he was obsessed with having perfectly clean teeth. Indeed, his long-standing title 'the mouth of Manchester' added to people's belief that this must be true, but those who knew him well knew that it wasn't. In reality, Drew had given up smoking several years before and the toothpick helped to dull the cravings. And he'd been dubbed 'the mouth of Manchester' in his earlier, wilder days, when he was known for picking rows just for the sake of it. Now, with the jobs they pulled being much higher risk, he picked them more carefully and made sure to stay off the police radar.

'What are we looking at?' Drew asked, as Richie secured the top of the roller door. He peered inside, his icy blue eyes quickly searching through the goods within.

'There's some dead good stuff in there, boss,' Richie replied eagerly, jumping up. He opened up one of the boxes and tipped it so that Drew could see inside. 'This lot was on the way to the designer depot. There's some Chanel coats, a crate of Zanottis and some Louis.' He pointed towards the handbags. 'Quids in.'

Drew looked at the products, his expression blank. 'Any high street?' he asked with a frustrated sigh.

'Couple of Ted Baker boxes but nah, nothing lower.' Richie glanced out towards his boss, puzzled. This stuff was worth much more than the usual high-street lorries they caught.

'Get word to Catriona – tell her she needs to come take a look at it. She'll have to sell it through the girls. I can't send this lot through the markets.' Drew turned away.

'Oh, right.' Richie put the box away and jumped down, dusting off his hands. Now he understood why his boss wasn't over the moon.

Every couple of weeks Drew planned a heist on an unsuspecting lorry full of retail goods. Sometimes it was local, but more often it was miles away from home. The days and times were always different, as was the process. That way it didn't look like they were all connected and there was no trail back to them. One they had sorted through the goods, they went down to the chain of market stalls that Drew ran throughout the city. It was an easy, paperless way to lose the products and bring in the cash. But they couldn't sell top-end designer gear that way – it was too suspect. Instead it would have to go through Drew's long-term shag-piece (girlfriend was too formal a term for what they shared) Catriona. She managed Drew's escort company and the girls in their employ had many skills. It wouldn't be hard for them to sell the goods to clients on the quiet.

Drew bit the toothpick, trying to hide his annoyance. 'Wait till after dark and take this up to Preston. Find somewhere on the outskirts to burn it out and make sure no one finds it till it's well on its way.'

'No problem,' Richie replied.

'Take Skidders with you – have him follow you in the car. After you drop the truck, you need to go to Preston Golf Club.'

'Oh yeah?' Richie asked, surprised.

'Yeah. You're picking up,' he answered with a meaningful stare.

'Ah, I see.' Richie nodded.

'Do not get caught, you understand?'

'Yeah, 'course.'

Drew nodded and walked out of the warehouse towards his car.

Flexing his fingers, he threw the toothpick to the ground irritably. There was a lot riding on this new direction they were going in and he could feel the pressure bearing down on him. But pressure was good, he reminded himself, rolling his shoulders. Pressure was the catalyst that formed diamonds from lumps of coal. London and its current rulers didn't know it yet, but soon there would be a new king in town. Life was about to change for them all.

CHAPTER NINE

Freddie sat on one of the stools by the breakfast bar in his and Anna's home and stared into the tumbler full of whisky. It was his third but it wasn't helping to relax him at all. He had barely slept the night before, tossing and turning as he reeled from the news that he'd possibly fathered a son. Thankfully Anna hadn't come home. He recalled her mentioning that she was having a night in with Tanya to discuss business plans and would probably just stay over. He had never been so glad of her absence.

Now, though, it was coming up to the evening again and he knew she wasn't working tonight. She had texted him to say she'd be home early if he wanted to grab a takeaway and spend some time together. He could have lied and claimed he was busy, avoided seeing her until he got his head around things, but he knew he couldn't do that. It wouldn't be fair. He had to be straight with Anna, even knowing how much this news was likely to hurt her.

The day before, as he'd stood in silent shock, staring down into the all too familiar eyes of the boy in front of him, Jules had handed him a piece of paper. '*These are the details of where I'm staying and my number. Get in touch when you want to talk,*' she had said. Not knowing how to respond, Freddie had just watched them walk out.

The men on the tables around him had stared, waiting to see what he would say. Freddie had slowly turned and told them very clearly that they were not to tell a soul what they had just witnessed. That if he found out that news of this had spread to Anna before he had told her himself, he'd cut out the tongue of whoever was responsible. They had all nodded and quickly agreed. They all knew who Freddie was – most of them worked for him in some way. This would be enough to make sure his threat was taken seriously.

Freddie heard the sound of the front door opening and waited, closing his eyes momentarily in dread. When he opened them, Anna walked into the kitchen, a bright smile on her face and a bulging bag of Chinese food in her hand.

'Let's get fat,' she said with a laugh. 'I bought two of those big chicken rolls this time as I'm starving and I just don't want to share.' She placed the bag on the side and walked over to Freddie.

Frowning, she paused as if to take a proper look at him. He was slumped over in a defeated way, his shirt messily untucked and unbuttoned at the top. Anna glanced at the whisky in his hand and up to his drawn, stressed face.

She kissed him lightly on the lips. 'Bad day?' she asked softly, wrapping her arms around his waist.

Freddie looked down into her dark blue eyes; eyes that were so full of love and trust. His gaze swept over her peachy skin, the natural glow over her high cheekbones and up over her dark shiny hair. He pulled her close, savouring every detail of her as she was now – happy, content and at one with him. When he told her about Jules and Ethan, that fragile happiness, which was only just resurfacing after their dark recent history, would be crushed.

'Yeah.' Freddie steeled himself to tell her. The words hovered on the tip of his tongue, but he couldn't bring himself to say them.

A little voice inside his head reminded him that it still might not be true. Sure, the boy looked like him, but so what? That could just have been what sparked the idea to con him. This could still be just an elaborate hoax to get money out of him. It wouldn't be the first time something like this had happened to a man like him.

Freddie forced a smile. 'It's just been a long one. I didn't sleep last night. Too much coffee.'

Anna rolled her eyes and kissed his cheek. 'I told you it was a bad idea drinking it so late.' She pulled away from Freddie and walked back over to the Chinese to unpack it. 'We should get some decaf maybe.'

'Sure,' Freddie replied. He stood up. 'I'm going to get changed – be back in a minute.'

Freddie ran his hands down his face as he walked down the hallway to their bedroom. He needed to see Jules and quickly, and put this whole thing to bed once and for all. Because more importantly than anything else, he needed to save Anna from more heartache.

CHAPTER TEN

Freddie took a couple of deep drags on his cigarette as he stared at the block of flats across the road. This was the address Jules had given him. Flicking the cigarette away tensely, he crossed the road and pressed the buzzer. After a few seconds he heard the door click open and he made his way up to the first-floor flat.

As he reached the flat, the door opened and Ethan ran out past him down the stairs. Freddie paused, unsure whether or not to speak to him.

'Come on then, you going to stand there all day?' Jules said, her tone betraying her nerves.

Freddie glared at her as he walked past her into the small living room and she shrank back a little. *Good,* he thought. *She damn well should be nervous after that stunt at The Black Bear.*

Looking around, Freddie had to stop himself pulling a face of disgust. The whole room was a mess and there was a full ashtray on the arm of the sofa. A small waft of smoke indicated she'd just stubbed a cigarette out. Not that Freddie had any issue with smoking itself, but he strongly disagreed with smoking in the same room as children. Walking to the balconette doors, Freddie opened them to let some fresh air in and watched as Ethan crossed the road to the small park opposite.

'He's a bit young to be out there alone, isn't he?' he asked, with a frown.

'Why, what's he going to do?' Jules replied sarcastically. 'Run away? He's old enough to know to stay where I told him.'

Freddie turned to face her. 'Anyone could just take him.'

'Well, they haven't yet,' Jules replied with a tired look.

Freddie felt his anger intensify but was careful to keep it in check. If Ethan really was his, there were going to have to be some changes. Before he said anything though, he wanted to find out for certain. He rubbed his hand over his face, stressed.

'Tell me what happened. From the beginning. I want to know why, if what you say is true, you've only come forward now. Because I don't believe you one fucking bit.' Freddie sat down on one of the chairs, keeping one eye on the boy in the park as he waited to hear what Jules had to say.

Jules sighed heavily. 'Do you want a drink?' she asked. Freddie shook his head. 'OK, well, I need one.'

He waited as she disappeared into the kitchen, then came back with a full glass of wine. Jules sat down on the sofa opposite and began talking.

'When I found out I was pregnant, I knew it was yours straight away.' She ignored the look of disbelief on Freddie's face. 'I know you weren't the only one I slept with. We both know I was tomming on the side. But I was always very careful with clients. I was always careful with you too. But the night you opened Ruby Ten, we all got really drunk. You were celebrating, so a whole load of us got absolutely wasted, do you remember?'

Freddie nodded, casting his mind back. He'd been sick as a dog the next day; by far the worst hangover he'd ever had.

'You and I ended up in the office after everyone had gone. From what I remember, we had a lot of fun.' Jules half-smiled. 'But we fell asleep and when I woke up I found that the johnny we'd meant to use was on the floor next to us. I don't know if it had fallen off or what, but we hadn't used it. It was the only time I was unprotected.'

Freddie closed his eyes. 'So, why didn't you speak to me then?'

'I was going to,' Jules answered. 'I went to find you one night, went up to the office in Club CoCo. You weren't there, but Vince was. He could see I was in a state, told me to sit down and poured me a drink.'

Freddie's head snapped up at Vince's name. Vince had been the one who had brought him into the firm when he was just a boy. He had trained him up, groomed him to take over in time, had helped make him who he was today. What did Vince have to do with this?

'I told him I was pregnant and that I knew it was yours. He asked me to give him twenty-four hours before I told you. Said he had an idea, but needed to run it by someone first. He was being so nice to me I agreed. I thought he was trying to help me,' she added bitterly. 'The next day we met again. He offered me a hundred grand in cash if I got an abortion and disappeared. He said I could start over new somewhere with the money, but that no one could ever know about the pregnancy.'

Freddie's eyes widened in shock. Why would Vince do that, without talking to him?

'I took the money and left. But I didn't get the abortion. I had this romantic notion that being a mum would be this great adventure filled with love and happiness. Huh!' She laughed with a sneer and drank deeply from her wine. 'It's not. It's fucking terrible, actually, being a single mum to an ungrateful little brat who spent his baby years screaming and who's done nothing but moan and cost me a fortune ever since. But I made my bed, so here we are.'

Freddie balled his fists, angered by the way she was talking. He had no doubt that her situation was difficult at times, but that wasn't Ethan's fault.

'I'm sure the money helped along the way at least,' Freddie said, his voice clipped.

'That ran out years ago,' Jules replied. 'And I've struggled every single day since.'

'Like I said, why wait until now?'

Jules coloured slightly. 'When I took the money Vince warned me that if I went back on my word there would be consequences. I'm not stupid; I know what that meant. But then I heard that he's finally given in to his old age and gone into a retirement home.' She shrugged. 'Not much he can do to me from there.'

Freddie stared at her. She didn't know Vince at all if she thought that. He might be retired but he still had the contacts and reach that he always had. He also still had the temper. But he kept this to himself. 'And what exactly are you here for now then?' He was pretty sure he knew the answer already.

Jules jutted her chin out. 'I need money. He ain't cheap and I can't exactly work with a kid at home.'

Freddie shook his head. It wasn't easy, but there were ways and means if she did want to work. His mother had worked every hour God sent when they were kids, after their dad died. He had no time for those sorts of excuses. 'So what sort of thing are you thinking? A maintenance payment each month?'

'No,' Jules answered a little too quickly. 'I want a lump sum. The same again.'

'Why?' Freddie asked, suspicious.

'I want to start over somewhere new. We've seen an opportunity in Spain for a little beach bar. It could be a gold mine.'

'We?'

'I mean I. I saw it.' Jules looked away, pushing her dull blonde hair behind her ear.

'You meant we,' Freddie replied firmly. 'Don't lie to me, Jules.'

'Fine, I meant we,' Jules said irritably. 'My boyfriend, Liam.'

'And what does he do for a living?' Freddie asked, smelling a rat.

'Not much right now. He has a bad back, but with some money we could set up our own little money-spinner. He wouldn't be doing nothing then,' she answered, defensively.

Ah, Freddie thought. *So they're both scroungers.* He stood up and Jules jumped slightly.

'There's no point discussing this yet. You ain't getting jack shit until I have proof this is the truth. Because part of me is still convinced that you're pulling a con.' He looked out the window at Ethan, who was sitting alone on the swing, hunching his shoulders against the cold through his thin jacket. Freddie's heart reached out to him, but he turned his gaze away. He couldn't let his emotions run riot. It still may not be true. He pulled a piece of paper from his pocket. 'This is the address, date and time to take Ethan for a paternity test. It's all paid for and the results come straight to me. I'll be in touch afterwards.'

Jules's mouth flapped open and shut as he turned to leave. 'And what am I supposed to do with him in the meantime?' she asked.

Freddie's eyes flashed with anger as they turned on her. 'What do you mean *what are you supposed to do with him*? He's your son. Be his mum, for Christ's sake.' He walked out before he lost his temper with the woman completely.

As he crossed the road and got into the car, Freddie let out a long, hard breath. His mind was reeling from all the information and he still couldn't believe this was all happening. One thing was for certain though: he needed to speak to Vince – today.

CHAPTER ELEVEN

Freddie's shoes clipped loudly on the hard floor as he walked down the hallway of the retirement home towards Vince's living area. He'd been here a couple of times before to make sure Vince was comfortably settled and kept up to date with the business ventures he still held a stake in.

Until recently Vince had been enjoying his retirement out in Surrey with his second wife. She was much younger than he was, but although they seemed oddly matched, Freddie knew it was genuine love that had brought them together. Then one day Celia had been driving back from a yoga class when a truck driver had fallen asleep at the wheel and crashed head first into her. She hadn't stood a chance; she'd died on impact. The stress had been too much for Vince in his older years and he had suffered a heart attack. It had weakened him severely, and after fighting against it for a while, he had finally given in and accepted a place in the retirement home.

Freddie turned the corner and entered the large living area for this particular wing. A TV blared away with the news in one corner, and what appeared to be a sewing circle had gathered in another. But Freddie ignored these and all the other activities, making a beeline for the group of men around a table at the far end of the room.

'Royal flush – have that, ya bastards,' Vince's deep guttural voice called out. There was a groan of annoyance around the table and Vince chuckled as he pulled in the pile of change from the middle of the table. 'Ah, what you bitching for, eh? You're lucky we're playing for fag money. You'd be bloody crying if we were playing for real stakes.'

Freddie had to hide the grin that threatened to spread across his face. 'You fleecing them for all they're worth again, Vince?' he said, as he reached the table.

'Freddie! Now here's a man you want to be careful of on the poker table.' Vince beamed, his deeply lined face lighting up at the sight of his protégé. 'I wasn't expecting you, son. Everything alright?' His smile turned to a frown of concern and he looked him up and down critically. It had been a long time since Freddie had turned to him for help, but old habits died hard.

'Maybe. I'm not sure. I need to talk to you about something.'

Vince clicked his fingers at the table, his expression all business. The men around him immediately stood up and moved away, without a word. Freddie sat down next to Vince with his back to the wall and waited for the last retiree to shuffle out of earshot. Vince pulled all the stray cards in and began shuffling the deck, waiting for Freddie to talk.

'I've had a bit of an interesting week,' Freddie began. 'An old flame turned up out of the blue with a boy she claims is my son.' Freddie watched as Vince's hands paused in their shuffling momentarily. 'She reckons you paid her to disappear and get rid of the baby. I've got a paternity test booked, but she seems pretty convincing so far.'

Vince continued shuffling the cards but slower than before. His expression was grim. 'Jules,' he said eventually.

'You don't deny it then?'

'Why would I?' He shrugged, still focusing on the pack of cards in his hands. 'You were young, up and coming in our world. You were riding high and finally starting to live life after years of hardship and hard graft. You spent your youth looking after your little brothers and sister and your mum. It was your time to shine, to take your real place in the world and to enjoy it. Women…' Vince waved his hand dismissively. 'There was a time and place for that someday, but not back then. Not seriously anyway. And yet there she was. Jules.' Vince's tone changed as though her name left a bad taste in his mouth. 'She turned up in your office that day like a bad penny.' He shook his head, remembering. 'She was thrilled to find herself knocked up by you. She tried to hide it, but I could see it in her eyes. That girl would have been the end of you, if I'd let her tell you. You're too good a man, you see. You'd have done the right thing.' He gave Freddie a wry half-smile. 'I couldn't let you do that, Fred. You were the son I never had. I had to protect you.'

Freddie blew out a long breath. Part of him had hoped Vince would deny it, tell him Jules was a liar. But he hadn't even tried to. What could he say to all of this? The fact that Vince had kept something like this from him was a huge betrayal. But he'd been trying to protect him, in his own unique way.

'Jules said you asked her to wait until you spoke to someone else. Who was it?' Freddie had been wondering about this on the way over. Who else knew this secret?

'Oh that.' Vince shook his head. 'I just needed time to think and to make sure I was doing the best thing. It wasn't a decision I made easily, Freddie.' He turned his gaze towards the younger man.

'It wasn't a decision you should have made at all,' Freddie said flatly.

'Perhaps not. And I did it knowing that this day might come. But even knowing that, I still believe I made the right choice. Without her holding you down, you've built an empire. And you've met someone worthy of you,' Vince pressed, raising his eyebrows. 'Anna isn't just any woman, Freddie. And chances are you wouldn't be with her now if I hadn't done what I did.'

Freddie didn't reply. Vince did have a point. But it didn't make it any easier to swallow.

'Still.' Vince frowned. 'Jules was supposed to have got rid of it. We had a deal. And I gave her a lot of money to uphold that deal. I'm surprised that there's a kid involved.'

'Ethan,' Freddie said.

Vince nodded. 'Well, at least she picked a half decent name for it. Look, Freddie, if you're looking for an apology from me for dealing with the situation and keeping it from you, you ain't gonna get one. I stand by my decision. Your life is better because of it. But I am sorry that this is coming back to bite you in the arse now. If you need me to talk to Anna…'

'No, I think you've done enough,' Freddie replied. 'I need to go. Thanks for your honesty.' He stood up and straightened his jacket. 'I'll see you later.'

Vince watched as Freddie walked out with a grim expression. So, the bitch was back. Anger bubbled under the surface at the audacity she'd shown. He had given her fair warning back then – get rid and stay gone, or else. It was a lot of money he'd handed over. He didn't expect to be treated like such a joke in return.

He narrowed his eyes. He might be old and retired, but that didn't mean he wasn't still a powerful man. Jules had made a big mistake coming back. He would bide his time and let Freddie deal with things. But there was no way Vince was going to let a snub of this magnitude go unchecked. Not a chance in hell.

Picking up his mobile he scrolled through the contacts. Before he did anything else, there was an important call he had to make. He'd been quick to throw Freddie off when he'd asked who Vince had needed to speak to all those years ago. He hadn't exactly lied; he *had* needed time to think about things. But he had not made the decision alone. And now that the game had changed, so had the stakes. He pressed the dial button and waited for the call to be answered.

'It's Vince. Look, we have a slight problem…'

CHAPTER TWELVE

The gates to the Westway gypsy site were pulled open by two teenage boys and the big old caravan rumbled through. As it made its slow way down the main track, in between the closely packed dwellings, many of the residents sidled out to watch what was going on. The gates were pulled shut, the metal groaning as they clanged into place. Jacko pulled neatly into the space that he was being waved towards and turned off the engine. Stretching up and cracking his back, he jumped down and grinned widely.

'Alright, mate?' he said to the nearest man. 'Can ya point me in the right direction for O'Callahan?' The instructions had been to make contact with this man and leave the caravan under his protection. And right now he wanted to get the caravan settled as quickly as possible so that he could get back to his B&B and have a nice cold beer. It had been a long journey.

'Sure,' he answered with a smile that didn't quite reach his eyes.

Jacko felt a prickle run up his spine as he caught the coldness in the man's response. He glanced at all the other faces around him and realised they'd surrounded him in a circle. None looked friendly.

He frowned, his senses sharpening. 'I'm Jacko; Drew Johnson sent me,' he said warily. Perhaps they didn't realise who he was – though there couldn't be that many strangers showing up with caravans full of cocaine.

'Yeah, we know,' another one of the men answered. Still no one moved.

Jacko bit his lip as he tried to work out what was wrong – and he could sense that something was very, very wrong. He needed to find this O'Callahan figure. But he had already asked once and hadn't been answered, and there didn't look to be a way through the circle of men without a confrontation.

A door opened a couple of trailers down and a broad man with wild hair and a deep frown stepped out. Three other men followed him. Jacko's attention was drawn to them. They didn't look to be from the site – two of them were in suits, for one thing. The circle silently opened as the broad man made his way towards Jacko.

'So,' he said, an Irish twang colouring his gruff tone. 'You're here to deliver the cocaine to us. We thank ye very much for your generosity.'

Jacko blinked, unsure he'd heard correctly. 'You what?' He swallowed. 'Are you Teddy O'Callahan?' he asked.

Teddy grinned. 'In the flesh.'

'Oh, sound.' The small wave of relief at meeting his contact was tinged with worry. 'I think there's been a misunderstanding, though. I'm not here to deliver the coke to you. The agreement was that we're paying for use of the pitch and for your protection whilst it's here. I'll need to come and go to distribute, until we find somewhere permanent. But after that I'll be out of your hair.' Jacko's gaze flickered between Teddy and the two suited men standing behind him. They were staring at him intently and the slightly smaller one's gaze turned his insides to ice. He swallowed again, reminding himself that he was a hard man, not someone to be intimidated.

'The *agreement* is whatever I decide it is, lad. And right now the agreement is that you're going to hand over the keys to that there caravan behind ye and leave my site.' Teddy crossed his arms.

'What do you mean?' Jacko's mouth flapped open. 'I'm not handing it over to anyone. This is *ours*. If you don't want us here that's fine, but if I'm leaving, this van's coming with me,' he replied indignantly.

'Oh, it's yours?' Teddy feigned surprise. 'Did ye hear that, lads? He says it's his.'

The man whose gaze had sent ice through Jacko's stomach stepped forward. 'I'm afraid that's where you're wrong, mate,' he said. 'You see, you're in London now. West London to be exact. Which just so happens to be within *our* territory for all chemical distribution. And that means' – he stepped closer – 'that the massive stash of cocaine in that caravan is now ours.'

'And who the fuck are you then?' Jacko blustered. His words were confident but his heart was sinking like a stone as he put two and two together. He'd never seen him in the flesh but it could only be one person.

'Oh, where are my manners,' Freddie replied with a cold smile. 'I'm Freddie and this is my brother Paul. We're the Tylers. And you're Jacko, here on the orders of your boss Drew Johnson. You see' – keeping eye contact as he slowly circled the man in front of him, Freddie's tone turned deadly – 'this is *my* city, Jacko. No one in our line of work so much as takes a *shit* in my city without me knowing about it. You were fucked from the off, mate.'

Jacko groaned internally. Freddie was right – he was well and truly fucked right now. *Ahh well*, he thought. *In for a penny, in for a pound.* He straightened up and tensed, keeping an eye on the men closest to him. 'Yeah? If you knew all about us why'd you let us get this far?'

Freddie hid a smirk. Jacko had spirit; he'd give him that. Many a man would be quivering in their boots in the same position, surrounded by unfriendly gypsies and pissing off powerful people miles from home.

Stepping forward until his face was just inches from Jacko's, Freddie's tone turned hard. 'Well, if I hadn't let you get this far I'd never have got my hands on a whole caravan of product, would I?'

Jacko's gaze flickered around as he tried to work out what to do. Eventually he took a deep breath and shook his head strongly. 'You ain't getting it now either.'

Curling his lip, Freddie lunged forward and knocked Jacko backward. The other man almost crashed to the ground but managed to right his footing just in time. Freddie came at him again, smashing his fist into Jacko's face.

Paul's eyebrows shot up in surprise. Freddie was usually so calm and calculated; he didn't lash out until necessary. He exchanged a confused glance with Seamus.

Freddie smashed his fist into the other man's face again, anger and frustration clear in his own expression. Jacko stepped back and put up his fists. Freddie had taken him by surprise but now he was ready.

Without warning, Freddie twisted and kicked Jacko in the stomach, sending him backward and to the ground this time. He had clocked Jacko as a boxer straight away, from the way he held himself. If you knew what you were looking for, you could easily tell. However good a boxer he might be, though, Freddie was better. Years of training from the age of five had honed his skills to a fine point, and though he might not get in the ring anymore, he was still sharp.

'You still think you're walking out of here with that product, do ya?' Freddie spat, kicking him viciously in the side. Jacko yelped in pain and kicked back from the floor but Freddie sidestepped and he missed. 'Think I'm that much of a mug, do ya?' He kicked him again, putting all his weight behind the action and Jacko grunted, scuffling back, holding his stomach with one arm and trying to stand using the other.

Not ready to let him get up, Freddie lurched forward and began raining hard punches down on the other man, over and over, exerting all his energy. He hit the man again and again, each impact of his fist on Jacko's face feeling like a welcome release as the blowback pain travelled up his arms.

Blood began to flow as Jacko's mouth burst open. He hit back in self-defence and landed a few blows on his attacker, but he wasn't in a position to place any force behind them so they barely made an impact.

'You don't get to come in here,' Freddie roared, 'bringing your *fucking* product into my *fucking* gaff and expect not to suffer some *fucking* consequences!' Spittle flew from his lips as he raged, and the veins in his neck bulged as the stress from everything else he was dealing with came to the fore.

'Freddie,' Paul called out curtly. The whole gypsy camp was watching this breakdown. The last thing they needed was for word to travel that Freddie was acting like a livewire.

As if suddenly remembering he had an audience, Freddie looked around and noted the look on his brother's face. He sniffed and pushed his hair back into place, stepping away from Jacko. He hadn't planned to lose his temper with the man. The stress of everything else going on must be getting to him, he realised.

Paul relaxed, seeing that Freddie had curbed whatever the hell had driven the unnecessary attack. Jacko stood up with difficulty. One eye was already swelling shut and blood ran down his face from a gash on his forehead.

Acting as though nothing had happened, Teddy O'Callahan sauntered over casually and pointed towards the main gate. 'We thank ye again for the gift. The exit is there. You'll be on your way now.'

Jacko clamped his mouth shut and limped back down the road towards the main gate, his head held high. Drew would be furious when he heard what had happened here, but there was nothing Jacko could do about it on his own.

Teddy whistled and tilted his head towards the man holding the keys. He stepped forward and handed them over to Freddie.

'She's all yours,' Teddy said. 'The offer is still there. You can keep it here if you like – no one will touch it.'

Freddie nodded respectfully. 'Thank you, Teddy, I appreciate it, but we have somewhere.' He turned to Seamus, who had been silent during the exchange. 'Here, take it over to the yard. We'll meet you there.'

Seamus nodded. 'No problem. I'll see ye later then, uncle.' He waved goodbye, before getting into the cab of the caravan and pulling the tired old vehicle back out onto the track.

'Thanks again for all your help,' Freddie said as he and Paul made their way over to the car.

'Anything for family,' Teddy said. His clear blue eyes studied Freddie and he gave a small half-smile. 'We'll be seeing you again, I think.' He returned to his trailer and the remaining men melted away back to their business.

Freddie joined Paul in the car and they pulled off.

'What was all that about?' Paul asked quietly, nodding thanks to the boy opening the gate to let them out.

'He hopes to do more business,' Freddie replied. 'But it's not likely.'

'I wasn't talking about that.'

There was a short silence. 'That was nothing,' Freddie answered.

'Didn't look like nothing.' Paul paused and studied his brother. He was tense, his shoulders rigid and his jaw set in a hard line. He knew that look all too well. Whatever it was, Freddie wasn't going to talk about it.

Freddie gripped the steering wheel hard as they drove off down the road. He needed to get a grip on his temper. He was usually so calm when faced with challenges, but usually his problems didn't leave him in such a tight, uncontrollable corner. Like a caged lion, he felt a frustrated anger bubbling away inside of him, just beneath the surface. And he wasn't sure how well he could contain it.

CHAPTER THIRTEEN

The two resident guard dogs barked viciously as the car swept up towards the locked gate of the scrapyard, but they piped down as Freddie jumped out to put in the combination on the lock. This was their boss, one of the few men they'd been trained to let pass without issue. If it had been an intruder, they wouldn't have made it ten feet without losing a limb. It was one of the reasons Freddie liked owning this place. The chains fell away and he opened the gate for Paul to drive through, before locking back up behind them.

Pulling the car around the first Portakabin and a pile of rusted old car parts, they stopped beside Seamus, who sat on an upturned barrel waiting patiently. The dogs followed and sniffed around their bosses and Seamus with interest. Seamus ruffled one of their heads and got a lick of affection in return. One of the first responsibilities the Tylers had dished out to Seamus when he'd joined the firm was to feed and water these dogs daily and make sure they were OK. The general manager was only part-time, so they'd needed someone else to rely on. Seamus had always made sure to spend a few minutes playing with the dogs whilst he was there and they loved him for it.

'Pass the keys.'

Seamus threw them to Freddie who caught them and unlocked the door to the main body of the caravan. He stepped inside to look around.

As his eyes adjusted to the dark, he took in his surroundings. To a stranger's eye there was nothing out of place – it was a normal caravan. Freddie reached over to the sofa and pulled up the seat. It lifted easily and he chucked it to one side. Peering into the space underneath, Freddie's eyes rested on the neatly stacked bags of cocaine.

'Bingo,' he said softly.

Paul came up behind him and glanced over his shoulder at the stash, before lifting the seat of the second sofa bench. This was stacked full of product too.

'How much do you reckon there is?' Paul asked.

'I'm not sure.' Freddie stood up and moved down towards the back. Opening one of the cupboards, he found this to be full too. 'A lot,' he continued.

Despite knowing that this was going to be a big load, Freddie was surprised by the quantity. There was enough product on board to supply the whole city. He hadn't been expecting this Northern crew to go all out on their first run. 'Stupid,' he muttered, shaking his head.

'Hmm?'

'They've ticked more than their lives are worth on this one load. There's no way they had the money to pay up front for all this.' Freddie moved so that Paul could see the full cupboard.

Paul raised his eyebrows. 'That's one serious contract.'

'It is. With a very well set-up supplier who has very good quality product.' Freddie picked up one of the bags and weighed it up in his hand. 'We need to find out where they're getting this from and make a deal.'

'I'm not sure they're going to take kindly to the firm who stole from one of their biggest clients. And these guys must be big clients to have so much on tick.'

Freddie paused, considering this. 'They will if we deal with this the right way. They're businessmen after all.'

Paul pulled a face that let Freddie know he wasn't convinced. 'Well, I'll see if Bill can track some information down, but they'll be keeping their cards close to their chests, especially now we have the gear.'

'If anyone can find out, Bill can,' Freddie replied, placing the bag of cocaine back in the cupboard. 'Come on.' He edged past Paul and out into the sunlight. Paul followed. 'Seamus, I want you to count up all the bags that are in there. Call to let us know how many, then stay put. Dean will join you shortly with a list and between the two of you, you'll need to distribute. Make sure' – Freddie emphasised his words with a hard glare – 'that the fuckers you drop to know that it's from us and that all future drops will be by us. Remind them that *we* run this town and that whilst we turned a blind eye when our river ran dry, that problem has now been rectified and there is no further excuse for disloyalty.'

'Got it.' Seamus jumped down off the barrel and took the keys back from his boss.

Freddie got into the car on the driver's side and waited for Paul before pulling the car back out the way they came.

'Where to now?' Paul asked.

'I'll drop you off; I've got some things to do.'

'Oh, anything I need to know about?'

Freddie's expression darkened. 'Not yet, mate. Not yet.'

CHAPTER FOURTEEN

Victims. He hated that word. They weren't victims, not really. Alfie Ramone only ever took to this room those who were deserving of punishment.

Although the cravings he felt pushed him every day to hurt the people around him, he kept them at bay. He may be different to everyone else, but he wasn't stupid. He knew that if he gave in to self-gratification whenever the impulse took him, it would lead him down the short sharp path towards either jail or the nuthouse. Neither of which appealed to him. He enjoyed his freedom and the life he led with his family and his businesses. So instead, Alfie waited patiently for people to cross him or let him down. And luckily, in his line of business, he never had to wait too long. Cocaine distribution on the scale they were running meant that all types of opportunistic scumbags came floating his way. A fair percentage messed up and these were the ones with whom he indulged his pleasures.

Picking up the scalpel, he turned to face the whimpering man tied to the chair in the middle of the room. He shook with fear and beads of sweat began to form on his brow as he caught sight of what Alfie had in his hand.

'That's a lovely sleeve,' Alfie said, gesturing towards the extensive artwork on the man's right arm. 'I bet that cost a lot of money. Tell me, was it the money you were skimming off my product that paid for that?'

The man in the chair made muffled protests through his gag and shook his head, the terror on his face intensifying.

'Oh please,' Alfie said with a tut. 'Don't treat me like an idiot. I may be a lot of things…' He turned the scalpel over in his hand watching the light reflect off the small blade, momentarily mesmerised. He snapped back. 'But an idiot isn't one of them.'

He moved towards the bound man, shifting his considerable weight with surprising grace. 'I know you've been skimming. I even know how much and for how long. You see, your men are a lot more afraid of me than of you. So, when questioned, they sang like canaries.' He shrugged with an almost apologetic expression. 'But back to that lovely sleeve. It looks pretty fresh, which I guess means my money did pay for it.'

He sniffed and his gaze darkened. 'I don't like being stolen from, Reggie. It gives me a sort of hot red feeling right here.' He pointed towards his chest. 'You know?' He raised his brows as if expecting an answer.

Muffled sobs came through the gag as the man pleaded with his eyes. Alfie looked away towards one of the two men standing silently at the bottom of the stairs that led up out of the dark basement they were in. He tilted his head and one of them stepped forward and untied the arm with the tattoos on it. Reggie tried to scream and bucked and writhed, trying to get away from the tight grip but it was no use. The other man had him held fast. Pulling the tattooed arm out and holding it straight, he nodded to his boss.

Alfie smiled as the man's screams filled the room.

*

'So, what else have we got? Any other news or new angles anyone wants to push?' Sarah Riley stood in front of the main information board in the centre of the task-force office, her team gathered in front of her for the weekly strategy meeting. One of the men at the back raised his hand. 'Yes, George?'

George pushed his thick-rimmed glasses up his nose. 'They've switched the phones out again. I had Thea and James tapped, but they've gone dead. I didn't manage to get anything useful off them this time.'

'OK, not to worry, George, just keep trying to locate the new lines. Follow their routines, you'll get back on them eventually.'

'Yes, ma'am.'

'I feel like we should try and get another mole in,' someone piped up from the side. It was Veronica, a younger woman with a short auburn bob and a pixie-like face. She was fairly new to the team and eager to please.

Sarah pretended to consider it. 'The problem we have is that since DI Miechowski got herself caught out' – she allowed herself a quick glance at Holly – 'the Tylers are on high alert on this front. Anyone they hire, they'll go deep and they know exactly what to look for.' She shook her head. 'We can't risk it, not with the allegations of harassment on our desks. It could jeopardise the whole operation.'

There was a silence and Sarah could feel the meeting coming to a close. She turned her attentions towards Holly, who had, as usual, stayed very quiet the whole time. 'And what about you, DI Miechowski? We haven't heard your plans for this week?'

'I thought I'd go back over the old club footage again this week, see if there was anything we missed. There might be some small detail that was overlooked.'

'You wanted to try a car tracker this week too, didn't you?' Veronica piped up helpfully.

Sarah felt a stab of smug satisfaction as she saw the flash of irritated frustration cross Holly's face. Clearly this was something she'd hoped to hold back and carry out without Sarah's knowledge.

'Oh, yes, I was considering it,' Holly said in a falsely bright tone.

'Great idea,' Sarah enthused. 'We haven't tried that in a while; they might have relaxed their checks. Which car are you thinking? Or will you try multiples?' Sarah crossed her arms over her cream turtleneck top and waited.

'The black Merc,' Holly replied, her tone flat with resignation that her idea was now a bust.

'Great idea. Get onto that one today if you can. No time like the present,' Sarah said chirpily. 'And actually, I want to try something new this week, as a team.' She grinned. 'They say two heads are better than one, so instead of working individually, I want you to work together in pairs. Still carry on with what you're doing, but share the load. Perhaps one of you will see something the other hasn't. Holly, you and Veronica can pair up; Adam, you go with George; Helen, you and Isobel can team up; Alex and Chris; Kim and Noelle. And I think that's everyone sorted, so off you go, crack on in your pairs. Let's use each other's heads here along with our own. We might discover something we've previously missed. Let's try to make some real headway this week.'

Sarah watched them all scurry off back to their desks, everyone's energy renewed from the pep talk she always worked into this meeting. Everyone's except for Holly's, of course. Sarah watched her walk away, her shoulders tense and her expression moody. Holly flicked her long, blonde hair over her shoulder and for a second their eyes met across the office. Holly's big blue eyes shone with resentment before she quickly averted her gaze.

Irritation shot through Sarah. Holly was a thorn in her side, and her presence made her more and more nervous by the day. Up until now she had been as rude and as difficult as she could be with her, without being too obvious to the rest of the team, but the bloody woman was still here. The sensible thing for Holly to do under such circumstances would be to leave and start afresh in a clean team somewhere, forget all this had ever happened. If she went willingly, Sarah would happily give her a glowing recommendation. But stubbornly she held on, always trying to catch Freddie out under Sarah's radar. Well, Sarah was never going to let that happen. Because that was *her* job, to keep Freddie from being caught. And she refused to lose.

She took a deep breath and exhaled slowly, pushing her irritation aside. It was time to try a different tack, get Holly talking, perhaps find out a little more about her.

Following Holly out of the office and down the hallway to the kitchen, Sarah pretended to be getting herself another coffee. Holly was busy texting someone on her phone and didn't hear Sarah come in behind her. She jumped slightly when Sarah cleared her throat and opened the cupboard to grab a coffee cup.

'Want one?' she asked, with what she hoped was a winning smile.

Holly frowned suspiciously. 'No, ta. I'm just grabbing some water.'

'And texting.' Sarah gestured towards her phone, which Holly promptly put back in her pocket. They weren't supposed to use mobiles for personal calls in the office and it was Sarah's job to police this. Seeing the opportunity, Sarah jumped on it. 'Oh, don't mind me,' she said with a small grin. 'I don't mind you guys texting. We all have lives outside of here.'

'Don't we just,' Holly replied, sarcasm practically dripping from her words.

Sarah chose to ignore the dig and instead passed a clean glass over. 'So, got any plans for tonight?'

Holly just stared at her, as if she'd grown two heads.

'Oh, come on, Holly,' Sarah said, dropping the fake smile and holding her arms out. 'I know this isn't an ideal situation, not for any of us.' She glanced out of the door, checking that they were still alone. 'But it is what it is. And I'm not a monster; I'm just as human as you. And we have to work together in front of everyone else, whether we have the same agenda or not. We might as well try to get on?' She held out the olive branch, hoping Holly couldn't see what a strain it was for her to do so.

After a few moments of silence, Holly stepped forward and stared at her levelly, her big blue eyes icy and full of accusation. 'I might have no choice but to walk into my office every day and pretend I don't know exactly who you are and what you're doing,' she said quietly in her melodic Northern accent. 'But that doesn't mean for one second that I have to pretend to like you. You know I talked to people about you,' she said, her eyes narrowing in anger. 'Oh don't worry,' she added, seeing the look of shock pass over Sarah's face. 'I didn't mention a word about your private dealings with our most wanted criminals. But I found out quite a lot. Top of your game for your whole career. You climbed the ladder faster than I've been managing. Countless arrests, awards for bravery. One of Ben Hargreaves' chosen few to lead at the very top. You were known as someone to be admired. Right up until the day you quit. And now you're back, you're just a scumbag who protects the people you're supposed to be taking down. People who murder, people who peddle drugs and pimp out girls.'

She shook her head in disgust and looked Sarah up and down. 'I don't know what happened to you. And honestly I don't really care. I've got about as much respect for you as I do the Tylers. So do me a favour…' Stepping back, Holly picked up her glass. 'Don't come in here trying to be all pally with me. I won't tell tales and get you arrested. Not because I give two shits about you, but because I know Freddie meant what he said. I have no doubt that if I did the right thing he'd slit my throat in my sleep. And you'd let him.' She stared at Sarah accusingly. 'I have no doubt that not even witness protection could keep me from his reach. So, this time, I've been bested.' She mashed her lips together in frustration. 'But that doesn't mean we aren't going to catch him as a team. So, watch your back, Sarah Riley.' She pointed a finger at her. 'Because I'll keep my word but that does not mean I won't do my job to the best of my abilities.'

With that, Holly stalked out of the kitchen and back towards the office, her long, blonde hair swishing from side to side behind her. Sarah watched her go, her heart pounding. There was so much she wanted to say, so much she wanted to bite back at. But she couldn't. With a quiet growl of annoyance she turned back to the coffee machine. So much for playing nice.

Pushing her short, dark hair back behind her ears, Sarah took a deep breath and made the decision to talk to Freddie about everything soon. Something had to be done. Because this situation was getting out of hand and there were far too many uncontrollable factors for any of them to be truly safe.

CHAPTER FIFTEEN

Anna checked herself out in the mirror and ruffled her long, dark hair to give it some volume. She wore very little make-up, her overall look soft and subtle. Her usual striking war paint was not required this evening, as she wasn't off to work. Instead, she was heading over for a girls' night in at Tanya's. They had a rare evening off together and had decided to make the most of it, gathering together their close girlfriends and copious amounts of alcohol. Anna was looking forward to it.

Picking up her jacket, Anna turned towards the sound of keys in the front door with a smile.

'Oh hi, I hadn't expected to see you back.'

'Yeah, flying visit,' Freddie said, closing the door behind him. 'Can you do me a favour?'

'Sure, what?'

'Can you take my car?' He pulled the keys out of the inner pocket of his suit jacket.

'What, to Tanya's?' Anna frowned. 'We're drinking – I won't be driving home.'

'Yeah, I know. Leave it there.'

'Why?' Anna was confused.

'It's got a tracker on it. Got planted yesterday.'

'Ahh, I see.'

'So, drive it as much as you want for the foreseeable. I'll use yours for a while if that's OK.'

'Brilliant.' Anna grinned. 'I prefer yours anyway.' As she didn't need to drive very often, Anna hadn't bought a car as nice as Freddie's. It was still a good one, a little Audi hatchback, but it wasn't as powerful or as luxurious as Freddie's Mercedes.

Freddie grimaced. 'Yeah, I bet you do.'

Anna grinned back at him and Freddie felt his heart soften at the sight of her smile. Her dark blue eyes twinkled and her natural beauty shone through, now that she was dressed down for the evening. Once again he counted his blessings that Anna was finally getting back to her old self. The things she had been through had knocked her terribly and for a time he wasn't sure that she was going to make it back. But she had and she was getting stronger every day, as was their relationship.

The feeling of guilt and stress that had been hovering since Jules had confronted him in The Black Bear washed over him once more and he pulled his gaze away. Anna was a perceptive, sharp person. It was one of the things he most admired about her, but it did mean he struggled to hide things from her. As if on cue, she tilted her head and focused in on his face.

'Are you OK?' She frowned slightly.

'Yeah, all good. I've just got to shoot – I'm late.' Freddie walked to the sideboard in the hallway and fished Anna's keys out of the glass bowl they used for that purpose. He jangled them in the air with a bright smile. 'Off to take the speed machine for a spin.'

Anna laughed. 'You mock it, but it's really not that bad. You're just spoiled.'

'Probably. Catch you later.' With a wink, Freddie disappeared back through the front door.

As he waited for the lift to reach their floor, Freddie sighed and closed his eyes, fighting back the urge to punch the wall in front of him. Today had been the day Jules was supposed to take Ethan for the paternity test. He'd paid extra to fast track the results, so he would know by tomorrow evening whether or not she was telling the truth. His hand tightened around the set of keys in his hand.

If Ethan was his, he was going to have to find a way to tell Anna. It would crush her, not because of the unexpected addition to their family but because of her inability to carry their own child. It would bring back all the horrific memories of the day she'd lost their baby, and he dreaded the thought of what that would mean for her mental recovery. At best it would set her back, at worst... He didn't dare finish the thought.

If Jules had lied to him and had put him through all of this stress just to try and extort money from him, then his fury would know no bounds. He hoped that if this was the case, she had the sense to disappear where he couldn't find her, for Ethan's sake. Because if she'd lied to them – to him and to Vince all those years ago – and he found her, Freddie could not be held accountable for his actions.

*

Anna threw back her head and laughed as Amanda recounted the horrors of her latest date. She was curled up in the corner of Tanya's big comfy sofa with a chilled glass of wine in her hand and her friends around her, more relaxed than she'd felt in ages. Amanda was an old university friend, one who had met Tanya eighteen months before in rather dark circumstances. Unbeknown to Tanya, she had been dating a married man and Amanda had been the long-suffering wife in the background. When the truth had come out, they'd hatched a plan together to bring him down and had both left him high and dry.

On the other end of the sofa sat Amy, Bill Hanlon's wife, and across the room Sophie sat on a cushion on the floor, her back to the radiator. They'd invited Freddie's sister Thea along too, but she'd been too busy to join them.

Tanya walked back through from the kitchenette, carefully carrying a large jug of something bright and fruity-looking. 'This, ladies, is Carl's latest special. Or at least I hope it is. I just followed the recipe.'

'Ooh!' Sophie sat forward eagerly. 'I love Carl's cocktails.'

'Me too,' chirped Amy. 'I never even tell him what I want anymore, I just tell him to surprise me if I'm there.'

'I find that's generally best,' Tanya replied. 'Unless you're Anna, who had the nerve to tell him she didn't like a couple of them.'

'You never!' Amy exclaimed with a horrified cackle of laughter.

'I did,' Anna admitted. 'But it wasn't anything against his skills. I'm just particular with drinks.'

'Fussy,' Tanya corrected. She began to pour each of them a glass. 'Now, Carl won't let her taste any of the new ones until after he's had my opinion.'

There was a wave of laughter through the room and Anna shook her head with a grin. 'It's true, he won't.'

As the laughter subsided the door buzzer sounded. Tanya placed the jug down on the table and disappeared into the hall. Anna frowned. Had Thea changed her mind?

'Hiya.' Anna strained to hear Tanya's voice above the hum of chatter that had resumed around her. 'Come on up. I'll leave the front door open.'

Tanya reappeared and Anna looked up at her expectantly.

'Hope you don't mind, but I've invited my friend Jules to join us.'

'No, 'course not,' Amy said.

'The more the merrier,' continued Amanda.

'You met her in the club before, do you remember?' Tanya said to Anna.

'Oh yes, the one who's just come back to London,' Anna replied.

'She popped back in the other day after we'd arranged tonight, so I mentioned it to her.'

Anna smiled fondly at Tanya. She was a good person, always ready to include anyone. It had been Tanya who had first offered her a bed and her friendship when she had been the new girl in the area.

They heard the front door shut and a few seconds later, Jules appeared. She looked around nervously and Anna offered her a friendly smile. 'Hi, Jules,' she said.

Jules answered with a nod and Tanya stepped forward to guide her into the room. 'Come, take a seat.' She ushered her towards the empty armchair in the corner. 'You know Anna, this is Amanda, that's Sophie and this is Amy.'

Amy's forehead creased into a small frown and she tilted her head. 'I know you. But I can't think where from.'

'Jules and I were friends way back when. We used to work together at the Silver Star,' Tanya said, passing a drink to Jules.

'When you were dancing?' Amy asked, her gaze still on Jules.

'Yeah. I probably brought her along to a few of the parties you and Bill were at.'

Amy's gaze sharpened as things clicked into place and she finally located the memory.

'You haven't missed much,' Tanya said to Jules. 'Amanda here was just telling us all about her last date. It was horrific; the guy smelled of blue cheese and asked her if she wanted to climb Snowdon.'

'Which was obviously a no,' Amanda jumped in. 'Who wants to do that to themselves? I mean, really… Anyway, what about you, Tanya? You're on the circuit now, the meat market of lurrrve. What's new?'

'I actually have no new stories for once,' Tanya said with a shrug. 'There are a couple of guys I've been chatting to on Tinder, but honestly, it bores me. There's no challenge and no spark with online dating, you know? I just want to meet someone and be like, *boom*, hello Mr Good for Right Now.'

'Not Mr Right?' Sophie asked.

'Nah, he's far too much hassle, mate. Who's got time for that shit? Not me, that's for sure.' Tanya took a deep drink. 'Damn, this is good. Even if I do say so myself.'

'What about you, Jules?' Anna asked. 'Are you with anyone?'

'Yeah, I'm seeing someone. He ain't nothing special but he'll do. Haven't exactly had a lot to choose from. The market's pretty narrow when you've got a kid hanging round your neck.' She pulled a face and took a sip of the cocktail Tanya had given her. 'They're the biggest cock-blocker going.'

Anna took a deep breath in and tried to swallow the resentment that she felt at hearing the ungrateful way Jules spoke about her child. Jules had every right to make frustrated comments at a girls' night; motherhood wasn't easy. But Anna couldn't view things in an unbiased way, not when she was one of the women in the world who would never have the opportunity to be a mother. Out of the corner of her eye, she saw Amy had turned to look out of the window, a neutral mask over her face. Amy also couldn't have children, though she and Bill had known this for years. She was perhaps more used to this feeling by now.

Tanya's concerned gaze flickered over to her friend's face and then back to Jules. 'Oh,' she said brightly. 'I didn't know you had a kid.'

'Well, I had him after I left,' Jules answered. 'An unexpected present from his dad.' She looked across the room at Anna and smiled.

Anna forced a smile back, hiding her pain.

'I had a pretty funny date the other week,' Sophie piped up, changing the subject.

Tanya jumped on the lifeline. 'Ooh, do tell! You've had some corkers too, haven't you?'

'I have indeed.' Sophie offered a kind look across the room at Anna and Anna smiled back gratefully. 'So, I'm vegetarian right, and I always tell my dates before we go anywhere. Not that I mind *them* eating meat, but just so they know I need somewhere that caters for this…'

An hour later Tanya stood up to replenish the cocktail jug. 'I'm going to try another recipe Carl gave me. It's just as nice as that was.'

'I'll give you a hand,' Jules said, unfolding her legs from beneath her on the chair and following Tanya to the kitchenette. The rest of the group continued chatting and laughing between themselves.

Tanya smiled as Jules joined her. 'It's really nice to see you back around. I'm glad you came tonight.'

'Me too.' Jules glanced at the recipe on the paper Tanya was holding. 'I'll chop the limes.'

'Thanks, mate, knives are there.' Tanya pointed behind her. 'So, where's your little one tonight then?'

'We're staying with my mum, so she's got him,' Jules replied.

'Oh, really?' Tanya raised her eyebrows. Jules had always had a very rocky relationship with her mother in the past. The pair hated each other, though they used to live under the same roof. It was one of the things Tanya and Jules had found they had in common – bad mothers. They'd bonded over that one night with a bottle of tequila.

'Yeah. Still the same old story there, but she didn't turn me away when I turned up so it's somewhere to stay while we're here.' She shrugged.

'We'll have to go for lunch or something, you, me and your son – what's his name?' Tanya asked.

'Ethan. Yeah, that would be nice.' Jules stared back into the lounge with a strange look in her eyes that Tanya couldn't quite place. 'You should see if Anna wants to join us.'

Tanya bit her lip. 'Um.' She paused, feeling awkward. 'Thing is, with Anna, she's had a bit of a bad time lately. She lost a baby not long ago and…' She sighed. 'It don't look like she can have another one. So, she's not great around kids right now.'

'Really?' Sudden interest flashed across her face and Tanya frowned, confused by her reaction.

'Yeah, well, don't say anything, alright?' Tanya said sternly. 'I'm only telling ya so you don't get offended.'

'Yeah, 'course. I won't say a word.' Jules continued chopping the limes but her gaze stayed trained on Anna. Tanya had no idea how valuable that piece of information was.

She smiled nastily, hiding her expression from view. If she thought she could get money out of Freddie before, she was completely certain now. One thing she had gleaned from her research and her time watching him was that he idolised that prim little princess in there. She wasn't a local girl from the clubs, the sort Freddie used to roll with. She was something else, and the great Freddie Tyler had always chased things that weren't the norm for people like him.

Her eyes narrowed resentfully. She hated women like Anna, always thinking they were better than everyone else. And she clearly did think that, holding herself the way she did, speaking like she had a plum in her mouth. Why had she not stayed among her own hoity-toity people? Why did she have to pick up an East End bloke like Freddie? The East End dating pool was shallow enough already without outsiders coming in and taking their pick.

Now, though, Freddie wasn't about to let Anna go, but staying with her meant he could never have children. Her son Ethan was the one and only chance he was ever going to get. Which meant that her leverage had just increased tenfold.

She plopped the limes into the jug, her smile serene. She was going to get what she came for and Princess Anna was going to get the shock of her life.

CHAPTER SIXTEEN

Freddie's mobile rang and he stared at the screen for a few moments. It was the clinic calling with the results of the paternity test. Knowing that this call was coming, Freddie had holed himself away in the office at Club CoCo and told all the staff he was not to be disturbed. The last thing he needed was one of his men waltzing in as he was getting the news, either way. Other than Vince, nobody knew about this situation yet. His threats of violence seemed to have worked on those who were at The Black Bear when Jules had publicly announced that Ethan was his son; the rumour had not yet been spread. Freddie wasn't stupid – he knew this wouldn't last forever, but at least he had this time to get to the truth before it leaked.

Swallowing hard, Freddie answered the call.

'Mr Tyler? It's Dr Hassan from Sigma Labs.'

'Yes, hello.' Freddie cleared his throat.

'I have the results of the paternity test you ordered. Would you like to come into the office to discuss them or are you happy for me to confirm to you over the phone?'

There was a pause as he waited for Freddie's answer. Freddie swallowed again and sat upright in his chair. He was suddenly feeling hot, too hot. Had someone turned the heating up? Pulling at his shirt to let some air in, he glanced at the digital thermostat. It was set to twenty degrees just like always.

'Please, go ahead,' he said finally.

'OK. So, with these tests, dependent on the subjects, we always look at between twenty-one and thirty-one genetic markers within the DNA,' Dr Hassan said, his tone calm and professional. 'In your case we compared twenty-five genetic markers and the results have shown that there is over a ninety-nine per cent chance that you are Ethan's biological father.'

Freddie heard himself gasp and felt his jaw drop as the confirmation hit home. Ethan was his son.

His *son*.

Time seemed to freeze as Freddie's mind tried to process the realisation of what this meant. This was going to change everything. It was going to have an impact on everyone's lives, not just his and Ethan's and Jules's. What was this going to do to Anna? What would this do to his mother, Mollie?

'Freddie?'

Freddie vaguely heard Dr Hassan gently prompting him on the phone, but he still couldn't quite bring himself to speak. He just sat there, in stunned silence. There had been something all along about Jules's confidence that had led him to believe there was some truth in it, but he hadn't wanted to accept it. And the boy was the spitting image of him as a child, but he had rationalised it down to coincidence. Nobody could argue with DNA, though. Even with the best will in the world, Jules couldn't have faked that.

'Often these results come as a shock.' Dr Hassan was speaking again and Freddie tried to focus on his voice. 'No matter how much we prepare ourselves. If you would like me to run through the markers with you, go into more detail, please let me know. I am available all afternoon if you'd like to pop in.'

'No. Thank you.' Freddie found his voice. 'Have you given Jules the results yet?' he asked.

'Freddie,' Dr Hassan's voice was patient and kind. 'She doesn't need the results; she already knows. It was you who needed the proof.'

'Oh, of course.' Freddie shook his head. Of course Jules knew.

'I'll email you over a copy of the results shortly. Good luck with everything. Farewell.'

The line went dead and Freddie's hand slowly dropped from his ear. After staring at the screen for several seconds he straightened up and scrolled through to write a new message.

Results have come back. We need to talk. Freddie.

Locating Jules's number, he pressed 'send' and locked the phone. Within a minute a reply pinged up.

Yes we do. You'll want to see your son but first I want some money. Kid's not cheap. Ten grand up front. Then you can see him.

For the second time in ten minutes Freddie's jaw dropped. Was she being serious? White-hot rage flew through him as he realised he was now trapped in a tight corner with limited options and Jules was the one holding all the cards.

He shook his head. This was not happening. Freddie was a fair man and someone who would do anything for his family. If Ethan was now a part of that family, so be it, but he would not be extorted by the boy's mother as and when she felt like it. He began typing.

I will be over later this week to discuss Ethan. As for the ransom, I suggest you take some time to remember who I am.

Locking the phone, Freddie tried to calm himself down with deep breaths. As everything ran through his mind, round and round, his breaths grew faster until all the frustration and shock and rage finally burst out of him. With a roar he launched the phone across the room at the wall as hard as he could. It smashed and fell to the floor in pieces.

CHAPTER SEVENTEEN

Paul drove into the scrapyard and pulled around to the caravan. The day manager closed and locked the gate behind him and waved a casual greeting before walking straight back to the little shed he used as an office. He wasn't paid to bother the bosses when they were here; he was paid to keep an eye on the place and play dumb if he was ever asked questions about their business.

Dean stepped out of the caravan to meet Paul and greeted him with a wide grin. 'Alright?'

'Yeah, how's it going?' Paul asked, leaning back against the door of the car. He pulled his cigarettes out and offered one to Dean. He took it with a nod of thanks and they both lit up.

'It's going well enough,' Dean replied, blowing out a plume of smoke. 'About half gone, just waiting on the runners to come back tonight for the next load.'

'How long before all of it's gone?' Paul asked.

'If you move that smaller batch like you mentioned, just another day or two.'

Whilst the cocaine was in the caravan, Freddie had ordered that one of the men had to remain on-site at all times to guard it. Having used a more streamlined approach with their former supplier, they were not used to being in long-term possession of the product. With Marco they had ordered as needed and the runners had gone straight between Marco's factory and the top of the dealer tree. It had been simple and efficient and fairly low risk. Now, though, they had to stay alert to make sure no law enforcement came sniffing around. They also had to watch out for Drew's crew. At any point they could get wise as to where it was and make a grab attempt. So far there had been nothing, but that didn't mean they could relax just yet.

Paul glanced at the open door of the caravan. 'Where's Seamus?'

'Coming back later to take over. He's got a boxing session with Anna.'

Paul nodded and took another drag on his cigarette.

'There's something you should know,' Dean said, staring back down the track where it disappeared around a pile of rusting car parts. 'People have been sniffing around, trying to get a look in the yard.'

'Oh yeah?' Paul's attention sharpened.

'Couple of cars. They've been doing drive-bys, crawling as they pass trying to look in. One of them got out and walked the perimeter in the early hours. If it is them, I'm guessing they think it's here but don't know for certain.'

'Sounds like it is them. No one else would have cause to do that,' Paul replied, his face grim. 'You tooled up?' Dean nodded. 'Good. I'll send Simon as well as Seamus tonight. Up the odds a bit, just in case.' He bit his lip as he pondered the situation. 'I'll spread a couple of rumours that it's being held elsewhere. Confuse the fuckers.'

Paul's phone beeped and he looked at the screen to read the message. He raised his eyebrows as he saw what it said.

'Well, seems our Northern friends want to meet up for a chat.' He grinned coldly. 'Let's see if it is them, shall we? This should be fun.'

*

Jules sat slumped in the corner of the faded, sagging sofa in her mother's lounge with narrowed eyes and her mouth twisted bitterly to one side. The room was hazy where she had been chain-smoking and couldn't be bothered to get up and open the balcony doors. The TV hummed away in the background but she wasn't really watching it.

She was pissed off that her request for money had been met so coldly. Now that Freddie had the proof in his hand that Ethan was his, Jules assumed things would change immediately. In her mind, once he knew he'd rush over full of guilt, ready to hand her whatever she asked for. He'd never paid a penny towards his son so far and Freddie was nothing if not generous to his family – everyone knew that. So why had this not happened? She *deserved* it. She had *earned* it, looking after the little brat all these years without help.

Irritated, she shifted in her seat and picked up the bottle of wine she had been swigging from over the last hour. Swallowing down the acidic liquid, she pulled a face. She couldn't even afford decent plonk. This had been the cheapest shit in the shop and it tasted like it too. It wasn't even taking the edge off. Though this had nothing to do with it being cheap. She was craving something stronger, something much more expensive and effective than alcohol.

As she screwed the lid back on the bottle, the sleeping man next to her stirred. He sat up with a yawn and stretched, rubbing his bleary, bloodshot eyes. Turning to look at her, he coughed up some phlegm and blinked. Jules curled her lip in disgust. Liam was becoming more and more of a lazy waste of space by the day. But as much as she knew this, she still wanted to keep him around. He was the only one who was interested, and she craved male company like oxygen.

'What's your problem?' he asked, frowning at her.

Jules sighed, muting the TV. 'Everything,' she replied, bitterness colouring her tone.

'Yeah, well.' He sat forward and began rolling a joint from the little tin of weed on the coffee table in front of him. 'You know what to do about that. I've told ya. Get the money and we can leave this fucking dump, start again in Spain.'

'Why does it have to be Spain?' Jules asked tiredly. 'Why can't we just start again somewhere new here, in London?'

'Because, Jules,' Liam said irritably, 'my mate can get us well set up over there, with a bit of cash. You know that. There wouldn't be no more of this bollocks, having to go to endless interviews for shit jobs, just to get a few measly quid from the twats down the job centre.' He licked the cigarette paper and rolled the joint thinly. 'Here, that money won't last. Out there we can set ourselves up with a nice little bar on a beach somewhere. Chill out all day, pull in money from the tourists. It'll be pukka. You and me and the life of Riley.'

'Yeah, it does sound nice,' Jules said moodily.

'Then get the money, girl,' Liam said, slapping her on the leg.

'Ouch,' Jules protested. She shot him an angry look as he picked up the lighter. 'Get that thing out of here – go on. You know Mum won't have the smell of wacky baccy in the house.'

Liam pulled a face. 'Might actually improve the smell in here. It's disgusting. She don't clean shit.'

Jules snapped and slapped him around the back of his head as he stood up. 'Go on. Fuck off. Out you go,' she shouted.

She scowled at the wall as she heard him walk out of the small flat. As silence resumed, she took a long, deep breath and closed her eyes. Everything ached and life seemed dismal and grey. She needed an escape, but there wasn't enough money for that yet. There had to be some way of getting a decent wedge out of Freddie sooner rather than later.

'Mum?' a tentative little voice called out.

Jules opened her eyes and her head swivelled until she located her son. He was standing in the doorway, peering round at her. 'And what the fuck do you want?' she yelled, irritated.

Ethan swallowed. He hated it when his mum was like this. When she got in one of her moods, nothing he said or did was right. Usually he stayed out of the way, but he hadn't eaten all day and eventually his growling stomach got the better of him.

'I'm hungry,' he said quietly.

Jules shot him a scathing look and stood up, padding across the room and past him towards the kitchen. Opening the fridge, all she could find was a bottle of lemonade, a mouldy cucumber and some butter. She slammed the door and began rooting through the cupboards. She cursed her mother under her breath for not having any food in. She only had a tenner left until the next day, which she didn't intend to spend on food. There were only a few cigarettes left in her pack, and she'd definitely need another to get her through the evening at the very least. This was far more important.

'Here, eat these.' Jules chucked a half-empty box of cream crackers at Ethan and he quickly caught them.

His heart dropped as he saw what they were. 'Can I have some cheese with them?' he asked, his hazel-green eyes looking up at her nervously.

'Are you stupid?' Jules demanded, her cheeks turning red. 'Do you think if we had cheese I'd be giving you those? We don't *have* cheese, Ethan. We don't *have* anything, because your useless shit of a dad won't give me any money.' It didn't cross her mind for a second that this comment was unfair to Freddie, who until the previous day hadn't known for certain he had a son. Looking down at the bane of her existence, Jules shook her head with a look of disgust. 'Go on, get back to your room.'

When Ethan didn't immediately move, Jules's hand shot forward and slapped him hard around the ear. 'Are you deaf? I said get to your room, you naughty boy. Honestly, kids have no manners these days.'

Ethan stumbled back from the force of the slap and nearly dropped his crackers. With tears stinging his eyes, he turned and fled back to the safety of his temporary bedroom.

Walking back to her spot on the sofa, Jules lit another cigarette and re-settled into her pool of self-pity. When she had learned the other night that Anna couldn't have children she'd thought all her Christmases had come at once. Ethan was Freddie's only shot at being a father.

She figured she'd dangle Ethan in front of him and click her fingers and Freddie Tyler would deliver whatever she demanded. But she had stumbled at the first hurdle. Freddie had put her straight back in her place and not even made her a counter-offer. Instead she was supposed to wait around for him to come and see Ethan whenever he decided he wanted to show up. She made a sound of disgust and took another deep drag on her cigarette.

Freddie needed a wake-up call, something to remind him *exactly* who was in charge when it came to Ethan. As an idea formed in her mind, a vacant coldness crept into her narrowed eyes. Standing up, she slowly walked back out of the room and stared down the hallway at Ethan's door, her expression growing darker and darker as she walked forward and reached for the handle.

If Freddie cared about Ethan at all then he was going to have to pay up. Because she was about to show him what she was capable of if he didn't.

CHAPTER EIGHTEEN

Screeching to a halt outside one of the larger high-rise buildings in the Somers Town estate, Freddie turned off the ignition and jumped out. Sammy relaxed his grip on the handle above the door, which he'd been holding on to for dear life, and exhaled slowly. He stepped out and straightened his pale beige suit jacket. Freddie was waiting for him impatiently a few feet ahead.

'Come on, let's go,' he said.

'Fred…' Sammy frowned and held his arms out in question. 'What's going on with you?'

'What do you mean?' Freddie asked, agitated.

'I mean *what's going on?*' Sammy repeated. 'You're all over the place. I've never seen ya so pissed off over something so small. You've raced over here like you've got a fire up your arse. We nearly copped it at that last set of traffic lights.'

'A non-compliant dealer in my tree ain't something small, Sammy,' Freddie retorted, rounding on him.

Sammy stared him down, refusing to cower under his boss-cum-friend's thunderous expression. There weren't many people in the world who could stand up to Freddie and get away with it, but he was one of the few who had earned the right over the years. 'Nah, I ain't buying that.' He shook his head. 'Something's wrong. What's going on?'

There was a tense silence and for a moment Sammy thought Freddie was going to rip into him. But suddenly he retreated and shrugged, turning back towards the building.

'Buy what you like, but do your shopping later. We've got shit to do.'

With a deep sigh Sammy followed Freddie into the building, pulling his black leather gloves out of his pocket as they walked up the stinking run-down stairwell. He watched as Freddie mirrored the action in front of him. They weren't here for a cup of tea and a friendly catch-up – this dealer was in for a hiding and judging by his boss's mood it wasn't going to be a light one.

As they reached the third floor – and Sammy was thankful it wasn't higher up, as there was no lift – Freddie stepped back and with one swift movement kicked the door in. The thin wood splintered almost in two and the second kick finished the job. Straight away, the lazy silence of the decrepit estate was broken by complete uproar. Freddie hollered for Callum to come out and take what he deserved; a young woman began to scream in terror for the same man to save them and further inside a young child began to cry. It was bedlam.

Sammy shook his head and cursed under his breath as he looked around. This wasn't how Freddie usually did things. The man was well known for his control. He might have a temper, but he honed it and used it carefully. It was what kept them off the public's radar and out of jail cells.

Seeing two of the other front doors open and wary faces peer out, Sammy sighed heavily. Freddie was walking into the flat and he knew his boss would be expecting him to follow. Right now, though, he needed to work on damage control. The last thing they wanted was someone calling the police.

Walking towards the two open doors, Sammy cracked his knuckles deliberately and put on his hardest mask. He glared at them and pulled himself up to his tallest height.

'You didn't see or hear nothing, you understand?' he said, his tone quiet but menacing. They nodded. 'You know who that is?' he asked, pointing over his shoulder to the shattered front door behind him. Another nod. 'Good.' He turned away. If they knew who Freddie was, they definitely wouldn't call the police. Freddie was equally feared and admired around this estate, for his dangerous yet fair ways and for the professional opportunities he opened up for some of the residents. A lot of his dealers and runners lived here.

Freddie ignored the screeching woman in the hallway and made straight for the small living area. He whirled around, checking that Callum wasn't hidden behind a door or in the kitchenette. Marching back into the hall, he grabbed the woman by the arms and shook her.

'Where is he?' he bellowed.

'Please, don't hurt us,' she cried through her fearful wails.

'Tell me where he is and I won't have to.'

'Please,' she begged, shaking her head and pleading with her eyes. Her glance slid down behind Freddie and he looked back. A small child he hadn't noticed was cowering against the wall by the front door. Tears streaked down her face and small pudgy arms reached out for her mother, though fear had rooted her to the spot.

Freddie closed his eyes and exhaled loudly through his nose. He straightened the woman in front of him. He wasn't going to get anything out of her anyway and the last thing he wanted to do was scar the child for life.

'Get her and get out of here. Go on,' he ordered. 'And not a fucking word to anyone, you understand?'

The woman quickly nodded, then scooped up the little girl and bolted out of the front door, almost colliding with Sammy, who was on his way in.

A noise reached Freddie's ears from the back bedroom and he ran through, throwing the door open with a bang. Callum was at the window with one leg already half out of the small opening. He yelped as Freddie strode towards him.

'Freddie, please, man. Listen, I was just…'

Without pausing to hear him out, Freddie grabbed the man by the scruff of his shirt and threw him against the bedroom wall with force. His head connected with the plasterboard with a sickening crack. Before he had time to even register the pain, Freddie picked him back up with a roar and threw him across the room to the open door.

Callum groaned and reached out with his hand as Freddie came towards him again. 'Please, I was coming back to you, I swear.'

'Coming back to me?' Freddie repeated, reaching down and grasping a handful of his thick ginger hair. He yanked it viciously, dragging him by it through the small hallway and into the living room beyond.

Callum screamed out in pain, half of the hair pulling away from his scalp in clumps, the rest sending searing hot pain through his head as he was mercilessly pulled along.

Freddie felt the anger flow through his veins. He was furious at Callum and he had every reason to be. But if he was honest with himself, he knew that it wasn't just that. Sammy was right – he wouldn't usually get this het up over an errant dealer. This was just the vent he'd needed to get out all the frustration he was feeling over Jules and Ethan and the Manchester crew who'd had the barefaced audacity to try and take his business from underneath him.

Getting to the small breakfast bar that sat along the edge of the kitchenette, Freddie dumped Callum unceremoniously against it. He stepped back and began to pace, as he often did when agitated.

'Thing is, Callum, it was never your fucking choice to begin with. This is *my* city. I was the one who grafted, sacrificed and bled for the right to rule the distribution of chemicals around here.' He stopped pacing and stared Callum in the eyes. 'I've *killed* to be who I am,' he snarled, 'and you really think some jumped-up little shit from the estate like you has the right to *choose* who he

gets his product from? Like you're some sort of big fucking *I am*?'
He leaned down. 'Big mistake.'

Callum tried to focus in on Freddie, the room moving around
in his vision. The pain was searing from where his head had hit
the wall hard and from being dragged by his hair. He suddenly
wished to God he hadn't been so stupid. The Mancs had offered
superior product at a lower rate. It was just good business to go
with them. But of course this wasn't normal business. There were
no offices and rules and safe little HR departments in their line
of work. He'd momentarily forgotten who he was dealing with
and that, as Freddie pointed out, had been a big mistake.

Sammy watched from the door, keeping one eye on the opening
to the hallway. No one had dared come to see what was going
on. Commotions like this were not uncommon on this estate,
but more importantly Freddie Tyler in a rage was definitely not
something anyone wanted to get in the way of.

'You're right, I fucked up,' Callum said, gingerly trying to
stand up.

BANG.

Freddie punched him in the face, hard, and he reeled back
against the counter.

'You can stay down there, you treacherous prick,' he barked.
'From what I hear, the product we've supplied you all these years
suddenly wasn't good enough. *Inferior* I believe was the word
you used.'

'No, I…'

'Don't try and lie to me,' Freddie cut him off, his voice dangerously low and cold. 'You were heard talking about it to anyone
who'd listen down at The Grove the other night. You apparently
said that my brother and I had *lost our touch*.' Freddie glanced back
towards Sammy. 'Would you say we've lost our touch, Sammy?'

'Definitely not, Fred,' Sammy answered. 'I'd say you're top of
your game, myself.'

'Yeah, that's what I thought.' He rubbed his chin as though lost in thought as he stared at Callum. 'So that makes you either completely stupid or on a death wish. Which would you say it was?'

Callum swallowed and his eyes darted between the two men as he floundered, unsure how to answer.

'Whichever it is, I can't have someone like that working for me. Which means your career working with chemicals of any kind is over.' He reached down and grabbed Callum, pulling him upright. Callum nearly toppled over and barely kept his balance.

'Freddie, come on, man, it was a mistake. People make mistakes.'

'Not my people.' Grabbing the side of Callum's head, he bashed it down on the hard counter of the breakfast bar. Callum cried out in pain and tried to pull himself back and away from Freddie unsuccessfully. Freddie tightened his grip and smashed Callum's skull down again and again in quick succession until his nose exploded over the counter.

Blood spurted out and smeared all over the previously clean, white surface. Callum's hands helplessly flailed about, smearing the bright red liquid around, making it look even worse. He cried out, begging Freddie to stop and nearly choking on the blood that began pouring down the back of his throat.

BANG.

Again the broken nose made contact and for a second Callum thought he was going to pass out.

Feeling the slack in Callum's body as he wavered on the edge of consciousness, Freddie pulled him upright. The blood seeped down his front and his head lolled as the beating finally began taking its toll. He groaned.

Freddie glanced at Sammy, who was watching him intensely, without expression. He didn't need to see it to know what he was thinking, though. Freddie had known Sammy since they were kids; he could read him like a book. Sammy never usually questioned

Freddie's actions, but right now, Sammy would be wondering if Freddie was going to stop just short of doing any permanent damage like he usually did, or whether he'd throw caution to the wind as he had when he'd broken into the flat. Tempting though it was to unleash all his rage right here, right now, Freddie was still far too controlled to actually do it. This beating was going to have to do. He'd vent the rest of his frustration elsewhere. Freddie didn't kill without very good reason. Plus the inconvenience of clearing up and hiding a body just wasn't worth it.

Dragging Callum over to the window, he pushed the sliding glass open and hoisted him up so that his top half was sticking out. The man yelped and tried to grasp the window frame to stop himself from falling, but his hands were slick with blood and he couldn't get a good grip.

'You're *done* working for me, and you're *done* in this line of work, for good,' Freddie said through gritted teeth. 'I warn you now, if I ever get wind of you dealing inside London again, if I hear you've so much as sorted someone out with a fucking *joint*, I'll come for you,' he promised. 'And next time you'll go out the window head first. You got that?'

'Y-y-yes! Please!' Callum pleaded, terrified that he was going to drop at any second.

Freddie roughly yanked him back in and let him fall to the floor in a heap. He looked down on the shaking man in contempt. 'The drought is over. Our product is back in circulation. You pass on the message that the next dealer I hear scouting around as though he has options will get this' – he pointed a finger at Callum's face – 'and more to boot. You'll serve as my warning. And the next time I hear you've been slagging us off, I'll cut out your fucking tongue,' he added.

Staring Callum down one last time, Freddie turned and swept back out of the apartment, straightening his suit and pushing his hair back into place as he went.

Sammy followed Freddie out. As he followed him down the stairs, he wondered again what was really going on with Freddie Tyler.

*

Anna heard the front door open and shut from where she lay in a deep bubble bath, soaking away the aches and pains that now came with her rigorous boxing training. It had been two days since her last session, but day two was always the worst. She'd been surprised to learn just how many muscles throughout the body were used in the sport. It wasn't just her arms that were toughening up, but her core and her back – even the tops of her legs to a degree.

She played with the mountain of bubbles absent-mindedly as she listened to Freddie moving through their flat.

'Anna?' he called.

'In here,' she answered.

Freddie walked in and smiled down at her. Even with her hair pinned up messily on top of her head, barefaced and natural in the bath, she was still the most beautiful woman he had ever seen.

'I thought you were out tonight?' Anna said. She stared at the spatters of blood that had soaked through and dried on his white shirt and pursed her lips but didn't say anything.

'I am,' Freddie replied, sitting down on the lid of the toilet and facing her. 'But I had time to pop back first.' He gaze followed hers and he shrugged off his jacket and began unbuttoning the shirt. It would have to be incinerated.

'Well, that's good.' Anna forced herself to look up to his face. If he wanted to talk about it he would. But it was part and parcel of the life Freddie led. She'd accepted that a long time ago. 'Because I have some possibly exciting news.' Anna's dark blue eyes began to sparkle with excitement. 'I haven't shown Tanya yet, but I think I've found just the right premises for our after-hours house.'

Freddie hid a small grin. Ever since Anna had floored them all by telling them she wanted to open up a whorehouse, she had insisted on calling it an after-hours house. It seemed to sit better with her than the usual term. He didn't blame her; she was new to this game, to dabbling in the underworld. He'd been surprised she'd been up for doing it at all. Women like Anna didn't tend to walk down the darker paths that he did. But then Anna wasn't like most people, and even after all these years together she still surprised him regularly.

'That's good. Where is it?' Freddie balled up the shirt and added the white vest he wore underneath to it. Better safe than sorry. Keeping any clothes with bloodstains was an unnecessary risk.

'Literally just round the corner on Old Compton Street. It's above a little Italian restaurant, two floors, five bedrooms but two more that can be used as extra bedrooms, well kept. It's not cheap.' Anna pulled a face. 'We will definitely lose money until we're established, but I'm hoping that won't be too long.' She picked up her loofah. 'After speaking to the girls privately, about two thirds of them want to work there. I think we should have enough girls; we just need to bring in the clients.' She glanced at his bare torso appreciatively. Freddie kept himself in good shape and she was enjoying the visual.

'That won't be too hard,' Freddie said. 'Not with the club. The girls can advertise themselves without even trying. Plus you can do all the usual marketing. Under the radar, of course.'

'Hmm.' Anna looked doubtful and again Freddie forced his face not to crease into a grin. She was serious about doing this and he didn't want to belittle her journey. But it still seemed crazy to him that he was even having this conversation with Anna.

'We're going to need security. Can I hire one of your guys?' she asked.

'You can hire as many as you want,' he replied.

Freddie and Paul had built up a successful security company over the years. It was all above board and legal for the most part, except for the fact that all their staff were hired under the understanding that they turned a blind eye to any and all illegal operations they were witness to – and often part of. Security for Anna and Tanya's new whorehouse would be no issue.

'When are you showing Tanya?'

'Tomorrow afternoon.' Anna lathered some shower gel onto her arms and began exfoliating. 'So, what's going on with you? Anything interesting?' She glanced briefly at the balled-up shirt and vest, but then quickly averted her eyes, not wanting to force him to talk about it.

Freddie paused. For the last couple of days he had been trying to work out the best way to tell Anna about Ethan and Jules, but every way he thought of pitching it sounded terrible out loud. Freddie knew he was going to have to watch the horror wash over Anna's face, followed by pain and devastation, no matter how he broke the news. If this had come about a year ago it wouldn't have been so bad, but after the events of the last few months, it was going to reopen wounds that had barely even started to heal.

'There's, er—' Freddie took a deep breath. 'There's something I need to talk to you about.' He felt sick and struggled to find the right words. 'I was in The Black Bear,' he started but then stopped. How on earth could he explain this?

'There was – you know, I used to be so different to who I am now.' Why was he trying to excuse himself? He'd done nothing wrong. This was not the right approach.

Stressed, Freddie squeezed the bridge of his nose. 'I love you, Anna,' he said sincerely, his voice filled with heartfelt emotion. 'You mean everything to me.' How could he hurt her?

Anna's heart reached out to Freddie as she watched him struggle to express whatever he was trying to talk about. She reached out and took his hand in her own, ignoring the bubbly drips of water that dropped off her arm all over the floor.

'I know you're under a lot of pressure right now. There's been so much going on, what with the guys from Manchester and everything else,' Anna said gently. 'But you know what? Things are on the up. You know they are.' She smiled at him and forced eye contact. 'You are *Freddie Tyler*,' she said with force. 'You've got this.'

Freddie tried to force himself to tell her, but as he gazed into her trusting eyes, so full of their belief for him, he couldn't. He couldn't shatter the fragile bubble of contentment they had reached as a couple just yet.

'Yeah.' Squeezing her hand, he gave her a tight smile. 'You're right.' He glanced at his watch. 'I'd better go get dressed. I'll be late so I'll see you in the morning.' *And I'll tell her then,* he silently promised himself.

CHAPTER NINETEEN

Drew sat at a table near the back of the pub where they had been instructed to meet the Tylers, the beer in front of him untouched and growing warm. He faced the entrance and grew more tense and alert every time a shadow passed the frosted glass in the front door. Jacko sat beside him quietly brooding, and two more of his men, Richie and Steve, hovered nearby at the bar.

Drew's cold gaze moved around, assessing the situation. The barman knew who they were, this much was obvious by the subtle glances that kept being thrown their way and the quiet phone call he'd made as soon as they'd arrived. That was OK. Drew had expected this place to be on the Tylers' turf. So long as it was still a public place, he felt confident enough. He hadn't risen to his position up in Manchester by showing fear of those who were more powerful than him and he wasn't about to start now.

It had been a mistake, sending that much product down south in one go. He'd thought he had been cautious enough, testing the waters with small batches here and there, but logistically it made more sense to plant a bulk load there and have someone oversee the distribution. Drew had moved too fast and had severely underestimated the Tylers' reach. It was not a mistake he would make again but one he most certainly needed to rectify if he wanted to come out of this in one piece.

The doors opened and Skidders, the youngest member of their firm at only nineteen, came scuttling in and over to the table.

'They're here, I think,' he said, glancing back at the door.

'Cheers, our kid,' Drew said quietly. He tilted his head towards the men at the bar and Skidders melted into the background beside them.

The door swung open and three men in suits stepped in. The first two were clearly brothers, both with the same dark hair and brooding looks about them, and a hardness that only this type of life lent a man. The third man looked older, somehow rugged and reserved at the same time. He stayed one step behind the others as they approached.

'This them?' Drew asked quietly, barely moving his mouth.

'That's them,' Jacko murmured back.

The larger of the two brothers gave a nod to the barman, who made a shrill whistling noise. All but one of the tables immediately emptied, the patrons walking out of the establishment without a word. The last table in the corner still had two men sitting around it who turned to stare in their direction now that the pretence was over.

Drew shook his head slightly with a wry smile. As the last man left, the barman locked the door, before walking back around the bar to continue what he had been doing, as if nothing was out of the ordinary.

Freddie sat down opposite Drew, who had not yet moved or reacted to their arrival. Paul sat one side of him and Bill the other. Dean and Simon left their perch in the corner and moved to stand behind their bosses.

'Drew Johnson,' Freddie stated, taking measure of the thin, calm man seated across from him. 'Jacko.' He nodded at the man they had previously met at the gypsy site. He didn't bother to address the rest standing behind them. 'I'm Freddie Tyler; this is my brother Paul and colleague Bill, through whom this meet was arranged. Now' – he relaxed back in his seat – 'what can we do for you?'

Drew stared across the table at Freddie for a few moments, not a flicker of emotion in his expression. 'I understand there has been some confusion surrounding the ownership of one of our caravans, which currently contains a large amount of product.'

'I don't think anybody here is confused by the situation.' Freddie turned to look questioningly at Paul and then to Bill before turning back to Drew with a shrug. 'In fact, I think we made ourselves pretty clear already to Jacko here.' He leaned forward, his tone polite but menace appearing in his hard eyes. 'The central belt of London has always been under our jurisdiction, as you already know. That means all distribution and sale of cocaine here comes through us.'

'And yet your dealers were crying out for product for quite some time,' Drew replied icily.

Freddie's mouth twisted to one side in a bitter half-smile. 'They were. But again, that would be our business to sort out. Which now we have.'

'By stealing our product, because you have no access to a decent supply yourself anymore,' Drew shot back, his tone still level.

Paul balled his fist, angered by the disrespect with which Drew was speaking to Freddie. This was *their* city. *They* held all the cards here. Who was this Northern nobody to come in here mouthing off?

'I'm afraid the second you decided to try and steal our business from under us and brought that shit ton of coke into the city, it stopped belonging to you. Turf rights. Stupid move.' Freddie pointed at him. '*You* should have stayed up north, mate.'

Drew squeezed his own fist into a ball under the table where Freddie and the others couldn't see. He needed that coke back, no matter what. Their lives depended on it.

'Perhaps we could come to some sort of agreement,' Drew suggested.

'Like what?' Freddie asked, a glint of amusement in his eye. 'What could you offer me that I don't already have from this arrangement?'

'A supplier.'

Freddie narrowed his eyes. This was what he was really here for. The cocaine was extremely high quality, possibly even better than Marco's had been – and Marco's had been the best Freddie had ever sourced.

'Go on,' Freddie said.

Drew swallowed. He didn't want to say what he was about to say; he wanted to fight his corner and win like he had every other battle of his professional life so far. But one thing he had learned was that to stay in the game you sometimes had to pick your battles. And in this particular case he was hoping if he played to lose this battle, he would survive the war.

'You need ongoing product and I need to pay my supplier for this batch. You know we had that on tick,' he said openly. 'If you give me back the amount we owe from your sales and keep the profits for yourselves as you intended anyway, we can open a channel between you and our suppliers. I will personally act as the go-between and perhaps we can all come out with something we didn't have before.'

'What?' Jacko asked incredulously. Drew held a hand up to silence him. He was practically grovelling, something that did not come easily to someone like Drew, but he was also a smart man. This was the best chance they had.

A large smile slowly crept up on Freddie's face. He began to chuckle, as did Paul, as though they were sharing some sort of private joke. Drew's heart began to pound. If he was reading them correctly, they weren't going to go for it.

'The thing is, why would I do that, Drew?' Freddie asked, tilting his head to one side in query. 'Firstly, why would I give you anything back for product I'm already in ownership of – but secondly and more importantly' – his smile dropped and was replaced by a hard coldness – 'why on earth would I go into business with someone who has already tried to usurp me from my position in my own city?'

Freddie watched Drew's expression draw tighter. The man was fairly good at keeping a poker face, but even the hardest and most skilful of men couldn't hide the look of defeat. And Drew was defeated. He had nothing to bargain with, no solid knowledge to work with in this unfamiliar city and he was as good as dead when his suppliers found out what had happened. But none of that was Freddie's concern. It was all just business at the end of the day.

'I won't be going into business with you, Drew – not now, not ever. But I will make you a deal.' Freddie leaned forward, his hazel-green eyes boring levelly into Drew's pale blue ones. 'You'll give me your suppliers' contact details directly and bow out. You'll also give me fifty per cent of your profits from the gear you peddle in Manchester for the next year, as an apology for the absolute piss-take of trying to undermine me. In return I will then pay back what you owe for this batch and you can run back to your shithole of a city up north. You'll have to swallow your pride and run back with your tail between your legs – but at least this way you'll still have legs.' Freddie sat back, his manner relaxed as he watched the anger course through the men around Drew. 'It's up to you.'

'Is he for real?' Jacko spat.

Drew put up a hand of warning once more and with difficulty Jacko swallowed the rest of what he was about to say. He exhaled loudly and crossed his arms, shooting daggers at Freddie.

Drew cast his eyes away from Freddie's for the first time and looked down at his warm, untouched pint. His hand lay loosely around the bottom, though he had no intention of drinking it. In his mind he thought through the option he would usually be inclined to take back home. If someone had backed him into a corner there or spoken to him the way Freddie had, he'd have launched the beer out of this glass, smashed it on the edge of the table and slashed his challenger's face open. He'd have made sure to scar him for life and burn out his motor later on for good measure. Drew was a quiet man most of the time, but those who had seen him in action knew just how deadly he could be when provoked. The quiet ones were often the most deadly, and up in Manchester this was definitely the case. But not here. Here Drew was wrong-footed and way out of his depth – and he knew it.

Pushing the urge for violence aside with difficulty, Drew thought over Freddie's words again. News of the things the Tylers had done over the years hadn't just stopped at London's borders. Stories had been passed around the underworld of all the major cities and Drew had no doubt that they were true. This deal was far too clean to be all there was to it. The Tylers weren't going to let such an offence go away with nothing but a slap on the wrist. No, Drew thought, if he gave them what they wanted, that would be the end. They'd kill them. It would be for nothing.

'I'm afraid we aren't interested in taking that deal,' he said eventually.

Freddie narrowed his eyes. 'Perhaps you should think on it.'

'Perhaps we will,' Drew offered back.

There was a tense silence as they stared each other out. Finally Freddie smiled, but the smile didn't reach his eyes. He stood up and Paul and Bill followed suit.

'Our offer expires in two days.' With that, Freddie turned and walked out. The barman opened the door to let them through and shook his head at the group left at the table, before going about his business again.

Jacko turned to Drew as the others sat down in the seats the Tylers had just vacated. 'Well done, though you should have told them where to fucking stick it,' he spat.

'Are you mad?' Richie asked Jacko. He turned his attention to Drew. 'Why *didn't* you take it? We're all dead men walking now!'

'What?' Jacko asked. 'He didn't take it because he ain't no mug. He's going to get those Southern twats where he wants them, aren't you, Drew?'

Drew closed his eyes and pinched the bridge of his nose. His men fell silent. 'I didn't take the deal because if I had given them what they wanted, we'd all be dead anyway.' He faced Jacko. 'Do you really think *the Tylers* are going to let a snub like this go unchecked? We walked into their yard and took out their dealer tree from right under their noses. If we'd been successful we might have been OK. We'd have had the upper hand at least, could have protected ourselves. But we weren't successful. We *failed*. They took us out before we even got underway. Now *they* have the upper hand, *they* have the product and *everyone* has seen us go down. If they let us go now, people will think that anyone can have a go at taking over and that if they fail they'll just be sent home with their ball. It would make them look like an easy target who dole out no repercussions. They can't let that happen. *I* wouldn't let that happen. If we give them our suppliers' details they'll kill us. At least now we have some time.'

His face darkened and he balled his hand into a fist. 'Now what we need to do is locate the coke and get it back from the fuckers. We ballsed up, but that don't mean we have to take this lying down. We get it back home, sell it on and get the Ramones off our back.'

Richie and Steve nodded.

Jacko's frown deepened. 'What, and not continue our plans for London? This was supposed to be the firm's expansion, our big move.' He shook his head, unable to comprehend what he was hearing. 'You said this was for me to head up, my area to manage.'

'We messed up,' Drew said, anger flashing in his eyes. 'Don't you get that? The minute they took that coke, our plans meant nothing. We're in over our heads.'

Jacko stared back at his boss, his fury and rage bubbling hotter with every word Drew said. All his dreams of becoming his own boss, of standing in the limelight on his own projects, were fading before his eyes.

'We could take this town if we wanted to, Drew,' he said, pointing his finger at his boss aggressively. 'But you've become too soft. *That's* the only thing standing in our way.'

Jacko stood up abruptly and his chair clattered to the floor behind him. Grabbing his jacket, he stormed out of the pub.

'Fuck sake, what's he doing?' Steve said. His eyes flickered back towards Drew, worried. 'He don't mean that, Drew. Our kid's just letting off some steam.'

Drew held his hand up to stop him. 'It's fine.' He glanced back towards the bar where the barman was sending a text to someone covertly in the corner. 'Let's just get out of here.'

Without another word the small group left the premises and walked off down the street, away from the small pub and the swinging sign above the door that read The Black Bear.

CHAPTER TWENTY

Alfie Ramone rubbed his temples, trying to ease the hammering that was pounding through his head. It got like this sometimes, when he needed to release some steam.

Reaching forward he grabbed the packet of painkillers and popped two into his hand. He knew it wouldn't help. It wasn't an illness – or at least not a physical one – that gave him this pain. It was the anger that built up inside of him and burned red hot until he hurt people. Hurting people made him calm, took away the stress and fury. It was why he took so long, kept them alive and pulled them apart piece by piece. Every second was savoured. He felt no guilt afterwards. They were people who deserved it after all.

Andre Ramone looked up from his desk across the room. A stark contrast to his brother, he was as thin and tall as Alfie was round and short. Both had the same dark features and the same dead eyes above hollow rings.

'Everything OK?' he asked.

Alfie nodded and waved his hand dismissively.

Their office was above one of their largest legal enterprises, an auction house. It was here that they ran the cocaine through from their contacts in Mexico.

Andre and Alfie, born Andreas and Alfonso Ramone to a Mexican cartel worker and his British wife, had grown up in a cartel compound in Mexico. They were just teenagers when their father was killed in a raid and their mother had managed to smuggle them out back to England where she sought refuge. They had settled into their new lives in Liverpool but maintained their contacts, and once they were old enough, Alfie had set up trading links between their old cartel family and the north of England.

Known for his vicious nature, Alfie had quickly pushed all the big competition out of the way and within a few years had a chain of dodgy auction houses, through which he smuggled in about a third of the country's cocaine. Most of it came in through phony artwork.

Thick cocaine-filled paint was layered over and over on the canvases by South American painters, making them look as old and authentic as possible. These large paintings were shipped over as specialist cargo, all the paperwork in order, then they were set up at auction and bought by fake bidders. Alfie would launder the money from selling the previous lot of cocaine into the auction house via the bidder, then sent the painting off to a separation centre he had set up in a warehouse in the middle of nowhere. Here, the pieces went through a chemical process to dissolve the paint and strip it away. They would dry out the canvas and the residual cocaine could be extracted from the material in its powder form, clean and ready to be weighed for sale.

It always amazed Alfie how simple it was to extract a chemical which was immune to what was essentially paint stripper and water, and how blind the authorities had been to this process so far.

'The next shipment is a large painting short,' Andre informed his brother.

Alfie frowned. 'Why?'

'It got damaged en route. Do we have enough backlog?' Andre looked over questioningly.

'No,' Alfie said, twisting his mouth to the side in annoyance. 'Not since we sent that extra load with Johnson.'

The brothers stared at each other for a moment. They had called Drew a couple of times to see how things were going but he hadn't answered or called back. This was unusual – and Alfie did not like unusual.

Looking down at the small, elegant knife with an ornately carved handle that sat on a stand on his desk, Alfie's hand twitched. Maybe Drew might end up giving him a reason to use his tools. He was a good customer, but customers came and went. People in their line of business rose and fell. If Drew disappeared, someone else would take his place. He was expendable.

'I'll make some calls,' Andre said eventually. 'See if we can find out what's happening.'

'You do that,' Alfie replied, not taking his eyes off the blade. Part of him wanted his money. But a bigger part of him wanted his next victim.

CHAPTER TWENTY-ONE

Tanya walked awkwardly, nearly falling sideways as her stiletto heel caught the wrong part of a street cobble.

'Ouch, Anna, can I look yet? I'm going to break my neck in a moment, you lunatic,' she protested.

Anna was walking behind her with her hands covering Tanya's eyes.

'Oh, come on,' she said with a giggle. 'What's the fun in that? It's worth it, I promise. Plus, I'd never let you fall, you know that.'

'Well,' Tanya grumbled, 'you'd better not. Where is this place anyway? Surely you can't walk me all the way there like this…'

'We're here,' Anna interrupted brightly. She let go and Tanya blinked, looking confused.

'Babe,' she said flatly. 'We've literally walked about a hundred yards. Where are we going?'

'That's the beauty of it,' Anna said, her eyes shining. 'It's right here!' With fluttering jazz hands, Anna dramatically framed the building in front of them. 'This place it up for rent. I've already been in – thought it was going to be a dud so didn't want to bother you, but it's *perfect*.'

'Really?' Tanya blinked up at the building. It was so close to the club it had to be too good to be true.

'Honestly,' Anna continued, brandishing a set of keys. 'Come on, I'll show you.'

She led the way in through a subtle grey door next to a little Italian restaurant and up the stairs to the second floor. As they walked into the main entrance room, Tanya raised her eyebrows in appreciation. It was a bright, spacious room perfect for pre-bedroom entertainment. A small kitchen went off to one side and a hallway ran down the other.

Anna walked Tanya round and up onto the next floor, showing her all the bedrooms and talking through the possible layouts she had envisioned so far. As they wandered from room to room Tanya could see that Anna had been spot on about the place. This was exactly what they'd been waiting for – and they had been waiting quite a while. The girls were getting antsy, as Anna had put a firm stop on all activity until they had found a suitable place to set up.

Tanya had thought that it would be easy, that there would be all sorts of options to choose from, but she had been wrong. Every rental they had viewed had had some serious flaw; either it was falling apart inside or there weren't enough rooms, or it was too closely overlooked – which was a particularly hard one to escape in Central London. But this was one business on which they couldn't compromise on that side of things. The last thing a punter needed was an old granny across the way having a heart attack as she peered in, or calling out for the noise to be kept down whilst she let some air in the window.

This place was perfect. Modern, ideally proportioned rooms, a space for everything they needed and barely a stone's throw from the front door of the club. It was an absolute gem. Tanya looked away from the freshly re-plastered ceiling and zoned back in as she realised Anna was still talking.

'... and they've said they don't mind us painting so long as it's painted back neutral when we leave. Of course they don't know why we really want it. I said about the club, that you and I wanted to live nearby...'

'Anna, it's perfect,' Tanya cut her off with a beaming smile. Her green eyes sparkled with excitement as she looked around. 'We can do everything we'd planned here. I can get the painters in next week, if we can get the paperwork signed by then. I'm assuming it's vacated?' She looked around at the empty rooms.

'Yes, the last tenants had had enough of the noisy area apparently. Left quite sharpish so it's been empty since last week. OK, so' – Anna raised one shapely dark eyebrow in enquiry – 'shall we definitely go for it? Is this the one?'

'This is the one,' Tanya confirmed, her full lips curling up into a smile. 'This is most definitely the one.' Her voice rose to a shriek as they both began squealing in excitement.

'OK, I just need to get you to fill in a few things on the paperwork and then I can confirm it with them in the morning.'

Anna led Tanya back outside and made sure to lock up the front door securely, before she turned to tuck her arm into Tanya's.

As they walked away, Tanya shot Anna a sideways glance. 'It's nice to see you smiling. Lately you've seemed a bit… I don't know. Off, I guess. Everything OK?'

Anna sighed and her excitement dulled as Tanya's words brought her worries back to the forefront of her mind. 'I'm OK. I'm just worried about Freddie. Something's going on and he doesn't want to talk about it, so…' She shrugged.

Tanya frowned. 'What do you think it is?' She had watched the pair of them go through their fair share of secrets, both ways. Surely after all they'd been through together, Freddie would have no need to keep anything from Anna anymore. Unless he was doing something he shouldn't.

'I really don't know. I'm hoping he's just stressed about his supplier issue, but…' She took a deep breath and pushed away the niggling feeling that it was something more. 'Anyway. We have enough on our own plates to think about.'

'We do,' Tanya agreed and smiled brightly. 'So, are you ready to start peddling flesh to perverts then, Anna Davis?' she teased. 'Are you ready to become the madam of your first whorehouse?'

Anna narrowed her eyes at her best friend. 'After-hours club, if you don't mind,' she replied tartly.

'It's a whorehouse,' Tanya said with a throaty chortle.

'After-hours club has a nicer ring to it,' Anna continued, holding her head up a little higher.

'It's still a whorehouse,' Tanya replied, undeterred. 'Listen, I've got to pop home and feed Princess, but give me half an hour and I'll be back and we can celebrate our fantastic decision in style. Go get the good stuff on ice, yeah?'

'On it.'

Tanya and Anna unlocked their arms and they each swept off in different directions. Neither of them noticed the woman following them, in the dark jacket and bitter mask.

CHAPTER TWENTY-TWO

Anna walked into the club, her spirits as high as the sky. She was thrilled that Tanya was so happy with the place. As soon as the estate agent had opened the front door, Anna had just known that this would be the place for their next venture. It was as though it had been designed specifically for them.

'Carl,' Anna called down the busy bar to get his attention. 'Can you put some Dom on ice? The good stuff, the 2004.'

'Oh wow.' Carl's eyebrows shot up. 'The 2004 is not an everyday vintage. What are we celebrating?'

'I'll tell you later when Tanya's in. Can you get Rebecca to clear us a table? We'll have a little party after closing, pass it on through the girls.'

With a twinkle in her smile, Anna turned to walk towards her office and pulled her phone out of her pocket. She scrolled through the contacts to Freddie's name and was about to dial when she felt a hand touch her forearm. Turning, Anna took a moment to register who it was.

'Oh, Jules, hello,' she said, with a small smile of surprise. 'Are you looking for Tanya?'

'Actually no, I was hoping to talk to you,' Jules answered.

'Oh, OK.' Anna raised her eyebrows slightly. This was unexpected. They had only met a couple of times and had barely talked on those occasions. She offered a friendly smile anyway, curious as to what Jules could want. 'I was just heading to the office; why don't you join me in there?'

'Sure. Lead the way.'

The expectant way she said it made Anna wonder if she'd been hoping to get her alone anyway. Did the woman need someone to talk to? Surely her old friend Tanya would be better placed than she was, but Tanya wasn't here so Anna resigned herself to being whatever it was Jules needed at this moment. She reminded herself that Jules was only newly back to the area. Perhaps she was just lonely and wanted to get to know people a bit better.

Anna closed the door and offered Jules a seat on the small sofa at the side, before taking her own seat at the desk. She smoothed her long, dark hair down to one side in a subconscious gesture of awkwardness. Crossing her slim legs, Anna smiled broadly.

'So, this is nice. I can always make time for new friends. Can I offer you a drink? We should have got one before we came in really. Although—' Anna reached down to the lowest drawer built into the desk and felt around. Her hand touched cold glass and she wrapped her fingers around the neck of the bottle with a smile of triumph. 'Yes, here it is.' She pulled it out. 'Tanya tends to keep a not-so-secret stock of cherry vodka in here, for when she's forced to do the paperwork. It isn't her favourite job,' she said with a laugh.

Jules gave a sarcastic half-smile and looked around. Anna raised her eyebrows at the catty response but kept her counsel.

'Nice little set-up you've got here, ain't it?' Jules said, taking in the office.

Anna looked around. Their office wasn't up to much if she was honest. Magnolia walls with nothing but a plain mirror and one small painting mounted upon them. The desk was nice enough but not expensive and bought because of its practicality rather than its looks. The sofa was plain, with a couple of scatter cushions for comfort, but other than that it was all business. Filing cabinets and CCTV screens took up the rest of the small space. Anna couldn't understand why Jules was looking around so pointedly, as if this was some sort of opulent palace.

'It's alright,' she said eventually with a small shrug. 'It could do with brightening up a bit, though. We haven't really done anything in here since we set up—'

'I meant the whole club. The whole thing, it's a nice set-up.' Her gaze pierced Anna's accusingly and Anna felt herself frown in confusion. The tone behind the words took away any compliment.

'Well, yes, it is. We like it anyway,' Anna replied, feeling the urge to be cautious. The tiny hairs on the back of her neck prickled as Jules's level gaze didn't waver for even a second.

'So, did Freddie front you the money to set it up? I mean, it must have cost a fair bit.' Jules's words were quiet and silken, but her face was hard and Anna couldn't place the emotion behind her strange expression.

'No, he didn't,' Anna replied sharply. Her friendly smile dropped completely.

'Oh right. Your parents then? Oh, of course.' Jules's lip curled back, causing her features to distort into an ugly grimace and she nodded to herself. 'The bank of Daddy, I'm guessing. Yeah, you have that look about ya. The way you talk and hold yourself in such high regard.'

'Excuse me?' Anna felt rage wash through her at the sheer rudeness the woman was displaying. Who on earth was she to come in here and talk like this?

'Not that it is anyone's business, but I earned everything I have. I worked hard to build this club up from nothing, and I didn't need help from *any* man along the way.' Standing up, Anna drew herself to her full height and stared down at the other woman. 'Now I think you need to leave.'

As Anna walked around the table, Jules settled back into the sofa with a smug expression on her face. 'Oh, I ain't going anywhere. Not until I've been heard.'

'Not until what's been heard?' Anna asked irritably. 'You have exactly thirty seconds to say whatever it is you're here to say before I have one of my bouncers throw you out into the back alley.'

Anna took a deep breath and tried to calm herself down. These days her anger was always bubbling near the surface, just itching for a release. Usually she vented it in her boxing sessions with Seamus, but right now she could have happily shown Jules a couple of moves. She imagined pulling back her fist and smashing it repeatedly into Jules's face. Straight away she felt shame. The woman might be rude, but she hadn't earned that.

Jules licked her lips exaggeratedly. 'He's not bad in bed, old Freddie, is he? Is that why you're with him then? If not for the money?'

Anna's jaw dropped as she suddenly felt like she was the one who'd been punched. 'What did you just say?' she asked, her tone full of disbelief.

'It's been a few years, I'll admit, but he certainly had some moves,' Jules continued, baiting Anna coyly.

Anna rubbed her forehead. Had Jules really come here just to rub in that she'd slept with her boyfriend? The conversation was moving from rude to full-on bizarre.

'Especially that one move, you know the one – does he still do it?' Jules wriggled in delight, as if enjoying the memory. 'When you're stark bollock naked and you've been going at it for hours and he throws you, mid-fuck, up the bed and wraps his big, muscly forearms under your bum and just goes to town on your—'

'That's enough,' Anna snapped. Jules's words were making her feel sick. She wasn't stupid; she knew Freddie had had other lovers before her – she had a past too – but she didn't need a blow-by-blow description.

'Oh, come on, love, he's been around the block more times than you or I have had hot dinners. You shouldn't date a guy like him if you can't stomach the fact he's dipped his wick elsewhere,' Jules said with a touch of glee.

She was enjoying this more than she had thought she would. Anna had it all, this posh girl from the Home Counties who'd turned Freddie's eye. It made her feel better about the mess her own life had become, tearing down a little of Anna's. Anna's dark blue eyes grew hard as they locked onto Jules's.

'I know Freddie has a past. Who doesn't? But is that really what you've come here to tell me?' Stepping forward as the confidence grew in her words, Anna held her ground. 'Do you honestly think you're special because you're one of the many flings he had, before he settled down?'

Jules stood up slowly and closed the space in front of Anna.

'No,' she said serenely. 'I think I'm special because I'm the only one he has a kid with.'

It was like being hit by a speeding train. As the weight of Jules's words hit home, Anna staggered backward and only stopped when her hip banged into the desk.

'You're lying,' she whispered.

'Am I?' Jules retorted. 'And why would I do that?'

Anna sagged back against the desk and scanned the other woman's face for evidence that this was a lie, but there was none. There was just the cold, confident stare of a victor.

'What do you mean you had a kid with him?' Anna's voice quivered as she spoke.

'I mean exactly what it sounds like. Freddie and I have a son together.' Jules held her head higher and the smugness in her expression intensified as she saw the other woman weaken just a little bit more. 'His name is Ethan. He's seven and the spitting image of his dad.'

'And Freddie knows?' Anna heard herself ask.

'Oh, Freddie knows. It came as a surprise to me that he hadn't told you, I'll admit. I mean, after all…' Her lip curled into a mocking smile. 'He tells you everything, right?'

Anna swallowed the bile that rose from her stomach. It couldn't be true. She had to be lying. But why would she lie about that? And Freddie knew... why hadn't he told her?

Jules pulled a crumpled picture out of her pocket and held it up in front of Anna. 'Here's his last school picture. Look familiar?'

Anna took the photo with trembling hands and looked down into the face of her boyfriend's son. The eyes staring back at her were definitely Freddie's. They were unmistakable with their mix of hazel and green, amber flecks shining out right near the pupil. Anna felt her heart ache with a fresh feeling of loss and longing that the memory of her miscarriage always brought forth. Staring into this little boy's eyes was like staring into a picture of what her future might have held. But not anymore. The image blurred as her eyes filled with tears of shock and grief.

'You can keep that,' Jules said, her tone flat and unsympathetic. 'Tell Freddie it's time to start paying up. We ain't going to sit in the shadows anymore, not now Vince is dribbling into his porridge every day at that retirement home.' Hearing of the all-powerful, mighty Vince's decline had made Jules's year. Fear of what he would do if she came back had been the only thing standing between her and Freddie Tyler's money. 'You can tell Freddie his son is currently going without all sorts of things, because I can't work with him hanging around me neck.' She laid it on thick, for maximum effect. 'I'm only one person; I can't do everything myself. Surely the great Freddie Tyler can't be seen to have a son living in squalor, now can he?'

Opening the door, Jules turned with a final grin. 'Catch you later, *mate.*'

As the door closed, Anna crumpled to the floor and gave in to the shock and the pain. Great, heaving sobs wracked through her body as she tried to process what was going on. Just half an hour ago she had been on top of the world. She and Tanya were celebrating finding new business premises. She had been busy living her life and looking forward without the constant reminder of her miscarriage and the trauma she'd been through.

With a groan she put her hands to her face and tried to wipe away the tears that streamed down her cheeks. Crying wasn't going to help her. She wiped them more forcefully, angry with herself for what she saw as a weak reaction. Taking deep breaths, Anna straightened out her legs in front of her, smoothing her fitted, dark blue dress with shaky fingers. As she stared at it she thought about Freddie. He loved her in this dress, told her that it matched her eyes. Tears stung again as the pain of his secret child stabbed through her heart. She blinked them away angrily.

How could he not tell her? How long had he known?

Suddenly the door swung open and Tanya swept in with a dazzling burst of energy, a cloud of Chanel perfume following her in and settling around the room. Opening her mouth to speak, she froze and looked down to the floor where her best friend sat, defeated against the foot of the desk.

'Well, fuck me, I was only gone thirty minutes. You smashed already?' she joked. As she looked more closely at her friend she suddenly noticed the telltale track marks running down her face and the redness around the eyes. 'Anna?' Her smile disappeared and she dropped to the floor. 'What's happened?'

'Freddie,' Anna started, 'he… Jules came and, and…' The shock rose back up and Anna began to sob anew. 'Oh my God, Tanya,' she cried.

'Jesus!' Tanya grasped Anna to her and held her whilst she cried. 'What's this about Jules? Anna—' Tanya wiped the hair from her friend's face and straightened her up, extremely concerned now. 'Tell me what's happened.'

'It's Freddie,' Anna sobbed, heartbroken. 'He has a son. With your friend Jules.'

CHAPTER TWENTY-THREE

Freddie tried Anna's number for the fourth time and sighed as it rang through to voicemail. He had hoped to take her for an early dinner, maybe engineer a walk by the river afterwards. All day he'd been working up the courage to tell her and eventually realised that he was never going to feel ready.

He looked down over London from the balcony and breathed in the cold air. Closing his eyes, he let the sounds of the city wash over him. It had been a long day and he'd spent it mainly putting out fires before they took hold. Placing Sarah Riley into the task force was proving to be one of the best moves he had ever made. They were hot on his tail and trying everything they could to trip him up and find out information they could later use against him. Every step of the way, Riley was ahead of them. She compiled weekly reports, sometimes daily when the need arose, giving Freddie access to all of their plans. This week they had been close, but after pausing some shipments and rerouting a couple of drop-offs, he'd managed to keep everyone in the clear. For now, at least.

The noise of the front door banging shut sounded from inside and Freddie turned with an expectant smile. This was swiftly replaced by a look of confusion when he caught sight of Tanya storming through the living room towards him, her long, red hair swishing wildly from side to side.

'Hey,' he said as she stepped out onto the balcony. 'Is every-thing—'

A resounding clap sounded through the air as Tanya slapped Freddie hard across the face. He reeled back in shock.

'What the fuck do you think you're doing?' he demanded. He put his hand to his burning cheek. She had hit him hard enough to truly hurt and that was no mean feat. 'You're fucking lucky I count you as family,' he growled, struggling to contain his anger.

'Yeah?' Tanya shot back, her own anger flying free. 'Am I? Did you count me as family eight years ago when you and I were seeing each other and you were fucking my friend behind my back?' she screamed, her eyes wildly bright and her face red with fury.

Freddie stepped back, for once too shocked to know how to reply. As he stared into her hurt expression, he could have kicked himself for not thinking about what this would mean to Tanya sooner. It wasn't just Anna that this was going to hurt. Tanya had loved him at a time when they were all young and carefree and he hadn't wanted to settle down. He'd cut her loose without a second thought and moved straight onto the next one. Jules.

'Tanya, listen—'

'No, *you* listen,' she cried. 'I forgave you for breaking my heart. I let you back into my life as a friend. I stood up for you with Anna when you two first started out and I rooted for you. I put aside our past and my pain so we could all move forward. We became a *family*. I thought you of all people would understand what that meant.'

'I do understand what that means, Tanya,' Freddie replied, his eyes pleading with her to see how serious he was. 'My family means more to me than anything, *all of you*. I never wanted to cause you pain again. For Christ's sake, I love you like a sister.'

Tanya made a sound of disgust and wiped a tear that had escaped through the angry mask.

'OK, perhaps not quite a sister,' Freddie corrected. 'But I do, Tan. And if I could take back the hurt I put you through all those years ago, I would. But I can't. All I can tell you is this.' He stepped closer to her and looked her in the eye, his expression sincere. 'I wasn't fucking anyone else while I was seeing you. I might be many things, but I've never been a cheat.' He took a deep breath and exhaled heavily. 'Jules was afterwards. I didn't plan on it; I knew she was your friend. But she kept coming to the parties and I got drunk and it just happened.' He shrugged, looking tired, as though the weight of the world was suddenly on his shoulders. 'It was a very casual thing. We hooked up a few times over the next couple of months and then she disappeared. I thought that was the last I'd ever see of her. I'm sorry, Tanya. Believe me, I really am, now more than ever.'

Tanya shook her head and crossed her arms defensively across her chest. Her history with Freddie was long dead and buried. She had no romantic feelings for him anymore and had put to bed all her unresolved issues when Freddie and Anna had first met. But hearing this now, finding out that he hadn't just broken her heart but had betrayed her, *that* brought about a whole new world of hurt. Tanya could count the people she cared about on one hand and they meant everything to her. Finding out that any one of them could betray her felt like getting shot all over again. And whether or not it had been while they were together, it was still a betrayal. Jules had been her friend.

Freddie ran his hands down his face, stressed.

'Listen, I still need to tell Anna. I'm hoping to take her out tonight so I can—'

'Anna knows. She's the one who told me.'

'What?' The bright lights of the city seemed to swirl around his head as his whole world came crashing down. All the colour drained from his face. 'How did she find out?'

'Jules told her, about an hour ago. She just turned up at the club.' Tanya sniffed and stepped towards Freddie, her arms still folded defensively but her initial anger spent.

'She did what?' Freddie asked, aghast. He hands flew to his head and his jaw dropped in horror. 'Why the hell would she do that?'

Tanya narrowed her eyes. 'Because, Freddie,' she said, 'she's a cold, home-wrecking bitch who would sell her own mother to get what she wants. Surely you've figured that out by now. Friends like me don't get any special treatment, so why on earth would you?'

With that, Tanya walked into the flat. 'I'm here to get a bag of Anna's things,' she called over her shoulder. 'She's not coming home tonight; she's staying with me for a few days.'

'I need to see her, Tanya,' Freddie replied. 'I need to explain.'

'She doesn't want to see you,' Tanya responded. 'Not tonight at least.' She walked on out of sight.

Anger boiled up from his insides at the thought of Jules hurting Anna like that. He gave a strangled cry as he realised that he couldn't even hurt her in return, not without hurting his son.

His son. Even with all of this going on, he felt the need to meet Ethan properly, to get to know this boy who was his flesh and blood. *Was he like him? Did he have any of the same traits? Was Jules going to let him form a proper relationship with Ethan?*

Rage flowed through his veins at the corners she kept continually trapping him in. His eyes grew hard as he made a promise to himself. Jules would pay for what she had done tonight. One way or another, he would make sure she paid her debt of pain in full.

CHAPTER TWENTY-FOUR

Paul pulled up to the old barn nestled in a small valley between two hilly fields. If you didn't know it was here, you'd assume the dirt track leading to it was only there for access to the miles of farmland all around. It was precisely why they had purchased it from the elderly farmer a few years before. He'd needed the cash and they'd needed somewhere where no one could hear what was going on. They owned the track and the barn, and the farmer still owned the fields around it. It was a win-win situation.

Bill's car was already there, as Paul had expected. He looked at his phone screen one last time, but there was still no call or message back from Freddie. He tutted in annoyance. Surely his brother wanted to be here for this?

Grabbing the small black backpack from the passenger seat, Paul left the car and entered the big wooden barn. He rolled the door shut behind him and walked over to Bill and Simon, who were waiting patiently by a trussed-up captive tied to a chair. There was a hessian sack over his head blocking his sight and he visibly tensed as he heard Paul approach.

'He talked much yet?' Paul grunted. He hated doing this without Freddie. Freddie always found the perfect words for situations like these. Although sharply intelligent, communication wasn't Paul's strongest skill and he was well aware of that fact.

'Not really, unless you count random outbursts of abuse,' Bill answered.

Right on cue, the trussed-up man began spitting out expletives. 'Fucking let me out of here, you fucking twats.'

Bill tutted and shook his head. 'Honestly, did your mother teach you no manners?' He whacked the man around the head hard. 'And you really shouldn't use all your insults in one go. They lose all effect.'

Simon laughed and even Paul cracked a grin at Bill's mocking sarcasm. The man in the chair groaned at the hit on the head and mumbled to himself in self-pity, but didn't raise his voice again.

Paul tilted his head at Simon, who stepped forward and whipped the hessian bag off their captive's head.

'Fucking finally,' the man said, finding his voice again. 'I couldn't breathe in that thing; it gets all in your mouth. It ain't healthy.'

'And you think your health is at the top of my agenda?' Paul asked, his deep voice holding no trace of amusement.

The man in the chair finally looked up and focused on Paul properly. There was a flicker of recognition in his eyes, which Paul caught.

'Know who I am, do ya?' he asked.

The man nodded.

'Good.' Paul opened the rucksack and rummaged around inside. 'So, who are you then? I know you're related to one of Drew's men, used to be on the crew.'

'I'm Nige,' he said. 'And I ain't nothing to do with them anymore. Cousin or not, I'm a civilian now.'

'Thing is, Nige' – Paul found what he was looking for, threw the bag to one side and turned the small knife over in his hand – 'once you're in this life, you're never really out. Not properly. Know what I mean? You're part of things. Part of history. Jobs that have been pulled, conversations that you've been in on that have ongoing repercussions.'

'Any jobs I was part of had nothing to do with London.' Nigel stood his ground firmly. 'So whatever beef you've got with Drew, it's nothing to do with me.' He strained against the ropes that held his hands to the arms of the chair, frustrated. 'Come on, man. I've done nothing to you. I'm a foreman in a factory, for God's sake. I've got kids. I've been straight for years.'

'Yet you contacted Bill here to set up the meet.'

'As a favour to my cousin,' he cried. 'All I did was pass on a message because I happened to be here and know who's who.'

Paul nodded. 'Fair enough,' he said. 'You ain't here because we think you're still with Drew; you're here because we need some information.'

'What kind of information?' Nigel asked warily.

'I need the details of Drew's cocaine supplier.'

Nigel's face dropped and he shook his head, fear growing behind his eyes. 'You know I can't tell you that. He'd kill me.'

'Well…' Paul exchanged glances with Bill. 'We're going to kill you if you don't. Except we'll do it slowly in the hope that we can extract the information before you cop it. Because, you know' – he shrugged – 'saves on the clearing up.'

Nigel closed his eyes and the colour drained from his face. He knew what the Tylers were capable of. They hadn't become barons of the underworld for nothing. They'd fought their way to the top through a mixture of good business sense and limitless violence. He admired them greatly, but right now he feared them even more. The problem was, though, he also feared Drew. In Manchester, Drew had also fought his way to the top and his vicious outbursts were legendary. If there were two crews he would give anything not to be caught in the middle of, it would be these two.

'You know I can't just roll over and hand you what you want. You're right. I was part of the crew; I was part of their history. I can't grass them up. Would any of your men do that to you?'

Nigel asked. He swallowed, knowing full well that he wasn't going to like what came next.

Paul sighed heavily. He understood exactly where the man was coming from and Nigel was right in what he'd said. None of the Tylers' men would just turn over information to the enemy. This would have to be done the hard way. Paul wouldn't take pleasure in torturing the man, but business was business, and at the end of the day any man who entered this life knew and accepted the possible consequences.

Lunging forward, Paul plunged the small knife down through Nigel's hand and into the wood of the chair arm. There was a short delay as Nigel registered what had happened and then a blood-curdling scream as the pain set in.

'Who's their supplier?' Paul asked, his tone devoid of emotion.

'Argh, I can't. Argh, Christ!'

Reaching forward, Paul pulled the knife back out. Blood spurted out from the wound and stained his suit trousers. Paul tutted and with a deep breath lifted his arm and stabbed it back into the same hand again, next to the first wound.

Nigel screamed again, this time tears escaping his eyes as the pain intensified.

'Please,' he begged. 'I can't give you what you want.'

'You can,' Paul replied. 'You just won't. There's a difference.'

'I have a family,' Nigel pleaded.

'Then give me what I need so that you can get back to them. Come on, be smart about this.'

Nigel didn't answer. He dropped his head and sobbed into his chest, tears and snot mixing as they trailed down his face. His whole body shook from the shock of the stab wounds.

Shaking his head with a sad expression, Paul grasped the handle of the knife and slowly began to twist.

'No, no, argh!' Nigel's screams hit a crescendo and he bucked and twisted in horrified agony as the blade mangled his hand.

Simon quickly came forward and held the back of the chair secure, so that Nigel couldn't topple it in his attempts to escape the torture. 'Stop! Stop, please!' he screamed, a gurgling sound of anguish in his throat.

'You can make it stop,' Paul said, holding the knife fast. 'Just tell me what I need to know and you can get back to your family. No more pain.'

Nigel writhed around, his face distorting as he tried not to pass out from the pain. Paul twisted it a little bit more and he let out another feral cry.

'You're down to two options, Nigel,' Paul pushed, sensing the other man breaking. 'You can carry on protecting people you don't even work for anymore and I'll carry on limb by limb until your heart gives out. Or you can give us a simple piece of information and go home. Surely you want to see your kids again?'

Nigel felt the last of his resolve disappear. He was a dead man either way, but at least if he left now he might be able to run away with his family, start somewhere new. His survival instinct was stronger than his loyalty to Drew.

'Alfie,' he shouted through the pain. 'It's Alfie.'

Paul immediately let the knife twist back to its original position and yanked it out. Nigel screamed once more but then bit his lip, overwhelmed with relief. Bill threw a clean hand towel over to Paul and he hunkered down next to Nigel and pressed it over the bleeding wounds, applying pressure.

'That's good, Nige. Tell me more,' he said.

'His real name is Alfonso, but he don't like it so everyone calls him Alfie. Alfie Ramone.'

Paul nodded to Simon, who stepped forward and began untying the ropes that held Nigel so tightly to the chair.

'And where can I find Alfie? Who is he?' Paul asked.

'Liverpool. On paper he's an art dealer, owns a chain of galleries and auction houses. His real money comes from the coke.'

Nigel whimpered and winced as Simon untied his injured hand. Paul lifted it from the arm of the chair and quickly wrapped it tightly in the towel.

'Go on,' Paul prompted.

'He smuggles it in through the auction houses. He's connected to a cartel in Mexico. That's all I know. That, and the fact that he's bad news. Not someone you want to be on the wrong side of.'

Paul looked up to Bill who nodded and pulled out his phone. 'I'm on it,' he said, walking away to a quiet corner.

'Simon…' Paul turned to the younger man and threw him his car keys. 'Drop Nigel near a hospital – that needs to be seen to. Bring the car back to Ruby Ten tonight. Oh, and if there's so much as a scratch on my new motor…' He let the threat hang in the air as he stared Simon out.

Simon put his hands up in surrender. 'There won't be,' he promised.

'Nigel?' Paul gave him a hard stare. 'You had an accident. Fell off a wall and your hand came down on some scrap metal. I know where you live if that story changes.'

'It won't,' Nigel said, cradling his hand.

Paul nodded, satisfied. Nigel knew the score. He had been in the game himself for many years. There was no way the man would open himself up for more of this.

Nigel stood up stiffly. There was a time he would have turned on Paul and meted out justice for what had been done to him today. But that was a long time ago now. Since he'd had his daughters and settled down with his wife, things had changed. All he wanted to do was go back to his quiet life. There would have to be some changes now; he would have to go somewhere Drew couldn't find them. But that didn't matter, not in the grand scheme of things. All he cared about were his girls.

Simon led Nigel back out of the barn and into Paul's car. He started the engine with a roar and carefully backed it up and drove off down the dirt track. Paul waited patiently for Bill to finish his call and come back over.

'So?' he asked.

'Ramone Auction Houses, they're his chain. Main one based in Liverpool. Zack's going to pull as much info on the business and Alfie Ramone as he can. I'll get it back to you by tonight and we can go from there.'

'Perfect,' Paul said with an eager glint in his eye. Now they were getting somewhere.

Bill leaned down and began rolling up the plastic sheeting they'd laid underneath the chair. 'Come on then,' he said. 'I'll help you get rid of this. We'll have to burn the chair.'

'We will indeed,' Paul confirmed, eying the bloodstains that ran down one side. As he rolled the other end of the plastic sheet, Paul thought over the events of the last half hour. He hadn't needed Freddie's smooth words today after all. He'd extracted the information pretty quickly by himself. Perhaps sometimes, he thought, a blunt edge really was as effective as a sharp sword.

CHAPTER TWENTY-FIVE

Freddie stood under the trees in the small park near the block of flats where Jules was currently staying. He knew she wasn't at home when he arrived – he'd checked. The flat had been empty. Taking out another cigarette, he lit it and took a deep drag. It had taken every ounce of his self-control not to find her and launch, all guns blazing. It had been tempting, but with all things considered, Freddie knew he would have to take a much more calculated approach.

His mind wandered back to Anna, as it seemed to do every two minutes at the moment. She wasn't talking to him, wouldn't answer his calls or texts at all. He felt terrible, knowing how hard the news must have hit her and how betrayed she must be feeling, hearing the news from Jules instead of from him. He closed his eyes as guilt and pain washed over him once more.

After an hour of waiting in the shadows, Freddie spotted Jules coming down the road. With her hood up and her shoulders hunched tensely, she kept glancing back over her shoulder as she hurried towards her building. Freddie watched with narrowed eyes as she shouted impatiently to the young boy trailing behind her. When he reached the door, she shoved him roughly inside. Freddie shook his head and his mouth formed a hard line. He'd not heard her say one kind word to or about him. It was as though she didn't even like the child.

Waiting around for another five minutes until he figured they were settled inside, Freddie walked briskly over to the building.

He tapped in the code that he'd watched other residents enter and when the dull buzz sounded to let him know the door was unlocked, he went inside and climbed the stairs.

Stopping outside the cheap, thin front door of the flat, Freddie was tempted to repeat his actions from the other day: kick this flimsy piece of wood through and frighten the life out of her. In his mind's eye, Freddie watched himself grab her by the neck, push her against the wall and demand to know who the hell she thought she was. This imaginary version of Jules cowered underneath his fury.

But Ethan was inside and he didn't want to scare the boy. He also didn't want to alienate him straight off by hurting the person he loved most in the world – however much she deserved it.

Taking in a deep, frustrated breath, he let it out slowly, pushing the itch to cause havoc aside. Clocking the absence of a peephole, Freddie knocked and waited. He heard Jules approach the door and hesitate before she opened it just a crack. Her reluctant face peered round and when she saw it was Freddie, her eyes widened. She didn't try to close the door, but when she didn't open it either, Freddie's patience ran out and he shoved it hard enough to push her backward and create an opening to walk through.

'Ouch, oh, really! There was no need for that,' Jules complained, her gaze darting towards the lounge. Freddie wanted so much to think that she was glancing over out of concern for Ethan, but it seemed more like she was checking that there were witnesses. She almost scowled when she saw there were none.

Jules licked her lips and watched him warily. 'You could have texted first,' she said, fronting it out with fake confidence. 'We were just about to count our coppers, see how much we've got to spend on dinner tonight.' She jutted her chin out defiantly.

Freddie lunged forward and she quickly jumped back against the wall. Unable to stop himself he grasped her neck tightly and loomed over her. His eyes burned with furious intensity, filled with dark hatred.

'Who the fuck,' he said in a quiet, deadly voice, 'do you think you are, telling Anna about Ethan?'

Jules's mouth flapped open and shut like a fish, and guilt and fear flashed across her features. 'I thought she knew,' she squeaked through his vice-like grip. 'I assumed you'd have told her by now. I didn't mean no harm.'

'Didn't mean no harm?' Freddie repeated, raising his eyebrows in disbelief. He itched to squeeze tighter but held back.

'No, 'course not. I was just trying to get her to put in a word with you, about money.'

'About money...' Freddie barked a humourless laugh. Shoving her away from him and stepping back, he pulled a brown envelope out of his pocket and threw it on the small table in the hallway where they still stood. 'There's two grand there, to keep you going for now until things are sorted out properly. I *told* you that I would be coming over. You had no need to go shit-stirring in my personal life.'

Jules rubbed her neck where Freddie's fingers had left angry red marks and eyed him warily. 'You didn't answer my text about money, though, Freddie,' she continued to needle, not ready to give up on her story. 'I need food for my boy, money for clothes, a decent life, everything. You're his dad – it's your job to provide at least some of that for him. He's had nothing whilst you've had the life of Riley, all this time...'

'I found out *days* ago, Jules!' Freddie roared, his anger finally getting the better of him. He glanced behind him to check Ethan hadn't come out and lowered his voice again. 'I've known I'm a dad for *days*. I'm still getting my head around it. I still had to break the news to my family, my partner – because *you kept his existence from me all this time* – and then you completely fucked *that* up for me too.' He turned away from her, the hatred he felt towards her becoming too much to bear. 'If I had known about

Ethan before, then he wouldn't have *had* to go without. That's on *you*.' He swivelled round and pointed a finger at her accusingly.

For once Jules had the good grace to look down as her cheeks turned red. But as her eyes slid sideways towards the envelope full of money, her shame seemed to instantly disappear.

Freddie closed his eyes and took a deep breath before he continued. 'I want to meet him properly. Now.'

Jules just shrugged and picked up the envelope, distracted now. As she pulled out the wedge of notes, her eyes lit up, and she no longer seemed interested in Freddie or Ethan at all. 'Sure, knock yourself out. He's all yours,' she said, her tone cocky and indifferent.

Freddie stared after her for a moment, trying and failing to understand the woman. Eventually, he turned and walked towards the small, messy living room. Pausing at the door, he watched Ethan for a moment. Engrossed in some children's TV programme, he was sitting cross-legged on the floor in front of the sofa. If he'd heard their exchange, he wasn't making it obvious, though Freddie imagined it probably wasn't the first fight he'd overheard his mother in. He sighed, feeling like he was failing before he'd even begun.

His eyes moved back around the room. The sofa was covered in piles of clothes, casually thrown there unfolded after a wash. An overflowing ashtray was on the floor to one side of him, three empty beer cans on the other. The carpet was dulled with dirt and different bits of food stuck to it here and there. It angered Freddie to see Ethan sitting amongst this, having grown up with a mother who would never have allowed any room to reach such a state.

Eventually he stepped forward and made his presence known. 'Alright, Ethan?' he asked gently with what he hoped was a friendly smile.

Ethan turned, his face long and serious. 'Yeah, I'm OK.'

The two stared at each other for a moment, until Freddie moved closer and sat down on the floor nearby.

'So, what you watching?' he asked, trying to look interested.

'It's *Paw Patrol*,' he answered, then quickly looked down as his face coloured. 'It's for babies, I know. I should be watching something more older.'

Freddie frowned. He looked at the screen and tried to follow. 'Well, I don't think it looks like it's just for babies,' he said. 'Talking dogs who save the day, that sounds like a pretty good show.'

Ethan peeped up at him, surprise in his eyes and a small smile on his face. 'That's what I thought,' he said quietly, checking the doorway to check his mum hadn't come back. She always put him down for watching programmes like this.

'Though' – Freddie squinted at the screen as he carried on watching – 'I don't know where that kid gets the money from for all this.'

Ethan giggled and Freddie turned to him with a smile. Studying him up close and without the shock factor or Jules or an audience, he started taking in details properly for the first time. The eyes, the shape of his face and the dimples in his cheeks when he smiled – they were all Freddie. His hair was a touch lighter, somewhere in between Freddie and Jules, but other than that he couldn't see much of her in him at all.

Other details presented themselves which were not such a pleasant surprise. Ethan was overly thin, his arms like twigs. There were purple rings around his eyes and the clothes he was wearing had seen much better days. His hair was dirty and his fingernails were black. His bright eyes darted around uncertainly, alert yet tired at the same time. Growing up in a poor area, Freddie had come to know the telltale signs of neglect from an early age. Usually these kids were the ones with drunks or junkies for parents and often they would end up being taken away by the social.

Freddie frowned, concerned. He had already decided to help set Jules up somewhere and pay for anything Ethan needed, but the boy's needs clearly went beyond that. Jules needed help looking after him. The only problem was, Freddie hadn't exactly had much experience in this area himself. Whilst he figured he knew the basics, he wouldn't know anything about getting Ethan the right clothes, help with homework or anything else like that. He'd have to have a think about how he was going to approach this. One more fire to add to the pile he needed to put out.

'Do you like *The Avengers*?' Ethan asked.

Freddie's attention was brought back to the present. 'What, like superhero stuff?'

'Yeah. Like Hulk and Spiderman and Iron Man…' Ethan started reeling them off.

'Can't say I've ever really watched 'em. But I'll tell you what, you tell me which one of the films is the best and I'll watch it so we can talk about it next time we hang out.'

'Are we going to hang out then?' Ethan's young voice was so hopeful it touched Freddie's heart.

'I'd like to, mate, if that's OK with you?'

Ethan thought about it for a moment, shooting another tense glance towards the door. 'Can we go somewhere else next time? I don't like it here.'

'Yeah, 'course. How about we go out for some food,' Freddie offered. 'What's your favourite food?'

'Anything.' The reply was automatic and a look of acute hunger appeared in Ethan's eyes.

Freddie had a hard time controlling his expression for a moment. The poor boy – his son – was starving, right in front of him.

'What about pizza?' he said eventually. 'Do you like pizza?'

'I love pizza,' Ethan replied enthusiastically.

'What's your favourite one?'

'I like pepperoni and ham when I can choose. I went to a party once for Aaron Chambers' birthday and they let me choose.' Ethan's face was animated now as he talked.

'Do you ever get pizza with your mum?' Freddie asked.

'Sometimes. But we only get the chicken and mushroom ones because she doesn't like pepperoni.'

'Well…' Freddie pulled his phone out of his pocket and quickly found the local pizza-delivery site. 'Here's what we're going to do. I'm going to order you a pepperoni and ham pizza tonight, and then when I come next time I'll take you to this little place I know in Chalk Farm. It's called Marine Ices. All it does is pizza and ice cream and they are the *best* in London at both.'

'Really?' Ethan said, not sure which to be more excited about, the fact his favourite pizza was coming tonight or the promise of this magical restaurant. 'But Mum doesn't like pepperoni,' he said as his face slipped back into worry.

'Well, this pizza isn't for your mum,' Freddie replied, trying to keep his tone light. 'It's for you. From me. And it's all ordered and paid for, see?' He showed Ethan the screen of his phone. 'It will be here in about twenty minutes, so listen out for the door. Now, I have to go but before I do, I'd best go see if your mum minds me taking you out next time.' Freddie stood up and brushed down his smart trousers.

'Oh, she won't,' Ethan answered, his tone confident. 'She sends me out with anyone she can. It don't matter who. She just likes me out of the way.'

As Freddie listened to the words and saw the resignation on Ethan's face, his heart broke. How had the life of his child come to this? And how had his child been brought into the world by a woman as callous as Jules?

CHAPTER TWENTY-SIX

Alfie Ramone gripped the handle of the telephone he was holding so tightly that his fingers turned white. His expression turned darker and darker as his cheeks flooded with crimson rage. With a frustrated roar, he slammed the handset down, disconnecting the call.

'What's wrong?' Andre asked from his desk across the room.

Alfie turned to face his brother, thunder in his eyes. At five-nine he wasn't a particularly tall man, but what he lacked in height he made up for in stature. His shirt strained over his rounded stomach and his dark features were all but eaten up by his large, puffy face. Balding on top, just a few hairs remained, carefully combed over in neat lines, meeting each well-cut side. He was the polar opposite of his brother, who was both tall and slim with a full head of salt and pepper hair.

'Those fucking pricks have lost the extra shipment of coke,' he spat, his tone incredulous.

'What?' Andre dropped the chicken salad roll he had been about to bite into. 'What do you mean, *lost?*'

'I mean fucking *lost,*' Alfie fumed. 'As in had it swiped off them from right underneath their noses. That's why they've been dodging our calls.' He slammed both fists down angrily on the oak desk he stood next to.

'Was that Drew on the phone?' Andre asked, trying to understand.

'No, 'course not,' Alfie replied, rolling his eyes in irritation. 'He'd be fucking stupid to call here right now, and he knows it.'

'Right.' Andre stood up and took control of the conversation. 'What – *exactly* – has happened? Who's taken the coke and who was that on the phone?'

Alfie took a deep breath and sat down. His emotions sometimes got the better of him. He needed to calm down and explain everything to his brother properly.

'Wouldn't give me a name. Whoever it was informed me that after Drew tried to take the coke into London it was *taken off his hands*. Apparently, Drew didn't have the "in" that he thought he did after all and the powers that be decided to teach him a lesson.'

'Well, who are they then?' Andre asked, walking over and leaning against his brother's desk.

Alfie shook his head. 'It was Big Dom and Vince, back in the day, but Big Dom's dead and Vince is retired. Handed it down the chain a few years back to the Tyler brothers.'

'I see,' Andre murmured, fiddling with his bottom lip absent-mindedly. 'Where are Drew and his men now?'

'Still in London – I would imagine trying to get it back,' Alfie answered.

'They would be wise to succeed,' Andre said. He was as annoyed as his brother by this turn of events, though he was more reserved in showing his emotions. He began to boil away under the surface. They had been reluctant to give Drew what he'd been asking for. It was a very large increase to their normal order, more than double the size. The sort of money they would owe until the product was sold was substantial, not something that any man should take lightly. They had warned him of this, made sure that he knew exactly what he was letting himself in for, but the man had insisted. Drew had been so sure that they had everything tied up neatly, and indeed he *had* been convincing. It appeared that this had been a mistake, though – and neither of the Ramones could stand making mistakes.

Alfie stood up, the fury still simmering in his eyes. There was at least one thing he might be able to get out of this, if the situation continued to go awry. 'Contact the Killers,' he said. 'Tell them they're coming on a trip with us.'

'Good idea,' Andre replied, a cold smile creeping up his face.

The Killers were the Ramones' nickname for three people within their firm. These particular men were ex-special forces, who'd turned to earning through crime when their country had turned its back on them. Having fought their politicians' wars and fought their way through the most hellish of places and situations, they had returned home to nothing. There were no trumpets or cheering crowds, no rewards for what they'd done. All they were given were directions to the job centre and a half-hearted offer of mental-health help, as though the way of life they had been pushed to adopt and embrace was now somehow wrong and dirty. Alfie had given them a professional home and aside from using their unique skills to solve his own problems, he also contracted them out for specialist jobs. They were kidnappers, hunters, top-end security, but most famously they were ruthless killers. Alfie made sure that they were well compensated and rewarded, in a way that their country had not.

'Tell the Killers to find them and report their whereabouts,' Alfie said. 'But they're not to move in until I'm there. I want to see what the situation is. If it can be resolved then I want to make sure Drew understands the urgency.' Business still had to be the priority. The money needed to be paid. If he failed, that was a bonus, but Alfie had to be seen putting the business first. He cracked his knuckles. 'And if it can't' – his expression darkened – 'then I'm going to be the one to make them wish they'd never been born.'

CHAPTER TWENTY-SEVEN

Anna stared at herself in the bathroom mirror and sighed. Her eyes had hollow rings around them from the lack of sleep and seemingly endless tears that not even make-up could fully hide. Her long, dark hair hung straight and dull where she couldn't be bothered to style it, and her already pale complexion was as white as a ghost. She took a deep breath and closed her eyes, feeling mentally and emotionally drained already. She had only been up an hour.

Tanya walked in behind her and rubbed the tops of her arms comfortingly. She bit her lip and stared at her friend's reflection in concern.

'You don't have to go in, you know,' she said gently. 'Why don't you just chill here for another day? I can manage.'

Anna reached up and squeezed one of Tanya's hands with an affectionate half-smile.

'It's OK. I can't hide up here forever. Plus, it's driving me mad sitting with nothing to do. I just keep going round and round in circles in my head…' She trailed off.

It had been two days since Jules had told her about Ethan and about the fact Freddie was fully aware that he had a son. It had hit Anna like a ton of bricks. Jules had carried that child safely into the world, unlike Anna. Anna the murderer.

Anna closed her eyes against the pain. It was all so much to deal with and she *had* been dealing with it, slowly. But how could she get over what had happened when suddenly the one thing she could never give Freddie had turned up out of the blue? A son. His flesh and blood. She knew she should try to be happy for him, but all she could feel were crashing waves of devastation. Perhaps it might have been easier hearing it from him, knowing that they were a team through this just like everything else, but that hadn't happened. He had kept it to himself. Anna was suddenly the outsider – the barren, useless outsider. And it hurt more than she ever thought anything else could.

Anna stood upright and tried to fluff some volume back into her hair. It didn't work. She still looked as tired and defeated as she had for the last two days.

'Here,' Tanya said kindly, rummaging in the make-up bag on the side. 'This will give you a bit of colour.' She handed Anna the soft pink lipstick.

Anna carefully applied it and stood still whilst Tanya pinched her cheeks from behind.

'There you go. Not quite yourself, but not quite *Day of the Living Dead* either,' she joked.

Anna gave a small laugh, unable to resist her best friend's attempts at making her smile.

'I love you, Tanya Smith,' she said suddenly.

'Yeah, alright,' Tanya said with a laugh. 'It's only a bit of lippy.'

'No, I mean it.' She squeezed Tanya's hand again. 'You're the best friend anyone could ever ask for. Don't you ever forget that.'

Anna meant every word. They had been through some tough times, the pair of them, and no matter what, they had always had each other's back. She didn't know what she would do without her crazy, erratic, wonderful best friend.

'Well, you ain't too bad yourself, Anna Davis,' Tanya replied, giving her a hug. 'Now, are you absolutely sure you want to go in today?'

'I really am,' Anna said with feeling. It wasn't her style to stay cooped up brooding. She couldn't stand it any longer. There was a whole world out there and two clubs to run, and no matter what was going on in her personal life, she was never going to let anything get in the way of her business. Not even Freddie.

Walking into Club Anya, the first thing Anna noticed was the unhappy expression on Carl's face. He looked tense, which was unusual. Usually he was the most chilled-out person Anna knew.

'What's wrong?' she asked, with a frown.

Carl looked as though he was going to speak, but then seemed to hesitate. He exhaled loudly. 'Nothing. I'm fine.'

'Well, you don't look fine,' Anna said, pausing by the bar.

Carl studied her for a moment. 'Do you want a coffee?'

'Sure, thanks,' Anna replied. She realised she must look exhausted. She opened her mouth to speak again, but Carl cut her off.

'I'll bring it through to you.' He turned his back and walked off to the other end of the bar where the large coffee machine stood.

Anna raised her eyebrows, surprised. Usually Carl loved a chat. She shrugged mentally and continued through to the office. If Carl wanted to talk to her, he knew where she was.

The office door closed behind her before she caught the familiar scent hanging in the air. Whirling round, she reached for the handle but it was too late. There he was, between her and the only exit from the room and the situation she wanted to avoid for a while longer.

'Please.' Freddie held his hand up to halt her. 'Hear me out.'

'I can't do this right now, Freddie,' Anna said strongly, seething that she had fallen into the trap.

'Well, when can you do this, Anna?' Freddie retorted. 'Because I've been trying to talk to you for two days now and all I get it your voicemail and silence.'

'What do you expect?' Anna said, the emotion she felt beginning to creep into her tone. She stared at the man in front of her, the man she loved with all her heart and soul. Her body ached to be held by him; her mind begged her to give in to whatever platitudes he had in store. But she couldn't.

'I expect you to hear me out.'

Anna snorted. 'Why should I?'

'Because I'm your partner, Anna,' Freddie replied, raising his voice in heartfelt frustration. 'Because we're a team, you and me. And we get through things *together.*'

'And where was this team spirit when you found out you had a son, huh?' Anna shouted, her temper finally flying free. Tears stung her eyes and she blinked them away, refusing to let them fall. 'How long have you known, Freddie?' She stepped forward, her anger mounting. 'A month? A year? Five years? Have you known and kept him a secret for the whole time we've been together? Did it help you get over the loss of our child, Freddie?' She knew her words were barbed now just for the sake of it, but she couldn't help herself. 'Knowing you had another one already to fall back on? Please do tell me. Because I need to know *exactly* how long I've been the mug you've kept separate from your child, from your *family.*'

Freddie recoiled as though he'd been stung. 'Anna, *you* are my family,' he stressed. 'Please—' He reached for her hands but she snatched them away.

'No. Do *not* touch me right now,' Anna said, shaking. She was barely holding the tears at bay and knew if she felt Freddie's warm touch it would push her over the edge.

Freddie ran his hands down his face and took a deep breath. It was killing him, seeing Anna like this. Her words cut him deeply, but he tried not to be angry with her for them. They were thrown out of hurt – he knew she didn't really believe them.

'Listen,' he started again. 'I love you, more than I've ever loved anyone.' Taking the couple of steps away from her to the small sofa at the side of the office, he sat down tiredly. 'I didn't know about Ethan until recently. Yes' – he looked up at her – 'I should have told you straight away and I didn't. I wasn't sure if it was even true at first. I wanted to be sure. I sent them for a paternity test. When it came back positive it was the biggest shock of my life. And I knew it was going to hurt you.' Anna's hand moved subconsciously to her stomach. 'So, I've been putting it off. That was a mistake.'

Anna shook her head miserably. 'We are supposed to be a team.'

'You're right, we are,' Freddie replied. 'Which is why I didn't want to hurt you.'

'Well, you have hurt me, Freddie,' Anna cried. 'Finding out about Ethan would have been hard under any circumstances, yes. But you hiding him from me, keeping secrets about something so huge, that hurts even more. I had to find out from *Jules*,' she said, her voice wobbling. 'Can you imagine how that felt?'

'Actually, yeah, I can. She broke the news pretty hard to me too,' Freddie replied.

Anna closed her eyes. She felt so torn. There was a huge part of her that wanted to ask Freddie how he was feeling, show him support and help him process the fact he was a father. Teamwork went both ways and she knew that he needed her too. But all she could manage to do right now was hide away to prevent herself from falling apart any further than she already had.

'I'm sorry that this has been such a shock for you, really I am,' she said, her voice breaking. 'I know this must be hard for you, in so many ways. But I need a bit of space to get *my* head around everything. Because every time I think about Ethan, I'm right back at that farm losing our baby.' The tears started to fall and this time she didn't bother trying to stop them. 'And then everything else comes back. So, I need to find a way to think about all of this without that happening, before I can be there for you. I hope you can understand that.'

Freddie watched Anna's tears fall, desperate to walk over and hold her. All he wanted to do was make it all better and have her back by his side, but he knew it wasn't that simple.

Nodding slowly, Freddie stood up. 'You know where I am,' he said quietly. 'I'm not going anywhere. Just come home to me when you can, and then I promise you we will sit down and talk this all through before anything goes any further.' He stared at her intently. 'I promise you that, OK? Because I need you with me a hundred per cent, Anna. I need us to be *us*. More than ever.'

Not trusting himself to say anything more, Freddie turned and left the office. As the door closed, Anna crumpled to the floor for the second time that week and cried.

CHAPTER TWENTY-EIGHT

The black Bentley purred gently as it rolled into the turning circle at the front of the Royal Garden Hotel in Kensington. Two liveried doormen rushed forward, one opening the back door to let the occupants out and the other rushing round to instruct the driver where to find the underground parking.

Alfie Ramone stepped out of the car, followed by his brother, and the pair looked up through the revolving glass doors that led to the lobby. A man stood in the shadows just inside, his clothes dark and nondescript. As Alfie's gaze locked with his, he turned and walked away out of sight. Alfie mounted the steps and entered the hotel with purpose.

Andre followed him in and made his way to the front desk to check them in, whilst Alfie looked around for the man. He caught sight of him disappearing again around a doorway that seemed to open out into some sort of lounge area. Leaving his brother to deal with the formalities, Alfie followed him through to the lounge.

Inside there were a number of small tables surrounded by plush chairs, in an airy, opulently decorated space. A piano was being played softly at the back of the room and waiters wandered around serving afternoon tea to the smattering of guests that littered the room. Alfie sat down at a table with the man he'd seen and one other, similarly dressed.

'Lee, Brian,' he greeted the two men with a nod. 'Where's Dan?'

'Tailing Drew,' Lee answered.

'Good.' Alfie's face darkened. 'What's the situation?'

'They're working on a plan to get it back but no luck as yet. We could bring the Tylers in, if you'd prefer going down that route. It's an option.' The Killers had scoped out the situation already and updated Alfie on the parts he hadn't already been clear on.

'Perhaps. But not yet,' Alfie said. 'I want to see how this plays out for a while first. It could be interesting.'

It was Drew's screams he dreamed about filling the air in his special basement, where he took all of the men who had earned their punishment. But that being said, the Tylers had overstepped the mark, big time. That could not be seen to go unchecked. Taking a deep breath, he forced himself to focus on the present. Time would tell which direction this whole mess would go in. Whether it was Drew or whether it was one of the Tylers who ended up slaking his thirst for torture, only time would tell. Perhaps it would be both.

'Are you here for afternoon tea, sir?' one of the waiters asked, hovering politely.

Alfie stared at him. He wanted to tell him to piss off, that there was much more important business than afternoon tea going on at this table. Instead he smiled.

'Sure,' he said. 'Make it for four.'

'Right away, sir.'

As he hurried off, Alfie rolled his eyes. 'Come on then,' he said impatiently. 'Tell me the rest.'

'Drew and the others are in East London, lying low in a small hotel. They don't know we've found them. Jacko's been moving about, seems to still be tailing the Tylers, though pretty badly. He's not keeping the lowest profile.' Lee glanced at Brian, who had remained silent up until this point.

Brian leaned forward. 'I've located a disused barn within thirty minutes' drive, out of hearing range for the closest neighbours, fairly well concealed. Farmer doesn't seem to use it. It's a good spot whenever you're ready.'

Alfie nodded and he felt the familiar flicker of excitement run over his skin. This was the part he loved, the part of his job that he lived for. The art galleries, the cocaine, the money – that was all exciting up to a point, but after so many years in business it had lost its shiny edge. The risk no longer thrilled him the way it used to. The fear on a man's face as he was confronted by his imminent death, however – that did things for him that nothing else in the world could.

'Let's speak to Drew first, let him know that I know where he is.' A cold smile played across his lips. 'Let's watch him squirm and find out if he has any sort of backup plan. Perhaps we can recoup if he does. And if he doesn't…' He shrugged. 'Then we make use of that barn.'

'And the Tylers?'

'Make sure everyone in the underworld knows that we're here to deal with this issue and that we'll treat the Tyler thieves in accordance with underworld law.'

Turning to exchange a loaded glance with his brother, he smiled. 'We didn't step on their turf, and the product is still our property until the debt has been paid. So, we're well within our rights to kill them all. Make sure they know that,' he said, his tone deadly. 'Make sure they know that their time is nearly up.'

CHAPTER TWENTY-NINE

Jules stood just inside the dark, narrow alleyway where she had arranged to meet her old contact. Too long she'd gone without the good things in life, but things were on the up. Finally Freddie had started paying his dues and she knew that there was a lot more where that first payment had come from. For once the kid she'd spawned was more use to her than just the measly few hundred quid he brought in through benefits.

Having Ethan had been a disappointment to Jules in more ways than one. Initially she had planned to get rid of the baby, as per her agreement with Vince. In hindsight, she wished she had just gone ahead with it. But then she'd felt him move and her maternal instincts began to stir.

Ethan's birth had been difficult and traumatic and something Jules had never quite got over. He'd been a sickly baby from the very start, screaming at all hours of the day and night, never satisfied, never content. With no one to help her, Jules had been run ragged and post-natal depression had hit her hard, through the endless nights of sleep deprivation and the long lonely days. She'd grown to despise the creature who had brought her to such a low point, both physically and mentally. Ethan was not the mini-me companion she'd hoped for. When Jules looked at him, all she saw was a leech, sucking the life out of her, day after day.

In the distance Jules could hear the unhealthy chugging of Liam's battered old Ford Fiesta as it sat idling down the road. He was waiting for her there, not wanting to stand out in the cold like Jules had to. She scowled. He really was useless at times, but at least he was there and he was a solid companion through the good times and the bad.

Another sound broke through the chugging and she listened, with her head tilted to one side. It was footsteps coming towards the mouth of the alleyway. Peering out, she grinned eagerly when she saw who it was.

'Long time no see,' said the man in the dark hooded tracksuit. He checked behind himself cautiously. 'It was a surprise hearing from you after all this time, I tell ya.'

'Yeah, well, I've just come back to the area. I'm glad to see you're still in business, Nick.'

'They ain't caught me yet,' he replied, grinning. Two gold teeth gleamed in his neatly set teeth. 'So, what you after?'

'Ket and crack,' Jules answered.

Nick kissed his teeth and raised his eyebrows. 'Straight in at the deep end, I see. Someone's having quite the party.' He chuckled, subtly analysing the woman he hadn't heard from in eight years.

She'd changed a lot. Life had clearly not been kind to her. When he'd known her before she only came to him for recreational drugs for parties. Usually cocaine, sometimes ecstasy. She'd been a stunner back then, all boobs and lips and big blonde hair. Now she looked puffy and stooped, her hair was lank and age had slammed her hard. Eight years ago Nick would have given his right nut to sleep with her, but now he wouldn't touch her with a barge pole. Especially now that she was on the hard stuff. It was a downward spiral once a person started on that. Nick should know – he'd watched his clients slowly circle the drain over the years, one by one. Whilst he was quite happy earning a living from selling the stuff, he wouldn't touch anyone who hit it at that level.

'So how much you want?' he asked, checking the street behind him once more.

'Five or six rocks and three grams,' Jules answered with a bright smile. It had been too long since she'd last hit the good stuff and she was missing it like crazy. The thought of finally relaxing and forgetting her troubles in a haze of ketamine was exciting her beyond belief. The crack would pick her back up tomorrow. She might even go out, hit the dance floor once she'd had a pipe or two. Really live it up for a change. She deserved it, after all.

Nick sorted out a few bags of product, for the amount Jules had asked for, then named his price. Jules eagerly handed over the cash and stuffed the little bags down into her trouser pocket.

'Don't be a stranger now,' Nick said, with a friendly grin. 'I'm here when you want some more, alright? Nick will always look after you.'

Jules preened at his words, mistaking his interest in her custom for interest in her. She flashed what she thought was a flirty smile. 'Like I'd go to anyone else,' she said with a giggle.

Nick hid his disgust behind a cheeky wink. 'See ya around then, gal.'

He held his placid smile as she sashayed her rather round bottom from side to side as she went. As soon as Jules was out of sight the smile dropped to a hard glare. Pulling out his mobile, he quickly made a call. It connected after just two rings.

'I've got something you might want to know about.'

CHAPTER THIRTY

Drew moved the curtain in the window a couple of inches with his little finger and peered out from his spot in the shadows. They would be coming for him soon, for all of them. This much was a certainty. The message he had received last night had confirmed what he'd been praying would not yet happen – Alfie Ramone knew that they no longer had the cocaine.

Within minutes of receiving the text, Drew had gathered his men, checked out of the nice hotel they'd been staying at and had immediately delved into the back streets of the East End. Here they had found a tired-looking B&B run by an old lady with too many cats. She didn't ask for names or credit cards, just an upfront cash payment. Drew hoped that this would buy him some time before the Ramones found them. And time was what he needed.

All this time they had been watching and waiting, hoping to receive a solid confirmation of the location of the caravan. They had followed the Tylers, carefully watching from a distance to work out any patterns or catch any small nuggets of information that might come in useful when they eventually tried to steal their product back. But there had been nothing of use and they were still no closer to solving their issue than they had been a week ago.

Drew wasn't delusional; he knew that the coke pile would already be steadily depleting. But all they needed was half of it to make the money they owed back. At this point, even if they ended up without a penny in profit, he didn't care. He just wanted to fix this mess and be done with it. Alfie Ramone was well known for his love of violence. The man got off on the pain and suffering of others. A man without any kind of emotion and a cold, clinical view of the world, he was as ruthless as they came. It wouldn't matter than Drew had worked with him so efficiently for many years – to Alfie he was just another walking piece of meat who had cost him money. So right now, Drew needed to make damn sure he stopped costing him money.

By now, he assumed, the Killers would have been called. He had watched these men in action before, sat in the office listening as Alfie sent them out on tasks and looked on in horror as they dragged a body through the room, covered in blood. He had never seen anything like it, had almost thrown up on the spot. The memory had kept him up at nights for a long time afterwards.

Jacko sat behind him on one of the narrow twin beds, his back against the wall. 'This is fucking ridiculous,' he said. 'We need to stop pissing about and just get on with it. Who cares if they know we're after it? We should have struck as soon as we got wind of that scrapyard.'

'We don't know for certain it's there,' Drew answered, not turning around.

'Yes, we do,' Jacko responded, frustrated.

'There are talks of it being seen out east at one of their barns. There are also whispers of a basement in one of the clubs.' Drew took a deep drag on his cigarette and exhaled it through his nose. 'If we hit the wrong one they'll know we're coming and double the protection. And we can't hit all three at once – we don't have the manpower.'

'They won't be so stupid as to keep it in the club,' Jacko replied.

'Probably not,' Drew conceded.

'And I think the barn rumour was set to throw us off. No one mentioned anything about the barn until recently.'

Drew nodded. Jacko had a point.

'We need to move. Now,' Jacko pushed. 'We need to go for the scrapyard, hope it's there and take it back. What else can we do? Sit and wait to die?'

'No,' Drew said firmly, shaking his head. 'We are not doing that.' Stubbing his cigarette out on the window ledge, he turned around. 'Fuck it. Tell the boys we're going tonight. Midnight.'

Jacko stared off blankly into the distance for a few moments, lost in thought.

'Hey,' Drew snapped. 'Did you hear me?'

'I did, yeah.' Jacko tuned back in, a strange expression on his face. 'I need to go out. I'll be back by tonight.'

'Where you going?' Drew frowned.

'If this goes tits up we're going to need a fallback plan.' He grabbed his jacket and his lips formed a hard line. 'I'm going to go set one up.'

CHAPTER THIRTY-ONE

Sarah tapped her pen on the notepad in front of her as she stared at the back of Holly's head across the room. She still hadn't been able to unearth any further information on the boyfriend and it was bothering her. There had been no Roddy in her friend list on Facebook, or Instagram or any other social-media channel. There was no Rod or Roderick either. She'd searched for every possible link she could think of but nothing came close. From what she could gather, Holly didn't talk about him in the office and kept him well away from her civilian friends too. It was almost as though he didn't exist.

Ben Hargreaves walked into the office and up to Sarah Riley's desk. She looked up and filed away her thoughts on Roddy for later.

'Riley, how are things going?' Ben cut straight to the point, like always. He sat on the end of the desk next to her, which was currently vacant. Picking up a ball of elastic bands that had been left in a paper tray, he began to fiddle with it as he waited for Sarah to update him.

'Pretty much the same at the moment, sir,' she replied. 'We've gathered a few more bits of intel but nothing useful. They're getting better and better at covering their tracks.'

'Well, then we need to get better at *uncovering* them, don't we?' Ben answered. He turned to address the rest of the room. 'Come on, what have we got? You aren't paid to sit here braiding each other's hair and drinking tea; you're here to catch criminals. What's the new intel?'

Adam caught Sarah's eye from across the room and she gave him a nod to go ahead. He stood up and stepped forward.

'There's a new crew in town. Northerners, a Manchester firm, following the Tylers around for some reason. They're into the drugs trade and seem to have their fingers in a few other pies back home, but nothing that connects them to London, so at the moment we're still trying to work out what they're here for.'

'What do you mean *following*?' Ben asked.

'They don't seem to be in direct contact with the Tylers, but they have been tailing them here and there, watching their movements.' Adam pulled an expression of uncertainty, a deep frown settling on his forehead. 'I don't think they're here to challenge them – there's only five of them, one barely more than a kid. They don't seem to know their way about the city either.'

'Find out more about them,' Ben ordered curtly. 'What else have we got?'

'I managed to get a tracker onto Freddie Tyler's car,' a voice piped up at the back of the room.

Sarah's head swivelled towards Holly as she walked forward towards them. Her gaze narrowed slightly and Holly returned the expression defiantly, before switching her attention back to Ben. Sarah clamped her jaw shut, annoyed. Although Holly was too intelligent to fully cross the line, she was getting harder to control. She was a loose cannon and it was making Sarah more and more uneasy.

'And?' prompted Ben.

'And the very same day, Anna Davis began using it. They switched cars.' Holly's big blue eyes flickered over at Sarah with exaggerated innocence. 'It was almost like they knew.'

'They may well have done,' Ben replied.

Sarah tensed and she felt her heart almost stop in her chest. Her fingers grew cold and she suppressed a shiver. *Did Ben suspect that there was a mole in the task force?*

'It's not exactly hard to get hold of a bug tracker these days,' he continued. Sarah breathed out slowly in relief. 'After finding your bugs in his office' – Ben glared at her accusingly – 'I would imagine he does routine checks.'

Holly's cheeks burned scarlet and she stepped back, looking down. Sarah hid a smug smile.

'Is that all you've got?' Ben looked around questioningly.

'For now,' Sarah said eventually. 'They're going to do a huge digital push this week, and get a few people on the ground around their known hubs.'

'Be cautious with that,' Ben warned. 'The last thing we need is another shitty harassment accusation from their lawyers. If they keep barking up that tree I'll be forced to put on a limiter. And that will be the final nail in the coffin at the rate you're going.'

Sarah's attention perked up at Ben's words. Perhaps this was her way out of this whole thing. She'd heard of limiters causing teams to shut down open cases before. It was rare, but it did happen.

If a member of the public who was under investigation made enough legal complaints of harassment, their lawyer could insist that the team responsible show enough evidence to support it as a valid case within a certain amount of time. If the time limit was reached without a solid case, the team were forced to abandon it or face legal action against them for unjust harassment. It would make the Tylers pretty much untouchable – for a while at least.

Sitting back in her chair, she played absent-mindedly with the long pendant hanging over her crisp white blouse. Ben Hargreaves had unwittingly just given her exactly what she needed. A small smile made its way onto her face, as for the first time in a long time Sarah could see the light at the end of the tunnel for them all.

CHAPTER THIRTY-TWO

Freddie banged on the thin front door of Jules's flat and waited, cocking his ear to listen. The chilled-out tones of Fleetwood Mac drifted out to him, but other than that there was nothing. He banged again, harder this time.

'Jules?' he called, trying to keep his tone light, despite the fury that was mounting inside of him. 'Jules, I know you're in there. Open up.'

Leaning in, Freddie put his ear right up against the hollow wood and stilled his breathing.

The smooth melody of 'Little Lies' was the only thing he could hear within. He waited. *Thunk.*

The sound was soft but it was closer than the music. It sounded like it was just the other side of the door. Freddie exhaled through his nose and closed his eyes for a moment.

'Ethan?' he called in as soft a voice as he could. 'Is that you?'

There was a shuffling sound, as if someone was moving closer.

'Can you open the door, mate? It's your – er.' He paused, unsure what to call himself. 'It's Freddie.' He waited. Nothing happened. 'Was the pizza nice, the other night? Did it come with the pepperoni and ham, how you like it?'

The sound of the latch being taken off scratched across the door and Freddie stood back. As it opened, Ethan's gaunt little face peered round fearfully.

'I'm not supposed to open the door,' he whispered.

'That's OK, mate.' Freddie slowly but firmly pushed his way inside before Ethan could close it again. 'It's only me; I'm a friend.'

'You're my dad,' Ethan replied, with childish simplicity.

'Well, yeah. I am,' Freddie replied.

They stood and stared at each other for a few moments, each unsure as to what to say next. The song changed and Freddie looked over towards the lounge.

'I'm supposed to stay in my room,' Ethan said, the fear back in his eyes.

Freddie nodded slowly. 'Yeah, probably best to go back there for now, mate. Go on.' He gave him an encouraging smile and waited until he'd gone and the door was closed.

Entering the lounge, Freddie was immediately filled with shock and rage. When he'd got the call from Nick telling him that Jules had scored off him just that morning, he hadn't been hugely surprised, but seeing her like this with Ethan in the house was something else entirely.

Jules lay passed out on the sofa, a bloke Freddie assumed must be her boyfriend sprawled across her, only half dressed. The neglect in the room was at a more terrible level than ever except for the coffee table. Whatever had been piled up on there previously had now been removed so they had a clean surface to party on. A heap of little bags sat to one side, one of them open, a fine white powder spilling out into a mess on the clear surface. A card and two rolled-up notes lay nearby, evidence that whatever it was had been snorted. Judging by the comatose-like state of the pair, Freddie put his bets on this being the ketamine. They'd be out of it for hours.

His anger warred with a feeling of horrified sorrow. How could she do this with Ethan in the house? He was just a kid; he shouldn't have to see his mother getting off her head in the next room. And what if he'd picked some up to try himself? Freddie shuddered at the thought.

It had been just a few days since Freddie had known for sure that he was even a father. It was still new information that he was trying to process and now he had this to contend with too. He ran his hands through his hair, for once at a total loss as to what was the right thing to do. The new father within him wanted to beat seven bells out of Jules and protect Ethan from her at all costs, now that he'd seen her parenting skills in all their glory. But Freddie Tyler, the guy who had only just been introduced to this situation, was urging caution. Ethan didn't even know him and Jules was his mother. Was it right to just drag him off and call the shots? What rights did he even have at this point?

The music took a more upbeat turn as the first few bars of 'Go Your Own Way' chimed out and Jules's slack face morphed slowly into a smile of joy. Freddie watched, still not able to understand how she could forget her son so cruelly.

Looking around the room once more, his eyes clocking the mouldering plates to the side, the beer cans everywhere and the overflowing ashtrays amongst the dirt, Freddie made a decision. With one last hateful glare at the passed-out woman, he marched back down the hallway to Ethan's closed bedroom door. Knocking, he waited a beat before he opened it himself.

'Listen, mate…' Freddie looked around the tiny room. It was barely bigger than a closet, but that wasn't what stopped him in his tracks. One side had overflowing boxes of junk piled up from floor to ceiling. Against one wall there was an old dressing table with a cracked mirror holding up the peeling wallpaper and in the corner was a single mattress on the floor, upon which Ethan sat, hugging his knees to his chest. With no sheets to protect against the stained, greying mattress, all Ethan had was one pillow, a thin blanket and a small stuffed dog, which he had positioned to sit next to him.

'You're going to come and stay with me for a little while,' Freddie said firmly. If he had been warring with himself before, he wasn't now. 'Is that OK with you?'

Two grand he'd handed Jules. With that she could have at least got Ethan some sheets, some clothes, started to sort their lives out if that's what she'd wanted to do. That was what she'd *said* she needed money for. Instead she'd shut Ethan away in what was basically a cupboard, her seven-year-old son, and got high in the next room. What kind of mother did that?

Ethan's face lit up with hope. 'Yeah, 'course. We going right now?' He scrambled up from his spot on the bed and grabbed his stuffed dog. Seeing Freddie's eyes flicker to the dirty mattress once more, his cheeks reddened and he tried to hide it with the blanket.

'Hey, it's OK. It's not your fault,' Freddie said, frowning. 'Come on. We're going.'

He held his hand out and Ethan took it trustingly, without a second thought. Holding the boy's soft little hand in his own pulled at Freddie's heartstrings and he wondered again at a mother who could treat him the way Jules did. He led Ethan out of the flat and down towards his car.

As they walked, Freddie was reminded of his promise to Anna and guilt flooded through him. He had promised her that when she was ready they would talk, and that nothing would go any further until they had discussed things. He closed his eyes. Now, more than ever he needed to keep his promises to her, but at the same time he couldn't leave Ethan in that flat. It was child abuse. He prayed that Anna would understand, once he explained.

Noticing Ethan shiver as they walked out in the cold, he realised he hadn't even thought to find his coat. He shrugged off his jacket and draped it around his son's shoulders.

'Here you are,' he said. 'Don't worry. We'll go out first thing tomorrow and get you some stuff.'

'That's OK. Marshall's all I need,' Ethan said, hugging the stuffed dog tightly.

Freddie swallowed and didn't say any more, not trusting his emotions. Jules had come back to London to wheedle money out of him, to use Ethan as a pawn to get funding for her sordid lifestyle. She clearly hadn't counted on him finding out what sort of games she was really playing behind closed doors. She'd underestimated him, expecting that he'd pay over whatever she asked in return for being left alone. But that wasn't Freddie. The moment he'd found out that there was a child out there born of *his* blood, he'd made the decision to properly get involved. And now Jules was going to get a lot more than she'd bargained for.

Because whether she was his mother or not, there was no way Freddie was going to let her ruin Ethan's life with drugs and neglect. No matter what he had to do to stop her.

CHAPTER THIRTY-THREE

Drew ran around the east side of the perimeter fence, keeping his head low and his movements as silent as possible. He reached Jacko.

'You find anything?' he asked, in a whisper.

'Nah, nothing. Richie and Skidders haven't either – it's all clear,' Jacko replied.

Drew narrowed his eyes. 'Why is that?'

'What do you mean? The old man's gone home for the night is all. It's midnight.' Jacko shrugged.

'Where are the dogs? They had dogs here before.' Something wasn't quite right; it was too quiet.

'I don't know, maybe they were just here because they thought we were a threat before. Perhaps because we haven't tried anything they've let their guard down.'

Drew's jaw formed a hard line. Something was off, but they still needed to get the job done. He wished for the hundredth time they were dealing with this back in Manchester, back on their own turf. There, they wouldn't be swallowing this shit. There they would have already beaten those Southern thieves to a bloody pulp and made them watch as they took back everything that was theirs, and then some. But they weren't in Manchester. They were in London, outnumbered in an unfriendly territory.

'Come on. It ain't going to take itself, is it?' Jacko said irritably. 'Shall I signal the others?'

The others were hiding around the other side, having done their own planned checks too. Drew nodded.

Jacko whistled. Aside from not wanting to die, Jacko had big plans for his future and that all started with this batch of cocaine. He didn't want to be working under Drew forever, especially now. He'd changed.

In all the years Jacko had looked up to Drew, he'd never stepped away from a fight. It didn't matter how big or small the problem was, Drew had always gone in head first, guns blazing, and got things done. If someone was ever stupid enough to stand in their way, they were bulldozed down. Yet here they were being treated like absolute mugs and Drew was just pussyfooting around. If it had been up to him, he'd have gone and shown those London wide boys who was boss by now. They weren't all that, in his mind. Just because they dressed smart and had got one over them at the gypsy site, didn't mean they were any bigger or smarter than anyone else.

Three shadows moved along the ground towards the gate from the other side and Jacko ran forward to meet them. Drew followed, pausing whilst one of them used the bolt cutters and pulled the gates open just wide enough for them to slip through.

As they entered, Drew held his hand up to signal them to stop. He was eager to get on but there was definitely something not quite right about this. Why was it so easy to get in? This was one of the Tylers' businesses and the Tylers were not just anyone. They were dangerous people who played at much higher stakes than Drew did.

'Drew?'

Drew heard the hard edge of annoyance in Jacko's whispered tone and exhaled in frustration. Jacko didn't understand how delicate the situation they were in currently was. If they pissed off the Tylers too much, they would end up dead. If they didn't get their product back and sell enough to pay the Ramones soon, they would end up dead. They were walking a fine line through the middle of hell, and their chances of getting through unscathed were thin at best. They had to play this exactly right.

Pushing forward, Drew signalled for them all to follow him. Luckily it was a clear night and the full moon shone down over the piles of scrap metal and car parts, sending long, distorted shadows across the ground. Drew darted from pile to pile, peering around each one as he moved deeper into the maze-like yard. As he rounded a small mountain of rusting Ford carcasses, his eyes rested on the large white caravan parked up in the middle.

'Bingo,' he muttered, his mouth curling upward in a cold smile.

Jacko gave a chortle of excitement and rushed forward. Cursing under his breath, Drew followed him.

'Hey!' He grabbed his shoulder as they approached the vehicle. 'We haven't checked this out yet, it might be a trap.'

'What are you talking about?' Jacko shrugged him off. 'It's right here – we've bloody got it. Why are you being such a…' Seeing the dangerous flash in Drew's eye, Jacko trailed off.

'Such a what, Jacko?' Drew asked in a deadly voice, stepping forward into his friend's face.

'Nothing,' Jacko backtracked. 'Mate, nothing.' He forced an uneasy grin. 'I just think we should be happy, that's all. We've found it – we've got back what's ours.'

'Have we?' Drew asked, raising his eyebrows in question.

Jacko opened his mouth to speak but another, deeper voice cut through the silence.

'He's right, you have.'

Drew whirled around to see Paul walking up behind them in the dim light of the moon. Behind him were four other men, each of them large and unfriendly looking, two with guns held casually by their sides.

'Ah, shit,' Steve cried in surprise, before moving to stand a little closer to his boss.

Drew groaned. He *knew* this had been too easy. They'd walked right into the lion's den, though for the life of him he couldn't understand how the Tylers had known they were coming tonight.

And they must have known, because surely Paul Tyler had much better things to do with his nights than sit around a scrapyard waiting for them on the off chance they might show up. No, they knew.

Paul reached where they were standing and casually sat on the top of an upturned metal barrel. He smiled coldly at Drew.

'Well, what are you waiting for?' he asked. 'Aren't you going to take it?'

Jacko and Richie exchanged glances, but Drew kept his eyes trained on Paul. This was a trap; there was a catch. What was it?

'Oh!' Paul pulled an exaggerated expression of forgetfulness. 'Your keys.' He fished in his jacket pocket and pulled them out, chucking them over to Jacko. 'There you go. You're all set.'

Jacko glanced from Paul to Drew and then shrugged, before turning to walk towards the caravan.

'Wait,' Drew ordered, his tone cold. Jacko paused. Paul's gaze met Drew's, his smiling eyes filled with amusement. Drew narrowed his own, suspiciously. 'Why would you let us leave with it?'

'It's yours.' Paul shrugged. 'When we heard you were coming for it, we figured we might as well give you the keys back, save you breaking in.'

Drew's brain was racing. This wasn't right; they were up to something. But what?

'And how *did* you hear we were coming, exactly?'

'Now that,' Paul said with a grin, 'would be telling.' The grin dropped. 'And we don't tell wannabes our business.' Paul's tone was now cold, the pretence of friendliness gone.

There was a tense few moments of silence as Drew tried to work out how best to proceed. Eventually, not taking his eyes off Paul, he grabbed the keys out of Jacko's hand. Turning away reluctantly, he marched over to the caravan and opened the door, then stepped inside and began to search throughout. It took him less than a minute to confirm that every single last brick of cocaine had already been taken out.

Crouching down in the dark inside where no one could see him, Drew grasped his hair in both hands and squeezed his eyes shut. They were done for. He'd known they would already be circulating the product, but by his calculation at the rate it would sell, they wouldn't yet be halfway through it. He'd assumed – or perhaps it was just blind hope – that they would only remove what they were using at the time. But they hadn't. They'd moved whatever they hadn't yet used on to another location under the radar. There was no way they would ever find it now. Not in a city they didn't know, whose people were loyal to the Tylers.

Pulling a deep breath of air in through his teeth, Drew straightened up. He walked back out. His men were standing warily, watching Paul and his men. Everyone was silent as they waited for Drew to reappear. He walked back over to Paul and stared at him for a moment.

'What are you waiting for?' Paul asked, a hard edge to his voice. 'You've got your van back.'

Drew licked his lips slowly. 'I'm waiting for my product,' he answered. 'The deal I offered is still on the table. I can make a connection for you; I just want enough back to pay my debts. That's all.'

As he uttered each carefully contained syllable, Drew felt his anger grow stronger. He wanted to leap across the dark yard and tear into Paul Tyler, but he couldn't. He knew it was this lack of violent action that was angering Jacko so much and he didn't blame him. But that wasn't a viable option in the position they were trapped in right now.

Paul shook his head. 'The product is gone, mate. You knew the price if you wanted to take the chance. You played the game and you lost. That's what happens when you try to take down people who are bigger than you.'

Paul looked around at the men in front of him. He held no sympathy for them at all. They had been prepared to screw over him and Freddie and everyone in their employ without a second thought. Why should he care about them now?

Not trusting himself to say another word, Drew clicked his fingers and marched back out the way they'd entered. Jacko debated it for a moment before following. He'd realised the second Drew had come out that the coke had gone. The Tylers were playing with them, letting them know they were one step ahead and taunting them with the empty van. Jacko wanted Drew to lose his temper and go for them, but he hadn't, and Jacko wasn't stupid enough to think he could take them on by himself. With a growl of frustration he followed his boss out.

Paul watched them go with a smile of amusement. This should finally show them that they'd lost and make them give up. They could finally get back to their own problems and stop having to worry about this crew's next move. Dean stepped forward to his side.

'You sure you want to let them go? We could get rid of them tonight,' he said.

'Nah.' Paul shook his head. 'Leave them; they're done. There are others already on the warpath. Let them take care of the mess.'

Bill nodded in agreement. He'd received a call earlier in the day from Zack. He'd been listening in on Drew's phone and had hacked through so that he could listen to conversations through the microphone even when the phone wasn't being used. He'd heard them decide they were coming tonight and had immediately informed Bill. Unable to reach Freddie, Bill had called Paul and they'd come up with this plan.

Jacko finally caught up with Drew as they exited through the front gate. He rounded on his boss, finally tipping over the edge.

'What the fuck are you doing?' he demanded.

'What do you mean, what am I doing?' Drew growled, already stressed to the max. He could do without Jacko's shit right now.

'Back there! Where's the Drew from Manchester gone, eh?' Jacko squared up to Drew. 'All we've done down here is get fucking whipped. They're laughing in our fucking faces.'

'Enough!' Drew roared, pushing Jacko backward hard. Jacko hadn't been expecting it and fell to the ground. Drew leaned over him, fire in his eyes. 'We're completely and utterly screwed, Jacko, don't you get that? If we make so much as one wrong move, more so than we already have, they will kill us. I'm actually surprised they haven't already. These are not some fucking street fighters gunning for an argument; these aren't territorial gangs guarding their block – these are the *Tylers*. They run the biggest city in the country and we've been caught trying to fuck them over.' He ran his hands over his face, stressed. 'We should never have even tried it. I fucked up. But now here we are – and we aren't here to fight with them, we're here to try and keep our fucking hearts beating. Why can't you get that through your thick skull?'

Jacko stood up, his expression still furious. 'What I get,' he said, 'is that we need to get out of this mess and the only way to do that is to force those Southern fuckers to give us our product back. And if you don't have the balls to make them, then I will.' With a determined glare, Jacko turned and walked away.

'What do you mean, you will?'

'Exactly what I say,' Jacko shot back over his shoulder. 'And unlike you, I don't care if I have to get my hands dirty to do it.'

CHAPTER THIRTY-FOUR

Tanya reached the front door of the flat Freddie shared with Anna and hesitated. The key was in her hand. Usually she'd just let herself in, but with everything that was going on and with the clear divide between Anna and Freddie, she felt awkward waltzing in as though it was just another normal day. Plus, the last time she'd come here, she'd slapped Freddie around the face. Although it had been entirely warranted, she wasn't sure he'd quite forgiven her for it yet. Dropping the key into her bag, she pushed her hair back and knocked, standing back to wait.

Freddie opened the door, his face drawn as though he hadn't slept, his stance tense. He blinked, surprised to see her there.

'Sorry it's so early, but Anna needs some things. I've come to get them,' Tanya said.

'Oh, er…' Freddie glanced inside and then back to Tanya, his arm barring her entrance. 'It's not the best time.'

Tanya frowned. 'Is someone here?' she asked sharply.

Without waiting for an answer Tanya pushed him out of the way and marched down the hallway. She turned to glare at him before heading through to their bedroom.

Freddie suddenly realised what she was looking for. 'Oh my God, Tanya, are you fucking *serious*?' he cried. 'As if I would ever do that to Anna. How could you even think that?'

Tanya stopped short as she reached the bedroom door and closed her eyes. He was right – what was she thinking? She rubbed her forehead, stressed.

'I'm sorry,' she said, swivelling round and walking back towards him. Freddie shut the front door and faced her, annoyed. 'I'm sorry; I don't know why I just did that. Of course no one's here. It was just the way you were peering behind you, it looked—'

'Like I had someone in here. Which I do,' he fumed, still angry that Tanya could think he would cheat on Anna.

'What?' Tanya asked, blinking.

'In there,' Freddie said, pointing towards the kitchen.

She turned and moved to see who he was talking about and her jaw dropped in surprise as she saw the young boy sitting at the breakfast bar, clutching his small stuffed toy to his chest. His wide, solemn eyes appraised her and she stared back at him, not sure what to say.

'Now if you don't mind, I'm going to continue getting dressed,' Freddie said, irritably.

Tanya turned to look at him and realised for the first time that Freddie was in nothing more than a pair of boxers and a T-shirt. 'Oh. Yeah, probably best,' she said. 'Don't think you'd be very warm out there in that.'

Freddie rolled his eyes and walked off. Tanya turned with a cheeky smile back to the boy who was quietly tittering with laughter at her comment. In a carefully casual manner, Tanya sidled into the kitchen and along to the large American fridge. She pulled out the orange juice and two glasses before turning to Ethan with a raised eyebrow.

'Want some?' she asked.

He nodded and she poured them each a large glass. Handing one over to him, she sat on the other side of the breakfast bar and watched as he took a deep drink.

'I'm Tanya, one of Freddie's mates,' she said.

'I'm Ethan. He's my dad,' Ethan replied.

'So, you've come for a visit, have you?'

'Yeah, well, I think so,' Ethan answered, fiddling with the paw of his toy dog. 'Not sure how long for.'

'I see. Did your mum bring you over?' Tanya asked, wondering if Jules had yet wormed her way into the flat.

'No. She was having her special medicine at home and I was supposed to be in the bedroom, but then my dad knocked on the door, and I wasn't supposed to answer' – his cheeks coloured in guilt – 'but I did and he took me away. I don't think she knows I'm gone. But she won't mind. She likes it when I'm gone.'

Tanya felt a chill run through her at Ethan's words. She was pretty sure she understood exactly what that all meant. 'What's your mum's special medicine like, Ethan?' she asked carefully.

'I'm not sure. It looks a bit like sugar or flour and it makes her happy and sometimes she sleeps a lot.' He sighed, his mouth and eyes turning downward.

Tanya's heart began to hurt for the boy as her suspicions were confirmed. Jules was a junkie. And judging by the state of Ethan, she was going the way the rest of them did. She noticed the thin arms and the unhealthy complexion. He looked clean and his hair was slightly damp, so she assumed he'd just showered, but that couldn't hide everything.

'You know, when I was little, my mum liked it when I was out of the way too,' she said, allowing the memories that she usually kept locked away come through.

'Really?' Ethan said, glancing up at her before lowering his gaze again.

'Yeah.' Tanya nodded. 'She used to tell me off a lot.' Tanya felt a small prickle at the side of her eyes and blinked rapidly. No way was she ever going to cry over that woman again. 'So, I get it.'

There was a long silence before Ethan spoke again. Tanya let him take his time, knowing how hard it was for a child to voice the things they naturally try to hide.

'My mum tells me off a lot too. Sometimes it hurts. I don't think she means it, though – she just gets angry.' Ethan licked his lips as if nervous that he'd said too much.

Tanya could see the internal battle and she smiled sadly. His mum had probably told him it was his job to protect her and that he was never to say bad things about her. She'd been through those mixed emotions too. It was no load that any child should have to bear. Though sadly far too many did.

'How does she hurt you, Ethan?' She waited but he remained silent. 'It's OK; I'm not going to tell anyone. Not even your dad.'

'Promise?' he asked, still wary.

'Promise.' She watched him bite his lip. Undoing the top button of her blouse, Tanya pulled it down over one shoulder. 'See this?' She pointed to a thin silvery scar that ran down onto her arm. 'One time, I accidentally knocked over my mum's bottle of gin. She was so mad at me that she grabbed me by the hair and threw me onto the floor, telling me to clean it up. I landed on the broken glass and it stuck into my shoulder. The scar never went away.' She buttoned her blouse back up.

Ethan pulled the sleeve of his T-shirt up over his own shoulder, revealing a set of long, ugly black bruises in the shape of Jules's fingers. Tanya had to stifle a gasp. 'My mum never did that but she sometimes hits me or grabs me a bit hard if I get in the way. But' – he rolled the sleeve back down – 'they always go away.'

Tanya nodded. The situation with Jules was more complicated than anyone could have imagined. She cleared her throat. 'Have you had breakfast yet?'

'Not yet, Dad was going to get it after he got dressed.'

'OK.' Tanya jumped down and opened the cupboard where she knew the cereals were kept. 'Let's have a look then. What do you fancy?'

*

Outside the kitchen door, Freddie stood to the side just out of sight listening to the conversation with a sinking heart. He ran his hand over his face. Ethan had told Tanya in confidence, so he couldn't address it. But he was going to have to do something. The question was, though, what was that something going to be?

*

Seamus walked up to the front door of the big warehouse gym and paused, wondering why it was already unlocked. The lights were on too, he realised as he opened it. He frowned and walked inside, looking around to see who was already there before him. This was a very unusual occurrence, seeing as it wasn't even open to the public before 8 a.m. He made use of the early peace and quiet to get additional training in.

Dull thumps sounded over from the big boxing ring that was his domain and a look of recognition passed over his face as he saw who it was, punching the life out of the bag hanging in the middle. Walking over, Seamus slung his backpack to the ground, unzipped and threw off his hoody, then hopped up into the ring. He arranged his stance to take the blows and moved forward to hold the bag still.

'You're too straight – move your feet,' he instructed.

Anna did as Seamus said, not taking her eyes off the bag. She hit out again, putting her weight behind each punch.

'Lift your arm. That's it.' Seamus watched her correct herself and appraised her critically. There were rings around her eyes and she looked pale. A sheen of sweat covered the parts of her body he could see and her energy was depleting. She'd been here a while already. 'OK, give me a combo. Right, left, right, right, upper cut.'

Anna did this, grunting with the exertion.

'Again,' he barked. 'Faster, three times.'

Gritting her teeth, Anna pushed forward, speeding up and fighting with all she had.

'Come on, again. Faster.'

Feral cries escaped Anna's mouth as she carried on through the exhaustion. She continued, never slowing, giving every single last drop of her energy over and over until eventually, with a loud cry, she pulled back and stopped.

She leaned over onto her knees and caught her breath as Seamus let go of the bag. He walked over to the corner and picked up the bottle of water she'd put there earlier.

'Here,' he said, giving it to her. 'Sit down a minute, catch your breath.'

She nodded her thanks and sat down, drinking deeply from the bottle. Seamus leaned back against the ropes next to her.

'It's pretty early for you to be here, isn't it?' he asked.

'Couldn't sleep.' Anna gave him a tired smile. 'Sorry, I hope I haven't disturbed your morning routine.'

'No, it's fine,' Seamus replied. 'What's stealing your sleep?'

'Oh, just…' Anna blew out a long breath, unsure what to even say.

She'd not been sleeping well anyway with everything going on, and tossing and turning in Tanya's spare bed each night was just making her yearn to be back home next to Freddie. She missed the intimacy between them, the love, the special bond they shared. She'd lain awake for most of the night feeling cold and alone and warring with her demons. Eventually, as the weak morning sun began to creep up into the sky, she'd given up trying to sleep and decided to come and fight it out instead.

'There's just a lot on my mind at the moment,' she said finally.

Seamus nodded slowly. 'I hear ya.' He glanced over at her, measuring his words carefully. 'This world is so full of stress and strain, eh? Thank the good Lord that he gave us each other, to help us get through it.' He reached over the edge of the ring and grabbed the straps of his bag, hoisting it up. Reaching in, Seamus pulled out his bandages and began wrapping his hands. 'Now

I'd ask you to hold the bag for me like I do for you, but I don't fancy sending you flying across the room now. I'm sure Freddie wouldn't take too kindly to me leaving you black and blue. He'd have my neck, being so fond of you and all.' He winked jovially.

Anna laughed politely, wondering how much Seamus actually knew. The jibe was there, however softly it was positioned. He'd most likely know about Ethan by now. And he'd know that Anna wasn't staying at home; he was around the house often and the boy didn't miss a thing. With quiet reserve and a sharp eye, Seamus was shaping up to be one of Freddie's most loyal and efficient men.

'Freddie's lucky to have you, Seamus,' Anna said.

Seamus looked up from his binding and flexed one hand to see if he'd gone tight enough. 'He's lucky to have you too, Anna. A man needs the love of a good woman in his life. Especially when life is as tough as his is.'

There was a silence as Anna cast her gaze away and Seamus secured his second hand. He pulled his gloves on.

'Anyway,' he said, changing the subject. 'You're getting quicker on those sets. I may have to move things up a notch if training's going to continue challenging you. When you come tonight I'll sort out some new ideas.'

Anna stood up from the corner stool. 'Sure, sounds good,' she said. 'Catch you later then.'

Leaving Seamus to his morning session, Anna jumped down and walked towards the exit. If she had hoped to feel better for her spontaneous boxing session, she had not achieved her goal. Usually it cleared her head and pushed away her demons, but that was the problem – Freddie wasn't a demon. Aside from Tanya and the clubs, he was everything she loved in this world.

Shivering as she stepped into the early-morning chill, Anna took a deep breath and sighed. It didn't matter what she did or how hard she worked, there was just something missing, a part of her soul that couldn't be replaced without Freddie. She needed him like she needed oxygen, and it was killing her staying away. But could she go back and move on from the secrets and ignore the new living reminder of her failings as a woman? Could she look into the eyes of a little boy who was Freddie's and not hers?

CHAPTER THIRTY-FIVE

Thea's eyes widened and her hand flew to her open mouth as her eyes darted back and forth between Ethan and Freddie. When he'd woken her up early and asked her to come over urgently, she'd not known exactly what to expect, but after years of working in the family business she'd assumed she would be walking into a newly acquired business with dodgy paperwork or perhaps a few bruises to clean up and an alibi to learn. She hadn't expected in a million years to be faced with a new seven-year-old nephew.

'What the hell, Freddie?' she said finally, in a squeaky voice through her fingers.

'Hey, language?' he replied with a stern look.

'Oh, right, yeah. Sorry, mate,' Thea said to Ethan, shaking her head to try and dispel her shock.

'That's OK,' he replied with a shrug. 'My mum says a lot worse.'

'And who exactly is your mum, Ethan?' Thea asked, with a concerned look at Freddie.

'That can wait until later.' Freddie headed off the conversation and guided Ethan back into the lounge where *Paw Patrol* was currently blaring out of the television. 'You chill out, mate. I've just got to pop out for a bit, but Auntie Thea's going to stay with you until I'm back. Is that OK?'

'I am?' Thea asked.

'You are,' Freddie confirmed.

Ethan eyed Thea warily and she quickly picked up on his underlying fear. She took a deep breath and smiled kindly. Holding her hand out, she winked.

'Well, we'd better get better acquainted then, hadn't we? I'm your auntie Thea and I'm *very* pleased to meet you. I'm also super fun and I'm going to let you have all the chocolate you want.'

Immediately Ethan grinned. 'I don't usually have chocolate, but I like it lots.'

Freddie frowned. 'Er, he's only just had breakfast…'

'Well, we'll just have to pop to the shop and buy it all up for later on then, won't we, Ethan?' Thea said. Ethan nodded eagerly.

'OK, well, thanks, Thea,' Freddie said gratefully. 'I shouldn't be too long, an hour or so. Just, whatever you do, don't tell anyone. Especially Mum.'

'Ho-*hooo*-no.' Thea belly laughed, shaking her head and raising her eyebrows. 'I wouldn't *dream* of jumping on that landmine. That conversation is *all* yours, brother.'

'Yeah, thanks,' Freddie replied sarcastically.

'Just promise you'll fill me in when you get back, OK?' Thea said. 'This is… well, it's huge.'

'Tell me about it,' Freddie replied, looking back at Ethan. He was once more engrossed in his programme, curled up on the sofa in one of Freddie's gym T-shirts and hugging the stuffed dog that he wouldn't put down. 'See you in a bit.'

'Well, Ethan,' Freddie heard Thea say as he walked out the door. 'I just want you to know that everything you think is cool about your dad, he learned from me…'

Freddie shook his head with a small smile as the door shut behind him and silently thanked the heavens for having family around him that he could trust.

*

Twenty minutes later Freddie stood outside Jules's front door once more. He took a deep breath and composed himself as best he could. All was quiet within and he doubted that the pair of drugged-up lovebirds had even risen for the day yet. The thought that if he hadn't intervened Ethan would still be in there, cramped up in that tiny room with no food or parental care, ate away at him. The sight of the dark bruises Jules had inflicted still burned the inside of his eyelids. He squeezed his fists as the anger threatened to take over once more.

The boy had been slowly starving and had eaten enough to feed a small army before passing out exhausted in Freddie's bed last night. Freddie himself had slept on the couch. He made a mental note to sort out a proper bed for Ethan today. Their spare room was used as an office, so they weren't exactly kitted out for unexpected guests.

He knocked loudly on the door and waited as someone slowly shuffled through to the hall.

'Who is it?' a groggy, wary voice called out.

'It's Freddie. Let me in. I want to see Ethan.' He kept his tone carefully neutral. He heard Jules pause.

'It's a bit early, Freddie. Can't you come back later?'

'No, I can't.' It came out sharper than intended and he softened his words a little. 'I want to take him out for the day, to the zoo perhaps, or something like that.' It was winter, but Freddie hadn't had time to sort out a more viable story. Luckily Jules was too hungover to be suspicious.

'Well…' He heard her whispering to the boyfriend to clear away the drugs and bit back the urge to smash down the door, and Jules with it. 'Give me a minute, yeah? I'm not dressed.'

Freddie waited as she moved away and could picture the frantic tidy-up of the lounge as he listened to the clanks and clunks of bottles and cans and everything else in there being moved around.

Eventually Jules opened the door and, with a fearful look behind her, she finally let Freddie in.

Pushing past her with a tight smile that didn't reach his eyes, Freddie walked straight into the lounge. The man he'd seen sprawled over Jules the night before was in the chair in the corner, looking pasty and worried. Freddie hid the disgust he was feeling as he took in the man's lank, greasy hair and general uncleanliness. Glancing at the coffee table, he could see it had been quickly wiped clean, the evidence gone and magazines freshly strewn across the top. He laughed without humour and shook his head.

'What?' Jules asked, on edge.

'Where's Ethan, Jules?' Freddie asked.

'I'll go get him,' she replied tiredly.

With Jules gone, Freddie turned towards the weedy man in the chair and glared icily down at him.

Jules reappeared with a small frown creasing her forehead. 'Um—' She licked her lips and her eyes slid to the side. 'I forgot, he's gone to school today. He ain't around.'

'He's gone to school?' Freddie asked, his tone casual. 'But you've just got up; how'd he get to school?'

Jules licked her lips again. 'The bus, it goes just from the end of the road so I watch him from the window. I just fell asleep again, that's all. I can sort out something for later on when he's home if you want to see him then?'

'Right, right…' Freddie began pacing, running his hand over his stubble as he did so. 'Which school is it? That he goes to. I can pick him up from there.'

Jules began to pale and she swallowed hard. 'You can't just pick him up – they only let parents they know pick kids up. I'd have to put you on their list and all that.'

'But you just said he gets the bus.' Freddie slowly walked closer to Jules, his eyes boring into hers.

'Well, yeah, but they meet the bus.'

'Who do? Which school did you say it was?'

'Well, I didn't…'

'So what school is he in, Jules? It's a simple question.' Freddie felt his anger mounting and he breathed heavily, trying to control it.

'It's called Birchmore,' she said, an irate edge to her voice. 'But I might be moving him anyway as I don't really like it there—'

Freddie's hand connected with Jules's throat and he slammed her back against the wall, hard.

'You don't have a fucking *clue* where your son is, Jules, do you?' he roared. 'And on top of that, instead of being concerned about that, you're fucking lying to me too.'

'Ouch,' she squealed, grasping at Freddie's hand with both of her own. 'What are you doing? Get off me.'

The man in the chair made a small sound of shock and for a moment looked as though he might stand to help his girlfriend, but as Freddie's dark gaze swivelled towards him, he froze.

'Get out,' Freddie growled. 'Unless you want to be next.'

With a brief look at Jules, the man ran out of the room. Freddie heard him lock himself in the bathroom and he laughed.

'Not exactly your fucking hero, is he?' he taunted.

'Freddie, you're hurting me,' Jules squeaked through Freddie's vice-like grip.

Freddie itched to squeeze tighter, to do some real damage. He leaned into Jules's face, right up to her frightened eyes.

'You lying junkie bitch,' he snarled. 'Did you really think I wouldn't hear about your habits, considering I run most of the drugs in Central London? Hmm?' He curled his lip. 'I came by last night and found you and your boyfriend passed out, off your fucking rockers in the lounge. Ketamine all over the table, just waiting for some little boy to try out for himself.'

'He wouldn't,' Jules whimpered.

'He hasn't so far,' Freddie roared. 'That don't mean he wouldn't. He's a kid – kids are curious, especially about things their parents think more of than them. And even if he didn't, what the *fuck* are you doing, getting high when you're in charge of him? Eh? He's just a kid, Jules! A frightened kid dependent on *you*!'

Jules's face was turning redder by the second and her eyes began to bulge as Freddie's grip grew a little tighter. She tapped his arm, realising her strength was no match against his and she couldn't get him off. Freddie loosened his grip a little but didn't let her go.

'How does it feel, eh?' he snarled in her face. 'To have someone bigger and stronger than you pushing you around?' He saw the fear reach Jules's eyes. 'I saw the bruises on his arm. I heard him talk about the things you do to him. You're a fucking liability. He's a *boy*, a child. *Your* child. How could you hurt him like that?'

With a loud growl Freddie threw her across the room and she landed on the floor by the coffee table she'd been snorting ketamine from just hours before. The thought made Freddie's fury burn even hotter than before and, marching over, he grabbed a fistful of her greasy hair and forced her face up near his. She screamed out, true terror in her eyes now.

'I have Ethan, Jules. And I'll tell you something now: there is no way in hell I'm bringing him back to you like this. Not a fucking chance.'

'What?' Jules gasped. All her plans, all her dreams of a better future fuelled by Freddie's money began to crash down around her, as even now she couldn't think of anything else. 'You have to bring him back,' she cried, her voice wobbling in fear.

Freddie threw her to the side, releasing her hair, and she quickly put her hands out to soften her fall. Her scalp burned where Freddie had nearly ripped her hair from her head, but Jules was used to the odd beating from her previous profession. That wasn't what scared her right now. The thought of losing Freddie's money did. She needed Ethan. The picture she had of herself swanning around as the dutiful mother to Freddie Tyler's golden child began to wobble. The status she had spent all this time making sure she could use wasn't as solid as she'd thought. How could she have been so stupid? Why did she not go further afield to get her fix? And why had she let that little brat irritate her enough to leave marks? Freddie wouldn't have known and she'd still have the upper hand. She could have kicked herself.

Freddie shook his head, disgusted. He wiped his hand on his trousers feeling dirty after touching her. 'Why, Jules? Why do you want him back? You hate him. All you do is moan, abuse him and shut him away. You don't look after him, not really.'

'Because he's mine,' she snarled back, holding her head and looking up at Freddie warily. 'He's all I have.'

Freddie knew it was the truth. He was all she had to bargain with for a better life and she wasn't about to give that up. Not that she would ever say this out loud, of course. She needed to try to appear like a selfless, struggling mother so that Freddie would make things right.

'I need my boy. I ain't perfect, but you don't see the whole picture. We love each other. We're all we have.'

Freddie shook his head, the fight leaving his body as pure sadness took over. Sadness for his little boy whose mother cared more about her next fix than him.

'Jules, I hate you more than you can ever understand for what you've done to that boy. But you're his mum and I deeply want to believe there is a tiny piece of you that wants to change and do some right by him. Because he needs you to be better than this.' He rubbed his hands over his face in stress. 'There's a rehab centre in North London, The Priory. If you'll go voluntarily I'll foot the bill for as long as you need to get clean. I'll look after Ethan until you're better.'

'What?' Jules said, aghast. Her jaw dropped open and her frown deepened. 'No!' she cried. 'There's nothing wrong with me, for fuck's sake. I'm not a bloody junkie, just because I like to have a good time now and then.'

'That much ket and crack, taken the way you've clearly mapped out is not a one-off, Jules. That's a habit,' Freddie replied. 'Come on. I'm offering you a chance to start afresh properly.' He glanced through the hallway at the closed bathroom door. 'You can start again, away from scumbags like whoever that is.' He pointed through the hallway. 'Guys who think it's OK to get high with a kid's mum while the kid's in the other room.' He shook his head again, sickened by the whole situation.

Jules stood up slowly, jutting out her chin. 'I want my son back. *Now*. You have no rights to him. You ain't on the birth certificate.'

Freddie tensed and glared at her coldly.

'Oh, you can try and intimidate me all you want, but it's true. If I call the social on you right now, they'd have him back off you and with me in hours and there'd be fuck all you could do about it. I could even have you arrested for kidnap. And that wouldn't do you much good at all. No.' She pulled herself up to full height and walked away, back towards the sofa and away from Freddie.

'That's the last thing you need. You need to bring him back home to me, his *mother*,' she emphasised, 'and then I'll see what we can work out with access. I only told you about Ethan because we needed help. Not clinics and bullying tactics like this – *real* help. *Financial* help. For you to put your hand in your pocket like any other dad has to, and that's all. You ain't been around when he needed nappies changing and was up all night. You weren't around when he grew out of clothes every few months – that was all me. His *mum*. I'm a bloody good mum, me. He's here, ain't he? Alive and well, fed and dressed. That's what matters. And as for last night, it was a one-off and I thought my mum was watching him,' she lied. 'That won't happen again.'

Reaching for her cigarette packet, she pulled one out and lit it with an exaggerated casualness that she definitely didn't feel under Freddie's wrathful gaze. 'I want him delivered back here within the hour. Or I *will* call the social,' she finished firmly.

Freddie watched her for a second and took in the fake confidence that couldn't quite hide how tense she was, nor how wary her eyes were as they kept darting in his direction. After a few seconds, he walked towards her slowly and deliberately. As he reached her, he leaned down just over her head and grasped her face tightly with his hand. She shook slightly, but she stared up at him defiantly, holding her ground.

'If social services end up at my door today,' he said quietly, 'I'll explain exactly why I took Ethan and insist on a blood test, which you'd fail, and then you'd lose him. So, you and I both know that you can't play that card with me. Nappies and late nights on your own or not, you lost the right to that argument the second you decided not to tell me he existed. Ethan is staying with me for the time being. Perhaps you'll have a rethink of my offer.'

Turning on his heel, Freddie walked out. As he left the building and unlocked his car, he seethed with anger. The fear of the drugs test should keep Jules at bay for now, but it wouldn't hold her off forever. Somehow Freddie had to come up with a plan that kept Ethan safe and sorted the problem of Jules out for good. But if she refused to accept his help and play ball, what options was she really leaving him with?

CHAPTER THIRTY-SIX

'Thea! How are you?' Anna said in surprise, seeing her reach the bar all dressed up. This wasn't usually where Thea hung around on her nights out. It was late and the acts were in full swing, the customers nice and merry and the dance floor was filling up. Anna had just popped out of the office to grab a drink and check everything was running smoothly.

'I'm good. How are you? Haven't seen you in ages.' There was a tinge of accusation in her tone, which Anna chose to ignore.

'I'm… OK.' Anna nodded and looked away, feeling suddenly depressed. 'So, what brings you here?'

'Actually, I'm on a date,' Thea said with a small laugh.

'And you brought him *here*?' Anna said in surprise. She glanced at the scantily clad dancers up on stage.

'Well, we were out to dinner just around the corner and they shut early, so I suggested we pop in here for a drink or two before we end the night.' She eyed the woman who had been her sister-in-law in all but name for many years now. 'And I would be lying if I said I wasn't also hoping to bump into you.' She bit her lip and Anna gave a tired sigh.

She decided to jump straight to the point. 'Anna, Freddie needs you right now. I know that this must be hard on you, probably harder on you than on him, even, all things considered.' She noted how Anna's hand automatically touched her flat stomach. 'But you're a family. And family gets through things together, no matter how hard. I *know* you love him still.'

'Of course I do, Thea. I love Freddie more than I've ever loved anyone, more than my own life,' Anna replied, her tone strained and unhappy. 'But the flashbacks are happening again,' she said, deciding to be openly honest. 'And I can't control them. How can I tell Freddie that I'm up for trying to play happy families with some kid he's just found out about, when I know that every time I look at him it's bound to put me right back there in that farmhouse?'

'You could try,' Thea replied gently. 'No one is asking more of you than that.'

She bit her lip. Anna still didn't know that Freddie had taken the boy home. Perhaps it was better that she wasn't there right now. Though she was going to have to come to terms with it soon, if they had any chance of making it through this. Because now they all knew about him, Ethan wasn't just going to disappear again. He was part of their lives now.

Anna folded her arms over her chest defensively and seemed to collapse in on herself in front of Thea's eyes. Thea thought back to the conversation she'd had with James earlier that day. Her babysitting shift had gone on longer than expected, so he'd joined her at the flat to work there. Ever the optimist, all James could see was the happy side of the situation and he'd said something that Thea decided to repeat to Anna now.

'Maybe, even though it's not what you imagined, this could be the chance you guys have for a family. It's not what you'd planned but what in this life ever goes to plan?'

Anna laughed, the action not reaching her eyes. 'Have you met Jules, Thea? There is no way that woman is going to make this that easy for anyone.'

Thea sighed sadly. 'Just think about it, Anna. You and Freddie are the strongest couple I know. If anyone can get through this, you can. And he really does need you right now. I've never seen him so lost.' She paused. 'I mean, if it was you who needed him, you know he'd move heaven and earth to be there. Just like he has before.'

The truth was harsh as it hit home. 'Listen, the VIP booth is free tonight. Take your date in there and order whatever you like. It's on the house.'

'Anna…'

'Thea, go and have fun. Seriously,' Anna insisted. She smiled gently. 'Please. You never get out on dates so this guy must actually genuinely interest you. Go and enjoy yourself. I mean it.' She squeezed Thea's arm affectionately and Thea gave her a sad smile.

'OK. I will. But just think about it. Please.'

Anna nodded and watched as Thea approached her date and took him over to the VIP booth. His eyes never left her face as she talked animatedly and Anna found herself smiling, happy for Thea. Thea had never been particularly interested in dating, always too busy with the family and the businesses and her friends, and far too cynical to fall for the usual lines. So this guy must have put forward a very convincing argument to get her to go out with him.

'Hey, Carl,' Anna called over the bar.

He looked over from where he had been pretending not to listen to their conversation. 'Hmm?' he asked innocently.

'Take Thea over a bottle of champagne, will you? Just put it on my tab and anything else she wants to order.'

'Sure thing.' He hurried off.

The music changed and another act moved onto the stage, but Anna couldn't seem to tear her eyes away from Thea and her date. They'd got comfortable, sitting close in the curved booth. He was pretty good-looking, stocky and muscular, well turned out with a cheeky face. As Carl set down the ice bucket and two glasses Thea leaned forward with a smile of thanks and held the glasses for him to pour into.

The man she was with put his hand on the small of her back. It was a small gesture, but one that made Anna's heart leap. Freddie always did that to her, without thinking. It was an unconscious gesture of protectiveness that she'd always liked. Unexpected tears filled her eyes and she turned away quickly to hide them.

She couldn't do this anymore. Thea was right. They were all right. She should have gone back home after she and Freddie had talked, but she'd been too afraid. A shiver ran through her and she closed her eyes. She was still afraid now, terrified of reliving the moment she'd lost their baby over and over again. But she had to try, like Thea had said.

Wiping her eyes, she marched through to the office to grab her phone and keys. It was now or never. If she didn't find Freddie whilst she still had the courage, she might talk herself out of it. Taking a deep breath, Anna pushed back her hair with determination. As she left through the back door she just hoped and prayed that she could be as strong as she needed to be, for all their sakes.

CHAPTER THIRTY-SEVEN

Anna unlocked the front door of the flat and hesitated. It felt strange coming back here without at least first letting Freddie know, but it felt even stranger that she felt like this about her own home. She may have been staying with Tanya for a while, but it wasn't like she'd moved out. Shaking off the feeling that she was somehow intruding, Anna opened the door and walked into her home.

Placing her keys in the bowl, she made her way through to the lounge where she could hear the television. The flickering light from whatever Freddie was watching lit up the dark hallway. He hadn't heard her quiet entrance.

She paused just inside the lounge door and drank in the sight of the man she loved and had missed so dearly. Freddie sat half turned away from her, watching a film with a tumbler of whisky in his hand. He still wore his suit, minus the jacket and with the top few shirt buttons undone. He looked tired and drawn and, above all, lonely. Anna's heart broke as she registered that this was mainly her fault.

Something alerted Freddie to her presence and he looked up towards the door. When he saw who it was his eyes widened first in shock and then in sheer joy. He cast his whisky aside on the coffee table and jumped up, crossing the room in just a few short strides. Anna moved forward straight into his open arms, dropping her handbag on the floor without a second glance.

Their lips locked hungrily and Freddie held her tightly to him, as though he would never let her go again.

It was several minutes before their passionate reunion finally simmered down a notch and Anna pulled her head away from his. Freddie put one hand up and stroked her face, a mixture of sadness and love etched into his own.

'I'm sorry,' she whispered. 'I have to be up front with you. I don't know if I can do this yet… but I'm going to try. I love you.' She closed her eyes for a moment. 'We've been to the edge of hell and back more than once, you and I.' She raised her own hand and touched the back of her fingers to his hard cheeks. 'What's one more trip?'

'I can't tell you how glad I am to hear you say that,' Freddie murmured, an emotional tremor in his deep voice. His eyes flickered behind her towards the hallway and he tensed.

Anna felt the change in his body and frowned. 'What's wrong?'

Freddie gently unwrapped Anna's arms from around his waist and led her over to the couch. She sat down and he sat next to her, twisting his body so that he could face her.

'A lot's happened in the time since we last spoke. It ah…' He exhaled wearily. 'I found out Jules is using, Anna. Ket, crack, the lot.'

Anna gasped and her hand flew to her mouth. 'Shit,' she said.

Freddie nodded. 'I went round there, found her passed out. There were drugs everywhere and Ethan was left to fend for himself with no food, nothing.' His hazel-green eyes met hers levelly. 'I couldn't leave him there, Anna.'

Anna felt a prickle of warning run up her neck and she pulled back.

'You should have seen where she had him. I wouldn't house my dog like that.'

Anna swallowed. Her heart was beginning to beat faster and she could hear it beginning to roar loudly in her ears. She already knew what Freddie was about to say and she hated it – but she hated herself even more for hating it. Ethan was just a little boy and if what Freddie said was true, then he had done the right thing. She just wished it wouldn't trigger her this way. But it did. She pulled in a breath and tried to focus on the room around her.

'So, he's here,' she said, her voice coming out flat as she tried to remain calm.

'Yeah,' Freddie replied gently. 'He's here.'

'Where?' Anna looked around, trying to ignore the alarm bells ringing throughout her entire body. This was her home, her safe place. How had the thing that had turned their lives upside down already ended up here? Freddie had promised her that they would talk things through before anything else happened. Her mind whirled as she felt like she was losing control of the elements in her own life. Shaking her head, she tried to focus.

'He's in the study. I bought a new chair that pulls out into a bed. It's pretty comfortable actually. Better than what he was on anyway.'

Anna nodded and bit her top lip, glancing towards the hallway. 'And how long is he here with us?' Her voice was curt.

'I can't answer that yet. I can't send him back there, how things are. I've offered Jules help but she declined. I'm hoping she'll reconsider.' Freddie reached for Anna's hand. It was cold. 'I know this is a lot to come back to.'

'It really is, Freddie,' she replied, pulling back. 'I understand you were against a wall, but you *promised me* we would talk.' She walked away from him, running her hands through her hair in agitation. 'And suddenly he's here, in my home.' She looked at him with pain and frustration in her eyes. 'Freddie, I don't even know who we are anymore. When huge life decisions aren't something we even talk about. When promises mean nothing.'

Freddie nodded. He knew that breaking his promise to her at this point, after everything, was a bad move for their relationship. It killed him to do this to her.

'I know that I broke my promise and that this is unacceptable.' He held his hands out in defeat. 'In your position I'd be furious. I'd be hurt. I don't blame you for that. And I know Ethan being here is probably bringing back… well, everything. But I don't know what else to do. I couldn't leave him there, Anna. I couldn't have left the child of my worst enemy in that flat last night.'

There was a long silence as Anna warred with the feeling of betrayal and her moral conscience. She could see the truth in his words and she knew that she had no choice but to accept the situation. But that didn't make it any easier. She felt the emotional distance between them grow wider. Straightening up, Anna quietly built up the protective walls around her fragile heart, against the person she loved most in the world.

'You did the right thing,' she replied eventually. 'But that doesn't mean I'm OK with what it's doing to us.' She tried to quell the churning in her stomach.

They stared at each other in silence, each registering the shift that had occurred in their relationship. Freddie wanted to reach out to her, to hold her and feel close to her, but he knew he couldn't. Anna stood rigid, her expression detached and cold.

'I'm going to go to bed,' Anna said eventually. 'It's been a long day.'

'Sure.' Freddie nodded. 'I won't be long behind.' He tried to comfort himself with the thought that at least she hadn't left again, but the look on her face weighed his heart down heavily.

Anna forced a tight smile and walked out of the room and down the hallway. As she passed the partially open door to the study, she paused. She willed herself to carry on, to just walk into her room, but somehow she couldn't. As if in a trance, she slowly turned and peered through the door.

The corner lamp was on, throwing a soft glow around the room and over the small figure of the sleeping boy. As her gaze rested upon him, her breath caught in her throat. His little chest rose and fell as he breathed and his warm brown hair shone in the light. Long, dark eyelashes brushed his pale cheeks, just like Freddie's, and his expression was peaceful as he dreamed. He looked younger than seven, lying there in his new pyjamas, wrapped up under the thick duvet.

He was beautiful, Anna realised. Just like her child would have been. The thought turned to ash in her throat as the walls started to close in on her once more.

CHAPTER THIRTY-EIGHT

Tanya rolled the satin sleeves of her deep-green blouse up and looked around with excitement and glee. It was finally theirs. She was standing inside the premises for their new whorehouse. There was a lot of work to do before they could open but nothing they couldn't manage in a few days if they really put their minds to it.

Already she'd roped in the girls to help, promising to pay them well for their troubles. They had eagerly accepted the extra work, glad that it was all finally coming together. Anna had put a strict stop on all extra activities until the house was officially open, so those who relied on offering these services to supplement their income had felt the pinch.

She turned expectantly at the sound of someone climbing the stairs and gave Anna a dazzling smile as she appeared. Rushing forward, she enveloped her best friend and business partner in a huge hug.

'Oooh, it's good to see you. How are you doing?'

Anna had texted Tanya the night before about Ethan being at the flat. Tanya had already known, of course, but she wisely kept that to herself. This was Freddie's mess; she wasn't getting involved. She was still feeling sore towards him about the timing of Ethan's conception.

'OK, I guess. I didn't get much sleep. It felt odd having Ethan in the other room.'

Tanya pulled a sympathetic face. 'How's all that going this morning?'

'It's er—' Anna wasn't sure what to say. She wasn't really sure herself. 'OK, I guess. Ethan's a nice kid, it's just…' She paused, floundering.

'It's just he isn't yours, wasn't planned and doesn't fit in with either of your lifestyles?' Tanya offered.

'Well, yes,' Anna replied with a laugh. 'But that's not his fault.'

'Of course it isn't,' Tanya replied. 'And it probably feels all weird and fucked up for him too, poor kid.' She searched Anna's face. 'It'll be alright. You just need to find your feet, all of you. And what kid doesn't throw their parents' life into complete turmoil? Even those parents who've planned it and organised themselves and bought all the right equipment and the *How to Raise a Baby* books – even they don't know what's hit them when it actually arrives.' Tanya shrugged. 'I've never met one person who's told me otherwise anyway.'

Anna nodded with a tight smile. She took a deep breath and pushed Freddie and Ethan out of her mind. She wasn't here to talk about them. 'Anyway.' She grinned, her dark-blue eyes sparkling. 'I can't believe we finally have the keys.'

'I know!' Tanya squeaked. 'Did you speak to Thea?'

'Oh, yes, she's on her way over. She should be here any minute actually.'

'Perfect.' Tanya walked through to one of the rooms leading off the back of the lounge and beckoned Anna to follow. 'So now you're here, I was thinking that this could be the fetish room. Both Dana and Siobhan have said they want to take the fetish clients – bondage, weird fantasies and stuff – and they want enough shifts that they'll cover this room between them about five nights a week. If we dress the room quite gothic, then turn those alcoves into built-in cupboards, we could house all their equipment and their more specialist outfits in there.' She outlined her ideas with her hands for Anna to visualise.

'Then if you see up here' – she pointed at the ceiling – 'that beam is load-bearing – I think. I'd need to get that confirmed.

But we could place some hooks for their sex swing. Then on the nights it's empty for standard services we could unhook it and put it in the cupboards so it's not too crazy for the regular punters. What do you think?'

Anna covered her mouth as the giggle she'd been holding in finally escaped. 'I'm sorry,' she said. 'It's just the thought of some guy hanging from a sex swing in here.'

Tanya chuckled along with her. 'I know. But hey, if it floats their boats and lines our pockets I'm all for it.'

'Good point,' Anna agreed.

'Hello?' a familiar voice echoed through the empty flat behind them and they both turned back into the main room.

'Through here,' Anna called.

'Ah, there you are,' Thea greeted them with a warm smile. 'Wow.' She looked around appreciatively. 'Nice space.'

'Yes, we think so,' Anna replied. She and Tanya exchanged looks. 'But we can get into that in a bit. There's something far more pressing we need to discuss first.'

'Oh?' Thea questioned, a small crease forming on her forehead.

'Yeah, your date,' Tanya said, jumping in with a grin. 'The great Thea Tyler *finally* goes on an actual date with a guy, instead of brushing him off like every other poor sod who's made an attempt. We need details. Like, *now.*'

'Oh my God.' Thea laughed. 'I thought you meant something serious then.'

'This is very serious,' Anna replied. 'I have never known you to go on a date with anyone. Not in all these years.'

'I go on dates,' Thea protested. 'Well, occasionally. I just don't tell anyone.'

'Why?' Tanya asked, aghast. She couldn't comprehend how their friend could keep something so juicy from them.

'If you had Freddie for a brother, would you share your dating life?' she asked, raising one dark eyebrow in question.

There was a short silence as they considered this. Finally, Tanya gave a grudging nod. 'Yeah, fair.'

'Well, anyway,' Anna butted in impatiently. 'Now that we know about this one, you have to tell us how it went! What do you think of him? Are you seeing him again?'

'Did you go home with him?' Tanya added.

'Was he a good kisser?' Anna shot.

'Is he a big boy?' Tanya winked saucily.

'What does he do for a job?' Anna asked, narrowing her eyes.

'Is he funny? That's so important. They have to make you laugh,' Tanya said.

'Ooh yes, it is,' Anna agreed, nodding seriously. 'Does he?' They both tilted their heads to the side, waiting for an answer.

'Whoa, OK,' Thea said with a laugh. 'Slow down. That's a lot of questions in a really small amount of time.'

'Sorry,' Anna replied. 'But we still need answers.'

Tanya nodded in agreement.

'Yes, it went well. And yes, I'm seeing him again. He just texted to ask me out again. But—' Thea blushed. 'I'm not talking about sex stuff. I don't ask you that,' she said, looking at Tanya accusingly.

Tanya shrugged. 'Oh, you don't have to – I'll just tell you.'

'She will,' Anna confirmed.

'Right now I'm sleeping with a rather sexy geek called Gavin.'

'Gavin?' Anna frowned and faced Tanya.

'Gavin,' Tanya repeated. 'And he is an absolute *beast* in the bedroom. Last night he had me screaming for the orgasms to stop, there were that many.'

'Gavin as in Gavin your therapist?' Anna continued, her tone flat.

'The very same.'

'Why didn't you tell me?'

'Because I knew you'd disapprove.'

'Damn right I disapprove,' Anna exclaimed. 'That is *such* a bad idea, Tan.'

'Actually, it proved to be one of my better ones,' she said. 'Anyway, back to Thea – that's what we were supposed to be talking about.'

'Ugh, I need a drink,' Anna said heavily, rolling her eyes in despair.

Thea laughed.

'Don't think you're off the hook,' Tanya warned her, pointing her finger.

'OK,' Anna said, 'let's go to the club and have a drink or two, get up to date with everyone's dating life and *then* get back to sorting out how we're going to run the books afterwards. Does that suit everyone?'

'Hell, yes,' Tanya replied.

'Sounds good. Let's go,' said Thea.

Giving up on work, Anna led the way out of the flat towards the club round the corner. As the girls chatted away behind her she smiled. She'd missed this.

CHAPTER THIRTY-NINE

Drew peered through the greying net curtains of the B&B to the outside street. It was fairly quiet, a few cars parked up on the side of the road and an old man walking his dog. There hadn't been any signs that anyone was watching the place, but Drew knew that this didn't mean anything. He closed his eyes and sighed heavily.

All he wanted to do was go home. His businesses weren't going to run themselves and they were barely ticking by under the men he'd left behind.

Going home wasn't an option anymore, though – no matter how much he wanted to. Not whilst he had nothing to offer the Ramones. His only hope was to try and steal the product back from the Tylers and go to them voluntarily before they caught up to him. Alfie Ramone was a dangerous man, but he was still a businessman.

Jacko was no help – he kept disappearing off to sort things out for some plan that he wouldn't tell anyone about. He'd mentioned a few vague things, but he refused to share the details. This wasn't making Drew feel any better about the situation. As loyal as Jacko had been over the years, he was also a livewire, and when he kept plans close to his chest that usually meant that Drew wasn't going to like them.

He turned towards Skidders and Richie who were playing cards on the bed.

'I'm going to the corner to grab some fags,' he said. 'When I'm back we'll make a plan for the evening. We need to get out of this room and try and find ourselves some sort of opportunity to get those fuckers in a corner. Any word from Nigel yet, Richie?'

Richie shook his head. 'Nah, he's disappeared off the face of the earth. Haven't managed to get hold of him since we got here.'

'Hmm.' This was odd in itself. Richie and his cousin were close and usually spoke regularly, despite the miles between them these days. Nigel had worked for Drew himself for many years, before moving down here to settle down. Even though he didn't work for Drew now, he'd understand the situation they were in, so it was surprising that there had been no word or some friendly offer of help.

Picking up the front door key, Drew set off to the corner shop, lost in thought. Leaving the property, he stepped down the couple of steps just outside the front door and out onto the street. The early winter's evening held a sharp chill but he embraced this, breathing the cool air into his lungs. It was cramped and stuffy in their room.

Zipping his bomber jacket up to his neck, Drew dug his hands into the pockets and began to walk briskly down the road. Too busy wondering why Nigel had gone so quiet, he didn't notice the soft purr of the car turning down the street behind him. It wasn't until he looked up and locked eyes with a man he knew to be one of Alfie Ramone's killers that the sound suddenly registered.

Lee walked steadily towards him, neither speeding up nor slowing down. Genuine fear flashed across Drew's face and he swivelled round in a panic, setting off at a run in the opposite direction. He swiftly pulled himself up short as he saw the second man, standing a few metres ahead.

'Shit!' Searching for any way out, Drew considered trying to dart into the park across the street but already the car was pulling up alongside him, barring his way. The black tinted window buzzed down and Alfie's thick jowls and cold eyes appeared out of the darkness within.

'Get in,' he growled.

Lee reached them and opened the back door, indicating that Drew should get in next to Alfie. Cursing under his breath, Drew slipped onto the soft leather and tried to work out what he could say to get out of this situation. The door was slammed shut and the driver set off.

Alfie twisted his large frame to the side, so that he could face the younger man. He waited, enjoying the tension that was building up and the speed at which the vein in Drew's neck was throbbing, betraying his fear.

Drew licked his lips. 'Listen, Alfie...'

'No, I don't think I will, Drew,' Alfie cut him off. 'You had plenty of time to ask me to listen, but you didn't. You had time to answer my calls; you ignored them. You had time to come to me and tell me what happened so that I didn't have to hear it from some *anonymous source*, but you didn't. So, after having to bring my men all the way down here to find you, I don't really feel like listening now.'

The car turned a corner and carried on at the same slow pace it had before. It seemed to Drew as though they weren't in any big hurry to get somewhere. He hoped this was a good sign.

'What I *feel* like doing...' Alfie continued, as he pulled out a long, thin, ornate blade from inside his jacket pocket. He touched it, almost lovingly.

'Shit.' Drew jumped and pushed his body as far away as the seat would allow.

'... is using this beautiful instrument to separate your skin from your body while you're still alive. It won't bring me my money back, but it would certainly serve as a soothing distraction.'

'Alfie, let's just calm down here, alright?' Drew held his hands up and tried to settle himself. He needed to take control of this situation, but he wasn't yet sure how. He took a breath and blew it out slowly, his heart beating against his ribcage like a hummingbird.

'But I already am calm, Drew. That's the beauty of it. You can't perfectly separate a man's skin from his body if you hack at it in a rage now, can you?'

'I can get the money back,' Drew spluttered. 'I can get it. I just need some time. That's what we're doing here.'

'You already tried and failed,' Alfie replied, his tone bored.

'Yes, we did. We did,' Drew wracked his brain for anything but they'd come up with nothing so far. All their ideas were dead ends.

His mind suddenly shot to Jacko and his plan. *What had he said to them? There had been some vague comments. He just needed to think…*

'The coke had already been moved by the time we found the van,' he said, 'but that doesn't mean we can't get it back. By my calculations their dealer tree couldn't have used more than forty to forty-five per cent of what was in there. That means they're storing it somewhere – it's still around. All we need is half to make back the money we owe you.' He swallowed again, trying not to look at the knife that had utterly mesmerised Alfie. 'We just need to get that back and we can sort this whole mess out.'

'Trying to take London was a stupid idea in the first place. It was a mistake ticking you the product to try it.' Alfie pursed his lips. 'I don't like making mistakes. And I don't like it when I see people I work with make mistakes. It doesn't give me much confidence in their plans. And what even is your plan? I'm pretty sure the Tylers won't just hand it back to you.'

'No, they won't. But…' He thought back over their conversations. 'That's OK,' he said finally. 'Because we're going to make them.'

'Make them?' Alfie repeated, with a snort of amusement. 'And how are you going to *make* the Tylers do anything?'

'By taking something they love and holding it ransom until they do.' Drew held his head up. 'That's the plan. That's what we're scoping out right now. It takes time, that's all.' He'd taken a gamble telling Alfie this much, as that was all he had gleaned from Jacko's ramblings. If he asked for details, Drew's bluff would become apparent. He moved on quickly. 'We want to make things right, Alfie. We've worked with you for many years and we want to continue this mutually beneficial arrangement for many more. Just give us the space to fix this and we can all get back to normal and put this learning curve behind us.'

'Learning curve,' Alfie said with a deep chuckle. 'You certainly have a way with words, Drew. You should have been a salesman.'

Eying him hard, Alfie twisted the knife in his hand, over and over as he considered Drew's words. Eventually he began to speak.

'I don't trust that you have the capability to force the Tylers to give you that coke, but I'm going to give you a chance. Just one.' He eyed the younger man. 'And we're going to turn this into a little game, because I'm also going to try to get my coke back. That, or the money owed against it. If I manage to get there before you do, you're dead,' he said simply. 'And if neither of us have succeeded in the next ten days, you're also dead. In fact the only way that you win in this game and walk away with your skin still intact' – his gaze travelled down to Drew's bare forearm and Drew suppressed a shudder – 'is if you deliver what I'm looking for first. And soon.'

He grinned, an evil glint shining in his smiling eyes. 'I think this could be quite entertaining. Don't you?'

The car came to a stop and the door opened.

'Now fuck off.'

With surprise, Drew realised that they had only driven around the block and were right back where they'd started. He stepped out onto the pavement, feeling shaky. Alfie leaned over and looked up at him with a cold glint in his eye.

'I'll be keeping an eye on you, Drew. Don't forget that.'

Drew nodded and the two killers who'd waited patiently on the side of the road slipped into the car, closing the doors behind them as it pulled away. He watched it drive down the road and disappear around the corner. A feeling of dread washed over him as he thought back over Alfie's words. The man was a psycho and this game was just another way of feeding his sick enjoyment of other people's suffering.

His jaw formed a hard line. This game might not be weighted in their favour, but they still stood a chance. They had time and they had whatever plan Jacko had been working on in secret. That was something. It was more than the Tylers had going for them anyway. The Tylers were now a hot target on two fronts. They might understand that there were people out to get them, but they had no idea what sort of sick, deadly game they had just been entered into.

CHAPTER FORTY

Sarah glanced up from her desk and took a look at the busy team around her. Half of them were out of the office, trying to get some information on foot. The rest were engrossed in whatever tasks they were doing. Reaching down into her new burgundy Coach handbag, courtesy of the double pay she was currently receiving, she pulled out her second phone.

She tapped out a quick text to Freddie. There hadn't been an opportunity to tell him yet of her new idea, but she needed him to get the wheels moving if they were going to pull it off. She made a mental note to try to catch him for a meeting over the next couple of days. It was getting harder for them to meet in person, with her team watching his every move.

Two sniffing round Ruby Ten today. Get manager to kick up fuss. Build harassment case.

Switching the phone back off, Sarah slipped it back into the depths of her bag and turned her usual phone off silent. Standing up, she smoothed down the front of her grey trouser suit and walked out of the office towards the small kitchen in search of coffee.

As she rounded the corner, Sarah had to stop herself from groaning out loud. Holly glanced around at the sound of someone entering the small kitchen. For once she didn't shoot evils at her boss, and instead her cherry-red lips curled into a small half-smile.

Her big blue eyes twinkled as though they held a secret and the quiet confidence of the woman began to make Sarah feel uneasy.

Sarah looked Holly up and down suspiciously. Noticing this, Holly was quick with the sarcasm.

'Oh, you like my shirt?' She fluffed up the ruffles around the wide collar and at the end of each sleeve. 'Karen Millen. It wasn't cheap but I'm sure your murdering drug-lord boyfriend could afford to take you shopping there.'

Sarah gave a humourless laugh. 'Actually, I'm single and quite happy to be so. But even if I did like this shirt – which I don't by the way; I find frills like that more suited to children below five – I'm more than capable of buying my own designer clothes. You see…' She pulled two mugs out of the cupboard and handed one to Holly. The coffee was nearly ready. 'I'm a much higher-ranking officer than you, which means my salary is also significantly higher. This also means' – her stare turned icy – 'that you have to remember your place and talk to me with a level of respect. I don't expect to have to remind you of this again, DI Miechowski.'

'Yes, ma'am,' Holly replied with a mock salute, the knowing smile still playing on her lips.

'What are you so happy about anyway?' Sarah asked, rounding on Holly after a quick check that they were still alone.

'Me? Oh, you know' – Holly shrugged – 'just life. The winter sun is shining, the city is buzzing and I just feel like there's going to be a very interesting breakthrough in the case soon. Don't you just love that feeling? As a police officer, someone who's sworn to uphold the *law*. That feeling of winning against all the evil in the world.'

Sarah snapped, bored of the pretence. 'I'd watch yourself if I were you,' she said in a low growl. 'You're treading dangerously close to the edge and you know what will happen if you open your mouth or go near the Tylers again. It's not my neck on the line with them, Holly. It's yours.'

Holly narrowed her gaze at her boss and seemed to consider her next words for a few moments. 'I know my hands are tied. I wouldn't have kept quiet this long if they weren't. When they get caught, I won't be the one behind it. And they *will* get caught, that's a certainty. Because I'm not the only one after the Tylers. I'm far from the only person who would like to see them go down. Especially on *this* team. That's the reason each and every one of them are out there.' She pointed towards the office. 'And they're smart officers, ma'am, way smarter than you give a lot of them credit for.' She watched as Sarah raised her chin a little higher. 'You can't dodge all the bullets forever.'

Holly stepped back and picked up the coffee jug. Pouring the hot, dark liquid into both of the mugs, she pushed Sarah's towards her.

'I think you'll find some of your team are a lot closer than you realise. And the minute they get a solid case, there's nothing you'll be able to do to stop it. And at that point' – Holly picked up her mug and gave Sarah a hard stare – 'questions will start being thrown around about the DCI in charge. *Why didn't she see this? What was she doing all that time?* All they need to do to figure out what you're doing is scratch just a touch beneath the surface.' She shook her head. 'It won't be me that takes the Tylers down, Riley – or you for that matter. You'll send yourself there all on your own.'

Sweeping past the thunderous expression on her boss's face, Holly allowed herself a smug smirk on her way back to the office. As she walked away with purpose, she held her head high.

Sarah's heart rate quickened. Since she'd been on this team she'd watched Holly closely and the woman had been stressed and deflated almost the whole time. But today she seemed different. Today she sounded hopeful. And nothing seemed more dangerous to Sarah right now than Holly feeling hopeful. Because that meant she had figured a way around her to the Tylers. And that was very bad news indeed.

CHAPTER FORTY-ONE

Anna stood outside the Italian restaurant Freddie had invited her to and took a deep breath. The busy Camden street was alive with noise and colour and all she really wanted to do was turn around and melt into the crowds, but she knew she couldn't. Freddie was inside with Ethan and this was their first official meeting. That morning Anna had made an excuse to be up and out the door early, not ready to properly acquaint herself with her lover's surprise child yet. Now, though, there was no putting it off any longer.

'OK, here we go,' she muttered as she pushed through the front door determinedly.

Plastering a smile on her face, she made her way over to the little round table where they were waiting for her patiently. Freddie squeezed her hand as she reached them and sat down. As her gaze landed on Ethan, her heart constricted. If his hair was just a couple of shades darker, she might have been looking at a young Freddie. His dark, fringed eyes were the same mesmerising mixture of hazel and green and his solemn face had the same calm yet wary confidence about it. He was almost exactly as Anna had imagined their own child would look. Yet Ethan wasn't hers and never would be.

'I know you guys met briefly this morning, but there wasn't enough time to get properly introduced. So, Ethan, this is Anna, who I was telling you about. And Anna, this is Ethan.' Freddie made the formal introduction and passed Anna a menu so that she could pretend to look at it whilst she collected her thoughts. He could see this was hard for her already.

'Lovely to meet you, Ethan,' Anna said with a quick grin, before looking down at the menu.

'You too,' Ethan replied. 'And, um, thank you for letting me stay in your house,' he added politely. He glanced nervously up at Freddie, who gave him a little smile of approval.

Anna immediately felt terrible for being so locked in her own selfish thoughts and put the menu down, facing him with a small smile. 'You're welcome, Ethan. It's nice for your dad to have you there and get to know you a bit,' she said honestly, before exchanging a strained look with Freddie. He was trying so hard, but the tension between them was so thick it could have been cut with a knife. A waiter walked past and she stopped him. 'Excuse me, could I please get a large Pinot Grigio to start with and…?' She raised an eyebrow at Freddie.

'I'll have the same, and what would you like, mate?' Freddie asked Ethan.

'Can I have a Coke?' Ethan asked cautiously, as if he was still testing the waters.

''Course. A large Coke Zero please,' Freddie confirmed.

The waiter walked off to get their drinks and there was an awkward silence at the table. Looking up through his lashes without moving his head, Ethan snuck a better look at the glamorous lady who'd joined them. She was very smartly dressed and her dark hair looked shiny and clean. Pretty eyes stared at his dad and perfectly polished fingers rested over his hand. He noticed that she wore red lipstick and decided that this looked nice on her.

Usually Ethan hated red lipstick. His mum sometimes wore red lipstick, but it didn't look very nice on her. Her hair would still be greasy and frizzy, and she'd wear clothes that smelled bad and looked even worse. But when she brought out the red lipstick, his mum somehow thought it transformed her into some beautiful superstar. She'd parade around like the lady of the manor and ask Ethan what he thought. If he told the truth, that it was smudged like a clown's or that it didn't look right, she'd repay him with cruelty and call him a bully. Days would go by with continual rants and ravings about how evil and abusive he was. She'd hit him and pinch him in return for his honesty. Tears would be followed by angry outbursts, and his life would be made a misery. He'd learned long ago just to lie and tell her she was perfect, no matter what the truth was.

'Do you like Coke?' Ethan asked, trying to draw Anna into some kind of conversation.

'Sorry?' Anna's eyes widened as if in surprise and this confused Ethan.

'My drink. Do you ever drink Coke?'

'Oh.' Anna laughed. 'Er, sometimes. Yes.'

Anna shook her head. She was so used to talking to Freddie about cocaine and his supplier problem that it took her a minute to remember there was an innocent version. This realisation worried her for a second. What sort of environment was this for a child? She immediately chastised herself. It was a good one. Freddie was going to be an incredible dad. Everything he ever did was for his family. Her heart hurt as she thought of Freddie as a father.

'So, tell me a bit about you, Ethan. Have you liked staying with your dad these last few days?' Anna smiled encouragingly.

Ethan relaxed. Anna was pretty when she smiled. He hoped he could make her smile more and maybe become friends. 'It's been really nice. He bought me these new clothes, look.' With a look of pride, Ethan pulled at the shirt he was wearing and the V-neck jumper over the top. 'I never had a shirt before. I only wear T-shirts at home.'

'Well, T-shirts can be nice too,' Anna offered.

'Yes, we bought some more of those. But they're nicer than my other ones. And they fit better. And look at my shoes!' He pointed down and kicked out one of his feet.

Anna couldn't help but smile at the smart new Converse trainers. 'Now they are seriously cool,' she said.

'Obviously,' Freddie interjected, happy that the ice was finally breaking. 'I'm a cool guy.'

'You are indeed,' Anna replied.

The waiter reappeared and Anna busied herself with picking her food whilst the others ordered. Sitting in a restaurant with Freddie and Ethan, looking like the perfect little family, felt strange. In reality she was the outsider. Part of her wanted to correct the waiter, tell him that she was a fraud, that it wasn't as perfect as it looked. But instead she carried on smiling and picked her pizza quietly.

Could she do this? Live a lie? Anna still wasn't sure. Only time would tell.

*

Seeing the Bentley on the side of the road, the spokes of the wheels gleaming brightly in the sun indicating that it had just been taken for a wash, Freddie turned his attention to the front door of his building. A familiar face smiled back at him.

'This is a surprise,' Freddie said.

'Well, I like to keep you on your toes,' Vince replied, a twinkle in his eye.

They both knew that this wasn't true. Vince had retired from the life a few years ago, leaving everything to Freddie on the condition he still get sent his cut every month. Freddie had dutifully abided by this, never once sending late payment and often adding a little something extra. Vince and Big Dom, before he'd died, had been his mentors. Back in the day, they had run Central London and were still infamous for their adventures now.

This begged the question as to what Vince was now doing here – Freddie knew it wasn't just a social call.

'This is a snazzy little block you're in here,' Vince said, looking up at the building. 'You got the penthouse, have ya?'

'I do.'

'Blindin',' Vince replied, his wide smile showing off his expensive veneers. 'You done well for yourself, son.'

Freddie tapped in the code and led the way inside. 'Well, I had a little help along the way,' he answered graciously.

'Nah.' Vince shook his head as they entered the lift. 'I gave you the job but you was the one who put in the work. And you're savvy.' Vince tapped his own head to get his point across. 'You wouldn't have lasted two minutes if you weren't.'

Freddie turned his level gaze onto his old boss and held eye contact. 'So, what's this about then, eh? We both know you ain't here to stroke my ego.'

Vince grinned and gave a low chuckle. 'Nah, you're right. I had some business in town. Some personal stuff.' They walked out of the lift and into Freddie and Anna's flat. 'I just thought I'd pop and see how things were with the whole Jules situation, while I was in the area. How's it going?'

They reached the kitchen and Vince took a seat on one of the bar stools. Freddie held up a decanter of whisky in question. Vince nodded, and he poured them each a generous measure, adding a couple of ice cubes.

'It's going OK,' Freddie said carefully. He passed one of the glasses over and sat opposite Vince.

'You don't sound over the moon about it,' Vince answered, searching his old protégé's face for any clues as to how he really felt.

'Well, it's been a shock, as you know. Finding out I had a son. But Ethan is an amazing little boy,' Freddie said with feeling. 'Whatever the circumstances, I'm glad he's here.'

'And what are the circumstances now?' Vince asked, sipping at his whisky.

Freddie paused. He was in two minds about telling Vince the whole story. His old boss might be retired, but he still had sway and connections and he was still as ruthless as ever, despite appearances. Jules had crossed him on a deal he'd paid out a lot of money for. For this she was already on his shit list. Freddie wasn't sure he wanted to give Vince any more reason to go for her. But he also knew that anything he didn't tell Vince himself, he'd only find out elsewhere. There was no point hiding it.

'Jules is using. I found Ethan there while she was on a session and took him back here.'

Vince gave a low whistle of surprise. 'Jesus,' he said.

'Yeah.' Freddie twiddled the whisky tumbler around on the breakfast bar. 'I've just dropped him at Thea's for a few hours or you could have met him. Jules, though… she's now demanding I take him back or she'll have the social and police round.'

'She what?' Vince asked aghast, with a deep frown. 'Who the fuck does she think she is?'

'His mother,' Freddie answered simply.

'Mother or not, she should know better than to send pigs round to people like you. What you going to do about it?'

'If it was anyone else I'd have broken her fucking legs already,' Freddie replied. 'But she's his mum.'

Vince exhaled in frustration but nodded his understanding. It was a very difficult position Freddie was in.

'Not that she gives a shit about him,' Freddie added, shaking his head. 'He's got nothing. She batters him about and acts like he's a nuisance. All she wants is money.'

Vince's gaze sharpened. 'How much?'

'When I first met with her she wanted another hundred grand. Wanted to move to Spain and start again. But that was before I met Ethan and now she just seems to be after a regular wedge.

But a hefty one. It ain't doing Ethan no good, though. It's all for her. And that's what I'm not sure how to handle without ending up in court.'

'You can't do that,' Vince said automatically. He stretched out and scratched his head, thinking. 'What about if you paid her to disappear again? Without Ethan. Do you think she'd go for it?'

Freddie bit his lip. He had been wondering the same thing, but that would mean him taking on Ethan full-time. He also wasn't sure Jules would go for it. Not that he thought she'd miss Ethan, but she was an opportunist and giving Ethan up would mean she couldn't tap Freddie up for anything else again. Then there was Anna to consider. Even accepting Ethan's existence had been hard for her; he wasn't sure how she'd react to him living with them permanently.

'There's a lot to consider with that,' Freddie answered eventually.

'There is. But the money ain't one of them.'

'What do you mean?' Freddie asked with a curious frown.

'If you offer her money in exchange for her son, all signed and sealed legally, and she goes off, she ain't his mother anymore.' Vince's pale, watery eyes grew hard. 'Which means she's fair game. You could set a trap, take the money back – however much you had to pay – and make her disappear. Your boy would be none the wiser. She'd be off making her new life in Spain without him for all he knew. Everyone's a winner.'

Freddie shook his head firmly. 'I can't be the guy who killed his mum, Vince. However tempting it might be.'

Vince sighed regretfully. 'Fair enough. But you still could send her off into the sunset, for the right price. Just keep it in mind. I know a good family court lawyer who can get everything written up all official pronto, for the right price. Once she signs the papers, the boy's yours and you don't have to worry about her again, if that's what you want.'

Picking up his glass, he knocked back what remained of his drink. 'That's nice stuff, that. I wouldn't complain if you got me a bottle for Christmas.' He winked. 'I've got to go. I've had enough of the city for one day. There's a big poker game waiting for me back home and I stand to make a killing.'

Freddie laughed, walking Vince to the front door. 'Poor buggers. Bet they didn't know what hit them, the day you moved in.'

'Cheeky bastard,' Vince replied with a low chuckle. 'But you're right, they didn't. I'll catch you later, son. Don't be a stranger.'

Freddie shut the front door and walked through to the lounge. Stepping onto the balcony, he moved to the corner and leaned over, resting on his folded forearms. Rubbing his forehead tiredly, he felt his troubles pushing down on him like a heavy cape. Vince had given him a lot to think about.

CHAPTER FORTY-TWO

The next day Freddie opened the back door of the car and Ethan stepped out onto the pavement. He was all dressed up in his new smart suit and he puffed his chest out, feeling special.

It wasn't a birthday or a wedding or any of the usual events that a young boy might wear a suit for. They were currently parked up outside Mollie's house, where they were about to inform her that she was a grandmother. It was a momentous occasion.

Right now, she had no idea about Ethan. Freddie had told her they were coming over for a family dinner. Everyone would be there. He'd explained to Ethan that it might be a shock for his nan to meet him and the boy seemed to have taken it in his stride, as he had everything else. Now that they were here, though, he began to look nervous, his proud stance falling back to insecurity. Freddie placed a comforting hand on his shoulder.

'She's going to love you,' he said. 'Won't she, Anna?'

Anna rounded the end of the car and joined them. She nodded encouragingly.

'Come on then,' Freddie continued. 'Let's go inside.'

As they reached the front door, it opened and Paul stepped aside to let them in.

'Is that Freddie?' Mollie called through from the kitchen at the back.

'Yeah, it's us,' Freddie called back.

'Come on in then and make yourself at home. I've done a nice roast leg of lamb,' she shouted, her voice slightly muffled under the sounds of pots and pans being moved about.

Freddie guided Ethan into the lounge where Thea, Paul and James all said quiet hellos to him. Thea ruffled his hair and winked and Ethan felt his spirits lift a little. He was trying to be brave for his dad's sake, but he could tell this was a big deal and he already felt so out of his depth even before he had to meet his nan. He looked down to the ground, trying to hide how worried he felt. All he really wanted to do right now was go back and find his stuffed dog. He wished he'd thought to bring him along.

'If you all want to go and wash up, I'm just setting the table,' Mollie shouted.

Freddie took a deep breath. 'You might want to set another place,' he called.

'What?' The sound of cutlery being pulled out of the drawer halted and there was a long silence. Eventually the kitchen door opened and Mollie bustled through, cutlery in one hand and a tea towel in the other. 'Who's with you?' She paused as her gaze landed on Ethan.

'Mum, this is Ethan,' Freddie cut straight to the point. 'It's a long story, but he's my son. We've only recently met and I've brought him to meet you,' he said, keeping his tone level.

'It's nice to meet you,' Ethan said quietly, as he'd discussed with his dad, his voice shaking a little.

Mollie put the tea towel and the cutlery down on a side table and walked forward with a wobbly smile. She reached Ethan and Freddie watched her eyes wander over his face, taking in the same similarities he had been in awe of himself not long ago.

'It's lovely to meet you too, Ethan,' she said brightly. Looking up to Freddie, her smile widened. 'He's the spit of you, you know.' She turned back to Ethan, cupping his face.

'I know,' Freddie replied slowly. His attention sharpened and his eyes narrowed slightly as he watched his mother interact with Ethan.

'I'm your nan, or nanny if you'd prefer. Up to you,' Mollie said. Her eyes darted between Ethan and Freddie. 'What a wonderful surprise this is,' she continued. 'I can't believe I'm a grandmother.'

'Really?' asked Freddie, his tone suspicious. 'Only you don't really seem surprised,' he added with a small frown. 'In fact, I think you seemed more surprised the time I told you I was changing tailors, or the time you found out Mr Singh at the post office was retiring.'

'What are you on about?' Mollie blustered, her cheeks growing pink.

Guilt shone through her expression and Freddie's eyes widened in amazement as he realised he was right. Mollie wasn't surprised at all. Which meant someone had already told her. He looked around at the rest of his family and searched their faces.

'Did one of you tell her?' he asked. They all shook their heads and Freddie could tell that this was the truth. 'Where did you hear about him?' he asked Mollie. 'It's not common knowledge.'

'I didn't. Where would I have heard that?' Mollie responded, trying to hold her ground. She fiddled with her apron nervously and didn't meet Freddie's gaze.

The cogs in Freddie's brain began turning until a conversation stuck out in his mind like a shining red beacon. He'd found it odd at the time, something Jules had said when she'd revealed why she'd disappeared. When she spoke to Vince, he'd told her to wait, that he needed to speak to someone else first. When Freddie had asked him who this was, he'd dismissed it, said there was no one. But there had been. He'd shared the burden with someone who could help him decide on the best course of action. He'd told Mollie.

'Vince,' he whispered, the room around him deadly quiet as everyone tried to work out what was going on. 'He came to you. Back then.' Freddie watched as Mollie's expression confirmed his suspicions. Mollie had known all this time, since before Ethan had even been born.

Mollie looked up at her eldest son beseechingly. 'Freddie, you were so young and you'd been working so hard to make something of yourself.' She glanced down at Ethan, not wanting to say too much in front of him.

Thea stepped forward, and put an arm around Ethan's shoulders. 'Come on, mate, let's go in the kitchen. I've got some cake we can get into before dinner if you like.' She led him away from the tense situation. 'We can be proper food rebels…' The door closed behind them.

Mollie swallowed and lowered her voice to make sure the sound didn't travel. 'Vince came to me and told me what he was thinking but said he needed to be sure he was doing the right thing. She was a stripper, Freddie. Just some girl you'd been knocking around with. She wasn't even your girlfriend.'

Freddie held his hand up to stop her from continuing and Mollie paused, closing her mouth and staring at him in misery.

'So, you thought it was OK to make that decision for me?' Freddie asked, his tone deadly quiet.

'Vince told me that she was out for all she could get. It would have ruined you, Freddie, ruined your chances of building a proper family, when *you* were ready, with who *you* chose.' She glanced at Anna. 'Look at what you have now. You wouldn't have had this if you'd known. You're a good boy; you'd have stuck by her.' She took a deep, wobbly breath. 'This was never supposed to happen. She was supposed to get rid of it.'

'Him,' Freddie cut in icily, horrified rage rippling through his expression. 'There is no *it*, only *him*.'

'Him,' Mollie repeated, looking down in shame.

Freddie groaned and ran a hand over his face. There was a short silence as he tried to process what was happening. Vince's actions he understood, in a strange way. But his own mother lying to him all these years about her own flesh and blood – he couldn't get his head around it. He felt completely betrayed.

'How long have you known?' he asked eventually.

'Yesterday. Vince came to the house.'

Freddie thought back to when Vince had turned up at his flat. This must have been the business he was in town for. He pinched the bridge of his nose.

'I can't believe you did that,' he said, his voice heavy. 'That you lied and hid it from me all this time.'

'Freddie, I was just trying to do what was best…' Tears began to roll down Mollie's cheeks.

'That wasn't your call to make,' Freddie growled.

He glared at her, raw resentment in his eyes. Mollie cowered back, her tears falling faster. She'd never seen Freddie like this before.

'Ethan,' Freddie called, marching over to the kitchen door and opening it. 'Change of plan, mate – we're going to go out for lunch instead.'

'Freddie,' Mollie wailed, grasping at his arm, her expression pleading. He brushed her off and turned his back, unable to even look at her.

Ethan joined his dad and looked around at the sea of stressed faces and his crying grandmother worriedly.

'Don't worry, mate,' Freddie said, straining his voice in his attempt to sound light-hearted for his son's sake. 'Everything's fine. Come on.' Without even glancing at Mollie, he gently guided Ethan towards the door, trying hard to contain his fury.

Anna followed him out in shocked silence. This was an unexpected turn of events and one Freddie was going to take very hard. He lived for his family and loyalty meant everything to him.

But Mollie lived for her family too and although she primarily agreed with Freddie that it hadn't been her call to make, she could see why Mollie had done it. The pair were more alike than either of them realised.

Anna swung her slim legs into the passenger seat and closed the door. The car pulled off and disappeared around the corner.

No one noticed the small, dark car parked across the road in view of the front room. From the reclined driver's seat where Jacko lay low, peeping through the bottom of the window, he'd seen everything. The front windows were wide and the curtains fully open. He'd watched as Freddie had taken in his son and saw how the family meeting had turned from a joyous occasion to one of heightened, strained emotion. He had no idea why but he didn't really care. It was clear there wasn't going to be an opportunity to pull off his plan here.

Restoring the seat to its usual level, he glanced down at the bottle of chloroform next to a small rag and a roll of rope on the passenger seat. Starting the car, he pulled off and out of the street. He would use them soon and Freddie would have no choice but to give them what they wanted. Jacko was going to make sure of it.

CHAPTER FORTY-THREE

Later that day, after her tears had dried and the rest of the family had left, Mollie knocked on the door of Thea's bedroom before opening it and walking in. Thea glanced up at her through the long mirror she was twisting and turning in front of, as she tried to decide on an outfit.

'Oh, that's pretty, love,' Mollie commented quietly. 'Not often I see you in a dress these days.'

'No, I know.' Thea wrinkled her nose. 'It's not really me, is it?'

It was a figure-hugging little red number, which still had the tags on even though she'd bought it nearly six months before. It was the type of dress that Anna and Tanya always wore. They seemed to pull the smart, sophisticated look off effortlessly, never seeming ill at ease in the restrictive garments. She'd often admired their sense of style and had bought this in a bout of confidence that she could pull it off just as well as they did. But it had sat at the back of the wardrobe ever since, collecting dust behind the T-shirts and leather jackets.

'Maybe not, but it does look lovely on you,' Mollie replied. 'What's the occasion anyway?'

Thea bit the inside of her cheek. She didn't like to share her love life with anyone, not even her mother. But after a quick look at the sad expression on Mollie's face she decided to tell her. It would perhaps cheer her up and distract her from all this Freddie business.

'I'm actually going on a date tonight,' she said.

Mollie's face opened up in surprise. 'Oh finally! I was beginning to think you were never going to find a man.' She smiled for the first time since Freddie had left the house in anger.

'What?' Thea asked, her eyebrows shooting up. 'Why would you think that?'

'Well, you know, love…' Mollie busied herself with folding the clothes Thea had discarded on the bed. 'It's just you've never brought anyone home. You just always seem too busy with work and you've never seemed bothered by being on your own. I'd started worrying you might end up a spinster.'

Thea rolled her eyes in disbelief. All she'd tried to do was cheer her mum up. Now she wished she'd just kept her mouth shut.

'Which is totally fine if that makes you happy, of course,' Mollie continued. 'I thought maybe you might end up one of those that has loads of cats instead of kids. Like old Mrs Pendle, down the road.'

'Alright, OK, Mum.' Having had enough, Thea gently pushed her mother out of the room.

'Oh, but wait, who is he? Or she. Is it a she? Is she nice?' Mollie called, desperate for more information.

'Goodbye, Mum,' Thea said firmly, shutting the door. As she heard Mollie tut and walk away, she rolled her eyes and let out a long sigh. Over on the bed her phone buzzed. Opening up the text, she smiled.

Still on for tonight? X

She quickly tapped out a response, confirming their date and chucked the phone back on the bed whilst she wriggled out of the dress. Reaching into her wardrobe, she pulled out a pair of her favourite Levi's and a dressy top. Happy with her choice, she nodded. This would do nicely.

About to slip into the top, Thea paused and bit her lip. Better change to the good underwear, she thought. It was a third date after all.

CHAPTER FORTY-FOUR

'You can't be fucking serious!' Drew shouted furiously across the small bedroom in the B&B.

'I am deadly serious,' Jacko responded, not at all deterred by the look on Drew's face.

'That's not OK. It ain't done.'

'I don't give a shit if it's not done,' Jacko replied with a deep frown. 'I ain't going to die playing by the rules when I can win another way. I'll take my chances to end this game still breathing, thank you very much.'

'This is messing with other people's lives, people who don't have anything to do with any of this.'

'It's *our* lives, Drew,' Jacko shot back with an angry glare. 'Have you forgotten that? Because I feel like you have.'

'Of course I haven't forgotten; I've been trying to figure out a way to fix this.'

'But you *haven't* fixed it,' he yelled back, 'and now Alfie's here and we're all fucking dead soon, or worse, if we don't get one over on the Tylers. So…' He shook his head and pulled a face. 'I'm not going to sit here and do nothing. I don't give a shit if this is playing dirty.'

'Well you still can't do that, Jacko, especially not…'

'Especially not what?' Jacko stepped up into Drew's face. 'I'm not playing anymore. I'm getting this done.'

Drew shoved him back with an angry roar and there was a short scuffle. 'Don't be fucking stupid,' he spat as he slammed Jacko against the wall. 'I'm telling you now, this isn't happening and you're *damn* lucky that we're stuck together in this mess because if we weren't I'd be tempted to kill you myself right now.' The muscles in his arms bulged as he pushed Jacko's neck up high in fury. Jacko struggled but he was no match for Drew once he'd lost his temper.

Suddenly Drew found himself being pulled back.

'And what do you think *you're* doing?' he roared, rounding on Richie. Jacko coughed and spluttered, leaning forward onto his knees.

Richie's face remained hard and steady as he locked eyes with his boss. 'This ain't the time to turn in on ourselves. And whether you like it or not, he's the only one with a plan.'

The others nodded from their seats on the sidelines. Drew stared around the room at his men, one by one. He could see in their faces that they were losing faith in him and part of him didn't blame them. He'd got nowhere so far and they were all facing the prospect of death and torture. But Jacko's plan was out of the question. There had to be another way.

Closing his eyes, Drew decided on a course of action. It was possibly the most foolhardy thing he could think of, but desperate times called for desperate measures – and these were definitely desperate times. He shook his head, not liking what he was about to do at all. The chances of it working were slim.

'I have an idea.'

Richie sat back down, relieved to not have been given a hiding from Drew for pulling him off Jacko. He'd seen his boss react much worse for much less.

'I need you to all lay out whatever weapons and tools you've got, right now,' Drew said with a grim expression. 'Because I think we're going to need them all.'

CHAPTER FORTY-FIVE

Thea checked her face in the hall mirror and topped up her pink lip gloss one last time. Her shoulder-length dark hair was shiny and voluminous, styled with a few loose waves just the way she liked it and her smoky eyes and fitted leather jacket gave her the look she'd been going for. She felt good in herself tonight and allowed herself a small smile of satisfaction in the mirror.

Hearing her phone buzz, she checked it and saw that her date, Jay, was right outside. He was taking her to Primrose Hill for a late-night picnic and a few beers, looking down over the bright lights of the city. It was exactly the kind of date Thea liked best. Jay was bringing the food and she'd bring the beers. She'd packed a thick blanket too, very aware that it was winter and they'd probably be freezing. This didn't put her off, though. In fact, Thea wondered if that might be just the opportunity that drew them closer together. Perhaps they'd need to huddle for warmth and he'd finally kiss her.

Shouting goodbye to Mollie, Thea quickly shut the front door behind her and skipped down the path to the waiting car before her mother could follow her out. She jumped into the passenger seat, threw the bag with the blanket and the beers in the back and grabbed her seat belt, grinning over at Jay.

'Hey, how's it going?' He greeted her with a wide grin.

'Great.' She glanced back at the house and saw Mollie peering out of the lounge window. 'Let's go, though, shall we?' she urged. 'If you hang about much longer, me mum's going to be out here asking your middle name and your shoe size,' she said and laughed. 'Come on, quick, let's go!'

Jay sped off with a chuckle, as if amused at Thea's description of her mother.

'So how have you been?' Thea asked, settling back into her seat once they were around the corner.

'Yeah, so-so. Work's been a bit stressful, but other than that I can't complain. How's your project going?' he asked.

Thea had told him all about the photography project she was doing in her spare time. Not that she had much spare time around work these days, but she was making an effort to get at least one night in a week with her camera.

'It's going OK. I've got some new spheres coming, different sizes this time. They should magnify really well. Maybe you could come out with me sometime, on a shoot. If you fancied it,' she offered shyly.

Jay smiled. 'That would be nice, yeah.' He glanced at her sideways and turned into a small alley running in between two rows of houses towards the garages at the back. Pulling to a stop, he put on the handbrake and turned to her, looking slightly awkward.

'What are we doing?' Thea asked, tilting her head in question.

'Um, there's something I wanted to do last time we met up. But things didn't exactly turn out as I'd planned.' He bit his lip and stared into her eyes intently.

'Oh, I see.' Thea felt herself blush and a bubble of excitement rose up in her stomach.

She took a deep breath and smiled, turning in her seat to face him head-on. Jay was finally going to kiss her. He laughed nervously and looked away for a second, before turning back to her.

'Can you close your eyes?' he asked.

'Sure,' Thea said with a giggle. She shut her eyes and tried to relax the muscles in her face. He couldn't kiss her very well if she was full-on grinning. She breathed in his sweet musky scent as he leaned in close to her and frowned slightly as she heard a small rustle by her feet. He was reaching for something, something that sounded like it was inside a plastic bag.

Jay's hand slipped around the back of Thea's neck and she instinctively leaned forward. As she moved her mouth towards what she had thought were his lips, something coarse and wet pressed against the lower half of her face. She jerked back but Jay's hand pushed her forward. Her eyes flew open and she realised he was holding a rough cloth over her face, his hand clamping down hard so that she had no choice but to breathe through it.

Even before her brain registered the cloying smell of the chloroform, Thea knew what it was. She'd been around in this world of theirs long enough to know it could only be one thing. She kicked out, scratching at his arm in an attempt to get him off of her, but he was much bigger than she was and though her nails drew blood, his arm didn't move an inch.

As she fought against the drowsiness, her actions grew weaker and slower. His face, so still and calm, seemed to move further and further away in her darkening vision, until suddenly there was nothing.

CHAPTER FORTY-SIX

Freddie marched through the main floor of the busy club and up the stairs with a quick nod of greeting to the staff as he passed the end of the bar. The sharp beats coming from the DJ booth began to dull as he reached the next floor and the door to his office. Opening this, he reached across the wall and flicked the light switch on as the door closed behind him. Light flooded the opulently decorated room, over the warm mahogany desk, his collection of first-edition books and collectible sculptures – and over the man sat in Freddie's oversized leather desk, lying in wait.

Freddie's eyebrows shot upward and he hesitated, tilting his head to one side in silent question.

'Mr Tyler,' Drew said. 'Please take a seat.'

Freddie barked a humourless laugh. 'You're sitting behind *my* desk asking me to take a seat in *my* office?' he asked in disbelief.

'I am,' Drew replied, his tone serious and calm.

Richie stepped out from his position and pushed a knife against Freddie's back. Freddie twisted to see who it was and then turned back, shaking his head. He sighed and took a seat opposite Drew. Richie moved to stand behind him, the knife still in his hand just in case.

Freddie caught this out of the corner of his eye and settled back into the comfortable chair. He glanced over at the grandfather clock in the corner.

'You realise,' he said, 'that this is a really stupid thing to do, right?'

Drew conceded with a nod. 'Well, you've given us no choice.' He held his arms out in helplessness. 'We're in a corner and the only way out of that corner is if you help us. I've asked nicely. Now I'm demanding.'

'Oh, you're demanding?' Freddie mocked. 'And how do you think that's going to play out?'

'I think it's going to play out like this,' Drew said, leaning forward. 'You're going to sign in to one of your accounts, here, tonight. Offshore, personal – I don't care which. You're going to wire me the money I owe my supplier, so that me and my men can go back to our lives. Once that's done, we'll leave London and never return. You'll make that money back on the coke you stole from us, plus a lot more, so you won't be out of pocket.' Drew sat back. 'You'll still be better off than before we came. It's a reasonable hold-up, Tyler. I'm not asking for anything more than that.'

A slow grin crept over Freddie's face and he chuckled in amusement. Taking his cigarettes out of his pocket, he lit one and pulled in a deep drag before blowing out a long plume of smoke.

'A reasonable hold-up,' he repeated with a slow nod. 'Holding anyone up over anything makes the situation *un*reasonable before you've even got to the whys and whens and whos. At least to the party being held.' He took another drag, holding Drew's gaze steadily. 'I get that you're in a sticky corner right now and I have to say, I wouldn't want to be in your shoes at all. I've heard all about Alfie Ramone, his penchant for torture. I hear he enjoys it more than anything else on the planet.'

Drew froze, his breath catching. Freddie knew about the Ramones. That had been the last true card he had to play, the fact that he had an in with an anonymous supplier. He'd been hoping to get into some sort of negotiations, now that he had Freddie at the end of a sharp blade. It might have swayed him, getting a little more out of this deal.

Freddie smiled at him, the cold, confident smile of a predator. Drew took a deep breath and pushed forward. This didn't mean he was out of the game yet. He still had the upper hand.

'So, you've figured out where we get our product,' he said flatly. He shrugged, as if this didn't matter. 'It won't do you much good. Alfie's a volatile man who doesn't trust easily. I've been in business with him for years. He's not going to take kindly to the man who stole his product from his long-term distributors. If you even get an audience, I wouldn't count on coming out in anything other than a body bag.'

Freddie nodded and took another drag on his cigarette. This was something he was concerned about, and although he knew Drew was using anything he could to gain an advantage, he also knew there was some truth in his words. He'd been hearing similar whispers elsewhere. That, coupled with the fact that the Ramones had shunned the unspoken rules of underworld engagement by coming to the city and not announcing themselves, was pointing Freddie towards caution. Though it hadn't yet put him off. He'd overcome the hostility of much bigger fish than Alfie Ramone in the past. He had twice come up against the wrath of the Mafia and had managed to come out on top on both occasions.

'I'll keep that in mind,' Freddie said eventually.

'Keep in mind whatever you like, but you need to log on right now.' Drew grabbed a laptop bag from the floor next to his chair and pulled out a slim grey laptop. 'And you need to send the money over.'

'You want me to wire it? You don't want it cash?' Freddie asked, leaning on the arm of the chair in a casual manner.

'That would mean you leaving this room or calling someone, neither option I'm OK with.'

'But a wire this large with no paperwork between two criminal firms who are under constant surveillance, you don't think that's going to create other issues?' Freddie asked, raising one mocking eyebrow.

'I don't have time to clean it,' Drew snapped. 'I don't have time for anything other than saving my neck and you're my last fucking chance. So just *do it*,' he yelled, standing up and leaning over the desk, pointing the knife in Freddie's face. '*Now!*'

Drew held the knife close to Freddie's cheek, willing the other man to show some fear, but he didn't. Freddie Tyler was one hard bastard, he had to give him that. He didn't so much as flinch, his gaze level and challenging.

'Knowing the situation you're in,' Freddie said, the mockery gone from his tone now that Drew was getting so close to break- ing point, 'part of me wants to feel pity for you. It really does.'

Strategically moving to put out his cigarette in the ashtray on the desk, Freddie's face was no longer under the pointy tip of the blade. Drew withdrew it, forcing himself to calm down.

'But then I'm reminded of how you came down from your little nook in the north and tried to overtake my business from right underneath my nose.' Freddie stared at Drew hard. 'You saw an opportunity and you took it. But there were other opportunities you could have explored, before making that fatal decision. For example, you could have approached us about middle-manning with your supplier, as you've since offered. We could have struck up a working partnership built on trust and good product. But you didn't.' Freddie's tone grew colder. 'And instead you became the enemy. So, I have no interest in helping you out now. You made your bed. Now it's time to lie in it.'

'I don't think you fully understand the situation here,' Drew snarled, tired of the ongoing discussion. 'So, let me make it clear. You have two options. Either you log on and wire me that money right now, or Richie and I will gut you like a fucking fish and leave you to bleed out in this lovely office of yours.'

Freddie sat up and stared at him, his eyes half smiling as though they held a secret. Drew maintained his gaze, refusing to be fooled by his outward confidence. Surely by now the man knew that he was cornered.

'Thing is,' Freddie said, 'there is a third option that you haven't considered.'

Drew frowned. 'What are you talking about?'

Freddie glanced at the clock again and smiled. 'Do you know what the difference is between a moderately successful, middle-of-the-road criminal and a man who runs the fucking show?' He waited but Drew didn't answer. 'It's attention to detail. You see, when you start trying to play at the top levels all it takes is the slightest oversight and you could go crashing back down, all the way to the ground. And the higher up you are, the more painful the landing. So, you have to pick up things a fucking *microscope* would have problems noticing.'

'Stop riddling, Tyler, and pay the fucking money,' Drew spat, getting tired of all the talk. Freddie was clearly stalling in the hope he could wriggle his way out, but that wasn't going to happen.

'For example,' Freddie continued, 'what you should have noticed when I walked in here is that I didn't stop to even try and unlock the door. The door that you boys had to break the lock on. Which means I already knew that the door I keep locked was open.'

Freddie watched as Drew grew still, the cogs in his brain turning.

'You should have also noted my lack of surprise at finding you here. Was that not even slightly odd to you?' He pointed at a small bust on a wooden pedestal to one side. 'You see, there's a camera in there. It's actually not an antique like the rest of the stuff in here; it's plaster of Paris, built up around the camera to hide it from view. If you look closely you can see the lens in the left eye.'

Richie and Drew exchanged glances and Drew tilted his head towards the bust. Richie walked over and leaned down, squinting into the lens. He turned with a look of horror and nodded.

'It's motion censored and linked to my phone. You can imagine my surprise when it went off. Especially as I'm the only one with a key. But now you're wondering why I came. Right?'

Drew didn't answer, his expression darkly worried.

'I came to see what exactly it was that you were here for. What angle you were plugging. And now I know. But knowing all I'd need was ten short minutes, I've had your friends downstairs thrown out while we've been talking and my men should be coming up to deal with you at any second.'

Right on cue, the heavy thuds of footsteps approaching began to sound down the hall.

'Fucking grab him,' Drew cried. Richie leaped back to his position behind Freddie, who still hadn't attempted to move, and placed his knife against Freddie's throat, holding him down in the chair with his free hand.

Freddie didn't flinch, just waited with his eyes trained on Drew. In a panic, Drew's gaze kept jumping from Freddie's calm unwavering expression to the door and back again. He made a sound of exasperation.

'I *knew* this was a bad idea. This is all fucking Jacko's fault,' Drew seethed.

Freddie's eyes narrowed slightly. He wondered what Jacko had to do with this. He'd figured Drew was the head honcho, the brain behind the operation. Jacko had always seemed more like the brawn. He filed the comment away for later thought.

The door was swung open with force and Paul marched in, Seamus hot on his heels. Sammy walked in last, closing the door behind him. It took Drew less than a second to clock the gun Paul was holding by his side as they fanned out. Seamus swung a long wooden baseball bat around a couple of times, just to make sure this was noted by everyone in the room, and Sammy took his time carefully fitting his fingers into a set of knuckledusters. He made a fist and grinned darkly at Freddie before shooting icy daggers at Richie.

Richie swore under his breath and looked over to his boss for direction. Drew hesitated, trying to calculate what chance they might have to get around these three. But they were outnumbered and out-tooled. Even if he had Rambo holding a knife to Freddie's neck instead of Richie, he still doubted they'd get as far as the door.

The fact that this plan had been stupid from the beginning had never been in question, but once he'd managed to get into the office without resistance, Drew had allowed himself a little hope. But that hope had been naïve.

He cursed Jacko again, wishing he hadn't acted out of desperation. Like Freddie, Drew lived by a code and he honoured the rules of their world. What Jacko was planning was abominable. It went against everything they stood for and it couldn't be allowed. If Jacko could do that to the Tylers, he could do it to anyone. And it meant that anyone could do it to them. Drew had made this move tonight in the vague hope he could fix everything himself and stop Jacko doing something so utterly stupid.

Paul cocked the gun and pointed it at Drew's head. His stance was calm and confident, his hold steady. 'Get your performing monkey off my brother and tell him to drop the knife right now, or I'll blow your fucking head off,' he said simply.

There was a tense moment as Drew considered it and Richie waited for his boss's decision. Eventually he gave a curt nod and Richie did as Paul had bid. Seamus stepped forward and picked up the knife, giving it to Sammy, who weighed it up in his hand before slipping it into the waistband of his chinos.

'Move around the desk,' Paul ordered Richie.

Richie walked around to stand by Drew, his expression sombre now that they were on the other side of things. Drew didn't try to talk his way out. He knew that they were finished. The second they'd walked into this room their fate had been sealed. All Freddie had done since he came in was lead them right into the centre of his neatly sewn-up trap. Not breaking eye contact with Paul, Drew dropped his own knife on the desk with a clatter.

'Good choice,' Paul said. He stepped forward himself this time, picking up the knife but not lowering his gun. 'You alright, Fred?' he asked without looking round.

Freddie stood up and brushed down the front of his smart suit jacket. 'Never better, Paul,' he answered, walking over to stand next to his brother.

'OK.' Freddie clapped his hands. 'So here's how this is *actually* going to go. We're all going to go for a nice little drive to a warehouse of ours. There is no second option; there will be no negotiations. Everyone understand the plan?' Freddie looked around questioningly and saw all of his men nod. The colour drained from Drew's face. Neither he nor Richie said a word, their expressions stony. 'Good,' Freddie snapped. 'Let's go.'

CHAPTER FORTY-SEVEN

Drew and Richie were facing each other, just a few feet apart, their hands tied to a low metal joist that ran through the centre of this part of the warehouse. Their feet were still touching the floor but barely and these were tied together also. They were all trussed up and Drew knew that whatever Freddie had in store for them, it wasn't going to be fun.

Drew had kept his mouth shut on the way over. The hot-headed crime baron of Manchester part of him wanted to tear into his captors, let loose all of his frustration, but he knew that this wouldn't do him any good. If anything it would just give them satisfaction and make whatever was coming even worse.

He wasn't sure yet whether they meant to kill them. Nothing had yet been threatened or promised and he wasn't about to ask. His in-built survival instinct fought against this possibility, but the small voice of reason and logic underneath actually hoped that they did. Whatever the Tylers were, they weren't anywhere near as sadistic and twisted as Alfie Ramone. They might be criminal overlords, but he doubted they took much pleasure in the torture of other men.

Richie stared at him, naked fear in his eyes as he silently pleaded with Drew to do something. Drew just shook his head in defeat.

'So!' Freddie grinned, seemingly in good spirits. 'You thought you could break into my office, wave a knife around and I'd just quake in my boots and hand over a vast amount of money. This was your whole plan?' Freddie waited for an answer. When he didn't get one he turned to the rest of his men and shrugged, pulling a face. 'What about afterwards?' He turned back to Drew. 'Eh? What then? Did you think we'd just say, *Ahh, fair dos, he got us?*' He paused and shook his head. 'You don't just walk into another man's domain, steal his money and waltz back out into some sort of rainbow-coloured sunset.'

'You stole our coke!' Richie blurted out, incensed by the unfairness of the situation.

'Ah, but that's an entirely different situation, isn't it? You were on *my* turf peddling chemicals that were under *my* jurisdiction, to *my* dealers, behind *my* back.' He tutted and started pacing with a disappointed expression. 'That's just plain outrageous. You had that coming.'

Paul and the rest of their men nodded to each other sagely in agreement.

Drew closed his eyes in despair, wishing Richie had just not bothered speaking. He pulled on the tightly bound ties around his wrist and tried to wriggle a hand out but it was no use. When he opened his eyes it was to see Freddie had stepped in front of him. His expression was unreadable, but there was no warmth in his eyes.

'You realise we can't just allow you to take the piss the way you have tonight without retribution, don't you?' Freddie asked.

'Oh, just fucking get on with it then,' Drew responded, irritated. 'Stop drawing it out – just do whatever you're going to do.'

'What?' Richie gasped, horrified.

'OK then,' Freddie responded.

Paul walked forward with the baseball bat Seamus had previously wielded in the office and with a wide swing smashed it into the back of Richie's head.

'Fuck sake!' Drew roared.

Richie's head lolled forward and his eyes drooped as he blacked out. After a couple of tense seconds he came back round, lifting his head with a deep groan of pain.

'Not nice, seeing your men take a beating for your bad decisions, is it?' Freddie asked, pulling a cigarette out. He lit it and took a puff, staring Drew out.

Drew suddenly laughed, a low, bitter laugh. 'You really think they're going to work with you, don't you? The Ramones. They won't. They'll chew you up and spit you out and they won't give two shits who you are. Getting in with them is hard, mate. It took me years.'

Freddie nodded. 'Well, I guess I'll just have to find out, won't I?' He turned his back and gave Paul a nod.

Paul circled around Richie and pulled the bat back up in the air. Drew bit his lip to stop himself from saying anything as Richie begged for Paul not to do it. Harder this time, Paul swung the bat into Richie's stomach, sending his body reeling backward until the ties around his hand jolted him to a sharp stop.

Harsh wheezing sounds came out of Richie as he struggled to take in a breath. A mocking smile played on Freddie's face as he turned back to watch Drew.

Drew could have been exaggerating, trying to save his own skin or it might be true. Maybe the Ramones wouldn't take kindly to them muscling in and trying to force an alliance. From what Freddie had heard, Alfie Ramone was a sadist at best – to give him an excuse to exercise his passions could be a very stupid move. But they were experienced in dealing with all sorts of people in the underworld and at managing tricky situations. If anyone could make sure their meeting went the right way, it was Freddie. He was confident in this. He took another deep drag on his cigarette, then threw it to the ground.

'You should have stayed at home, mate.'

Pulling back his fist, Freddie punched Drew in the face as hard as he could. As his fist connected with Drew's nose, he felt it explode under his knuckles, heard the crunch of bone and cartilage and felt the warm wetness of blood as it began to gush out. Drew rocked back and then forward again, in his suspended state from the metal joist. As he steadied himself, he roared out in pain.

'Come on then,' he spat. 'Fucking do it.'

Paul handed him the bat and in one swift movement Freddie pulled it up and smashed it down onto Drew's forearm. He howled like a feral dog as the bone broke clean in two.

Pulling back the bat, Freddie smacked it down onto the same arm a second time, forcing another bloodcurdling scream from Drew. Tears ran down his face as the pain became unbearable. He gritted his teeth through it all and squeezed his eyes shut.

'Come on,' Drew cried. 'Finish it.'

Freddie stepped back and took a deep breath, rolling his shoulders back. He was tempted to go to town on the two men. A concussion and a couple of broken bones was nothing compared to what they deserved. He itched to hospitalise them for trying to kidnap him and hold him to ransom. But he also knew that a much worse fate already awaited them. There was no point in exerting themselves and leaving a violent trail that had to be carefully covered up when they were already dead men walking.

Freddie turned to Bill and nodded curtly. Bill immediately moved forward and cut Drew loose. Drew fell to the floor in a puddle of his own blood, cradling his broken arm. Sammy cut Richie loose and helped him down to a sitting position. Slightly concussed, Richie wobbled around, groaning incoherently. He gingerly touched the back of his head and moaned even louder when he saw blood on the tips of his fingers.

'My men will escort you back to your hotel. And I suggest you get on the next train home. I don't want to see you around my clubs or any of my other businesses again,' Freddie said calmly.

'What?' Drew asked incredulously. He stared up at Freddie with a look of confusion. 'So that's it?'

'That's it,' Freddie confirmed in a dismissive tone. He wiped Drew's blood off his hand with a rag given to him by Seamus.

'You aren't going to kill us?' Drew asked.

'Drew,' Richie groaned. 'What are you doing?' He looked over to his boss, despair in his eyes.

Freddie smiled at Drew coldly. 'He's hoping I'll finish the job before Ramone gets to you, aren't you, Drew? Because he's scared.' He watched Drew bristle at this and ignored it. 'But why would I do that and saddle myself with all the hassle of the clean-up and the stress of getting rid of your bodies, when I can just leave it to someone else?' He wrinkled his nose and shook his head. 'Nah. You've already got a target on your back. It makes more economic sense to just wait and let the wheels that are already in motion run their course.' He paused and stared at each of them pointedly. 'Well? What are you waiting for? Off you go.'

Sammy helped Richie up, sensing he was still too wobbly from his head injury to walk unaided. Bill nudged Drew, who still sat on the floor staring up at Freddie with a mixture of anger and fear.

'Come on. Move,' Bill said gruffly.

Slowly Drew stood up, still cradling his broken arm.

'You'll want to get that seen to, mate,' Freddie said casually, as Drew walked past.

He paused and looked back at Freddie with a slow shake of his head. 'I was trying to sort this the civilised way, you know. Now...' He trailed off and clamped his mouth shut, as if stopping himself from saying any more. Careful not to knock his arm, Drew left and Bill closed the door behind them all.

Freddie and Paul were the only ones left now inside the small warehouse and Freddie set about picking up the loose bits of rope and rolling up the sheet of plastic they'd laid down underneath the two men. If ever an investigation came about after Alfie had finished them off, the last thing they needed was a trace of DNA on the warehouse floorboards – even as unlikely as the prospect was.

Paul stared at the closed door with a frown. 'Hey, what do you think that was about?' he asked.

'What?' Freddie didn't look up, busy making sure the plastic wrap was securely rolled.

'That thing he said about that this was the civilised way. He looked like he was going to say something else.'

'It's nothing, Paul,' Freddie said dismissively. 'People will say anything when they're in a corner. And that man's in the tightest corner I've ever seen.'

'Hmm, OK,' Paul replied, feeling doubtful. There was something in the man's tone that made him feel on edge. 'Come on then. I told James I'd be home hours ago.'

Turning to help his brother, Paul put all doubts aside. It was nothing. Drew and his firm had been dealt with. They shouldn't have any reason to see them again.

CHAPTER FORTY-EIGHT

Anna sat down on the old wooden bench at the side of the playground and crossed her slim legs, wishing she had thought to wear anything other than heels. Smiling tightly as Ethan ran over towards the monkey bars, she took the small takeaway coffee cup from Freddie's outstretched hand. He was as unsuitably dressed as she was, she noticed, his Savile Row suit already mucky from rubbing against the pirate-ship den Ethan had asked him to join him in. She smiled wryly as he noticed this with horror.

'Yeah, alright,' he said. 'Not my best decision.'

'Well, at least Ethan's enjoying himself,' Anna replied.

Things were still not right between them, awkward silences and a seemingly unbreachable distance between them where before there had only been easy companionship. Freddie was at his wits' end. If he had done something terrible and they were arguing at least they could have it out and he could apologise. But this time even Anna had admitted he had done the right thing. That didn't make it any easier, though; he had still hurt her and he had no idea how to make it right. So, for now they were stuck in a cold, awkward limbo, still living together, yet strangely apart at the same time.

Anna looked around at the small park. They were barely a stone's throw from their building, but Anna had never stepped foot inside this park before. She'd never had cause to, had barely even registered that it was there.

'Listen.' Freddie turned to Anna and touched her hand. 'We haven't had much time just to ourselves lately, especially with everything that's been going on.' He watched her strained expression soften slightly, underneath her flawless make-up. 'I was thinking we should go out for dinner soon, somewhere nice. Just the two of us. Talk things through. Properly this time.' He squeezed her hand. 'I want to make this work, Anna. I want us to be OK.'

Anna smiled at him sadly. 'We will be OK, Freddie. I'm not sure how, but you and me, this—' She pointed at him and then at herself. 'This will always get back to OK. It might take some time to make it work, but we'll do it. I promise.'

Anna knew that no matter how she felt about the situation, she would never leave Freddie. She also knew that this was what he was afraid of and she didn't blame him. She'd been cold and distant. It was her way of coping with things; it always had been. But it didn't mean she was going anywhere. Freddie was the love of her life. And she'd already resigned herself to the fact that she'd rather live with some unhappiness by his side than live a day without him. He was part of who she was, heart and soul.

'And dinner sounds good,' she said, her red lips turning upward in a genuine smile. Leaning in towards him she kissed him gently on the lips.

Freddie's phone beeped and he looked at the screen. After a second his eyebrows raised up in surprise. 'Er, can you stay with Ethan for a bit? I've got to pop back to the flat to make a call.'

'Oh, um…' Alarm ran through Anna at the thought of being left in charge of Ethan, of being trapped with him with no option to leave. She looked up at Freddie in panic; he was already standing up to leave, but he was still preoccupied with his phone, replying to whoever had just texted.

'I won't be long, I promise.' He leaned down and kissed her on the top of the head and then quickly marched off back towards their building.

Anna's wide eyes turned back to Ethan. What was she supposed to do now? What if something happened? What if she had another flashback? Her heart rate spiked and she raised her hand up to her chest.

CHAPTER FORTY-NINE

Holding the blankets back off the bed, Anna waited for Ethan to climb in before she draped them over his lap. It hadn't been as bad as she'd thought, watching Ethan at the park earlier. She had panicked thinking that the memories of her trauma would once again overwhelm her and that she'd somehow fail in the task of looking after him. In her mind, she played out a hundred ways he could get hurt and all of them would have been her fault for not protecting him. But nothing had happened. Ethan had played quite happily, life had continued on at its normal, placid pace and Freddie had returned to the same two normal people he had left. It occurred to her that perhaps she could get through this after all. Perhaps the biggest obstacle in her way was nothing more than her own irrational fear. Instead of lying down, Ethan stayed sitting up, staring at her. Anna hesitated.

'So, you OK then?' she asked.

'Yeah. I was just wondering something,' he replied.

'What are you wondering?' Anna asked warily.

'What's on your pyjamas?'

'Excuse me?' Anna blinked.

'When we went shopping Dad said everyone should have ones with things they like on, not just boring plain ones.' He pointed down at his new Spiderman set. 'So, I picked Spiderman. What did you pick?'

Ethan was still getting used to his dad's ways. Everything was completely different here to how it had been with his mum.

Having choices and special clothes and nice outings and even being allowed to act his age were all alien concepts.

He was also still trying to make friends with Anna. Sensing that she wasn't completely happy about him being here, he desperately wanted to change that. The last thing he wanted was his dad to stop seeing him because he made Anna unhappy. At home, if one of his mother's boyfriends didn't like him, she'd just shut him away out of sight and pretend he wasn't there. But that was because she had nowhere else to send him. His dad did. His dad could just send him back to his mum and stop having him over if Anna didn't end up liking him soon.

Anna's mouth curled into a half-smile of amusement. 'Well, I didn't actually pick a character. Mine are just purple.'

'Oh, OK,' Ethan replied. He glanced up at her nervously through his thick lashes. 'Do you like the Avengers?' he asked, trying to find some common ground in the only way he knew how.

'Actually yes. I think they're pretty cool,' Anna answered. She'd seen a couple of the films with Tanya, when they had girls' nights in. She suddenly felt a pang of longing for her best friend. She hadn't spoken to her properly in a few days, which was highly unusual for them.

'Who's your favourite?'

'Iron Man. Definitely,' Anna replied straight away. 'No contest.'

'His suit is really cool.' Ethan grinned. 'But I like Spiderman best. He can shoot out webs with his hands.'

'He can. Anyway—' Anna gave him a tight smile. 'You'd best get some sleep.'

About to stand, Anna was taken by surprise when Ethan leaned forward and tentatively hugged her. She froze for a moment, her arms suspended mid-air. Awkwardly she rested one arm over his back and patted him with the other. Part of her yearned to lean in and cuddle him properly, breathe in his sweet child smell and show him some love. But the bigger part was pointedly aware that this wasn't her son and was too scared to get close in case the memories of her miscarriage overwhelmed her once more. Anna was getting good at keeping the flashbacks at bay. She could be around Ethan now. All she had to do was keep an emotional distance.

The buzzer sounded in the hallway and Anna heard Freddie pick up the phone. His tone changed from calm and curious to hard and cold in a split second.

'What do you want?' she heard him ask curtly. There was a pause. 'Come up.'

Gently pulling back, Anna tucked the sheets neatly around Ethan's legs once more. 'Goodnight,' she said. She pulled the door almost closed and went to find out what was going on.

Watching her go, Ethan felt the tears rise in his eyes. He snuggled down into his bed and pulled his stuffed dog close to his chest, wrapping his thin arms around it like a shield. The tears fell silently down his cheek and into the pillow. At least at home he knew where he stood and he'd accepted his position. When his dad had taken him here he'd thought perhaps he and Anna would want him; that perhaps things could be different. He had allowed his hopes to rise. But when he'd taken his chances and hugged Anna, she'd turned stiff under his arms. If he hadn't been sure of her feelings towards him before, he was now. However polite she was for his dad's sake, Anna didn't want him here.

Closing his eyes to try and stem the flow of tears, Ethan turned over to face the wall. It was time to face facts – it didn't matter where he was. He wasn't wanted anywhere.

*

As Anna walked down the hall she saw Freddie's tense stance, his arms folded defensively across his chest. She frowned.

'What's up?' she asked, as the front door opened.

Mollie walked in, worry written all over her face. Her gaze darted from Anna to Freddie and she began to fiddle nervously with the cuff of her jacket.

'I know you don't want to see me right now…' she started.

'You're right, I don't,' Freddie said, cutting her off.

Mollie's lip wobbled and Anna looked away, feeling awkward. Mollie took a deep breath. 'Well, I had no choice but to come,' she said. 'I wanted to say something earlier, but I couldn't reach Paul and I was hoping it would be alright, that she'd come home…' The tears that had been threatening behind her brave composure finally began to fall.

Anna stepped forward and put her arm around her, shocked. Mollie Tyler was a thick-skinned woman at the hardest of times. It was rare to see her cry over anything.

'Mollie, what's wrong?' she asked in dismay.

'What are you talking about?' Freddie questioned, his attention sharpening.

'Thea,' Mollie replied. 'She went out last night and never came home. I tried calling and texting this morning but she's not answering.'

'And you're only telling me now?' Freddie exclaimed, looking at his watch. It was already gone seven.

'Well, I'm not exactly welcome right now, am I?' Mollie countered, pulling herself up straighter. 'And like I said, Paul ain't answering for some reason. Otherwise I'd have said something earlier. But I was hoping I wouldn't have to, that maybe she just stayed out and went straight to work or something. But I've still heard nothing. And now I'm getting really worried that something might have happened.' Mollie's voice broke and fresh tears fell.

Anna guided Mollie through to the lounge, exchanging a worried glance with Freddie as she passed him. Freddie's mouth formed a grim line.

'Don't worry, I'll find her. She's probably just lost her phone or something,' Freddie said. He watched Mollie nod and walked away to the kitchen to call Paul, a deep feeling of unease settling in the bottom of his stomach.

If Thea had lost her phone she'd have already been at the club to get a new one from him. He had loads of burners waiting to be switched out at a moment's notice. And it wasn't like his sister to just disappear. She had never done that before. Something was up and whatever it was, it wasn't good.

CHAPTER FIFTY

Jules answered the door with a tight expression and peered around Freddie into the empty hallway behind him.

'Where's my boy?' she demanded. 'I told you to bring him home or there'd be trouble. I ain't just giving him up to you just like that.' She put her hands on her ample hips and stared at him stonily.

'Oh, just don't, Jules,' he replied irritably. With everything going on right now and as they still hadn't managed to get hold of Thea, Jules giving him crap was the last thing he needed.

Despite this, though, Freddie was still aware of the power she held over his contact with Ethan. He forced himself to bite his tongue, clenching his fist down by his side. 'Listen,' he said, as calmly as he could muster. 'I'd like to spend a bit longer with Ethan. To get to know him.'

'You've had him for days, surely you've got to know him by now,' Jules said with a tut. 'Surely you've got tired of him by now and all,' she added with a snort. 'I can't imagine he fits very well around all you've got going on.'

When Freddie glared at her Jules stepped back, her expression suddenly uncertain. She'd been sure after a few days Freddie would be begging to hand him back, that taking him was just one big ruse to get out of paying her what she wanted. But perhaps she'd been wrong. Licking her lips, she looked away and tried a different tactic.

'You know it's been strange not having him here. I'm so used to him being by my side. He's my little man. I've missed him terrible.'

'Yeah?' Freddie asked sceptically. 'If you missed him so much, how come you haven't even rung to ask how he is? To check he's OK?'

Walking in, Freddie closed the front door behind him. He didn't need the whole building knowing his business.

'Well, I—' Jules stuttered at the question. 'I knew he was with you, didn't I? He's perfectly fine with his own dad.'

'A dad who's never looked after children, who only met him recently?' Freddie pulled a face. 'I'd be wanting to call and make sure everything was OK, if that was me.'

Jules didn't answer and Freddie stalked past her into the lounge. The place was still a mess but it was in a lot better shape than the last time he'd seen it. Jules had at least cleared away the dirty plates and mugs and empty beer bottles.

'I want to keep Ethan for another week,' Freddie said, turning around to face Jules. 'This is for your troubles,' he continued, passing her another envelope containing a wad of cash. She opened it and pulled it out eagerly, her eyes bright with greed. 'If you can bear to be without him for that long, of course.'

Freddie watched her reaction, willing her to show some sort of care for the boy, to give him some hope. Instead she smiled happily.

''Course. If that's what you need, that's fine,' she said. 'Just make sure you look after him, won't you? He's all I have in this world,' she added, widening her eyes for dramatic effect. 'But just for a week, mind,' she said sharply. 'I need him back after that.'

Jules couldn't quite hide the calculation from her eyes. Whilst she had Ethan she had control and this was of the utmost importance if she was going to get what she wanted from Freddie.

Not trusting himself to reply without launching at her, Freddie turned on his heel and walked out. He couldn't stay a moment longer for fear his temper would finally get the better of him and he'd do something he'd later regret.

As he left the small flat, Jules narrowed her eyes and smirked at his retreating back. The extreme effort it took Freddie to utter such a polite request had been exactly what Jules needed to see. Finally, the great Freddie Tyler was beginning to understand who held the cards in this situation. Jules. *She* was Ethan's mother and *she* was the one who could legally decide whether or not Freddie had any access to him.

This still didn't seem to be quite enough, though. Freddie still needed a little extra push to realise he would need to pay her a lot more to keep things sweet in his life. It was time to ramp things up a little. Her grin widened nastily.

CHAPTER FIFTY-ONE

Sarah Riley moved the mouse on the desk and the three screens in front of her came to life. Light flooded the corner of the large, dark office and she tensed, looking over to check that no one outside had seen and come to check out what was going on. They hadn't and she allowed herself a small breath of relief.

Tapping in the password she'd swiped a few weeks before, Sarah logged into the CCTV system and began methodically searching through the cameras nearest to Mollie's house. Taking off her chunky silver bracelet, she unscrewed the centre piece of it, revealing a small USB device. She plugged this into the hard drive ready to save any clips that could be of any use to Freddie's search for Thea.

Engrossed in the footage, she almost didn't notice the door opening and the person coming through it. Just as the door closed, she caught a glimpse out of the corner of her eye and looked up.

'Oh my God, Adam!' she exclaimed, holding a hand to her heart. She gave a small tinkling laugh to cover her nerves. 'You almost gave me a heart attack.'

'Oh hey, ma'am, likewise,' he said with a grin, showing even white teeth. His piercing blue eyes sparkled in the low light of the screens and held Sarah's gaze for longer than they usually would.

Taking advantage of this, Sarah smiled and subtly leaned forward, slipping the USB bracelet out of the port and down under the table where she quickly placed it back into its normal position on her wrist.

'You look different out of work clothes,' she observed.

In place of his usual shirt, Adam Chambers wore just a simple black V-neck T-shirt, which showed off his muscular arms and extensive tattoos in all their glory. Around his neck hung a long, thick silver chain with a chunky cross hanging off it. His dark hair was pulled back in its usual bun but it suddenly seemed a lot more attractive on him now that he was in more casual attire.

To her surprise, Sarah found her body responding to him in a way it hadn't responded to any man in a long time. She reminded herself that she was Adam's boss and was also in no position to let anyone too close to her secrets right now.

A grin crept up on Adam's face as though he was able to read her thoughts and Sarah felt herself blush. She was eternally thankful that the limited light in the office would mean this was not obvious.

'You don't seem to be out of work clothes yourself yet, though, ma'am. Have you been here all night?' Adam asked, looking pointedly back towards her desk and then at the one she was snooping on.

She hadn't been there all night; in fact she'd only just come back, certain that the place would be empty, but it seemed as good an excuse as any to jump on. 'I have. We still aren't getting anywhere and I wanted to go over everyone's data, see if a pair of fresh eyes could help.'

'In the dark?'

'Migraine,' Sarah responded with a self-pitying wince. 'No rest for the wicked, I'm afraid.'

'Ouch. Fair play for sticking it out. Still…' Moving nearer, Adam sat back against the desk next to her, his body now in close proximity. 'You can't burn a candle at both ends and expect it not to burn out. Maybe what you really need is a break.' He bit his full bottom lip and Sarah had to stop herself from mirroring his body language as she briefly wondered what it would be like to bite his bottom lip herself. 'Fancy a drink?'

The invite was tempting – more than tempting. For a moment Sarah allowed herself to imagine what might happen if she said yes. The thought of those arms wrapping around her waist almost made her resolve waver, but not quite. She still had work to do tonight, important work. Thea had already been missing for over twenty-four hours and there hadn't even been a ransom call yet. This was what worried Sarah the most. Without a call for ransom, they couldn't be sure if she was even still alive.

She smiled regretfully. 'I wish I could, but I'm just not going to sleep until I know I've gone through all I can. Sorry.'

Adam shrugged and backed down gracefully. 'Well, you can't blame a guy for trying,' he said.

'What are you doing here so late anyway?' Sarah asked, realising he hadn't said.

'Actually, pretty much the same as you,' he said with a guilty laugh. 'I'm too agitated tonight. I just feel like we're missing something, you know? Something really big and really obvious.'

'Mhm.' Sarah nodded along.

'So, I came to grab one of the work cameras. I'm going to do a late-night recce, see what I can find.'

'Oh yeah?' Sarah's heart rate quickened. This was unplanned; she'd had no time to warn Freddie. 'Where are you thinking of going?'

'Not sure yet. It's late so chances are Tyler's at one of the clubs.' He shrugged. 'I'll check out both, see if I get lucky.'

Walking over to one of the store cupboards, Adam opened it up and rummaged around, coming back out with one of the high-spec DSLRs the team used. He waved it up in the air.

'I haven't officially signed it out but I'll have it back safe and sound by morning. That OK?' he asked.

'Sure, that's fine,' Sarah answered. 'Good luck. You never know, you might stumble across that big break you're looking for.'

'You never know,' he replied.

As he walked back out the door, Sarah swore underneath her breath and quickly pulled the second phone out of her handbag. Dialling Freddie's number she waited and then cursed again when it went straight to voicemail. Switching to text she wrote out an urgent message and pressed 'send'.

'Come on, Freddie,' she pleaded. 'Pick up!'

CHAPTER FIFTY-TWO

Finally finding the file she was looking for in the cabinet, Anna opened it up and slipped in the flier she'd just received. A new rival had opened up in South London and was trying out some new acts. It was nothing to worry about just yet, but she liked to keep a record of what other clubs were up to. She stared at the paper for a moment, unseeing, as her thoughts once again wandered to Thea. Where was she? What had happened? No one seemed to have any idea.

Closing the filing cabinet, Anna ran her hand through her hair tiredly and walked through to the bar. She needed a drink.

The club was buzzing with activity and Rhonda was on stage, amazing the customers with her fire-breathing act. Pausing to watch as Rhonda pulled a particularly daring move, Anna leaned over the bar waiting for Carl or one of the barmaids to spot her when they were free.

Almost immediately Carl made a beeline for her, a grim expression on his face. Anna frowned as he reached her.

'What's wrong?' she asked.

'Er—' Carl glanced down towards the other end of the crowded bar. 'There's a bit of a situation. I was just about to come find you.'

'What sort of situation?' Anna asked.

Carl sighed. 'Tanya's mate, the one who came back to town recently. She's sat at the bar with some bloke, shouting her mouth off.'

Anna felt her blood turn cold. 'Saying what?'

Carl looked uncomfortable. 'That she's got a kid with Freddie. Keeps demanding her drinks for free, saying you owe her. She's off her nut.'

Anna took a moment to compose herself, then smiled tightly at Carl across the bar. 'The kid bit's true.'

'What?' Carl looked genuinely surprised.

'He only just found out.' Anna was irritated. It wasn't exactly a secret anymore, but they'd been keeping news of Ethan quiet, until things were more settled. Of course Jules wouldn't care about that, though. Anna could only imagine how much she'd love the kudos that came with being Freddie Tyler's baby-mamma.

'She's not getting a fucking ice cube free off me,' she continued resentfully. She hadn't forgiven Jules for the way she'd relished breaking the news to her and she never would. 'So, don't give her any special treatment.'

'Not likely, don't worry,' Carl replied. 'She's causing havoc down there, though. I was about to ask you if you're OK with me chucking her out.'

'Tempting,' Anna said with a wry smile. 'But don't worry. I'll deal with her.'

Bracing herself, Anna pushed her shiny, dark hair back off her face and stalked down the bar towards Jules. Now that she knew the woman was here, she could hear her loud, screeching laugh cutting through the music and general chatter. It grated on her nerves like sandpaper.

Anna curled her lip in disgust. The woman was draped over her stool and half the bar as though she was at home on her sofa. Her lank, greasy blonde hair hadn't seen a brush in days and her bright red lipstick was smeared around her mouth as though a five-year-old had applied it.

As Anna looked closer, she noticed how small Jules's pupils were. They were like pinpricks in her flat, pale eyes. It was something they all looked out for on the club scene. Here, in the dark, where most people's pupils were more dilated than usual, it was a clear sign of drug use. The pair of vacant eyes Anna was studying suddenly swivelled towards her and focused. Jules's round face changed, the smile of amusement turning to one of smug nastiness.

'Well, if it isn't my son's new stepmother,' she called out in a sarcastic, sing-song voice. 'Have you come to open me a tab? None of these people here seem to know who I am.' She tutted as if disappointed. 'Hiding your new stepson are you, Anna? Like he's something to be ashamed of? Disgusting. My poor boy.' She raised her voice, looking around for an audience. 'I'll have a right time when he comes back, undoing that mental damage.'

'Perhaps,' Anna said coolly. 'But hopefully not as long as it takes Freddie to undo the mental damage caused by watching his mother get high whilst he's left to rot in the background nursing the bruises she's inflicted,' she said, her dark-blue eyes flashing with challenge.

Jules blinked, taken aback. She clearly hadn't expected any response.

'What are you doing here, Jules?' Anna asked, jumping straight to the point.

'I'm enjoying a rare night out with my boyfriend here,' she said, tapping the equally unimpressive man next to her on the leg. 'Seeing as I'm child-free for once. For the first time in seven long years. Some of us don't have the freedom of just doing whatever we want when we want. We have responsibilities. Even when we're tired and sick and could really do with a break.' She snuck a sideways glance at Anna to see if her words had gained her any sympathy. It appeared not, as Anna's stony expression had not changed. 'But you wouldn't know about that, what with not being a mother, like me.'

Anna felt the barb hit home, and she braced herself against the sharp pain that always came with the reminder of her inability to have children.

'And why are you *here* exactly? In *my* club?' Anna pushed forward, ignoring the mocking look on Jules's face.

'Well, I figured a few drinks was the least you could do for me, seeing as I've looked after and provided for Ethan all on my own all these years, without any help.'

Anna had had enough. Ethan or not, she didn't need to pander to this bitch for any reason. 'Get the fuck out, Jules,' she demanded. She watched the confusion spread across Jules's wide face as she realised her idea wasn't working out. 'I don't owe you anything. No one does.'

She stepped closer, her stance menacing. 'If you really think you deserve some sort of medal for the neglect and utter abuse you've shown your son, you need your head looking at. That boy would have been better off anywhere else but with you. *Anywhere*. As far as I'm concerned you're lucky Freddie hasn't already called social services on *you*.' Jules's eyebrows shot up. 'Yeah, you heard me,' Anna persisted, her voice getting stronger and louder with every word. 'You thought you could play Freddie, play us – well, it's not happening. You don't get to rock up, pull a sob story after keeping Ethan a secret, demand money and waltz around like Lady Muck. I mean, it's not like you even care about him, is it?'

Anna felt herself growing more and more angry as she defended the poor boy against the woman who was ruining his life. Ethan was just a child. He might not be hers but he was Freddie's and he deserved better than this.

'It's not like you're on a crusade for Ethan. This is all about you. You haven't even asked if he's OK since he's been with us,' she spat. 'All you care about is money and getting high. As you clearly are tonight.'

'You bitch,' Jules screeched back. She got up off the bar stool and pushed her face into Anna's. Anna didn't move. 'You think you're all that, but you ain't. Looking down on me like some shit on your shoe, well, you can keep your shitty drinks, sweetheart.

And your skanky club.' She turned her nose up pointedly as she looked around. 'This place is crap anyway. You might own this little bar, but you know what you'll never have?' She leaned in and smiled like a snake, the nugget of information she'd gleaned from Tanya coming in useful. 'A baby of your own. Because your womb's shrivelled up like the old prune you really are under all that make-up and designer gear.'

Anna took a deep breath in but forced herself to stand tall and not waver in the face of such spite. Two of the bouncers came up and hovered behind her, having heard the commotion.

'You'll never feel a first kick or hold your brand-new baby in your arms, because you're dead on the inside.' Twisting her mouth spitefully, Jules went in for the knockout blow. 'Not like me. I felt the kicks. I held my baby. Mine and Freddie's. *Our* child. I gave him what you *never* can, you sad, dried-up— Argh!'

Having heard enough, Anna's hand shot forward and grasped a handful of greasy hair and yanked down hard. Jules toppled over and landed hard on her side on the floor.

'Hey!' The man she was with began to protest but the two bouncers grasped his arms as he started forward.

'OK, come on, buddy. You OK there, Anna?' Mickey, one of her bouncers, asked.

'Perfectly fine,' she replied grimly, ignoring the searing pain Jules's words had inflicted.

Jules writhed and cried out underneath Anna's vice-like grip. Anna yanked again, this time upward, forcing Jules to stand.

'Ouch, get off me, you crazy bitch, that hurts!' she yelled. She clawed at Anna's hands, trying to free her hair but it was no use. Anna was too strong.

The customers around them stared with wide eyes as the beautiful young club owner dragged the other woman towards the exit, still somehow retaining her composure in her fitted dress and heels. Although seething with embarrassment at the spectacle she herself was taking part in, Anna revelled in the power she held at that moment. The boxing had been paying off in more ways than one. She might look slight, but she was strong and agile. Jules, for all her bluster, was nothing but hot air and soft padding. And she had more than asked for this.

Anna braced her body at the door to take the extra weight and with all the force she could muster flung Jules out onto the street. Jules landed on her knees with a hard bump and quickly stood up, staggering as she regained her balance and holding her head with her hands.

'That hurt, you fucking cow!' she shouted, looking to her boyfriend for support. He was standing just down from her, keeping quiet as he eyed up the size of the bouncers who'd ejected him from the building.

'Good,' Anna shot back. She raised her chin. 'And you're barred. Don't ever show your face here again.' Turning away, she began to walk back inside.

'Yeah?' Jules gave a humourless laugh. 'Well, I guess I'll have to rethink Freddie's access to my boy then, won't I?' she shot back. 'Two can play at this game.'

The feeling of elation and satisfaction that came from throwing Jules out was beginning to wear off and Anna felt her heart plummet as she registered Jules's threat. She turned back with an icy glare.

'That's the problem with you, though, isn't it, Jules? You really don't care about Ethan at all. He's just a game to you.'

Knowing that no good would come of further arguments, Anna walked back inside and tuned out the angry gush of expletives Jules hurled after her. Ignoring the looks of some of the customers who'd witnessed her argument, Anna marched straight through to the back office and closed the door. The loud music dimmed to a low hum through the wooden door. With her hands on her hips, she replayed Jules's words in her head.

A deep, wracking sob echoed around the small space and she realised in surprise that it had come from her. She pulled air into her lungs as another one escaped and she tried to stem the river of emotions that had broken through the dam she'd so carefully constructed. Another one escaped and then another and another until she wasn't sure whether she was just crying or having a full-on anxiety attack. Taking deep breaths, Anna paced around the room, refusing to give in. She couldn't.

But Jules's words kept resounding in her ears and pierced through her heart. Jules knew her weaknesses, her failings. And she was right. Whatever else Anna was, whatever Jules was, Jules had been the one to give Freddie a son. Jules had experienced something that Anna never would. And that killed her.

A knock sounded at the door and Anna shouted out between sobs for Carl to go away. There was a pause and then the door opened. Freddie walked in, horror forming on his face as he found Anna in such a state.

'What's happened?' he asked, quickly closing the door behind him. He'd popped in on his way through to check she was OK with everything that was going on, but clearly she wasn't.

Anna tried to wipe away her tears but they kept falling. 'Jules. I can't do this anymore, Freddie. I can't do it.' Her voice cracked. 'She knows I can't…' She swallowed, not able to finish the sentence. 'I just can't see her and listen to her poisonous bullshit. I can't go through every day knowing I can't avoid her. I just, I just…'

'Shh, it's OK.' Freddie pulled her into his embrace and held her tight, kissing the top of her head. 'Don't worry. I'm going to deal with this. I know what to do.' His expression turned hard and dark above her head as he rocked her gently. 'I'll make sure you never have to see her again.'

CHAPTER FIFTY-THREE

Sarah walked into the office of Ruby Ten and closed the door behind her quickly. Taking off the woolly hat and unwrapping the thick scarf she'd used to obscure her identity, she chucked them down on the desk. She took the last vacant seat among the gathering of his most trusted men and leaned towards Freddie, who was seated behind the desk looking drawn and thoroughly pissed off.

'I've been through the footage. There's not much, a possible car driving away a couple of streets down, but I can't get a positive ID off the cameras. It's too dark. There's nothing closer and your mum's description was pretty vague,' she said, not bothering with the formal niceties. Time was of the essence.

'I figured.' Freddie pinched the bridge of his nose. 'So what now?'

'Bill and Zack are trying to track her phone, but...' Paul trailed off as Freddie's phone beeped, waiting as his brother checked the screen.

Freddie sat up, suddenly alert. He glanced at Sarah. 'It's them,' he said heavily.

'Let me see,' she demanded. He handed his phone over to her and she stared down at the picture of Thea Tyler tied to a chair. A text came through as she held the phone and she read it aloud. 'You have forty-eight hours to deliver the money from the coke to the following address or your sister pays the price.'

She glanced at the address. It was for somewhere in Manchester. Exhaling heavily, Sarah shook her head.

'Finally, a fucking text at least,' Freddie said, trying not to focus on the state of his little sister. She was alive and right now that was the most important thing. 'We need to work out where the bastards are holding her,' Freddie said.

'And which bastards are we talking about?' Sarah asked.

'Drew and his crew.'

'You definitely don't think it's Ramone?'

'No.' He shook his head. 'Not his style.'

Sarah nodded grimly and looked back down at the picture. She pinched the screen to zoom in and looked around the edges. 'They're in a house. Thick carpet, tidy room, nice enough furniture.' She looked up, puzzled. 'But where would they have access to a house here? Or do you think they've taken her to Manchester?'

'If they have we're screwed,' Freddie answered. 'We don't know the city and we have no pull there.'

Sarah took another close look and frowned. 'What time did your mum say she left again?'

'About eight.'

'There's a small clock in the background that's displaying the time as ten past nine, when the photo was taken. Look, here.' She reached over and pointed to the small clock on the side table behind Thea. 'It might be wrong, but then again if it's correct and if he took this last night not long after he kidnapped her, which' – she squinted – 'I think judging by how tidy she still looks, that may well be the case, then he wouldn't have had time to get her to Manchester. Which means she could still be in London. He probably waited until tonight to send it to throw you off, make you think he'd travelled.'

'He could easily have taken that at ten past nine this morning, or this evening,' Paul piped up.

Sarah shook her head. 'Not this morning – it's dark light. It could have been tonight,' she conceded, 'but she just doesn't look to me like someone who's been tied for a whole day already. Not from past experience anyway. But I could be wrong.'

Freddie nodded. 'The fuckers were here trying to extort money from me by around eleven, so I doubt they would have had time to get her to Manchester and back.'

'That was only two of them, Fred,' Paul replied. 'Where were the rest of them?'

There was a long silence as everyone considered the options. Eventually Freddie nodded. 'Well, we ain't got nothing else to go on, so I guess let's go with that and pray to fucking God that we're right. Riley, can you look into Drew, see if he's rented anywhere, or been seen anywhere unusual over the last few days? I'm assuming the team has been keeping tabs on them, since they've been around us.'

'I'll see what I can find, but I'm going to have to be careful. Miechowski's just waiting for an opportunity to help me slip up.'

'OK. Dig around their Northern properties too, just in case.' Freddie turned to the rest of the room whilst Sarah started wrapping herself back up. 'Dean, Simon, team up and see what you can find out. Sammy, Seamus, you too. Maybe start at The Black Bear. Paul, Bill, go and find Zack, see if there's anything he can do with this text. Here.' He threw his phone to Paul who caught it and slipped it into his pocket. 'I'm still on the same number for now in case anything more comes through. Now go.'

Freddie waited as they all filed out. Paul was the last to go and they exchanged worried glances.

'We'll find her, Fred,' Paul said darkly. 'And we'll fucking kill Drew and whoever else touched her when we do. They'll rue the day they ever came here.'

CHAPTER FIFTY-FOUR

Yawning after a long night of tossing and turning, Anna reached the top of the stairs to their new premises and handed Tanya a coffee. The place was a hive of activity, electricians in the main room fitting the new soft lighting, carpet men walking through to the bedrooms with brand new rolls on their backs and carpenters banging away on the second floor.

'Thanks, that's exactly what I needed,' Tanya said gratefully.

One of the workmen walked by and slowed down, giving her an appreciative once-over and her smile dropped. 'Hey, am I paying you to fucking ogle, mate?' she demanded, hand on hip. 'I think not. Get the fuck back to work.'

'Alright, alright,' he said, raising his paint-covered hands in surrender. 'Keep your knickers on.'

'Oh, I will, don't you worry,' she confirmed. She turned her back on him and faced Anna. 'What's going on with Thea then?' she asked, drinking deeply from her coffee.

'I have no idea,' Anna replied, her tone troubled. 'Freddie got in at dawn and passed out so I haven't had a chance to ask him. I left a note offering to watch Ethan for him when I get back, so at least he doesn't have to worry about that.'

'That's progress,' Tanya said, over the brim of her coffee cup.

'Just trying to help,' Anna replied. 'But it means I'll have to stay in with him tonight. I'll be climbing the walls there on my own all night, waiting for news. Come over?' she asked. 'Bring a bottle and we'll wait and stress out together?'

'Yeah, of course,' Tanya replied. 'Goes without saying.' She bit her lip as they watched the workmen in silence for a few moments. 'God, I hope she's OK,' she muttered worriedly.

Anna gave her a sad smile. 'Me too. But she will be. We need to focus on that. If anyone can find her, it's Freddie. You and I know that better than anyone.'

'True,' Tanya replied with a nod.

She bit her lip and glanced at Anna.

'Listen, I've been meaning to speak to you about something.'

'What is it?' Anna picked up a pile of colour swatches they were supposed to be choosing paint from. It all seemed unimportant suddenly.

'The Last Laugh. It isn't a huge earner and it takes up a lot of our time. Too much, really. With this opening I was wondering what you thought about selling up? We could increase our time and effort here and maybe even look at expanding Club Anya.'

She trailed off, hoping that Anna wouldn't dismiss the idea out of hand.

'Oh.' Anna was taken by surprise. She'd known Tanya didn't enjoy working their comedy club almost from the second they'd opened it, but she hadn't realised she wanted to be rid of it altogether. 'Can I think on it?'

'Yeah, 'course.' Tanya flapped her hand. 'Whatever, take your time. It was just a thought.'

'OK.'

One of the workmen called for Tanya's attention and she walked off to deal with whatever he needed help with. Anna stared at the room around her. People buzzed and moved and made noise and she just stood still right in the middle of it, feeling like she wasn't even really there.

For so long they had been so excited about this new venture. It had been all they'd talked about. Now all of a sudden it meant nothing. Thea was family and she was missing. And what was any of this worth without family?

*

Freddie walked through the hotel foyer and into the tea room to the side. The two men flanking Alfie and Andre Ramone saw him about the same time that he saw them. Freddie made a beeline for their table by the large front window and they stood up, stepping in front of their boss with hard expressions.

'It's OK, boys,' Alfie said, taking a sip of his tea. 'Let him through. Not much he can do unarmed and alone in a nice place like this, is there?' They stepped aside reluctantly and Freddie took a seat opposite the two Ramones. He undid his suit jacket and made himself comfortable. Alfie watched him, his dark eyes unwavering. 'I'm guessing this is why you've sought me out here. I can't exactly do much to you here either.'

'With all due respect, this is my city. There isn't much you can do anywhere, if you want to leave with the same number of extremities you came with.' Freddie smiled politely.

Alfie chuckled as he smothered a scone in clotted cream and added a blob of jam.

'Do you want one?' he asked, gesturing towards the plate on the table between them. 'They're really very good.'

'I'm OK, thank you,' Freddie declined graciously. He stared at the man across from him. Was he wrong? Was it the Ramones who had taken her? After all, they weren't exactly on the same side either. He needed to play this very carefully. 'I'm merely here to issue you an invitation.'

'An invitation?' Alfie repeated through a mouthful of scone, crumbs spraying everywhere.

'My brother and I would like to discuss some business with you. See if perhaps we can work out some sort of arrangement going forward.'

Alfie chuckled again and rubbed his hands together, wiping off the smudge of jam on one finger. 'And why would we want to do that, Mr Tyler?' he asked. He exchanged an amused glance with his brother. 'We've already had to travel all this way to chase stolen product that our fuckwit of a customer managed to lose down here to you. From what I hear, it didn't make it five minutes in the city before it was taken. Is that true?'

'That is true,' Freddie confirmed. 'We already knew it was coming.' He stilled his hand, not wanting to show how irritated he truly was. He was itching to be out there with the others, searching for Thea. But there was nothing he could do yet, not until they had some more intel. In the meantime, business still needed to be handled. And that's why he was here.

Alfie looked impressed and smirked. 'He was a fool, him and that ponce he had set up to run it. And I don't suffer fools, so they'll be out of your hair very soon. But that still leaves us with the small matter of business. Whilst I appreciate you believe you had the right to seize the load, this whole issue has left my brother and I significantly out of pocket and that isn't acceptable to us at all.' He shook his head and took another bite of his scone.

Andre narrowed his gaze and drank his tea quietly, observing the exchange.

'I completely agree. Which is why we will be paying you what was owed on the load, plus ten per cent extra to compensate you for the hassle you've had to deal with.' Freddie sat back and waited, his cards now on the table.

Alfie shook his head with an amused expression. 'All you young fuckers. You think you're so smooth, don't ya? A few pretty words, some cash thrown on the table and everything's all squared away.' He picked up another scone and cut it in half. 'I'll take that, Tyler. But as for us being square and as for doing further business with you, I ain't so sure.'

'Well, then let me convince you,' Freddie said, not surprised by Alfie's initial refusal. If they were going to reel them in it would take some coaxing. 'Tomorrow night at my club, CoCo. We'll host you at the VIP table, get the caterers in, the lot. Let us show you a good night at least.'

Alfie turned towards his brother with one raised bushy eyebrow. After a few moments, Andre nodded. Alfie turned back to Freddie. 'OK then, why not. We'll come. But that don't mean nothing, mind,' he warned. 'I might still decide to take what I feel you owe me in other ways.' His eyes glinted with something dangerously feral and Freddie's heart almost stopped beating.

What other ways? Did he have Thea?

Careful not to respond, Freddie nodded with a tight smile. 'So we'll see you tomorrow night then. And now that's settled I'll leave you to finish your lunch. Enjoy.'

As he walked away, Freddie pulled his phone out of his pocket. Dialling Paul's number, he checked behind him to make sure none of their men were following closely enough to hear.

'I take back what I said,' he said darkly, as Paul answered. 'I think it might have been the Ramones. It was something he just said. I want his lot followed; you need to get our men on it right now. Because if it is him, then she's in more danger than we could have ever realised.'

CHAPTER FIFTY-FIVE

Knocking on the front door of the run-down flat Jules was staying in, Freddie was surprised when an older, haggard-looking woman answered. She sneered up at him, her lips pursed tight as though she was sucking on a wasp.

'What do you want?' she rasped, her voice hoarse from decades of smoking. 'If you're from the leccy company I've already told you, I ain't having no meter in here.'

Freddie frowned. 'I'm not from any company. I'm here to see Jules.'

'Oh.' The woman turned her nose up. 'Lazy bitch is in bed having a nap. As if naps in the middle of the day are fucking normal.' She moved aside. 'Go on then, go sit down. I'll get her up.'

Freddie walked through to the lounge and immediately opened the balconette doors. It stank to high heaven of cigarettes and BO. He didn't know how any of them stood it. He thought back to the fun, carefree girl Jules had been and tried to think of that girl in this environment, but he couldn't, though he had never actually seen where she lived back then. A couple of minutes passed and Jules shuffled into the room, wrapped in an old dressing gown, bleary-eyed with her hair sticking up all over the place. Freddie felt a fleeting moment of pity for what life had done to her, before reminding himself that she'd made her own choices.

'Oh,' she said, when she saw who it was. 'I thought you weren't bringing him back for another day or two.' She seemed put out.

'I'm not,' Freddie replied. 'But I've had some time to think and I wanted to put another offer to you.'

'Oh right,' Jules said warily, her calculating eyes darting from him to the large brown envelope in his hand and back again. 'What's that then?'

Freddie looked away, suddenly tempted to rip into her for what she'd said to Anna and for being such a terrible mother to Ethan. He couldn't, though. It wouldn't do him any favours. He needed to be civil if he was going to get anywhere with her today. Instead he thought back to the lines he'd so carefully rehearsed on the way over.

'I know you've not had it easy. Whatever the circumstances were at the beginning, raising Ethan alone must have been tough.'

'Well, yes, it was,' Jules said self-righteously, nodding along to his words.

It grated on Freddie to say all this. 'It must have been even harder to form your own life with Ethan around, not being free to live how you want.'

Jules tensed suspiciously but kept listening. Moving further into the lounge, she flopped into the armchair and pulled her legs up under her.

He took a breath and looked down at the envelope in his hands. 'I want to make a deal with you that I think will make everyone happy. When we first talked, you told me you wanted another hundred grand. I'm prepared to do better than that.' He locked eyes with her, trying to read her expression. As expected it was alight with interest and greed. 'I'll give you two hundred, in cash, a new car and a ferry ticket to the South of France where you can continue to Spain, just how you wanted. I'll even hook you up with my contacts down there, if you want help with opening up that beach bar I know you've dreamed of. You can go right now and start a whole new life.'

'And what do you want out of it?' Jules asked, though she had an inkling she already knew.

'I want custody of Ethan,' he replied. Exhaling slowly, Freddie wandered over to the balconette and stared out for a moment. 'You don't want him around, Jules. You feel like he's tying you down.'

'He's my baby boy,' she replied guardedly.

'He is. And he always will be. But the lifestyle you want to live, it don't fit with having a kid.'

Jules snorted. 'And yours does?'

'No. But I'd be willing to change it. For Ethan.' He turned to face her. 'It's only been a short time but I've grown genuinely fond of that kid.'

'And your barren missus can't produce you another one,' Jules added nastily.

Freddie's eyes flashed dangerously and Jules blinked, reminded of who she was talking to.

'Watch your mouth,' he said in a low voice. 'Or I might just remember a few things I need to pull you up on.'

Jules swallowed and looked down, for once having the sense to stay quiet. She mulled over Freddie's offer. It was certainly a juicy prospect. Far more than she'd thought she could get out of him before. Palming Ethan off too would be an added bonus if she was honest with herself. She played with a loose thread on the arm of the chair.

When she'd first found out Freddie had taken Ethan to stay with him she had expected to miss him. Indeed, it had been strange having the flat so quiet without his programmes on or him irritating the life out of her. But once she'd grown used to this, she'd found to her surprise that she didn't really miss him at all. There was no one bugging her to get up in the mornings – save for her mother – and no one whining to go to the park, or hogging the TV or complaining they were hungry. For once she had no one to look after but herself and it had been a welcome break. She'd felt like herself again, Jules the person rather than just Ethan's mum.

Eying up Freddie, she wondered if she could get anything more out of him. 'Three hundred,' she said, testing the waters.

Freddie's anger increased but he held his tongue, unwilling to rock the boat until the papers were signed. He needed her for that first. Then she couldn't wiggle out of it. The family court lawyer Vince had hooked him up with had come up trumps. A trip to the theatre and one expensive handshake, and he'd managed to get all the official stamps in place without so much as one court appearance.

'Two fifty,' he countered.

Jules twisted her mouth to one side as if considering the amount. 'It's not much to replace my son, though, is it? Hmm. I'll think about it.'

Freddie narrowed his eyes and dropped the envelope down on the overflowing coffee table.

'In here are all the documents. The first is to officially declare me as Ethan's father. I've got the DNA results already; it just needs your signature. The second is the custody agreement, naming myself and Anna as his two legal guardians. It states that you still have access rights, of course,' he added. 'I'm not paying you to disappear; I just want custody. You can still have Ethan for visits as regularly as you want. He'll always be your son,' he stressed.

Although Freddie firmly believed he could give Ethan a better life than Jules, he didn't want to break any bond they did have. He was still holding on to the hope that they shared a love he hadn't yet witnessed, though that hope was fading with every visit.

'The third document states that I will deliver the two hundred thousand, the car and the ticket upon full completion of the first two documents. If you accept the two fifty offer, you can just edit the paperwork yourself and we can both sign beside it. That will make it legal.'

Standing up, Freddie walked out into the hall and stared back at her with a hard expression. 'You have until tomorrow night to accept. The offer expires at midnight.'

CHAPTER FIFTY-SIX

Freddie walked through the door and tiredly slung his keys in the bowl. It had been a long night, not least because after leaving Jules he had dropped in on every shady rat he could think of that might have picked up some information on Thea's whereabouts. But his searches had come to nothing. The crew had gone underground.

The stress of all the balls he had to juggle was truly getting on top of him now. As if dodging the task force, discovering he had a child and finding a way to protect both that child and his relationship wasn't already bad enough, now his sister had been taken. It had now been two days and he was running out of time. He needed to find her by tomorrow – that was the deadline on the text. He rubbed his face in agitation. Worry and fear sat in his stomach like a stone. Why would they take Thea? She was a civilian.

The task force was hopefully not going to be an issue much longer. After Sarah had shared her idea of sending enough harassment letters so that Ben was forced to issue a limiter, Freddie had put his lawyers on it straight away. They'd now sent enough letters that the one arriving tomorrow should put the final nail in the coffin. Ben would be forced to issue a wind-up order with a time limit on it. If they had nothing on him by then, the coast was officially clear. All they had to do now was wait it out. So that was one thing that would be taken off his plate.

Walking through to the lounge, he found Anna cradling a book, staring off into space.

'Good book?' he asked.

'Mhm,' she replied. 'It's a new author, Noelle Holten.' She flashed him the cover. 'Amy's been raving about it, thought I'd try and take my mind off everything for a bit, but I can't concentrate. I can't stop thinking about Thea.' She glanced at the clock on the mantel. 'Christ, I hadn't realised the time.'

'Ethan OK?' Freddie asked, sitting down next to her.

'Yes, he was really tired. Passed out by seven thirty—'

Freddie nodded. 'Listen, I wanted to talk to you about him. The whole situation really, with Jules and everything.'

Freddie watched her jaw tighten at the name of the woman who had taunted her cruelly only the night before.

Freddie's phone beeped and he glanced at the screen. He sighed and rubbed his head.

'Bill might have made some headway with Thea's phone. I've got to go. But we'll continue this later, OK?'

'Sure, just go. Find her.' Anna ushered him out.

Freddie left, grabbing his keys and mustering whatever energy he had left to keep searching for his little sister.

CHAPTER FIFTY-SEVEN

Everyone in the task-force office paused as a roar of fury erupted in the office next door, where Ben Hargreaves had placed himself for the day. Wary glances were exchanged as everyone tried to guess what was going on. Sarah gently put down her pen and leaned forward on her desk, waiting for what she knew was about to come. Making sure to look as confused as the rest of the room, she hid her excitement. It was finally happening. She had finally managed to bring down the task force from within and keep her reputation intact at the same time. That and her freedom, of course. It had been a tense few weeks. The end of this team couldn't come fast enough, as far as she was concerned.

The door flew open, hitting the wall behind it with a bang as Ben stormed out, the lawyer who had brought the bad news scurrying behind him. He marched to Sarah's desk and slammed the papers down in front of her.

'Sir?' she asked innocently. 'What's going on?'

'I'll tell you what's going on.' The colour rose up his neck as his rage took flight. 'We've had a demand for a wind-up order, straight from the Tylers' *fucking lawyers*,' he yelled, looking around at the team of people in the room.

'What?' she gasped. 'Surely we don't have to pay any attention to it?'

'Actually, we do,' Ben said, groaning in despair and rubbing his face with his hands in stress. 'They've played the game perfectly – collected photos, witness statements, made claims that their mental state is being affected by the undue attention caused by this team. They've got more than enough. And as so far we have sweet fuck all to show for our efforts, if we refuse and go to court, we'd be held fully accountable and be charged for harassment. I have no choice but to issue the wind-up order.' He turned to address the room. 'The team is being shut down.'

There was a chorus of shocked exclamations and frustrated curses as the devastating realisations hit. Everything they had worked so hard for was for nothing.

'We were so close,' George spat, throwing his pen at the wall in anger.

'Were we, though?' Ben asked. 'You've been on this case for weeks and you've come up with *nothing*. These guys are dirtier than the bloody Thames, and you couldn't even pin a parking ticket on them.'

Sarah watched as George's face turned red and he looked down, embarrassed. Ben was right, of course, but no one knew that this was all down to Sarah sabotaging their efforts the whole time. In truth, they'd come very close to nailing the Tylers several times. If she hadn't stepped in, they'd have been bang to rights weeks ago. She felt a fleeting moment of pity for George and the rest of the team. But at the end of the day she'd had a job to do.

Her gaze drifted to Holly, who was staring at her with a strange expression. It wasn't full of accusation or anger as Sarah would have expected. It was something else that she couldn't quite place. Those piercing blue eyes bored into her filled with a mixture of challenge and interest. Sarah narrowed her own eyes suspiciously.

What was Holly up to?

Her attention was pulled back to Ben as he barked out the rest of his orders.

'You have a week from today to find something we can pin on them. After that point, the case is closed and we can't so much as look in their direction again unless they decide to drive down the motorway holding a dead body in their arms, screaming *I did it, I did it* out the window whilst the BBC are live streaming. We can't follow them, we can't bug them, we can't even pull them in for questioning without being penalised.' He stared around the room, his face haggard and full of anger. 'So, get to it. One week,' he repeated, as he stormed back into his office, slamming the door behind him.

There was a silence as everyone looked to Sarah for instruction. She shook her head and blew out a long breath.

'Well,' she said with a grimace. 'You heard him. Get to it. If there's anything you think might come off that you haven't yet brought up, now is the time. I want you all to go and make a plan for this last week – a detailed one. And you need to make the time count.' Sarah stood up as she delivered the depressing pep talk. 'Team meeting in one hour; I want to hear everyone's plan then. Go.'

'Yes, ma'am,' they muttered, each going back to their desks and pulling out pads and laptops to complete the task.

'Oh, Adam—' Sarah caught Chambers on his way back to his desk. He turned around, raising his eyebrows in question. 'That camera you borrowed the other night, it doesn't seem to be back in the cupboard.' She knew because she'd looked. She'd wanted to see if anything incriminating had been caught, but it hadn't been in its allotted place.

'Ah, sorry, ma'am, it's still at home,' he replied apologetically. 'It was a late one and I completely forgot I had it. I'll bring it in tomorrow.'

'OK,' she replied. 'Did you get anything?'

'No, no one was about.' He shrugged. 'But at least it helped me get a good night's sleep after.' He grinned.

Sarah nodded. She knew that feeling better than anyone. They were quite alike, she and Adam. They both took the job too seriously. In another life she might have even taken him up on his offer of a drink and allowed that path to take her where it wanted. But there was no point dwelling on that now.

'Great. Well, good luck with your plan of action.' Putting on her best game face, Sarah smiled. 'Let's get these bastards.'

CHAPTER FIFTY-EIGHT

Anna chewed on one of her long, polished nails. She watched Freddie style his hair in the hallway mirror next to her, his jaw locked in a hard line of stress. He, Paul and the rest of their men had been up through the night once more in their search for Thea. After a couple of hours' sleep, Freddie had gone back out searching again all day, but still they had come up with nothing. If it was Drew and his crew who had taken her, the advantage they held was that nobody knew them and they had no habitual haunts. They might not know the city but they could move around fairly undetected. If it was the Ramones who had taken her, they had a team of ex-special forces on their side. Either way, whoever had her was doing a good job of staying hidden and time was running out. They had until tonight to deliver the money the ransom had demanded. Freddie had made arrangements for the drop if necessary but he was praying it didn't come to that. Because at that point, Thea Tyler was expendable.

Having spent the last couple of hours driving himself crazy and pacing the hallway, Freddie had decided to go ahead with meeting the Ramones at the club. If it was they who had taken her, perhaps they would finally play their hand. There wasn't much else he could do until one of his team came up with something.

Ethan was already tucked up in bed and Anna was set to stay home to watch him once more.

'You sure you're OK here?' Freddie asked.

'Yes, Tanya's coming over again in a bit,' she answered. 'If we're going to sit home worrying, we might as well do it together. You'll call me if you hear anything?'

'Yeah, 'course,' he replied.

Freddie disappeared into the bedroom and Anna heard the en-suite door lock. The buzzer sounded behind her and she jumped. She shook her head, berating herself for being so silly. *Tanya's early*, she thought, looking at her watch. Lifting the receiver, she buzzed the door open.

'Come up,' she said, before putting it back on the hook.

Wandering through to the kitchen, she opened the fridge and pulled out a bottle of wine. Leaving it on the counter, she opened one of the cupboards and rose up onto her tiptoes to reach the wine glasses. As her fingers curled around the first stem, there was a knock on the front door.

'It's open,' she called out, not sure why Tanya hadn't just walked in like she usually did. Tanya never knocked. In fact, if she even tried the buzzer they were lucky. And the only times she did that were when she forgot the keys Anna had given her.

When the door didn't open, Anna put the glasses down and walked through with a frown. Opening the door, her eyebrows shot up in surprise when she found Jules standing there. She opened her mouth, about to demand she leave at once, when she remembered that they had Ethan staying with them and that this was probably why she was here.

'He's asleep,' she said tightly. 'But if you want I can go and wake him.' She stepped aside to let Jules in, furious that she had no choice but to admit the woman into her house.

Jules shot her evils as she passed, still not having forgiven Anna for throwing her out on the street by her hair.

'I'm not here to see Ethan, I'm here to see Freddie,' she said, folding her arms.

Anna narrowed her eyes. 'If you think you're going to extort yet more money out of him, you've got another thing coming. He's already told you he'll pay maintenance and for anything else Ethan needs, but…'

'Oh, actually that's *exactly* what I think I'm going to do,' Jules said with a sarcastic smirk. 'I'm here to accept his offer.'

'What offer?' Anna asked.

Jules's mouth dropped open and she stared at Anna for a second before bursting into hysterical laughter. 'Oh my God, you don't know, do you?' She covered her mouth with her hand, still laughing, enjoying the moment.

'What the hell are you talking about?' Anna demanded, her heart rate increasing as she realised from Jules's glee that she wasn't about to enjoy whatever she was about to hear.

Freddie strode through from the bedroom, having heard the exchange. 'Jules,' he said heavily. 'Anna, listen. I was trying to talk to you about this last night when I came in. But then Bill messaged about Thea's phone…'

'Tell me what, Freddie?' Anna demanded, the volume of her voice rising.

'That he's bought you a kid, sweetheart,' Jules said in a mocking drone. 'Ethan's your early Christmas present.'

'What?' Anna cried.

'Right, just stop it, Jules,' Freddie demanded, shooting her a warning look. 'That ain't how it is at all and you know it.' He turned his back on her and faced Anna. 'Listen, he can't go back there. It's worse than you can ever imagine. If he goes back, he'll end up in a bad way, Anna.'

'Oh, charming,' Jules shot, bristling in anger. 'I can always change my mind, you know. In fact, maybe I will.' She stepped back towards the door and Freddie quickly skirted around her, blocking her exit.

'Jules!' He took a deep breath, wishing it was going down any way other than this. Getting Jules to agree and breaking the news to Anna were already difficult tasks in themselves, but juggling them both at the same time was something akin to the hell that the priests of his childhood had described. 'I'm not blaming you. And what I think shouldn't matter to you anymore, if you want to go and start again.' He could see the envelope in her hands. He was so close. 'Hand me those papers and I'll give you the money and the keys right now. I have it all here.'

'What, in cash?' she asked, her sly gaze sneaking sideways at Anna, who stood frozen in shock.

'A cheque. Here—' He pulled it out of his inner pocket. 'It's cleared with my bank; you can deposit it wherever you like.'

Jules narrowed her eyes. 'How do I know you won't cancel it?'

'Because I'm a man of my word,' Freddie replied. 'And because those documents are legally binding. That's why I had them drawn up. If I cancel the cheque, you can take Ethan from me.' He held his hands out. 'I have nothing to gain by doing that.'

'Freddie,' Anna uttered, aghast.

Jules looked her up and down and smirked. Taking the cheque from Freddie's hand, she passed him the envelope. He quickly opened it and scanned the pages whilst she folded the cheque and placed it into her inside jacket pocket. They were all signed.

'The keys and the ferry ticket?' she asked, holding her hands out.

Freddie walked over to his coat where it hung by the door and reached into the pocket. Pulling out a Mini Cooper key fob he handed it to her along with an envelope.

'Car's on the road out front. Pink slip and ticket are in there,' he said. It galled him handing over so much of his hard-earned money to a woman who'd sell his son for a packet of peanuts if she was hungry enough. But family was worth more than money and if this was what it took to get his son, he was prepared to take the blow.

'Pleasure doing business with you, Freddie Tyler,' she said sarcastically.

'He's through there if you want to say goodbye,' Freddie said, moving aside.

Jules hesitated. She'd gone to and fro in her mind a million times before signing the papers. In her own way she loved Ethan, though even she had to admit it was probably more the fact she was just used to having him around than anything else. A new start was exactly what she needed. But suddenly the thought of seeing his little face looking up at her in accusation, a face filled with betrayal, flooded her with guilt. If she was going to walk away and be done with it, she needed to just go. The last thing she wanted was some hormonal pull on the heartstrings stopping her at the last minute.

She sniffed and lifted her chin. 'Nah, I don't want to wake him,' she said quietly. 'It's best if we just let it be. Break it to him gently, yeah?'

Turning to Anna, she couldn't help but get in one last dig.

'He's all yours now, love. Finally a kid of your own. Not that he'll ever really be yours. And he'll never love you like he does me. Blood is thicker than any court paper.'

Turning on her heel, she left and the hallway was silent for a moment.

*

Freddie took a deep breath as he watched Anna build up to explode.

'Freddie, what the *fuck* have you done?' she screeched. All of her usual composure and poise flew out the window as Anna finally cracked. 'How could you *do* this? How could you just *buy* him off her like a piece of meat? We haven't even discussed it! I was just getting used to the fact he'd be coming here for fucking *visits*! What the hell!'

She grabbed two handfuls of her own hair and began to pace the hallway as her heart threatened to push her into a full-on panic attack.

'Anna, I know this is big, and you're right, this should have been a joint decision…' He held his hands out to her, trying to calm her down.

'A joint decision? Ha!' Anna laughed hysterically. 'Are you joking? Freddie, a month ago we were in mourning for the loss of our baby, *our* child. And then suddenly you have a full-on seven-year-old, and then he's visiting to get to know you a bit and now suddenly,' she yelled, 'he's apparently living here! Are you *serious* right now?'

'Hey, keep your voice down,' Freddie said with a frown. They both glanced down the hallway towards the door to the study where Ethan was asleep. 'Listen, Anna, I am so sorry. I know this isn't fair on you, but it isn't fair on him either, leaving him there. Can't you see I've had no choice?'

Anna shook her head, covering her mouth with her hands as she paced manically, trying to take it all in.

Freddie's phone rang and he pulled it out of his pocket. They both glanced down at the screen and then up at each other. It was a number they didn't know.

'Answer it,' Anna said flatly. Thea was still missing; not even the argument of a lifetime was more important than that right now.

Freddie answered and put it on speakerphone. They waited.

'Freddie?' a crackly voice came through.

'I'm here,' Freddie replied.

'It's Drew.'

Freddie tensed and balled his free hand into a fist, but he stayed silent.

'Can you meet me on the Golden Jubilee bridge?' he asked, sounding tired. 'London Eye side.'

'I'll be fifteen minutes. Don't move.'

'I won't.'

The call ended and Freddie stared at Anna, not sure how to leave with things how they were. He opened his mouth to speak but she cut him off.

'Just go, Freddie,' she snapped. 'Find Thea. But this conversation is not over.' With a cold glare, she turned her back and walked into the kitchen.

Freddie sighed heavily, then picked up his coat and walked out. His life might be falling apart but right now he needed to focus on Thea. Because if he didn't, there was a high chance she wouldn't make it home.

*

Anna bit down hard on her fist to stop her sobs from making their way out. Tears blurred her vision but she wiped them away angrily. She took a deep breath and looked up towards the ceiling, blinking hard. She had never felt so out of control as she had since Ethan and Jules had been around. She wasn't stupid; she knew Jules had been manipulating the situation to her advantage and this had caused Freddie to become preoccupied. But these decisions he was making were life-changing and not just for him, for all of them. And he wasn't letting her in on any of it. She was just expected to go with the flow, as if inheriting a stranger's kid was somehow normal.

She reached for the bottle of wine she'd taken out and poured herself a large glass. Taking a few big gulps, she refilled it. A stray tear rolled down her cheek and she wiped it away before picking up the glass and taking another deep drink.

*

Down the hallway in his makeshift bedroom, Ethan sat with tears rolling down his own cheeks. Big fat hot tears of pain fell fast, one over the other. He squeezed his stuffed dog until it was almost flat against his thin little body, as he shook under the weight of the emotions he was feeling.

He'd heard the whole conversation. It was his mother's laugh that had woken him. At first he thought he'd been dreaming. It wasn't unusual that he dreamed of Jules. Staying still and silent, he'd listened and learned that his mother had sold him off like he was nothing but an old pair of boots. She hadn't even come in to kiss him goodbye. As the pain had coursed through him, like nothing he'd ever felt before, he'd then heard his dad and Anna. She didn't want him here either. Even his dad sounded like he'd only done this because he felt sorry for him.

Shaking with shock and sorrow, Ethan slowly stood up. He couldn't stay here, he realised. He'd already spent years in another house where he wasn't wanted and he knew how that ended. There had to be somewhere out there where people would like him. He needed to go and find it, be brave like Ryder from *Paw Patrol* was. He couldn't bear to spend another second here, not like this.

Quietly he pulled out his clothes and put them on, one by one, sliding his new Converse on last. Slipping his arms into his coat, he did up the zip, struggling as his thin fingers shook in the dim light. He picked up his dog and wrapped his arms around it.

'Come on, Marshall,' he whispered miserably through his tears. 'We need to go.'

CHAPTER FIFTY-NINE

Drew breathed in the cold air and watched the tourists and merry-makers over on the South Bank. It was a nice spot here. He'd discovered it following Anna once, when they were gathering intel on the Tylers. She'd come and stood here for nearly an hour, staring at the water as though she might find some answers in it. He was beginning to understand why she came here.

He'd sent his men packing. He knew that now Jacko had gone and done what he'd planned, the game was up for all of them. The Tylers weren't going to accept that sort of threat and that meant that things would only end up worse for Jacko when they finally caught up to him. And if the Ramones got to him before the Tylers did, it was all over anyway.

Richie, Skidders and Steve were now on the run and Drew hoped that if they got far enough away Alfie might forget about them and let them be. He wasn't one to chase small fry. It wasn't worth his time. It was himself and Jacko the Ramones would hold accountable for everything. They were on borrowed time and he knew there was no escaping the Killers once the deadline Alfie had given them was up.

Knowing what was in store in just two short days, Drew had finally made the hard decision earlier that day to take matters into his own hands. It wasn't an easy choice to make. A man's survival instinct was one of the strongest drivers. But he knew that by ending things himself, he would save himself a world of pain. And this seemed as good a place to go as any. His expression was sad and tired as he looked down into the dark, murky depths of the Thames. Soon he'd be down there too, weighed down by the small rocks he'd piled up ready to place in his pockets. But there was one last thing he needed to do first.

He'd been horrified when Jacko had told him what he planned to do with Thea. It didn't matter that they weren't in their own city or that they were in an open feud with the Tylers. The rules of the underworld were clear and absolute. Whatever you did to each other, you *never* harmed a civilian. If that rule was broken by one person, it could be broken by anyone. It was something he couldn't agree with, and although he wasn't exactly Freddie Tyler's biggest fan, he wasn't about to let Jacko needlessly kill his sister. Drew had a sister of his own back home and the thought that someone could do that to her made him feel physically sick.

The wind picked up and Drew closed his eyes, raising his face to it. When Freddie grabbed him, his eyes shot back open and he was met with a murderous expression. Freddie twisted him round and bent him backward over the rail, holding him by the scruff of the neck. Drew didn't bother trying to fight him.

'Where is she?' he growled, ignoring the startled looks they were getting from worried onlookers.

'That's what I'm here to help you with, if you want to put me down,' Drew said with difficulty.

Freddie released him but stayed right up in his face, hot anger radiating off him.

'Why would you take my sister?' he demanded. 'She was off the table, nothing to do with this.'

Drew blinked and frowned. 'I didn't; I had nothing to do with it. I warned Jacko against it, but he didn't listen.'

Freddie stepped back slightly, surprised.

'Not that I have any love for *you*, mind,' Drew said with a tired laugh, leaning on the railing to face the river. 'But I don't agree with messing with family. When you cross that boundary…' He shook his head sadly. 'Well, then nothing is sacred anymore.'

Freddie eyed him warily. Drew looked haggard, as though he hadn't slept in days and his clothes were rumpled. He wore a cast over the break Freddie had left him with just days before and his face was still black and blue. He was a complete mess. But it wasn't that which gave Freddie reason to believe him. It was the overall air of resigned defeat. His gaze fell to the small pile of rocks by Drew's feet and he frowned as he suddenly realised what the man planned to do.

'So, it was Jacko. You didn't have to tell me,' Freddie said eventually. 'You could have just jumped and left me to deal with my own problems.'

Drew nodded. 'I could have,' he agreed. 'But I'd like to think if it had been my sister, someone would have done the decent thing there too.'

There was a long silence until eventually Freddie reached into his pocket and pulled out a small pad and a pen. He scribbled something down. 'One good turn deserves another. If the information you give me pays off, I'll see you alright,' he said sincerely. 'Don't jump tonight. Come to this address tomorrow morning and tell them I sent you.' He passed the paper over to Drew. 'Ask for Raul. He'll set you up with a fake passport and send me the bill. You're on your own from then, but it will give you a chance if you want it.'

Drew hesitated but eventually took the paper. 'Thanks.' He took a deep breath and felt a glimmer of hope shine through the darkness. He couldn't go back to his life, that was done with now and he'd accepted that before coming to the bridge today. But perhaps with this, he could start again. It was certainly a better option than dying.

Freddie nodded and turned back to the water. 'Now,' he said grimly. 'Where can I find him?'

'He didn't tell me, but I think I know. There are only two places here that he'd think to take her. He was never much of a thinker, our Jacko,' he said with a wry smile. 'Did he send you a photo?'

'Yeah.' Freddie took his phone out and brought up the photo he'd forwarded to his new phone. He passed it over to Drew, who immediately nodded.

'Yeah, I thought so.' He sighed and faced Freddie. 'I know exactly where he is.'

CHAPTER SIXTY

The violent thumping in her head brought Thea round from her groggy state of nothingness and she groaned, trying to lift her arms to hold her scalp. Her arms stayed stubbornly by her side and it took her a few moments to gather her thoughts enough to remember that they were bound. Opening her eyes, she cried out and quickly closed them again as the pain developed a new sharpness.

The noise must have travelled as within a few seconds she heard a door open a few feet away.

'You're up,' Jacko said awkwardly.

He'd been in a few times over the last two days to feed her sandwiches and give her water, but other than that he'd mainly left her alone. Thea had kicked and screamed, trying to get help but she had quickly learned that each time she got too loud, he'd dose her up with the chloroform again and she'd be knocked out for God only knew how long. Judging by how hard her head was pounding, she guessed she was just coming round from it once more.

She had no idea how long she'd been tied up in this room now. Her joints ached from being stuck in the same awkward position and the stench from the bucket he allowed her to relieve herself in made her want to throw up.

Ignoring the pain as best she could, Thea opened one eye to stare up at him accusingly.

'You fucking pig,' she spat.

She pulled against the ropes but all that did was confirm that they were bound tight. For the first time in two days, Jacko sat on the single bed against the wall instead of ignoring her and leaving the room as soon as he could. She focused in on him.

'So why the fuck have you taken me?' she asked witheringly.

He laughed a short humourless laugh. 'Ballsy little thing, aren't you?'

She snorted and instantly regretted it, as it brought about a fresh wave of head thumps. She'd asked questions before but it was the first time she'd had a response. Her fighting spirit perked up. 'You don't exactly grow up scared of shits like you when you've got brothers like mine,' she said, staring him brazenly in the eye.

He nodded. 'Yeah, I've met your brothers.'

'I guessed,' she said, her tone dripping with sarcasm. 'I figured you weren't holding me for my photography skills.'

Now she was more with it, Thea's anger was growing. She was angry at Jay – or Jacko as he was now – she was angry at the situation, but mostly she was just angry at herself for not seeing it coming. She should have known there was something off about him. But she'd really liked him and for once wanted to believe that she could enjoy a normal relationship.

Jacko gave her a small smile. 'I was actually really impressed with your photography skills,' he said. 'And I really did have a good time, when we went out.' He picked up a small soft toy on the bed beside him and tidied its hair absent-mindedly. 'Maybe if we'd been in normal circumstances…'

'Maybe in normal circumstances you could eat my dick,' Thea yelled. She instantly regretted raising her voice. Strong as she might sound, however long she'd been in this chair and numerous doses of chloroform had left her weak.

Jacko's eyes widened in shock. *Good,* she thought tiredly. *Be shocked.* She no longer cared about the pain in her head or anything else for that matter, she just wanted to attack the man who had fooled her into thinking he really liked her, who had fooled her into letting her guard down. She was confused and embarrassed, but most of all she was furious.

'Don't talk to me about your fucking feelings or what you'd like out of life. Because I *do not* care.' She kicked out at the bed. 'You messed with the *wrong* family. That much I can promise you. My brothers are going to find me and when they do, you'd better hope you get a head start, because I can promise you, you will *not* enjoy what comes next.'

'You think your brothers are going to find you here?' Jacko laughed. 'They haven't got a clue where you are. How could they? This might be their city, but it's a flaming big one. This is just one house in thousands. Hundreds of thousands.'

Thea laughed, her mocking gaze still on her captor. 'You have no clue what you're up against.' She shook her head, a smile still playing on her lips. 'You have no idea the people my brothers have found under circumstances much worse than this. Or the things they've done. Your best hope right now is to cut me loose and run. Run as fast and as far as you can.'

'*My* best hope is getting the money your brothers owe us for the shipment of product they stole,' he said. 'And as a matter of fact, it's *your* best hope that they pay it too. Because if they don't' – he walked out the door, having had enough of Thea's taunts – '*you're* the price that's going to be paid.' He closed it behind him and walked away.

Taking a deep breath, Thea bit her lip and looked around. If she was being honest with herself, now that Jacko had gone she was scared. She'd be stupid not to be in this situation. But she had every faith in Freddie and Paul. They'd done things she'd never thought were possible and even eventually outwitted Michael, who'd turned out to be the worst psychopath they'd ever come across. If they could do that, out-thinking an idiot like Jacko would be a walk in the park.

Eying up a metal nail file on the small dressing table to the side of the room, Thea tilted her head in resignation. It wasn't much and probably wouldn't work even if she managed to get to it – but she had to try.

*

Anna rested the cool glass of wine against her forehead. She'd decided against drinking the third glass, wanting to keep her wits about her with everything so up in the air, but it still felt nice against her hot skin. She'd finally grown calm, the myriad of emotions slowing down to a more manageable pace as they chased each other around in her head.

Looking up, she caught sight of herself in the mirror on her dressing table. Her make-up was a mess, her skin blotchy from the tears. Tutting, she wiped under her eyes and pinched her cheeks to give them a bit of colour. She'd moved through to the bedroom to deal with her small breakdown in private, just in case Tanya walked in before she had regained control of herself. Sniffing, Anna pushed her hair back off her face and stood up. She decided to go back to the kitchen and wait for Tanya there.

Walking lightly so she didn't wake Ethan, she stepped out into the hall. Glancing at his door as she passed his room, she nearly continued into the kitchen before she paused and glanced back a second time. The door was open nearly halfway. It hadn't been like that earlier. Frowning, she peered inside and saw his empty bed, the sheets pushed back.

Wandering down the hallway to the bathroom door, Anna tapped on it lightly. 'Everything OK, Ethan?' she asked. Waiting for an answer, she tilted her head and slowed her breathing. Silence. She knocked again.

After a few more seconds of silence passed, Anna tried the door. It was unlocked and, as it opened, she could see the bathroom was in darkness. Taking a couple of deep breaths as alarm began to take hold, Anna swiftly rushed through the other rooms in the flat, checking to see if he was in any of those.

'Ethan?' she called, the panic rising. She twirled round and ran out onto the balcony. That was empty too. 'Ethan, this isn't funny. If you're hiding you need to come out now.'

Running back into his bedroom, Anna looked around more critically this time. His coat and his shoes were gone. So was his backpack. Her heart leaped into her mouth as she raced into the hallway to the front door. It stood open just a crack, the empty hallway outside just about visible.

'Shit,' she cried, putting her hands to her head in horror. 'Shit, shit, shit!'

CHAPTER SIXTY-ONE

Freddie stormed past the bouncers into Club CoCo and straight into the VIP area where Alfie and Andre Ramone were enjoying his hospitality. One of the waiters that had been hired for the occasion stood holding a plate of appetisers whilst Alfie picked out what he wanted. Another was busy pouring champagne into Andre's glass. Their men sat around with drinks, chatting and laughing between themselves. They all paused in their chatter as Freddie approached.

'Ahh, our host is finally here,' Alfie said, clapping his hands together.

'Jacko's taken my sister.' He watched as Alfie's eyebrows rose in distaste and the smile dropped from his face. 'This isn't acceptable in our way of life for anyone, not for any reason. So, I've got to go deal with that. Now I know where they are, my men are on their way to meet me here so that we can go and take the fucker down together. Unless' – he paused – 'you'd like to make a deal.'

Alfie's eyes narrowed. 'What do you mean? What kind of deal?'

'I know you were looking forward to the pleasure of exacting payment from these guys yourself. From what I hear, Drew's already on the run. Now your men might catch up to him, they might not.' He shrugged, ignoring the indignant mutterings from the men around him. 'And when I get my sister back from Jacko, I'm going to put a bullet in his brain.'

Alfie's gaze flickered and Freddie could tell he didn't like the thought of that.

'I know what you're thinking. *What a waste*, right?' Freddie stepped up in front of Alfie and went in for the kill. 'If you agree to partnering up with us on a cocaine deal for distribution in London and put the past behind us, your men can come with mine and once I have Thea, they can bring Jacko right back to you. He's yours to do what you want with. I'll even get one of my men to escort you to a secluded barn of ours to use as you wish as a little icing on top of the cake. What do you say?'

Alfie sat back and smiled in amusement and admiration. The boy had certainly done his homework. It was the best deal Alfie had been offered in a long time. Looking over towards his brother for his agreement, he was happy to see him nod. Chuckling, he leaned forward.

'Alright then, Tyler. You've got yourself a deal.' Clicking his fingers at his men, he dropped the smile. 'Dan, Brian, go with Tyler and bring Jacko back to me. Lee, go with his men to set up at the barn.'

*

As Tanya reached to open the front door of Anna's building, it suddenly burst open, knocking her backward with force. The bottle of wine in her hand flew through the air and landed with a smash on the hard pavement. As she regained her balance, Tanya looked up, ready to give whoever it was a mouthful of abuse, but she stopped short when she saw that it was Anna.

'Anna?' she asked, surprised. 'What are you doing? And why do you look like that?' She'd never seen Anna so ruffled.

'Ethan, have you seen Ethan?' Anna said, grabbing her best friend hard by the shoulders.

'Ouch, Anna,' she complained, shrugging her off. 'No, why? What's happened?'

'He's run away. Oh God, Tanya, he's run away and he's *seven*.' She burst into tears as she realised what he must have heard them all say. If something happened to him she was never going to forgive herself.

'Why would he run away?' Tanya asked, her eyes widening in shock. She began to look around for signs of the little boy she'd begun to grow fond of.

'No time to explain. I need to find him. Help me?' Anna pleaded.

'Of course,' Tanya replied. 'Come on. You go that way, I'll go this way.'

They set off down the road in opposite directions, shouting his name.

Anna ran over towards the big Biffa bins and peered inside and behind. He wasn't there. She grasped her hair with both hands and looked up and down the empty road in desperation.

'Ethan, please. I just want to talk,' Anna pleaded. There was no sound except for the white noise of the busy city in the background.

With a sudden moment of realisation, Anna swivelled round. They were right next to the river and Freddie had a small rowing boat tied up down by some rocks. It was a dangerous drop at the best of times, let alone at night.

'Ethan?' There was an undertone of horror in her voice now as she picked up the pace and sprinted towards the edge of the river. There was a low wall surrounding it, cordoning off the rocks from the general public. She reached it and peered over. It was dark but the edge of the water was dotted with street lights. Squinting, she scanned the water down near the boat and as her gaze rested on a small bobbing circle of red, her heart almost completely stopped. The bright red item bobbed up and down in the water, moving only with the current. It was the hood of Ethan's coat.

'Oh my God, Ethan!' she cried. Running down the path towards the rocks, she jumped over the wall.

Tanya raced over. 'What is it?' she asked frantically. 'Is it him? Is he OK?'

'Ethan, Ethan, please! Get up!' Anna cried, tumbling down the rocks in her haste and twisting her ankle. 'Come on, please!' she screamed, scrabbling along, her hands grasping at any place in the rock they could get a good hold. She pushed forward and jumped to the next rock as Tanya quickly caught up. 'He's there! Quickly, get him out.'

'Jesus Christ,' Tanya said, her voice wobbling in horror as she caught sight of what Anna had.

'Aargh!' Anna cried out as she went over on her foot again. 'Get to him!'

Tanya leaped over the last of the rocks and threw herself into the shallow water by the boat. Bobbing under, she righted herself and pushed forward through the murky river, willing herself to go faster. Every second seemed like an age. She prayed they weren't too late.

Finally reaching him, Tanya reached out and grasped the hood of Ethan's coat. As she pulled it towards her and looked down, she began to weep in relief. It wasn't his coat – it was a deflated football.

'Anna, it's not him,' she shouted. 'It's not him, it's OK.' She pulled herself out of the mucky water and back onto the rocks.

Anna paused and looked up to the heavens in relief. 'Oh, thank God.' Tears of relief began to fall and she wiped them away. Putting her hand to her beating heart for a second, she looked back to Tanya, her expression grim. 'He's still out there somewhere.'

She jumped as her phone rang and her blood turned cold as she saw who it was. Tanya glanced at the screen.

'Fuck,' she hissed. 'Anna, you have to tell him.'

'Shit.' Anna bit her lip and, taking a deep breath, answered the phone.

*

As Freddie heard the words that came down the phone, he stopped in his tracks.

'What do you mean?' he heard himself ask. As he heard her sob, Freddie's hand dropped to his side, Anna still connected to the phone.

Two of the most important people in his life were missing. Two members of his family, his flesh and blood, the people he lived and breathed for. They both needed saving. Neither was safe, both were vulnerable and unable to save themselves from the danger they were in. The clock was ticking and the world was closing in on him.

How on earth was he supposed to pick between them?

With sudden clarity, Freddie lifted the phone back up to his ear. He closed his eyes and made the decision. He couldn't get to them both, but he didn't need to. He wasn't alone in this.

'Anna, you need to listen to me.' His voice grew stronger as he spoke. 'I trust you more than anyone. I know that you can find Ethan and you can fix this.' The line grew quiet and he knew that she was listening. 'I know you doubt yourself and that this situation is fucking terrifying, but there is a little boy out there that needs you. *My* little boy. He's part of me. And I know that's why you'll do whatever it takes to get him home safe. Find my boy, Anna.' Freddie heard his voice wobble as his worry and fear began to shine through. 'Just find him. For me.'

Seconds passed and Freddie squeezed his eyes shut. He needed her to be there for him tonight, more than ever.

'I will,' she whispered. 'I'll find him. I've got this.' Her voice grew louder. 'Just get Thea. I'll find Ethan. I'll bring him home.'

CHAPTER SIXTY-TWO

The house was in darkness, save for a dull glow coming from one back bedroom. Freddie and Paul crouched down behind the back fence watching through a hole as a shadow passed over the curtain. Sammy and Seamus were watching the front and none of them knew where the two killers Alfie had sent with them were. They'd melted into the shadows as soon as they'd all arrived.

When Drew had told Freddie where they were, he'd almost kicked himself for not thinking of it sooner. The one connection they knew the other crew had with London was Richie's cousin, Nigel, who they'd forced into hiding after questioning him about the Ramones. Drew told Freddie that they'd figured out what had happened after they couldn't find him and therefore knew the house to be empty. It was the only place other than the caravan that Jacko would think to go.

'Is it definitely him?' Paul whispered. The curtains were closed so they hadn't actually seen his face. For all they knew, Richie's cousin might have come home and settled his family back in.

'It's definitely him,' Freddie confirmed. 'Come on. I'm not waiting here all night.' Now that he was sure she was here, Freddie just wanted to get Thea and get home. He couldn't stop worrying about Ethan. He wasn't a particularly religious man, but he found himself praying that Anna found him safe and sound. Freddie had never felt so torn and terrified in his life.

Jumping up onto the bin that stood against the back fence, he quickly scaled it and jumped down the other side. Paul followed and as they walked through the garden in the soft moonlight, they each put on a pair of leather gloves. It wouldn't do to leave fingerprints.

They reached the French doors at the back of the house and peered in. There was no movement inside, just eerie darkness.

'Hey,' Freddie whispered to Paul. 'Give me some light.'

Paul switched on the torch of his phone and shone it down onto the lock and handle. Freddie pulled out two long pins from his inside pocket and set to work jimmying the lock. As he worked, Paul grinned and gave a small chuckle.

'It's been a long time since we last did this, eh, Fred?' he said quietly.

Freddie smiled wryly. 'Well, lucky we haven't lost the skills, I guess.'

The lock clicked into place and he retracted the pins, slipping them back into his pocket, then opened the door. The hinges on the door were creaky and they cringed as the high-pitched sound of it opening carried through the house. Leaving it open, they crept through the kitchen.

'You tooled up?' Freddie whispered suddenly.

Paul paused. In all the mayhem he'd forgotten to pick up a weapon. He shook his head with a grimace. Freddie pointed towards the set of kitchen knives on the side. Paul picked two of them up and handed one to Freddie. He weighed it up in his hand as they continued through the house.

As they reached the bottom of the stairs, they cocked their heads to listen, but there was nothing but silence. Freddie narrowed his eyes. The guy had been pacing up and down just a few moments before; they must have alerted him to their presence.

'Gah!' They suddenly heard an exclamation of pain. 'You fucking bitch!'

Racing forward, the brothers took the stairs two at a time, stealth forgotten. As they reached the top, they heard Thea's voice down the hallway.

'Through here,' she called out. The sounds of a scuffle ensued but Freddie couldn't see a thing. Scrabbling along the wall, he tried to find a light switch but he was out of luck.

Paul switched the light on his phone back on and suddenly the hallway appeared in front of them. The light was weak and threw shadows all around, but it was enough to see Jacko pulling Thea out of one of the bedrooms into the hallway. He struggled with her as she kicked and writhed in his grip, but as he pressed the knife he held tight to her throat, she stopped and tensed with a curse.

Jacko shook his head in annoyance. 'How did you find me?' he asked.

'It wasn't exactly hard,' Freddie replied, twisting his own knife in his hand. The sight of his sister being held by this idiot made his blood boil. He wanted to sink his knife into the other man's neck badly, but he knew he couldn't rush forward and do that for two reasons. The first being that Thea could end up being hurt in the crossfire and that wasn't worth the risk. The second was the deal he'd just made with the Ramones. He needed to deliver Jacko back to them in one piece. But it wasn't going to be easy getting hold of him without causing any damage in the process.

Jacko glared at the two of them down the hall. 'You know *you* caused this,' he yelled. 'I wouldn't have had to do this if you hadn't stolen our shit in the first place. Now we're on a death sentence.'

'You're on a death sentence,' Freddie said stepping forward slowly, 'because you were stupid enough to try and cheat your way into the big boys' game. That's on you, mate.'

'Stay where you are!' Jacko bellowed, his eyes darting from Freddie to Paul and then back again. 'Or I'll fucking kill her. I will, I swear.'

Freddie stopped and put his hands up, glancing down at Thea. She locked eyes with him and he could see the steely determination behind her fear. He nodded at her slightly, to let her know he had this.

'You don't want to hurt her, Jacko,' Paul said gently. 'Not really.'

He could see the other man was close to the edge, having run out of options. Jacko wasn't a killer. But desperate men went to desperate measures and this was the most desperate man he'd ever seen.

'Of course I don't,' Jacko snorted. 'But what option have you left me with?' He sniffed. 'I want the money sent to that address, right now. I want you to make a call on speaker and get it sent over. Go on, do it.'

'And how is he supposed to do that,' Thea asked witheringly, 'when you're holding his accountant to a fucking knife?'

'Thea,' Paul said warningly, shaking his head.

'What?' Jacko asked. 'Surely he can access his own accounts.'

Freddie sighed. 'Jacko, come on. Let her go and we can talk. But I'm not doing anything whilst you're threatening my little sister. Surely you can see how unreasonable that is.'

'Ouch,' Thea cried as Jacko jammed the knife harder into her skin.

'I'm not fucking playing anymore, Freddie. Do it now or she fucking dies,' he screamed, losing all sense of reason.

His eyes were wild and his whole body shook. Paul looked at Freddie fearfully. He'd seen that look before. It was the look of a man who had snapped past the point of return.

'I mean it, right now. I'm going to count to ten. If you ain't dialling, I'll slit her fucking throat,' he roared.

Freddie hesitated as he tried to work out what to do. They were too far away.

'One, two…'

'Jacko, come on,' Paul yelled. 'Don't be fucking stupid.'

'Three, four…'

Freddie stepped forward but all it did was make Jacko retreat and count faster.

'Five, six, seven…'

'Freddie,' Thea cried, genuine fear in her voice now as she realised like Paul that Jacko had lost the plot. Something caught Freddie's eye in the darkness of the bathroom behind Jacko and Thea, a flash of something moving, and the outline of a man appeared. Dan, one of the men Alfie Ramone had sent with them, began slowly stepping forward as silent as a ghost.

'Eight…'

Freddie cast his gaze back to Thea, about to try and somehow communicate that it was going to be OK, but she was sending him a silent message of her own. Flickering her eyes down towards her hand, she gave him a look of steely determination. Freddie glanced down and saw the small metal nail file in her hand. Turning it over, Thea got a better grip on it. She must have grabbed it earlier and kept it at the ready to use if necessary, Freddie realised. Alarm bells went off in his head and he shook it wildly at her, trying to warn her not to do anything stupid. Dan was just a few steps away, but of course she didn't know that. If she tried to fight Jacko now on her own, she wouldn't win.

'Nine…' Jacko screamed.

With a deep breath in and a strangled war cry, Thea lifted her lower arm and plunged the sharp end of the metal file into Jacko's thigh.

'Thea, no!' Freddie yelled, as she tried twisting out of Jacko's grasp.

For a moment time seemed to stop still as Freddie launched himself towards the knife.

Thea's face contorted as she strained against her captor.

Paul was just a heartbeat behind Freddie, having realised what his little sister had done.

Jacko roared out in pain and shock, a fresh wave of anger rippling through his expression as he tightened his grip on the young woman struggling to get away.

Dan hadn't seen what Thea had done, being behind them, but as he saw the brothers rush in he lunged towards Jacko's arm in an attempt to pull away the knife.

But it was too late. Already wound up and cornered into fight or flight mode, this final attack pushed Jacko over the edge. On reflex, he pushed the knife into Thea's soft neck with all his strength. Blood erupted as it pierced through the skin and muscle. In one swift movement he sliced it across, severing her oesophagus completely.

'No!' Freddie heard himself cry as his arms finally connected with Jacko's just a second too late. 'No! Oh God, Thea!'

Jacko suddenly flew back, Dan grasping him in a tight hold, forcing him to drop the knife and throwing him face down on the floor. Dan pulled his arms up behind his back and Jacko dropped his hold on Thea, the shock at what he'd just done setting in.

Freddie and Paul dropped to their knees either side of their sister, who lay choking on the hallway floor. Someone somewhere put on a light and it flooded the small hall, showing the extent of the blood which had already left Thea's body.

She clutched at her open neck, her hands slipping around, slick with blood, her eyes wide with fear and shock. She tried to speak but all that came out were thick gargles as the air in her lungs mixed with the heavy flow of blood.

'Her artery,' Freddie yelled at Paul. He grabbed his sister's neck and pressed down hard, trying to stop it from spurting out. It just kept running through his fingers and he began to cry.

'Freddie,' Paul cried.

Freddie pushed the hair back from Thea's face with shaking hands and locked eyes with her. 'It's going to be OK,' he said, his voice as shaky as his hands were. 'It's going to be OK. I'm going to get help, OK?' He pulled back and reached into his pocket for his phone. 'I'm going to call an ambulance. We'll get you help.'

'Ambulances bring questions you won't be able to answer,' Dan said urgently from where he was pinning Jacko down.

'I know that,' Freddie yelled at him. 'I don't care. I don't give a shit. All that matters is Thea.'

His own hands slippery with Thea's blood, which had formed a pool around them, he dropped his phone.

'Fuck!' he roared, picking it back up. 'It's going to be OK, Thea,' he said, trying to calm his shaking hands enough that he could dial the emergency services number. 'You're going to be OK.'

Thea's hands fluttered up and grasped at his forearm and he looked down at her. Her big brown eyes stared up at him intensely for a moment and then suddenly her arms dropped down and her body stopped moving. Her chest ceased rising, trying to draw in the air that couldn't make it past all the blood and her face fell slack.

The eyes that had locked with Freddie's just seconds before now stared right through him, vacant and unseeing.

Thea's struggle was over as quickly as it had begun.

Freddie blinked and shook his head, not wanting to believe what his eyes were telling him. He stared at Paul, whose face was ashen and wet with tears. He dropped his phone to the floor.

'No,' he said in barely more than a whisper, shaking his head fast. 'No, she's not gone. She ain't gone. Thea?' He placed his hands either side of her face and gently shook it. 'Thea, come on. Wake up. Please.'

Thea's face began to blur and swim around his vision as his eyes filled with tears of grief.

'Come on, Thea,' his voice broke as a sob erupted. 'You're OK. You're OK,' he repeated, willing it to be true. 'Please…' He squeezed his eyes shut as the wave of pain that washed over him was too strong to control. He felt Paul's arm pull him in and he gripped his brother back tightly as he finally gave in to the truth.

The grief he felt became tinged with guilt. This was all his fault. Thea was his little sister, the sister he had protected since she was just a baby. He'd watched her grow from a sweet little girl into a strong, intelligent, beautiful woman. He was so proud of her. And now she was dead. Drawn into a fight that was never hers to begin with, against the rules of their world, by an ignorant rat from up north.

Freddie's pain turned to fury, his sobs to ash in his mouth as he glared over towards the man underneath Dan's grip. The fire in his eyes burned hotter than hell and all of the boundaries he usually so carefully maintained disintegrated.

'You,' he growled in fury. 'You killed my sister. You killed my *fucking sister.*'

With a feral roar, he launched across towards the man, ready to beat him into a pulp, but Paul grabbed hold of him and barred his way.

'No, wait,' he said, his own face full of fury and grief too. 'We had a deal.'

'I don't care about the deal,' Freddie spat. 'I want revenge.'

'So do I,' Paul thundered, glaring at Jacko with pure hatred. He pulled his gaze back to Freddie. 'But with Alfie involved, from what I've heard, he'll pay ten times over.'

Freddie paused. Paul was right. Alfie's tastes for torture were not something they would usually want any part of. But in this case, Freddie was all for it. He felt as though Jacko had just ripped his beating heart out of his body. Nothing would ever be the same again. Their hearts would never recover from losing her. Nor would Mollie's, when she eventually found out.

His face grew hard and cold as he stared into Jacko's fearful eyes from where he lay on the floor.

'You're right,' he said. 'We had a deal and we're going to keep it. We'll give him to Alfie.'

'No,' Jacko uttered in horror.

'But I'm not just handing him over and leaving,' he continued, clenching his jaw. 'I want in. I want in on every single second of pain he goes through until his heart finally gives out.'

Freddie stood up and glanced over to the head of the stairs where Sammy and Bill stood silently, their faces ashen and grief-stricken. They had loved Thea too. Everyone had.

'Guard her,' Freddie asked of them. 'Don't move her, just stay with her until I get back.'

'Of course,' Sammy said solemnly.

'Bring him down,' Freddie said to Dan. 'We're going on a little trip.'

Dan hoisted Jacko up and he immediately began to wriggle.

'No, nooo!' he screamed, before Dan clamped a hand over his mouth.

CHAPTER SIXTY-THREE

Freddie's words spurred Anna on and whilst she felt more guilt than ever, she also felt more determined. They reached the park and Anna ran forward to the pirate ship. Pulling herself up the gangplank, she peered in and almost wept with relief as she found Ethan huddled up in the corner, clutching his teddy and his bag. Terrified eyes stared back at her in the dark and he shuffled back away from her as much as he could.

'Oh, Ethan. Oh, thank God,' Anna cried. 'You had me so worried.' Tears of relief began streaming down her face as all the terrible thoughts of what could have happened to him out there in the city alone melted away. 'Why would you do that? Why would you run away?' She climbed up into the pirate ship and faced him, on her knees.

'You weren't worried for me,' he said, his voice wobbling. 'You'll be happy I'm gone. Everyone will.' His own tears restarted and great heaving sobs wracked his thin little body. 'Nobody wants me. My mum's gone.' His voice cracked and his heart broke as he said it out loud. His sobs were so full of pain that it shocked Anna to the core.

What had she done?

The memory of when Ethan had tentatively tried to hug her and she'd kept him at arm's length flashed through her mind. She'd thought there was no particular meaning behind it, that perhaps he was just trying to get her onside, but he hadn't been. He'd just been looking for someone to give him comfort. And she'd shown him coldness. All the times he'd asked to sit with her or for a book to be read and she'd politely given the bare minimum, he'd been trying to form a bond. He'd been so strong and so brave and she'd been so tied up in her own selfish thoughts that she hadn't once stopped to really look at him.

The cold walls she'd constructed around her heart to protect herself melted away as she finally saw Ethan in a clear light. Leaning forward, she grasped his hands and put her forehead to them, before looking up into his face.

'Ethan, I am so sorry,' she said, through her tears. 'I have been so stupid and selfish. I know what you heard back there and I know that I haven't been the best person to you. But I need you to know that that has nothing to do with you. It was all down to me.' She turned and sat down next to him and rubbed her head. 'Before we met you, your dad and I lost a baby. It was growing in my tummy and it was supposed to be born and grow up into a beautiful little boy like you. But something happened and' – she took a deep breath – 'and he went to heaven instead.'

Ethan sniffed and wiped the tears off his cheek, listening.

'And that made us both very sad. And when you came along I was still very sad and I couldn't think about anything else. That doesn't make it OK, but I just wanted you to know that it wasn't anything you did. It's not you.' She reached up and pushed his hair back off his face. 'And I want you to know this. It sucks that your mum is gone.' Fresh tears fell from Ethan's eyes and Anna's heart ached for him. 'And nothing can replace her. But me and your dad *both* want you to stay with us. Not because we have to, but because we *want* you there.'

As she said it, Anna realised it was the truth. It was crazy but the opportunity was right in front of them. And they all needed each other. More than she had realised.

'I promise you that I will never make you feel like I did tonight again. I'm not perfect and I'll get some things wrong. But if you'll have me, I really do want to be your stepmum.'

Ethan's tears were still falling. It had been such a long, confusing and exhausting night and all he wanted to do was find someone who could make it all better. Gulping between sobs, he nodded and reached instinctively out to her for a cuddle.

Anna picked him up and pulled him onto her lap. Wrapping her arms around him, she held him tight and put her face to his head.

*

Tanya smiled in silent approval below them. *Thank God*, she thought as she walked back to the flat to wait for the pair of them. The family they had all become part of over the years was going to be OK. Ethan was going to be in a loving home and, finally, Anna was going to begin to heal.

CHAPTER SIXTY-FOUR

Alfie paced up and down patiently inside the dimly lit barn where they had taken Jacko to meet his fate. Jacko was tied up by his wrists to a supporting beam in the middle of the room and he hung limp, muffled moans of pain escaping through the thick gag that had been placed around his mouth from the injuries that had already been inflicted.

Freddie and Paul stood tall and still, each glaring at Jacko with a hard iciness that would make the strongest man's insides turn to mush. Around them in a circle were Alfie's men, Seamus, Dean and Simon – silent witnesses. Andre Ramone sat off to the side in the shadows, smoking a cigarette and quietly observing, as he usually did. He was calm and unruffled, used to his brother's exploits and the dramatics of other people.

Freddie had already given Jacko a thorough beating, only stopping when his brother pulled him away. It was Alfie's turn to inflict some pain and this was where the real retribution would begin. When they had arrived and the brothers had informed him that they intended to stay, they had expected to be met with resistance. Instead, Alfie had seemed quite pleased. There were very few opportunities in life where he was able to share his passions with others. Most people didn't have the stomach. He was looking forward to educating his new business partners.

The brothers didn't feel a flicker of pity for the man writhing in pain as Alfie began his routine. Their expressions were heavy with grief and anger, a sharp contrast to the look of joy that Alfie couldn't quite hide.

Freddie cast his gaze away as Alfie took things up a notch. Although he felt no sorrow for Jacko's suffering, this was something he couldn't watch. Their world was a brutal place and Freddie had no problem with violence, but what Alfie did was on another level. This was not normal. A promise was a promise, however, and they had promised Alfie that he could do whatever he wanted to Jacko. So, they would have to stand by and see this through.

Jacko's shrill screams filled the room and sweat formed on his face, dripping down and mixing with the salty tears that streamed from his eyes. Still, there was silence around the room as Alfie methodically carried out his long-awaited task. Jacko had lost control of his bladder, the acrid smell of urine wafting around the blood. Yet Alfie seemed to notice none of this. His placid smile stayed in place.

Freddie and Paul stood tall and unmoving as Jacko's screams reached a blood-curdling pitch. Alfie carried out his ministrations over what seemed like hours and still they waited without a word – waited for the point in time that Alfie was satisfied and they could finally finish the job. Because that's what they were here for – retribution. The monster currently writhing in pain under Alfie's hands had killed Thea.

As thoughts of Thea took over, Freddie squeezed his eyes shut in grief. The image of her lying on the floor covered in blood, her eyes staring into the distance, lifeless and unseeing, was burned onto the back of his eyelids. His hands clenched into fists and he took a deep breath.

'When I was a boy in Mexico,' Alfie said eventually, 'there was a rival cartel not too far away from ours. We lived in relative peace, but no slight was allowed to go unpunished. One day, one of the wives in our camp ran away. It was discovered that she had been having an affair with a man in the rival cartel.' He shook his head in disapproval at the memory. 'Her husband took a group of men and tracked the two lovebirds down. They had planned to leave and start a new life. But that was not acceptable. This other man had taken the husband's wife. She was not his to take.

Alfie stopped what he was doing and faced Freddie. Freddie locked eyes with him, ignoring the bloody mess of a man hanging behind him.

'When he brought them back to our camp,' Alfie continued casually, 'the wife declared that she could not be without her lover. That she could not bear to never feel his skin against hers again.' He smiled. 'So, the husband skinned the man, from head to toe. He forced her to watch and he made sure to keep him alive for as long as possible. When the lover's heart eventually gave out, he tossed the body in the river and handed his wife his skin as a gift.' He tilted his head as he paused. 'I always admired the skill and the careful balance it took to carry this out so well. When I grew up and met my first foe, I tried it myself. He died too quickly. I was too hasty. I needed to slow down, appreciate it for the delicate process it was. The second one lasted a bit longer, but I hit an artery.' He shrugged and shook his head. 'It took me some time to perfect. But now, all these years on, I have it down to an art.'

Freddie suppressed a shudder as he watched Alfie's face light up. The man was a complete psycho. No anger burned through his face, no thirst for retribution; what drove him was nothing more than love for the craft. He turned to Paul and they exchanged a grim expression. The sooner this was over the better. The Tylers believed in retribution; they were as Old Testament as men could come, here in London. But hurting others was not something they would ever take this sort of sadistic pleasure in. Especially not at this level. It was clear the man didn't even see his victims as human. They were just meat, waiting to be carved into what he saw as some form of art.

Jacko's breathing spiked and he began to shudder involuntarily. Alfie frowned and moved around to the front of his body. He placed his hand on the bloody area above Jacko's heart and waited, tilting his head as he felt the heartbeat underneath.

With a tut of annoyance, he stepped away and narrowed his eyes resentfully.

'Disappointing,' he said, shaking his head. He sighed regretfully and turned towards Freddie. 'He's weak,' he spat. 'His heart is ready to give out at any moment.' He carefully wiped his bloody blade and set it down neatly beside all his other tools. 'If you need further retribution, do it now. He'll be dead soon.'

Glad that Alfie was finally done with feeding his fetish, Freddie stepped forward, his lip curling up in anger. This was what he'd been waiting for. His last shred of mercy had disappeared the moment that bastard had slit Thea's throat. He didn't care that he'd been tortured or that his heart was about to give up. He wanted to be the one to do it, the one to end that murdering dog's life.

Thea's face flashed before his eyes. She'd stayed so strong, so confident even in the arms of her captor. She'd stared at him with steely determination, no fear. The Tyler way, right up until the moment she lay on the floor dying, trying and failing to draw in one last breath. She'd been beautiful, funny, clever and strong. And now she'd never look up at him or anyone else again. She'd never crack another joke or solve another problem. She'd never again go home to their mother.

Freddie's anguish broke through and he picked up a hunting knife from Alfie's collection. Jacko's eyes flickered wildly all around, his fear showing clearly in his pained expression. Freddie squared up to him, feeling the urge to rip him apart with his bare hands. But that wouldn't make this feeling of grief go away. It wouldn't bring Thea back. And this fuelled his anger even more.

'When we're done with you, I'm going to make sure your body is broken into a hundred little pieces,' Freddie growled. He plunged the knife into Jacko's stomach and yanked it back out as the man screamed once more. 'And every single one of those little pieces is going to be dumped in the dirtiest places I can find.' He stabbed Jacko in the stomach again, harder this time. His body rocked back from the impact and Freddie ripped the knife back out roughly. Blood spurted out, soaking through Freddie's already bloodstained shirt. He squared his face up to Jacko's, a cold, dangerously vacant look in his eyes as he stared at the other man. 'Pig troughs. Public toilets. Club urinals.'

Pulling his arm back, he plunged the knife back into Jacko's stomach again, with force. Blood was now pouring out of the wounds faster, and Freddie knew that they were fatal. Pulling his arm back, he stabbed Jacko one last time in the abdomen. Jacko's cries were pitiful but weaker now, as he stared fearfully into his killer's eyes.

'I promise you this,' Freddie spat through gritted teeth, 'not one bit of you will ever go back to Manchester. Your family will never bury you, you will never be absolved of your sins and your soul will never be put to rest.'

Grinding his teeth, Freddie twisted the knife around in Jacko's stomach, from one side to the other, inflicting as much internal damage and pain as he could. Jacko's face contorted into a look of utter shock and his body convulsed violently, before blood began to seep from his open mouth and his heart finally stopped beating.

Staring into his unseeing eyes for a moment longer, Freddie pulled back and dropped the knife to the ground with a clatter. Nobody moved. Dark bloodstains covered him, from chest to toe. He turned his hands over and stared at them, his eyes misting over as the realisation hit him that he didn't know how much of the blood on his hands was Thea's and how much belonged to her killer.

CHAPTER SIXTY-FIVE

Jules bombed it down the road in her new Mini Cooper and turned up the volume of the music she was listening to. It was Bon Jovi's 'Lost Highway', one of her favourite songs and at this precise moment it was very apt. She sang along happily, her tuneless voice booming around the small car.

The car behind her was getting right up her backside and she scowled, speeding up. Glancing at the dashboard, she could see that she was right on time to pick up Liam. He'd gone home to pack up the things he wanted to take with them on their new adventure. Once she grabbed him it would be plain sailing all the way to the ferry. She'd decided to book them into a swanky hotel for the night before they crossed. Maybe even spoil themselves with a few spa treatments to get them right in the mood.

The car behind was still up her backside and she narrowed her eyes. 'Alright, you twat – see how you like this.' She slowed right down to a crawl and smiled smugly. That should annoy them enough to overtake and leave her alone.

As the big black Bentley passed her she gave it the middle finger and waited for it to disappear into the distance. To her surprise it slowed down to a full stop instead, blocking her way. She beeped on the horn, hard.

'Get out of the way, asshole,' she yelled, winding down the window.

In her side mirror she saw another car come to a stop behind her, parking up close to the bumper so that she couldn't reverse away. Swallowing, Jules began to suspect foul play.

A man from the car in front got out and walked over towards her. Jules moved to lock the doors but she was a second too late as he yanked the door open.

'Get out,' he demanded.

'No,' she replied indignantly. 'I won't.'

'I said' – he pulled a gun out of his jacket and pointed it at her – 'get out.'

Paling at the sight of the weapon, Jules did as she was asked.

'Right. Now get in the back of that car,' he said, pointing towards the Bentley. 'Someone wants a word.'

Nervously, Jules walked towards the Bentley and opened the door. Getting in, she looked back. The man with the gun had got into her car and now both the Mini Cooper and the car behind it were pulling off. They had stolen it.

Turning to see who was in the car with her as she shut the door, Jules cried out in shock as she came face to face with another gun barrel and something far more dangerous. Vince.

'Well, well, well. Julie Carter. What a surprise it is seeing you around here again, considering our agreement,' he said as the car pulled off down the road. The doors locked and Jules whimpered in fear.

She swallowed. 'Vince, yeah, well I was just leaving actually,' she blustered. 'I had to pop back to town to see my mum. But I swear I won't be back again.'

'Really?' Vince asked. 'That's the story you're going with?'

Jules floundered, unsure what to say. Vince clearly knew why she was really here and the fact she was in his car put her in a very bad position indeed.

'Thing is, Jules,' Vince said, shifting in his seat, 'I heard a different story. I heard that you came back to town with a son in tow and that you publicly outed Freddie for being the father, then extorted quite a lot of money out of him.' He watched her puffy face pale to a sickly grey. 'Which is a surprise, really, considering

I gave you quite a lot of money myself to disappear and get rid of the kid, a few years back. Now, I'd say that this means you've not held up your end of the deal very well. Wouldn't you agree?'

'I can pay you back,' Jules said quickly. It would mean almost halving the money Freddie had given her to start over, but at least she'd still have the rest of it. 'I have the money.'

'Oh, I know you do,' Vince replied. 'But I'm afraid that ain't going to cut it this time. You see, I've been hearing other stories as well. Stories about your parenting skills. Jacking up while your kid watches. Leaving him hungry, battering him about. Now I don't have kids myself. But I've always thought of Freddie as the son I never had.' His cold gaze burned intensely into Jules's. 'And I've got this indescribable need inside me to protect him. That's why I tried to get rid of you all those years ago, in the nicest way I could. But that didn't work, did it? And now it appears you're trying to ruin *two* lives. Freddie's *and* his son's.'

'No, no, Vince that's not what it's like at all,' Jules said, her bottom lip flapping as she began to panic.

'Isn't it? I think it is, though. You know, if I thought you was a good mother to your kid, that you had some actual value here, I'd think twice. But you ain't. You're nothing but a cancerous leech, sucking what you can out of people and leaving behind nothing but stress and destruction.'

Reaching into his pocket, Vince pulled out a silencer and screwed it onto the end of his gun.

'Please, Vince, don't do this,' Jules begged. 'I'm Ethan's mother.'

'You're a mother he's better off without. And one who already abandoned him.' Vince stared her in the eye as he pressed the gun to her temple. She sobbed. 'Unlike you, I'll do anything for my family. And I won't let anyone get in their way.'

Pulling the trigger, he watched as the woman jolted and then slumped down in the seat. Her pale blue eyes stared vacantly into space, her face falling slack. Reaching forward, Vince searched her pockets until he found the cheque Freddie had given her for two hundred and fifty thousand pounds. Shaking his head, he ripped it up into small pieces then opened the window and scattered them to the wind.

CHAPTER SIXTY-SIX

Freddie paused outside his front door and rubbed his temple, feeling so lost and low that for a moment he was tempted to just sit down there in the empty hallway and give up the last bit of fight left inside him. The night before, he and Paul had cleared up the evidence of anyone else being in the house and had sent an anonymous tip-off to the police about Thea's body. It had felt like tearing their own hearts out, leaving here there on that floor, cold and alone, still drenched in her own blood. But they'd had to. If she wasn't found by the authorities and her death logged in an official capacity, they wouldn't be able to give her a proper burial. And that was out of the question.

After burning all their clothes and scrubbing themselves raw, they'd gone to break the news to Mollie. They'd held her close as she crumbled and cried for the loss of her daughter. They had no choice but to tell her some details, knowing full well that the police would not hold them back. They'd managed to force her to be strong, for their sakes, to pretend she was fine when the police later arrived and had even put on a show themselves. Mollie attested to them being there with her all night.

He'd called Anna briefly to tell her before she saw it on the news, but he hadn't been able to leave his mother and go home until now. Paul and James had agreed to stay with her for now, so that she wasn't alone. Anna had filled him in on Ethan and all he wanted now was to get back to his little boy and make sure he was OK.

Drawing on the fumes of whatever energy he still had left, Freddie opened the front door and walked inside. The sound of a film on the TV guided him through to the living room and he stood in the doorway. Anna and Ethan were curled up on the sofa together, under a blanket, watching a Disney film. She was stroking his hair and he leaned against her. He blinked in surprise but quickly hid his reaction as Anna looked up, realising they were no longer alone.

She gazed up at him, her expression full of sadness, guilt and sympathy. Her cheeks were wet from the sorrowful tears that were still falling and Freddie had a hard time not joining her in this. For so long he had been so strong, had let his anger carry him through. He wanted to keep fighting the wave of grief that threatened to overwhelm him, too scared to give in to such weakness. Walking over, he sat down next to them, placing a hand on Ethan.

'I'm so sorry, Ethan,' Freddie said, his tone full of grief. 'I'm so sorry we all made you feel you had to run away.'

Ethan immediately sat up and wrapped his thin little arm around Freddie, in comfort.

'I'm sorry about Auntie Thea, Dad,' he said softly.

These gentle words were finally Freddie's undoing, and rocking forward he placed his head into his hands and let the tears flow. Anna stood up and moved to his other side, wrapping her arm around him along with Ethan's, cocooning him in a circle of love.

Together they sat in silence, the three of them crying for the loved one they had lost and the hardships they had been through, united for the first time as a real family.

CHAPTER SIXTY-SEVEN

Closing his eyes, Drew felt the fresh sea breeze on his face and breathed in deeply. To the side of him a fisherman sat smoking a pipe, fixing a broken net. To the other side, two men were readying the boat that was going to take him away from England and this life for good.

It had been a week since he'd taken Freddie up on his offer and warily visited the address he'd given him. Raul had set him up with a new passport, just as Freddie had said he would, and had hidden him in a damp basement whilst he made arrangements to get him out of the country. Drew could have walked into any airport and used the passport, but with the Killers searching for him they'd have found him too easily. The plan was to hide in a concealed compartment within the fishing boat whilst it travelled to France and allowed him to sneak across the border. From there, Drew was on his own.

Looking up to the bright-blue winter sky, Drew huddled into his coat for warmth. He was sad to leave England. It was all he'd ever known and he'd lost everything he'd worked so hard for in the blink of an eye. All his businesses, the respect he'd gained, whatever it was he and Catriona had shared – it was all gone. And that stung. But that was the way of the world. He'd taken a risk and this was the price he'd had to pay.

At least he still had his life and his freedom, thanks to Freddie. It was a bitter gratitude he bore the other man. Because if Freddie hadn't taken their load in the first place, Drew would never have been in this mess. But despite that, and despite the fact he could have just turned his back, Freddie had thrown him a lifeline. Thanks to him, Drew had the ability to at least start again.

He'd seen the news, on the small ancient TV that had been in the basement where he'd been hiding. Thea Tyler was dead, murdered at an unconnected address. The news had shocked him to the core. Jacko had been desperate, but he'd never thought his friend would go through with it. Thea hadn't deserved to even be involved in this mess, let alone lose her life. Drew dreaded to think what they would have done to Jacko after that. Especially if the Ramones had got to him. He shuddered and pushed the thought of his former business associates away. It was a sorry situation indeed.

'Come on, let's get going,' one of the men on the boat shouted. 'You got any luggage?'

'Nah,' said Drew with a small smile. 'I got nothing but my two feet and the future lying ahead.' With one last look behind him, Drew stepped onto the boat and said goodbye to the past for good.

*

Freddie sat on Thea's bed and looked around. Gone were the dolls and the toys that had once littered this room whilst she was still a child. They had been replaced over the years with jewellery and photography magazines, pictures of her laughing with her friends and family. Memories, captured in silver frames. He picked up one of the three of them together, he and Paul dwarfing her in the middle as they posed for the camera. He rubbed his thumb gently over her face.

'Freddie?' Anna peered around the door. 'The cars are here.'

He nodded. 'I'll be right down.'

It was the day of Thea's funeral. The case of her murder had been cut and dry. CCTV picked up images of Jacko driving her in the direction of the house and his DNA had been all over her body and the knife. Although they obviously hadn't caught him yet – and never would, now – the coroner had decreed that with this amount of solid evidence, the body would not need to be examined further and could be buried. Freddie had been relieved, not sure that Mollie would be able to take the thought of Thea lying in the morgue for much longer.

Standing up, he paused, noticing that one small stuffed cat had made it through the years and still sat in its place on her bed. He picked it up. It could go in the casket to keep her company.

CHAPTER SIXTY-EIGHT

The service had been beautiful, her casket the most expensive money could buy and the church overflowing with her favourite flowers. All the seats and even the space at the back of the church had been filled with friends and colleagues, all wanting to say goodbye and show their support. Associates from all over the city had come to pay their respects to Freddie and Paul, knowing full well that in their world, to not attend such an event was an open snub. The Tylers were underworld royalty and one of their own had been lost.

Freddie and Paul had stood tall and strong, holding their devastated mother up between them as the prayers were said and Thea was lowered into the ground. Going through the motions, they had waited in line as everyone filed out to their cars, ready to head to the reception, which was being held at a small country club, just outside of the city. They had accepted the words of sympathy, the pats of comfort and the marks of respect afforded to them as people passed, hearing and feeling none of it as they gave in to the numbness of grief. It hit them all hard, the finality of the day. Thea was gone and she would never be part of their lives again.

Anna stood dutifully at the end of the procession, holding Ethan to her and giving her thanks to all the faces as they passed. The process exhausted her, ridden as she was by her own grief, but she knew that as Freddie's partner it was expected of her and she didn't want to let him down.

As the last of the guests trailed away, Tanya touched her arm. 'Why don't you let Ethan come with me, and you go with Freddie?' she offered.

Anna hesitated, looking down into the solemn eyes of her stepson. Her hands rested on his shoulders still, as she tried to give him comfort on what must be a confusing day for him.

Tanya looked down and addressed Ethan directly, seeing how torn Anna was, but knowing she was stretching herself too far. Anna couldn't look after everyone all the time. It was a lesson she still needed to learn, but one Tanya knew she probably never would.

'I was thinking we could stop off and get a milkshake on the way. What do you reckon?' she asked. She watched as Ethan tentatively smiled.

'Can I?' he asked Anna, twisting up to look at her.

She bit her lip and glanced over towards Freddie. His face was ashen and though he stood proud and strong, he looked lost and defeated, just like the rest of the family. He needed her the most right now. 'Sure,' she said. 'Why not? You know where to go?' she asked Tanya.

'Yeah, 'course. Just go. Be with Freddie, Anna.' She leaned in and squeezed Anna close. Anna grasped her back, subsiding against her best friend and drawing comfort for a few moments, before straightening back up. 'We'll see you there.'

Watching the pair leave, Anna turned her attention to Freddie. There was still a long day ahead for them all.

CHAPTER SIXTY-NINE

The door to the task-force office burst open and Ben Hargreaves thundered in. Sarah blinked and looked up at him in question. She'd not been expecting him, hadn't even realised he would be in the building today. He had steadfastly avoided the office ever since he'd been forced to issue the wind-up order. Now, though, as he marched towards her, his eyes held a manic gleam of excitement that made Sarah's stomach tighten in fear.

'OK, we're ready to go. SWAT team is on its way over there right now. This is it, guys.' He turned to the room with an exultant cry. 'This is what we've all been working towards. It might not be murder, but it's still bloody good.'

'What are you talking about?' Sarah asked, aghast. She stood up and rushed around the other side of the desk, where she had to stop herself from grabbing Ben and shaking him.

'The raid,' Ben said with a frown. 'What's wrong with you? The pictures Adam sent. It's solid proof – we've got them bang to rights. I signed off his request straight away. Well done, son,' he said, turning his attention to Adam, who was sitting behind his desk. 'You've done what no one else was able to. You're getting a promotion when all this is done.'

'What pictures?' Sarah asked urgently.

Ben frowned as if she was mad. 'Surely you've seen them? Surely you know what's going on in your own team?'

Both of them turned to face Adam, Ben confused and Sarah furious. He smacked his head with his hand and then shook it apologetically. 'So sorry, ma'am. I sent the email so quickly I thought I'd copied you in, but I must not have.' He clicked into his 'Sent' box and nodded. 'Yep, I accidently missed you off. Sorry.'

'Well, it doesn't matter now. It's done. They'll be picked up shortly and neither of them are getting out for a long time,' Ben said.

'But—' Sarah's mouth flapped open in horror and she quickly shut it. 'It's Thea Tyler's funeral. We can't hijack a funeral. Surely we can hold off until it's over, show them a bit of compassion?' she asked, trying to keep her tone level.

'Compassion?' Ben cried with a harsh laugh. 'Those bastards don't show compassion to anyone else; why should we show it to them? No.' He shook his head. 'They're done. And I for one will take *great* pleasure in bringing them in on a day where everyone in their world will be stood there watching. I can't wait to see their faces, Cos Christou, Ray Renshaw, Al Hynes… even retired veterans like Vince Castor will be there. He was Tyler's mentor, back in the day. They're all going to be there to watch us take the Tylers down. And it'll shake them all up big time, because you know what? They're next. As protectors of the law, we won't stop until we've brought down every single crime firm in this city. And now we know it *can* be done. This has just proven that. For so many years they've been confident working under the radar, but if we can get the Tylers, we can get anybody. So, let's go get these bastards, and then tonight, we celebrate!' With a grin of triumph, Ben walked back out.

Sarah watched him leave and then rushed over to Adam's desk. 'Show me,' she demanded.

He clicked open the email and pulled up the attachments. Grabbing the mouse out of his hand, Sarah leaned over him and scrolled through them. They were pictures of the Portakabin at the docks. Somehow he'd got inside and he'd taken pictures of a large block of cocaine hidden in the ceiling. There were pictures of him taking a sample for testing, pictures of the bag it was held in and pictures of Paul carrying the bag.

That, coupled with the DNA they would easily find on the bag was enough to put the brothers away for a long time. Dread filled her veins and Sarah shivered. The game was up – there was no getting away from this. She looked at Adam and he smiled back at her.

'Great news, hey, ma'am?' he said.

'Yeah,' she heard herself say faintly. 'Yeah, that's brilliant.'

She backed away and put her hands on her hips, trying to keep her breathing calm. All around her the office was celebrating Adam's big win.

'I need to pop out, but well done. This is truly great work, Adam.'

Trying not to have a full-on panic attack, Sarah forced herself to walk at a normal pace as she grabbed her bag and headed out of the office. She needed to find somewhere private to call Freddie. She had to warn him to run.

As Sarah disappeared out of the door, Holly sidled up next to Adam and squeezed his shoulder as they both stared after her.

'Well done, Roddy,' she murmured, using the nickname they only usually used at home. It was one that his friends used for him, after a few jokes surrounding his love for motorbikes. He'd gone from Adam to Hot Rod, then Hot Rod to Roddy. No one in the office knew that they were dating. It was something she'd insisted on right at the beginning, not wanting it to affect their professional life. 'You did it, babe.' She pulled back her hand, not wanting anyone to notice.

Adam nodded. '*We* did it,' he corrected. 'But just as long as she doesn't know that, you're in the clear.' He smiled.

Holly had kept her word; she'd not uttered a word to the police, officially, about Sarah. But after long sleepless nights at home she had decided to turn to the one person who could help her overthrow the Tylers without Sarah ever catching on to it being down to her. She'd told Roddy about the threats that tied her hands and the fact that Sarah was bent. Asking for his help, they had come up with a plan together that kept Holly looking clean and Sarah out of the loop. It was simple, but it had worked.

Adam had slowly gathered the evidence and kept it hidden at home, ignoring protocol and keeping it off the servers whilst he built the case, knowing that if Sarah found it, it would be wiped. The coke would have been moved by the Tylers and they would have ended up with nothing. By going behind her back he'd screwed her into a corner she couldn't get out of.

Taking a deep breath, he turned and accepted the string of congratulatory remarks that awaited him. All was good in the world again.

CHAPTER SEVENTY

Freddie and Anna sat close and held hands in the back of the limousine that was carrying them towards the funeral reception. Anna rubbed her thumb over his fingers and leaned her head on his shoulder.

'How are you doing?' she asked gently.

Freddie rubbed his forehead. 'As well as can be expected,' he answered. 'Mum's not coping well.'

'I know,' Anna said, pulling a sad expression.

They sat in silence for a few minutes, watching the world go past the tinted windows. Paul and James had gone with Mollie in the other limo, so they were alone.

'We need to think about registering Ethan for school,' Freddie said suddenly, changing the subject.

Anna sat up and turned to him. 'Yes, we do. Have you thought about what sort of school you want him to go to?'

Freddie fiddled with the button on one of his sleeves. Through the sleepless nights after Thea's death he had been worrying about what was best for his young son. 'Obviously I have the money to send him to the best private schools available. But...' He sighed.

'But you're worried he'll turn out like Michael,' Anna finished quietly.

Freddie had sent his youngest brother away to private school, years before, and after suffering severe bullying for his grass roots, he'd been thrown out of the school for violence and drug dealing. After this, Freddie had taken him into the family business and had thought things were going OK, but there had been something fundamentally broken in Michael that couldn't be fixed. They'd later discovered him to be a psychopath, causing all sorts of harm to people who hadn't deserved it.

Anna knew that Freddie blamed himself for this. 'It wasn't your fault, you know,' she said. 'And it wasn't the school either. It was just part of who he was. Sometimes people are just bad eggs.' She squeezed his hand. 'And Ethan is far from a bad egg. He's a lovely boy. We're lucky to have him.'

Freddie's grieving heart warmed at Anna's words and he looked at her with deep love. Since they'd decided to become a true family, she'd thrown herself into being a parent head first. He had never felt so grateful or so full of admiration for her. After all she'd been through, the emotional sacrifice she must have had to make, she had still done this for him. He thanked the stars once more for allowing him to meet such an incredible woman.

'I'm pretty lucky to have you too,' he said. 'Especially after everything—'

'Freddie,' Anna cut him off. 'No more of that. We agreed. We're not going to spend one more second looking back. This is our fresh start as a family. You, me and Ethan. Everything else, that's behind us. What's important now is creating the best future and a settled family for Ethan.'

'You're right.' He kissed her hand.

She smiled as the limo came to a stop outside the country club where the reception was being held.

'Come on,' Anna said, taking in a deep breath. 'Let's get this over with so we can all just go home.'

Freddie nodded and stepped out of the car. As he walked round to open the door for Anna, he saw Paul helping his mother out of the limo in front. She looked frail and old suddenly and this shocked him. He had never thought of her as either, but today she was both. He opened the door for Anna and waited as she got out.

'Where's Ethan?' he asked, looking around with a frown. He placed his hand in the small of her back and guided her forward towards the building behind Paul, James and Mollie.

'Tanya's stopping to grab a milkshake on the way. I think she just wants to give him a quick break from all this sadness…'

Anna trailed off and they both glanced over their shoulders as two cars screeched to a violent halt behind them. Her jaw dropped and her eyes widened in fear and surprise as half a dozen armed response officers jumped out and ran across the space between them, pointing their guns at Freddie and Paul and shouting all at once.

'Freddie Tyler, get on the ground!'

'On the ground, both of you!'

'Get down, *now!*'

'Shit,' Freddie uttered under his breath. He glanced at Paul who looked as horrified as he felt.

'You've got to be fucking kidding me,' he roared, turning back to the men shoving their guns in his face. 'This is my sister's *fucking funeral!*'

'Freddie and Paul Tyler, you are both being arrested for the possession and suspected distribution of a class A drug…'

'Freddie,' Anna cried, as she was roughly shoved out of the way. She tried to push forward through the men surrounding Freddie, but they beat her back once more, almost causing her to fall. 'What are you doing?' she yelled. 'Get off him!'

She clawed at one of the officers and he rounded on her as the others threw Freddie face down on the floor. 'Back off, ma'am, unless you want to be arrested too.'

'You do not have to say anything. But it may harm your defence if you do not mention when questioned something which you later rely on in court…'

Anna put her hands to her head and watched aghast as Freddie's hands were cuffed. He kicked out and writhed on the ground.

Mollie wailed as she watched the group of men accost her sons at her daughter's funeral. Unable to do anything, she began to shake and dropped to her knees. Two of her friends who had come out to see what was going on rushed forward to support her.

A large crowd had formed at the entrance of the country club, some of their guests inside having heard the commotion.

'Get your hands off me right now,' Freddie demanded loudly, still trying to fight his way out. His anger had reached fever pitch. This was not on, not today. 'You're going to fucking pay for this,' he added through gritted teeth as two of the armed men pulled him to his feet. 'I promise you this, I'm going to find out who each of you are and I'm going to make you pay.' They dragged him off towards one of the cars.

Paul was being pushed towards the second car, but he kept silent, leaving the threats to his brother. Bill and Sammy appeared through the crowd and Bill called out indignantly, starting towards them. Paul caught his eye and shook his head strongly. There was nothing he could do, and the last thing they needed was more of their men arrested.

'Just call the lawyers, Bill. Get them over to the station quick,' he shouted. He saw Bill nod, his face a mask of grim anger.

'This is a funeral,' Freddie continued. 'I don't care what you think you have on someone, you don't take them from a family funeral.'

Another car pulled up and Anna gasped, realising it would be Tanya with Ethan. 'Freddie,' she called, locking eyes with him as he looked back over his shoulder. He shot a look at the car and immediately stopped fighting.

'Shit.' He closed his eyes, guilt flooding through him at the thought of what this was going to do to Ethan. 'Anna, make sure he's OK.'

One of the men holding him shoved him forward, hard. 'Alright,' he roared. 'I'm coming. Just get me out of here, stop causing such a fucking scene in front of my son.'

Tanya stepped out of the car, looking over to Anna in shock. Ethan followed her out and she swiftly pulled him to her body, covering his face with her hand so that he couldn't see.

'Tanya?' he asked, trying to pull away.

'Trust me, Ethan. Just stay there for a sec, OK?' she replied.

'It's all alright, mate,' Freddie called to him as they pushed him down into the car. 'I'll see you soon.'

'I wouldn't count on it,' one of the officers said with a laugh as he slammed the door shut.

The door of the second car closed behind Paul and the last officer took his seat. The two cars pulled away and suddenly the only sounds that broke the silence were Mollie's cries of anguish. Anna looked around at the sea of shocked faces behind her and then to Tanya, as her friend came over.

Ethan broke free from Tanya and wrapped his arms around Anna, burying his head in her dress, terrified and unsure as to what had just happened.

Anna looked down at him and across to Mollie, who was still in pieces on the ground. None of it seemed real.

Surely this was some sort of terrible dream? It couldn't really be happening.

Her gaze turned to Tanya and she saw the horror she felt masked in her friend's face.

'What the fuck do we do now?' Tanya breathed.

Bill sidled up to them and put a hand on Anna's shoulder.

'We get him out,' he said in a hard voice. 'That's what.' Sammy and Seamus silently joined them. 'The Tylers have run this city for many years and their empire has never been taken down. One day their time at the top will be over,' he said, with a nod. 'That's the way of the world.' He gripped her shoulder harder. 'But that day is not today. Now—' His gaze pierced into hers. 'Let's get to work.'

A LETTER FROM EMMA

To those of you who have just joined the series here, thank you so much for buying my book and I really hope you've enjoyed being introduced to the Tylers. To those of you who have been on this journey with me from the beginning, I hope you have enjoyed the latest instalment and watching our characters grow and evolve. It feels crazy to look back at who they were at the beginning.

If you like my books, please do sign up to hear about new releases. Your email address will not be shared and you can unsubscribe at any time.

www.bookouture.com/emma-tallon

And if you have enjoyed *Reckless Girl*, I would greatly appreciate a review on Amazon. I read every single one and I love to hear what you thought. It makes the long hours and the moments of pulling my hair out worth it!

This series has been a total rollercoaster for me as an author. Some books have just flown from my fingertips and some have had to be dragged out of my brain, kicking and screaming. This one was one of the harder ones to write. I'm not sure if that was because the addition of Ethan really mixed things up – I think I needed to adjust to his presence as much as Anna did, in a way! It has been an emotional journey for us all. Because when I'm writing, I'm not sat at my desk, I'm there. I am in the moment, living it, feeling it; I become completely immersed.

I'm so happy to see this go out into the world so that everyone else has a chance to go on that journey too. Right now, I am working on book six in the series and, honestly, I'm just so excited about where the family is going to next. Hopefully you'll enjoy it too.

So, stay well and keep an eye on my page for further updates, and I'll catch you again in the next one!

All the best,
Emma X

 emmatallonofficial

 EmmaEsj

@my.author.life

www.emmatallon.com

ACKNOWLEDGEMENTS

I just want to say a big thank you to all of you who have read the book, especially those who have been on this journey with me since the beginning. Without you, these books would be nowhere.

I also owe a huge thank you to my editor, Helen. Through missed deadlines, heavy edits and even the occasional emotional breakdown, she has always supported me and been solidly there by my side. I couldn't do this without her.

And lastly, I want to thank all my incredible Bookouture author friends. Whether I need someone to laugh or cry with when the pressure is on, they are always there and the friendships I have formed with them are just priceless. Here's to many more books' worth of jokes and comfort ahead!

Milton Keynes UK
Ingram Content Group UK Ltd.
UKHW011601201123
432921UK00004B/340